Every Move You Make

Contents

Author's Note & Content Warnings

Stalking is bad in real life. Can we all agree on that? Alright. Good thing this is fiction then. Enjoy.

Just because this is a romantic comedy, doesn't mean the spice is lacking. There is a lot. I always try to make the spicy scenes hot, sweet, and a little humorous. If you've read my other works, you'll know what to expect. For a full list of content warnings, please click or scan the QR code and it will take you to my website.

To that one guy I met at a rugby tournament in college: this is mostly your fault. Thank you for being my forever teammate.

American Rugby Terminology

- **Boot** — Cleat.

- **Boot up** — Get ready to warm up.

- **Fifteens** — A full eighty-minute rugby game with fifteen players against fifteen players. Typically played in the fall and spring.

- **Full eighty** — Playing a full eighty-minute game.

- **Hospital pass** — A pass that is thrown to a player that puts them in danger of injury.

- **Kit** — Usually a duffle bag full of boots, uniform, and a change of clothes.

- **Line out** — A means of restarting play after the ball has gone out of bounds (into touch). Typically two players will lift another player into the air to catch the ball as it is being thrown back into play. The opposing team will do the same to try and gain possession of the ball.

- **Maul** — When the ball carrier is held by one or more opponents.

- **Pitch** — Field.

- **Rookie** — A first-year player.

- **Scrum** — An ordered formation of players, used to restart play, in which the forwards of a team form up, with arms interlocked and heads down, and push forward against a similar group from the opposing side. The ball is rolled into the scrum and the players try to gain possession of it by kicking it backward toward their own side.

- **Scrum cap** — Protective headgear.

- **Sevens** — A shortened version of the game, typically played in the summer tournament style. Seven players against seven players, played for seven-minute halves.

- **Shoot the boot** — Chugging alcohol out of someone's shoe.

- **Sir** — The referee, regardless of gender.

- **Social** — A little party right after the game with both teams. There's food, beer, and sometimes drinking songs. Everyone is dirty and tired. General comradery.

- **Vet** — A seasoned player.

THE POSITIONS

Forwards (very strong, tackle the most, members of the scrum) :
- #1 & #3 — Prop (Loosehead & Tighthead)

- #2 — Hooker

- #4 & #5 — Second Row (Number 4 Lock & Number 5 Lock)

- #6 & #7 — Flanker (Blindside & Openside)

- #8 — Eight man (Number 8)

Backs (fast and agile runners, score most of the game points) :

- #9 — Scrum Half

- #10 — Fly Half

- #11 — Left Wing

- #12 — Inside Center

- #13 — Outside Center

- #14 — Right Wing

- #15 — Fullback

Rugby is played at all different levels and age brackets throughout the world, and in most countries where the sport is popular, there are professional teams. At the time I wrote this, the US had one international men's team and one women's team, but the sport is growing in America and professional women's rugby has just started launching new teams! *Every Move You Make* primarily follows a professional women's rugby team. The college teams mentioned are not NCAA, they are club level.

Playlist

Every Move You Make – Spotify

TEXAS HOLD 'EM by Beyoncé
Somebody's Watching Me Remix by Rockwell & Syzz
Dip It Low by Ofenbach
Training Season - Chloé Caillet Mix by Chloé Caillet & Dua Lipa
The Motto by Ava Max & Tiësto
Scream Drive Faster by LAUREL
Wait by Alexi Murdoch
I Remember Everything by Zach Bryan ft. Kacey Muskgraves
This Could Be Good by Morningsiders
The scarlett empress by College
A Real Hero by College & Electric Youth
In One Ear by Cage the Elephant
I Will Follow You into the Dark (Instr. Version) by The O'Neill Brothers Group
Could Have Been Me by The Struts
Lil Boo Thang - Galantis Remix by Paul Russell

Chapter 1
Illegal Tackle

Isaiah

Every bone in my shoulder crunches as I'm tackled to the ground—illegally, I might add. The earth has barely thawed from winter, and the impact sends lancing pain through my body.

Fucking rookies and their hot heads.

We're playing against Trenton, New Jersey today, and I know this kid is a rookie. He can't be more than twenty years old, and he clearly has something to prove to his team. Who the hell tries to lift a prop? I'm six foot two, two hundred and eighty five pounds, and this dumbass managed to haul me up and slam me to the ground. If I wasn't in so much agony, I'd be impressed.

"Sir!" Pony shouts to the ref. "Where's the fucking red card? Are you kidding me?"

"I'm fine," I grunt back to my brother, trying to roll over.

"You're not fine," he snaps.

In the distance, I hear voices rising on the field—my team, I presume. No one says shit when it's an illegal tackle from one of your own.

"Are you blind, sir?" I hear my sister, Angie, yell from the sidelines.

"Trainer!" several teammates shout before I finally manage to roll onto my back and see the faces of my brothers, Dane and Jonah. Dane (a.k.a. Pony) is our team captain, and technically, he's the only one allowed to talk to the ref on the field. But my youngest brother, Jonah (a.k.a. JoJo), seems to have forgotten that rule as he sprints over to get in the sir's face.

I try to focus on the gray overcast sky above me, calming my nerves before everyone makes room for our trainer.

"Are you hurt?" she asks, her eyes assessing my entire body.

"Pain is subjective," I mutter.

"It's not," she says firmly. "Quit being an ass and tell me the truth."

Katrina has been with our team for a long time. Most teams have a rotating cast of trainers that come and go, but she's been with us through most of my injuries these last few years. She's basically my doctor so I can't bullshit her.

I try anyway. I have to.

With a hidden eye roll, I sigh, "It's my shoulder. And my neck."

"Can you rotate your head to the right?"

I scoff but don't move. "Yeah."

"So do it."

"Fine," I mutter. Slowly, I turn my head just the smallest amount before shooting pain rips through my neck, shoulder, and spine. "See?" I force out, unable to control the strain in my voice.

"Pony, call the EMTs over," she says to Dane.

"Not necessary," I grunt. "I just need a couple of minutes and I'll be good as new." But my brother isn't listening and leaves us to find the EMTs.

"Ha. You haven't been good as new since you were twenty-four. Shut up and listen to me."

"I'm only twenty-nine. I can still bounce back."

"Sure, Isaiah. Tell that to the three shoulder injuries you've had, the knee surgery, and countless broken fingers."

"Hey, I still have them all. I can count just fine."

"How many fingers am I holding up now?"

"Two," I say confidently.

"Follow my finger," she commands, holding her index finger straight up. "Good. I'm glad you started wearing a scrum cap. You hit your head pretty hard."

Just then, the paramedics arrive in a glorified golf cart and hop out. Katrina explains what happened and instructs them to double-check for a concussion. They stabilize my arm in a temporary sling and spine board me which seems excessive, and I try to tell them as much, but they insist. As I'm carried off the pitch toward the ambulance, the game resumes. I can't see it, but I can hear shouting and general ruckus before a whistle is blown and ignored. Knowing my brothers and teammates the way I do, they've started throwing fists.

Bloodthirsty idiots.

· · · ● · ● · · ·

An hour and a half later, I'm laying on a stiff hospital bed, waiting for my MRI results. My two sisters make themselves comfortable on the vinyl couch next to me as Angie, my oldest sister, nurses my four-month-old nephew, Domini-co. Boob totally out. Ivy, my youngest sister, watches them intently.

"Look at you go, little man," Ivy cheers softly.

How can she be so comfortable with our sister's boob so close to her face? I guess she was there to help deliver the twins. And she is a midwife—er, almost a midwife. I suppose she sees boobs a lot.

That's enough of that. Eager to redirect my attention, I start counting the ceiling tiles.

My soon-to-be brother-in-law, Rafael, holds my four-month-old niece, Zofia, and tries to burp her. Rafael, usually our team's eight man, is taking this rugby season off to care for his twins.

"Did the doctor come in yet?" My father, Neal, asks, walking in with a cardboard tray of coffee cups. He's still wearing our team's jacket—dark teal with white lettering and all of his sons' numbers embroidered on the sleeve, including my soon-to-be brother in-law.

"No," Angie says to our dad. "The nurse was just in here for vitals. He said the doctor will be in shortly."

"You guys really don't need to be here," I grumble.

"Nonsense," Dad says, setting down the coffee tray and taking his granddaughter in his arms before looking over at me. "That was a hard hit followed by a harder fall. You're lucky you can see straight."

"They're gonna kick you all out as soon as the doctor comes in here."

Raf takes his son from Angie as she tucks her boob away—thank god—and gently coos, squishing Dominico's cheeks. "How could they kick us out? Look at your concerned nephew. He needs to know his Uncle Zay is okay."

"He looks like he's five seconds away from passing out," I retort.

Rafael stares lovingly at his son. "Alright, so he's a little milk-drunk. Who doesn't want a relaxing brew after a game?"

A soft knock sounds off, and all of us turn when the doctor enters. She's a tall, slender South Asian woman with her black hair pulled back in an efficient bun. "Hi," she smiles, walking toward me while rubbing sanitizing foam on her hands. "I'm Dr. Shajahan. Isaiah, is it?"

"Yeah. Hi."

She opens her laptop and glances through my chart. "Rugby, huh? That's a tough sport. Tell me what happened."

Right as I'm about to tell her the details, Dane and Jonah come barreling in. Dane looks like he just wiped blood from his nose, and a black eye is already forming. Jonah's blonde man bun is disheveled, with sections of hair falling loose,

They're both covered in dirt and scrapes, and their tall socks have fallen down to their ankles.

"Is everything okay?" Dane asks, surveying me and the doctor.

"Will he ever walk again?" Jonah asks, and I can't tell if he's serious or not. "Oh my god, now you're going to have to join the wheelchair rugby team. Not that that's a bad thing. They're fucking animals. You'll fit right in. But I'm gonna miss you, bro."

"Jonah, shut up," Dane says, shaking his head. "He can walk. His legs are fine." He looks back at me. "Right?"

Before I confirm my legs do in fact work, Jonah cuts in when he refocuses his attention on the doctor. "Well, hello," he smirks, tone shifting lower while holding his hand out for her to shake. "I'm Jonah. What are you doing later?"

"Working," she deadpans, leaving his hand unshaken.

Tucking his arms back but smirking deeper, he leans against the plastic railing at the foot of the bed. "You're pretty."

"Jonah, shut up and get out of the way," Angie says from the couch. She pulls out a big plastic bag of orange slices. "Here." My golden retriever of a brother's eyes widen, and he silently plops himself next to her, rifling through the bag.

"As I was saying," the doctor continues, "Please tell me what happened."

"Illegal rugby tackle. They grabbed me at my knees, lifted me, and threw me down shoulder-first."

The doctor peers at her laptop. "Well, your MRI came in." She clicks a few keys, and the image is displayed on the TV screen in front of me. "As you can see here," she says, moving the cursor. "You have a dislocated shoulder. Have you had shoulder injuries before?"

"Minor."

"Major," Dad interjects with an authoritative boom, catching me off guard.

"He's had three previous shoulder injuries," Angie adds. "Rotator cuff twice, and a SLAP tear."

I bristle. "Stop paying attention to my medical history."

"And what about your neck?" the doctor asks. "Because this looks like a brachial plexus injury."

"I'm a prop," I say, as if that will explain things. "The neck injuries have always been pretty minor. I've never been checked out for them before."

Dr. Shajahan gives me a calm but serious stare. "I'm telling you right now, you need to take this seriously. Neck injuries like this can compound, resulting in permanent nerve damage, quadriplegia, and in some cases, death. You cannot ignore this, and you should not play until you seek out medical advice from a sports medicine and orthopedic specialist."

I gape at her. "What?"

"Even then, you still may not be able to play rugby. I would leave that call up to your specialist. They will be able to determine your range of motion better than I can through MRIs."

Holy shit. I may never play rugby again? What the fuck am I supposed to do? I mean, no, this isn't my career like it once was; this is just Division I club rugby. And sure, I have a great job working as the manager of a security company, but I've lived and breathed rugby since I was sixteen years old.

I can't be one of those players who retires early. A lot of guys play well into their forties, and I haven't even hit thirty yet. Suddenly, my whole body tightens, and my heart rate picks up. An electric chill zaps under my skin, and I can't breathe.

How am I going to...

Where will I even...

What will I...

"Isaiah?" the doctor probes. "Did you hear me? I said I'm

going to step out and make you an order to see a sports medicine and orthopedic specialist. I'm also giving you a prescription for pain meds. You're going to stay in a sling and a neck brace until you're told otherwise."

"Okay," I say on autopilot. I don't even recognize my voice.

"I'll be back shortly."

When she leaves, the room is eerily silent. The Johanssen family doesn't do quiet. All it does is fuel my intrusive thoughts.

Suddenly, the silence is cut through by the unmistakable rumble of one of the twins pooping, followed by a little sigh. Everyone, including myself, flinches when we see Zofia lay her head back down into my dad's neck, sleepy and pleased with herself.

Jonah snorts. "Nice."

"I'll just take care of this," Dad says sheepishly as he grabs the diaper bag.

"I'll join you," Ivy offers, standing from the couch and taking Dominico from Rafael. "They usually poop within five minutes of each other."

What I want right now more than anything is some kind of comfort, but I'm not always the best at asking my family for that. I'm actually the worst. But before Ivy steps out, I blurt, "Can I hold him for a sec?"

She gives me a wary look. "I don't think you're supposed to hold anything."

"Can you just," I grunt, "set him on my lap then?"

She nods, and I hoist my knees up to create a little cradle where Ivy lays our nephew in my lap. Yes, this is exactly the distraction I need. His newly brown eyes are so big and beautiful. I squish his little biceps and marvel at the weight he's put on in the last month alone.

"Look at you, bud," I whisper to him in Spanish. "Making gains. Is Papá sneaking you protein powder?"

Angie scoffs from the couch. "Hell no. That's all me, baby."

She winks and grabs her breasts but immediately winces and curses under her breath.

My anxiety thaws when I touch Dominico's soft, plump arms and watch his tiny little mouth glisten. There's not a lot that soothes me, but my niece and nephew have quickly wormed their way into my heart.

Suddenly, he tenses and follows his twin sister's enormous bowel movement. I can't help it when the corner of my lip curls up. I turn my head to survey the room. "Judges?" Everyone who has available hands pretends to hold up a sign, and I look at my nephew again. "Tens across the board, amigo."

"That's my cue," Ivy says, reaching out to take Dominico from me. She walks out of the room with our dad and the twins, but the hospital room is still too crowded for my liking.

"Can you all stop staring at me?"

"Are you okay?" Angie asks, her soft expression doing nothing to hide her concern. "That was a really big message the doctor gave you."

"I'm fine," I bristle.

"C'mon, Zay," Rafael says. "Stop acting like potentially retiring from rugby is even remotely fine with you." He gestures to Dane and Jonah. "We wouldn't be if we were in your position, and we're not the ones who used to play professionally," he adds pointedly.

"Well then, it's a good thing you're not in my position."

"We're just trying to help—"

"Well, don't."

"Bro," Dane cuts in.

"No," Angie says. "Guys, it sounds like he needs some time to process this. Why don't we step out for a while so he can think?"

"About time," I mutter.

She sighs but gives me a sweet look. "You can push us

away all you want, but no one in this family is gonna leave you."

"I might," Dane says.

Angie ignores our middle brother. "Okay, everyone out. Let's go."

Jonah stops before he leaves. "Hey, if the doctor comes back and I'm not here, can you give her my number?"

"Get out."

He puts his hands up in surrender and smirks. "Can't hurt to ask."

Once the door finally closes, glorious silence falls upon the room. Except it's not glorious. It's maddening because now I have no distraction. No meddling but well-meaning sisters. No dumb brothers. No tiny cherub to squeeze. Just the smell of cheap hospital cafeteria coffee, orange slices, and latex gloves. Just me and the tornado of worry in my head.

A notification buzzes from my phone, and I grab it from the mattress next to me, grateful for any distraction.

Robyn Cassidy has posted a video.

My mind relaxes when I press play, and her radiant face comes into view. "This is your daily reminder that you can be both." She takes a few steps back from her phone to show her bare, broad shoulders in a pale green dress that skims her strong, lean body. I know she works harder than anyone for it. "You can lean into your femininity and still do this." The video cuts to a clip of her stiff-arming an opposing rugby player as she absolutely plows over them. When she jumps over their body, she runs full-force to the end zone, sliding in with three players hot on her heels, and scores. The video jumps back to her, dressed to the nines again. Lips painted a color I would love to taste. Eyelashes long and fanned. With her head held high, she shows off her square jawline. "Knock 'em dead."

When the video begins to replay, I make my way to the comment section. It was *just* posted, but there are almost two thousand likes and dozens of comments.

Mommy? Sorry. Mommy? Sorry. Mommy?

Yes queen! Beast mode activated!

It's truly a crime that she's straight <sobbing emoji>

Robyn Cassidy could punch me in the face and I'd say thank you.

Marry me <diamond ring emoji>

But then a comment pops up that has me boiling.

Ain't nothin' feminine abt shoulders like that lol

I quickly report the comment as harassment, and it's removed. I know she deals with the haters in her own way, but I also do my best to moderate her comments so she doesn't have to see shit like that. *Secretly moderate* with my burner account. She has no idea how much I hover in her accounts. Or at all, because I don't like, comment, or favorite any of them.

I watch and I wait.

Scrolling through her videos, I replay them for the millionth time. I bounce to her other social accounts and her bright smile lulls me to a hopeful place. I've been doing this for years, ever since we parted after college. We went to separate schools: Robyn at Penn Valley University, along with Angie and Rafael, who were seniors when she was a freshman, and I at Brightwood College, about two hours away. At least twice a year, I made the trip to Penn to play rugby and hang out with Ang and Raf.

But one day, at a social when I was a sophomore, Robyn pushed her way through a crowd of filthy ruggers, bursting like a ray of sunshine. She was magnetic. She demanded attention without asking for it. She drew people in with her personality and playfulness—her whole-hearted goodness—and for some inexplicable reason, she liked me.

My girlfriend at the time? Not so much.

Chapter 2
Personal Best Training

Isaiah

I've been in a downward spiral ever since I went to the sports medicine specialist two days ago.

"Do you see here?" the doctor said, pointing to my neck on my MRI. "This is your spinal canal, and it's narrowed. It should be this wide." He indicated to an healthy part of my spine. But my world felt narrower than my injured spine when he told me if I took any more hits, it could leave me paraplegic.

For every injury I've ever had, I've been able to heal well enough. But to be told full-contact rugby was totally off the table—that was not something I was ready to hear.

Rugby has consumed my life since I was a teenager. Once I found out I actually had a shot at going pro overseas, I dedicated even more of myself to the sport. Everything revolved around rugby, and it paid off. I went pro. But after three years with the London Hornets, I suffered a shoulder injury that didn't quite heal all the way, and I wasn't picked up again. I came back to the states with my tail between my legs, unable to see the amazing opportunity I had been given and appreciate the time I spent playing professional-ly. I was in a dark state for a while until my family nudged me to try playing for the club team back home.

And it did help. Playing club rugby, especially alongside my brothers, made me feel whole again, regardless of the broken bones along the way.

But now, I can't even play at club level.

When I got home from the sports medicine specialist, all I could do was stare at the walls of my room looking for answers. But what is life without playing rugby?

I have to figure something out and that starts with the personal trainer I'm about to meet. He came recommended by the sports medicine specialist as someone who could help me transition from athlete to... well, a former athlete. The bottom line is I can't operate how I used to and now I need to heal and learn about this new version of my body.

Am I willing to accept this fate? I don't want to. But I see players come and go every year. Some retire. Some get caught up in their own lives and don't have time to play. Some have injuries so bad they can never play again. But more often than not, those same people make their way back to the team as spectators, or fans, or donors to the club. They're never truly gone for good. Rugby has a way of pulling you back into its orbit.

The retirement pill, as awful as it tastes, isn't as big and scary as it once was. Retiring from club rugby isn't as bitter as retiring from professional rugby. It still isn't easy to swallow.

Whether I accept my fate or not, I have to keep moving. So here I am, killing time before my first session at Personal Best Training. My appointment is at 1:00 p.m., which gives me enough time afterward to get home, shower, and make it to work on time.

With shaky legs and a heavy heart, I gingerly step out of my car, walk past the reflective windows, and pull open the door. When I find the suite I'm looking for, I'm greeted by an orange and white cat dancing around my legs and country music[1] playing in the background. I remember the website for this place having more cat pictures than would be expected of a personal training studio. In every picture of the gym, there were cats laying on the equipment and a full bio of the studio kitties including their likes and dislikes. Seemed excessive but... I like cats.

"You must be Isaiah," a tall, ridiculously buff and tattooed man in a white polo says. He stands taller than me by about an inch. His tan skin is a stark contrast to his shirt and smile. He's not body-builder-competition tan, but there's no way his white skin is naturally that pigmented. Even his tattoos are colorful. His blonde hair is pulled back in a bun, and his face has thick stubble and a proud chin.

"Yeah."

"Welcome. That's my son, Chester, at your feet. Hope you like cats. And that one scowling over there is BooBoo Kitty," he says, pointing to a black cat sitting on a perch suctioned to the window. Its tail flicks as it watches me like I'm its next meal if I'm not careful enough. "I'm Dell, and I'll be your personal trainer. I know you've already emailed your information and filled out all your intake forms, so thanks for that."

I nod.

"So for your first appointment today, I'd like to go over the layout of the gym, talk about expectations, and do a strength and mobility assessment."

"Okay."

Why is this cat obsessed with my legs?

"Do you have any questions before we start?" I shake my head, and he chuckles. "You don't talk a lot, do you?" I shake my head again. "Well, I do, so buckle up, buttercup."

Dell shows me around the gym, and it's a decent size. It's definitely designed for one-on-one interactions, but a small group could meet here. The equipment, rubber flooring, walls, and ceiling are all black, except for pops of yellow scattered throughout.

When we reach the end of the quick tour, orange and white cat in tow, he instructs me to sit down on a chair across from him in his office and pulls out what must be my file. That's when I notice the walls are covered in either body diagrams or paintings of his cats.

"You must really like your cats."

"Oh, my sons?"

"Are they always here?"

"They are," he beams. "And they can't be separated. Their bond is too strong."

Chester hops into my lap without my consent and nuzzles his head into my stomach. The painting above Dell's head shows each cat wearing some kind of historical gentleman's clothing in a regal pose.

"And before you ask, they're not brothers. They're boyfriends."

I don't know how to respond to that.

"So, this is a rugby injury, right? Says here someone picked you up and tossed you upside down? Jesus."

"Yeah."

"I know a few rugby players myself. What team do you play for?"

"Philadelphia Men's D1."

Dell's mouth hangs open before he smiles. "Oh, The Daddies? Nice."

My cheeks heat at the mention of our tournament team's nickname. "Sort of. The team turns into the Philly Fathers for summer sevens. I don't really play sevens often."

"Why not?"

I try to shrug, but there's a pinch in my neck. "Big guys like me aren't meant to run that much. It's a... faster-paced game. I'm meant for short bursts. Tackling. Rucking. The slow grind."

"Look at all those words you strung together. All for me? I'm flattered." Just to be obstinate, I stay silent, and he chuckles. "Alright, fine. What are you looking to achieve with personal training?"

"I want to be able to play again, but I know that's off the table."

He nods solemnly but with a small smile that tells me he agrees, and he knows that's a hard pill for me to swallow.

"So," I sigh. "I need to know what I'm capable of going forward, and where my limits are."

He writes that down. "Okay. What does that mean for your body?"

"I don't follow."

"I mean, how do you want your body to feel?"

"I guess... not in pain?"

"Good start. And were you in any level of pain before this last injury?"

"Just the normal amount."

"Which was? On a scale of one to ten—and don't lie. That's a huge turn-off." The way he bores into my soul with only a stare is both intimidating and weirdly comforting.

I swallow the lump in my throat. "Like a three if I wasn't playing or recovering from a game."

"Dude," he drawls, brows pinching together. "You shouldn't be playing if a three is your baseline pain level."

"I'm used to it."

Dell sighs. "Okay. One of my goals will be to teach you to listen to your body and not ignore pain."

I didn't exactly think my Greek god-like personal trainer would be asking such probing questions.

After our unexpectedly deep dive into my life, he takes notes while I tell him about my medical history. I follow him out of his office to the gym, and Dell drops Chester with his... boyfriend... on the window perch. Dell has me take off my sling and neck brace and go through a list of stretches and positions to demonstrate my range of motion, which are either incredibly easy or total agony. He doesn't let me stay in those poses as soon as he sees me wince.

"You can either tell me your limit, or I can watch you like a hawk and assume you're in pain. I'd rather you tell me, dude."

Nosy bastard.

When my body heats up, I zip off my hoodie and toss it to the side. Before I have the chance to try the next position, he guffaws. "Is that a *Twisted Sisters True Crime Podcast* T-shirt?"

I glance down at the logo across my chest, and pain shoots down my neck and spine. *Fuck.* "Yeah," I say, slowly repositioning my head.

"That's my favorite show," he cheers. "I have the same shirt. Did you listen to the one that dropped last week?"

I nod.

"Dude, I think Frank did it."

That has me riled up. "No way. They said he was coerced by the police into admitting he killed Shannon."

"Yeah, but Shannon's sister Wendy was sleeping with that detective," Dell muses, crossing his large tattooed arms over his chest. "I think Wendy was trying to get Frank back for breaking up with her all those years ago."

"You think?"

"Oh my god. I can't believe I found another *Twisted Sisters* fan! Who's your favorite host? Kate or Tiffany?"

"Tiffany, obviously."

Dell chuckles. "Obviously. Kate is only there to create mayhem."

"Yeah, but her mayhem is always what takes Tiffany down new avenues of thinking, which, more often than not, leads to fresh evidence."

My burly trainer looks taken aback, like he hadn't put that together until now, and I wonder if that's what he looks like when he listens to the podcast. I wonder how he listens. In the car? Working out? In bed? I wonder what he wears to bed…

"I never thought about it like that," Dell chuffs, "but you're right! Okay, stop distracting me from my job Big Rugby Daddy." His smile is so big and genuine and my gut drops like a lead balloon.

There's something else though—something I don't often feel. A quiet fluttering in my stomach. Like a single butterfly flitting about. That's unexpected. I usually only feel flutters once I really know a person and can trust them. There have only been three people I've been attracted to my whole life.

The first: my best friend in junior high, Conner, who quickly became my bully once I finally mustered the courage to tell him my feelings.

The second: my college girlfriend, Jessica, a religious girl who took me to church with her every Sunday and held my hand. She never pressured me for sex because she was saving herself for marriage. It allowed me time to develop my sexual attraction to her as our romantic attraction grew. It's fucking laughable looking back on that relationship now.

And then there was Robyn, the third. The woman who unknowingly consumes me whole. The wild freshman I met all those years ago, who snuck her way into my heart, and I've never let go.

No one has ever given me butterflies since. Not until this big blonde beefcake caught me in his smile like a live trap and called me Big Rugby Daddy.

One butterfly.

I'm going to ignore it.

He holds out a rubber resistance band for me to pull apart, and I have to shake myself back into reality when he says, "Next week we can talk about the newest episode. Twenty bucks says Detective Wilson gets murdered."

---

1. TEXAS HOLD 'EM by Beyoncé

Chapter 3
Team Meeting

Robyn

Eight weeks later

I'm thrumming with good energy as I walk into the USA Valor training facility for our team meeting. It's been about a month since everyone has seen each other. Women's professional rugby isn't set up like other professional sports in the U.S. Our games are scattered throughout the year, and sometimes we go through small periods of time between matches, like we just did. But with summer on its way, we have to get ready for three upcoming games.

Coach usually calls us all together the week before practices start to get us mentally prepared and discuss our team strategy for the season. The USA Valor picked me up four years ago. Before that, I briefly played for Minneapolis' Women's Premier League Rugby. And before that, I was playing in college.

A lot of my old teammates warned me not to put all my eggs in one basket when it came to making rugby a profession, but my parents had the opposite approach. They're both former Olympians. My father, Chris, was a soccer player, and my mother, Diedra, was a synchronized swimmer. They actually met at the Olympic games in Atlanta, and I was the result of that meeting, if you catch my drift.

"Birdie!" my teammate Serwaa cries out as she sprints toward me and launches herself into my arms. My nickname might be Birdie, but she's the one flying into me. My hands instinctively find her waist, and I lift her in the air for that signature *Dirty Dancing* pose.

"Hey, girl," I smile. "Missed you."

Serwaa carefully comes down, but then latches onto my back for a piggyback ride, and dozens of small braids flap over my shoulder. "Missed you, too."

"How was your trip to Denver?" I ask.

She sounds wistful when she says, "Amazing."

"Did you ask her yet?" Serwaa has been in a long-distance relationship with her girlfriend Dani for five grueling months, and she was supposed to ask Dani to move in with her.

"I was too nervous."

"Baaaabe," I drawl.

"I know."

Carefully, I drop her down as we approach the conference room. "She literally got your name tattooed on her under-boob. Arguably, the hottest part of the boob."

"How would you know?"

"I might be straight, but I appreciate the female form."

"The sooner you stop lying to yourself about being a lesbian, the better," she teases.

"You all just want me to join the club."

"Duh. Think of all the pussy you'd be drowning in if our fans found out."

I think of all the comments I get on a regular basis from my social accounts and snort. "More for you."

Serwaa opens the door, and most of the team is already here with ten minutes to spare. I give a few of them bear hugs before spotting a new player and making my way over to her.

Stretching out my hand, I give her a smile. "Hi. I'm Robyn

Cassidy. Team captain. Hooker."

"Hi," she replies. She's a couple inches shorter than me, about five-eight, with bright blonde hair pulled back in a ponytail. She's in casual team apparel like the rest of us, but she's wearing what looks like a tennis skirt. I like her already. "Hannah."

"Welcome to the team, Skirt." She smiles softly at my nickname for her. "This is Khaos," I say, gesturing for them to shake hands.

"She/They. Scrum-half." Khaos is a peppy, bizarre little human with short red hair and ivory skin. Her pregame ritual consists of sipping a Five Hour Energy shot while praying the rosary, immediately followed by screaming the lyrics to *Call Me Maybe*.

I introduce Skirt to the rest of the team and save my bestie for last.

"Serwaa Yeboah," she says, extending her hand. "Winger." Serwaa is Black, and she has her usual thin, waist-length braids falling behind her back. And, as always, her nails are perfectly painted. When Serwaa finishes playing a game, she looks more or less the same as when she started. Me on the other hand? Even with tight braids on game day, my flyaways take charge and I'm a blotchy mess. Serwaa will look like she went for a light jog.

Some people have all the luck.

When we get through the rest of the introductions, I take a seat next to one of our props, Casshole (real name Cassie), a white, masc lesbian with dark hair cropped close to her head. She's one of our quieter players, and most people find her intimidating, but she's actually a total sweetheart.

"Is that for our trainer?" I ask, peering over her shoulder and watching her edit a workout video.

She finally looks up at me. "Yeah. Thanks again for introducing me to him. I've seriously seen such an improvement in my core strength."

A couple of our other teammates see him too. "He's growing quite the collection of rugby players."

"If I were him, I'd be advertising that he trains Olympians."

I chuckle. "You and I both know he's not lacking in his marketing game."

Before Casshole can reply, Coach walks into the room. Laura Casey is slim and white, with strawberry blonde hair that's almost always in a tight bun. She played rugby in college like most of us, but picked up coaching after retiring from Premier League about ten years back.

"Good afternoon everyone," she says, coming front and center to address us. Leaning against the table, she crosses her legs and folds her hands in her lap. Her usual upbeat attitude is mysteriously missing. She swallows. "I hope you all had a nice break and were able to recover from any minor injuries. I'd like to welcome Hannah to the team," she says, nodding over to the rookie with a wan smile. "Normally, I'd be ready to get into this season right away with all of you, but there's been a change of plans. As many of you know, my wife Bridget has been suffering from migraines for the better part of this last year. It got so bad, she was hospitalized a couple weeks ago."

Oh my god! I didn't know about that.

Coach continues, her face turned down as she takes a deep breath, but it does nothing to help the crack in her voice. "They found a malignant tumor in her brain." There's an audible gasp and murmuring across the room in response and I'm certain all of our hearts have stopped beating. "She's been diagnosed with stage four cancer, and effectively immediately, I will be resigning as head coach to take care of her full time."

Before I can form another thought, I push out of my chair and round the table to hug her. A chorus of chairs scraping across the carpeted floor and falling over follows suit. We're soon surrounded by the entire team, all of us wishing this wasn't happening.

Laura has been more than a coach to us. She's been our friend, our mother, our rock. I can't imagine playing for anyone else.

Eventually, everyone gets back in their seats, and she continues. "Assistant Coach Wallace will step up as head coach until USA Valor hires a replacement. In the meantime, I'd encourage you all to put your feelers out in case you know anyone who might be interested."

I look over at our assistant coach and interrupt. "You don't want to be head coach?"

Bob's a white guy in his mid-sixties with a bald head and an addiction to sunflower seeds. "I was planning on retiring next year," he says with a shrug. "No sense in taking that position just for them to hire someone new again next year."

Laura cuts in. "Bob will help your new coach transition, but I expect each and every one of you to give the new coach your full attention, just the way you have with me and Bob. The USA Valor have come too far in recent years to let it all go back. It feels like we're finally seeing this sport grow in America, and I'll be damned if I see that slip away. So keep your heads on straight and stay focused."

"I'd prefer to keep my head on gay," Khaos interrupts, because she's Khaos and gets away with everything.

Miraculously, that gives Laura the first smile we've seen today.

· · · ● · ● · · · ·

After the coaches left the team meeting, us veteran players stayed behind to form a social media plan. I have the most followers by far, a combined total of about five million, so after talking with the team's social media manager, she approved me making the announcement with the team's to follow. I posted about finding a new head coach before

I left the training facility, and by the time I got home after my workout, it had forty-three thousand likes.

After a quick dinner, I had a long phone call with my dad about the announcement. It went about the same as I thought it would. He dug into me.

Be the best and make a great first impression. Establish your presence but be willing to listen. Show them why you deserve your title as captain.

It's impossible not to get tired of this same old spiel. He's been doing this for years, both of my parents have. He's ruthless about my athleticism and leadership, while Mom is ruthless about my appearance and brand.

I love them, I do, and I probably wouldn't be where I am today without them, but could they trust that I know what I'm doing? I'm twenty-eight, my whole prefrontal cortex is developed, and all I do is eat, sleep, and breathe rugby.

That, and read romance, usually something of the unhinged or sporty variety.

After a relaxing shower, I don my oversized *Bridgerton* T-shirt and slip into bed for an early night watching my favorite show. My Kindle is fully charged with a new dark romcom queued up so I can dig in the minute my show is over. With slimy under-eye masks pressed on, I settle in and press play. As the intro starts, I check my phone again.

TheGymBreaux has liked your post.

That makes me smile. Dell Breaux's online presence is how most people know him, but I met him long before his socials blew up.

Chapter 4
Cupid's Arrow

Robyn

Four Years Ago

Glorious clouds roll in, blocking the scorching sun as I hug a blue-haired fan. I'm in the Gayborhood of Philadelphia with most of my team for the pride parade, and it's been a hot one.

"I just love you so much," the teenager, dressed head-to-toe in rainbow attire, tells me. "I'm going to start a rugby team at my school."

"Do it," I cheer, letting go but holding their shoulders. "Start that team and DM me when you do."

"Really?" they ask, eyes wide.

"Yes! I'll come talk to everyone."

"Oh my god, seriously? That would be awesome!"

"Rugby isn't going to grow itself. It's people like us that need to make it happen," I smile.

When the teenager leaves, Serwaa bumps my shoulder and hands me a cold bottle of water. "That's the third team you've offered to visit."

"And that is the third team you're visiting with me."

"Um, I'm not the famous one," she remarks.

"Doesn't matter. You're coming with me. And if exposure is what they need, exposure is what I can give them."

"Alright," Casshole says, coming up to me and giving me

a hug. "Your shift is over, Birdie. Go see your man."

Everyone on the team signed up for a dedicated four-hour time slot to stand around and answer questions about rugby, the team, and spread our allyship in the community. A lot of players showed up with their significant others, who have been coming and going all day.

"That's right," Serwaa drawls, flipping her braids back and swaying her head. "It's your three-month fuckaversary."

I roll my eyes. "Don't say it like that."

"Like what? Is it special to you?" she asks knowingly, and my lips curl against my will.

"Yes."

"Then it's special." She smacks me on the ass. "Text me afterward and tell me everything. Get your fine ass outta here."

As I walk to my car parked a few blocks away, I pull my phone out of my dress pocket to check the time and send a text to my boyfriend, Derek. Well, he's kind of my boyfriend. I don't know. I guess he doesn't like labels.

I'm on my way!

When I look up and pay attention to my surroundings, a burst of warm summer wind whooshes over me, and my short sundress kicks up. After I fit it back into place, my eyes lock on a tall, golden man walking toward me. With the late afternoon sun behind him, his long blonde hair glows like an aura, and my heart stops.

It's impossible not to stare at him—he's beautiful. His shoulders are broad and muscular. Wearing a simple black T-shirt and pale pink shorts, it's nothing special, but I'm transfixed nonetheless.

It's then that I notice he's watching me, too. Our eyes meet and we both slow down—almost like we're moving in slow motion. When he's only a few feet away, I notice the cheap plastic rainbow beaded necklace he's wearing, indicating he's clearly coming to or from the pride event.

When he walks past me, for the first time in my life, I actually turn my body to shamelessly check him out.

He does the same.

Oh my god, he smells like mint. Colorful old-school American tattoos flow down his arms and thighs!

Am I drooling?

Big Handsome turns his whole body, stops, and removes his sunglasses. Unable to control my body, I mirror him.

I stop.

What am I doing?

"You're… beautiful," he says, like he was just struck by the same Cupid's arrow as me and he can't believe he's doing this either. When he takes a few steps closer, I do the same, like my body has its own agenda.

"Thank you," I reply, positive my cheeks are on fire.

He puts his hands in the pockets of his shorts and smirks. "Where are you going looking that pretty?" he asks, his voice husky and confident.

I huff a little laugh. "I was just at the pride parade."

He gives me a thorough body scan and takes his time. And I'm letting him. Why am I letting him?

"You wanna come with me to a friend's barbeque?"

A giggle bubbles out of me before I can't stop it. Who does this? Who meets a stranger and invites them to a barbeque? I've been catcalled before, but this is wholly different. I don't have an ounce of fear. He's staring at me like there's nothing more interesting to watch and I like it. I allow it. My mind has already shifted to attending with him—this perfect stranger—and flirting back and forth as I learn everything about him.

Something clicks, and it's like a wet blanket is thrown on me.

"I'm sorry. I have to meet… my boyfriend." Those last two words coming out slow and unsure.

My stranger lifts his chin in understanding. Every fraction of a second that passes tingles with electricity between us.

"Boyfriend," he repeats, like he needs to hear himself say it. "Of course. Does he know how lucky he is?"

All of a sudden, my hands ache and my throat seizes. I can't think—my brain doesn't want to picture anything outside of this moment. I'm transfixed by this beautiful, golden-haired man with the cheap rainbow necklace and a melancholy smile.

Does Derek know how lucky he is?

The truth hits me like I caught a hospital pass, but I can't show it. I have to believe in us. Sure, Derek has never fawned over me like this stranger just did, but it's okay. He has a quieter love. We're not a flashy couple, and I could never ask him to be.

But unloading my messy answer to the man in front of me is not a cute look. So I shrug. "I hope so."

"I hope so, too." His mesmerizing chestnut eyes lock on mine. He drags in a long breath. "Okay. I'm gonna walk away now before I say anything stupid."

"Okay," I say, toying with one of my gold earrings and trying to walk backward. I bump into the pole of a streetlight, and an unwarranted giggle bursts out.

Big Handsome bites his lip, stops, then walks toward me again. "Fuck, you're cute. No!" he says, lifting his hands up and chastising himself. "Leave me alone, you siren." He regains his backward steps and winks. "But think about me next time you kiss your boyfriend, okay?"

I roll my lips together and turn to walk away, but throw my chin over my shoulder to call back. "I promise no such thing."

His only reply is to blow me a kiss. It's harmless, but there's something so powerful in it that I can't explain.

Once I've safely rounded the corner of the building and

I'm out of his range, I close my hand around his kiss and slip it into my pocket.

Thirty minutes later, I walk into Derek's apartment and find him sitting in his room at his computer with his headphones on. He must be in the middle of a game because his concentration is fixed to his screen. I squeeze his shoulders, run my hands down his chest, and give him a weird back-hug.

Without looking away from his desktop, he gives me a quick kiss on the cheek. "Hey, I'll be done in a little bit."

"Could you be done now?" I whisper. I'm trying to ignore the lingering electric pulses that have been surging through me since the encounter with my stranger. But if I'm honest, it's one hundred percent the reason I'm worked up right now. I need to release this built-up tension.

"I... Can you just," Derek stammers, warring between his game, the people in his ear, and me. "Shit," he barks into his microphone. "Great job, team. Thanks for all the support, fuckers. Yeah, I gotta respawn."

"Does that mean it's over?" I ask, but I know the answer.

"No," he sighs. "I gotta start over. Make yourself comfortable, and I'll be there soon."

Without another word, I step away and head to the bathroom. While I wash my hands, I take a long look in the mirror. My long tawny hair is twisted up in a sleek bun and shows off my strong shoulders. The bow-tie straps of my dress and the delicate jewelry I wear mock me. My soft red lipstick is pointless.

I quickly remove all the bobby pins and hair tie and fluff out my hair, guiding it over my small chest. Then I fling it behind me. Then back in front. Over one shoulder, then the other, adjusting my posture.

Right when I'm about to grunt and throw my hair back up into another bun, I think of him. My stranger. His kiss burns inside my pocket and my fingers twitch.

When I look back into the mirror, his voice comes back to me.

"You're beautiful."

Chapter 5
Old Friend, Huh?

Robyn

"**G**ood morning, sunshine," Dell says. His knowing smirk would be a hell of a lot more annoying if he weren't holding an iced coffee for me.

"Nothing is good about 7:00 a.m. workouts," I grumble, taking the caffeinated blessing from him.

"Oh, come on," he drawls. "You love seeing my gorgeous face in the morning."

I swallow my first sip and deadpan, "There is absolutely nothing I love seeing before 9:00 a.m. on any day."

I'm not a morning person. But I switched time slots with Casshole when her baby was born a couple of months ago so she could get more sleep. Apparently, her son's prime sleeping hours are from 4:00 to 8:00 a.m. Knowing how booked Dell's personal training schedule is, I offered to switch.

And I regret it every Monday morning.

Dell finds it amusing. Thankfully, he sweetens the pot by always having my coffee order ready.

I take a long swig of my iced heaven, letting it soak into my sleepy bones. Dell busies himself with placing an agility ladder on the ground, and my mind replays our first encounter again. It became clear to me that he had no recollection of our first meeting when I hired him as my personal trainer two years ago. My last personal trainer was moving to Germany, and she recommended I hire Dell, who was *her* personal trainer. I knew I would be in capable hands if he was a personal trainer to personal trainers.

Of course, the moment I saw him, I recognized him, and all those old feelings resurfaced. When I tried to bring it up, I not-so-casually asked, "You look so familiar. Have we met before?"

But he hit me with, "You might have seen my videos."

And that's how we discovered each other's mutual, massive social media presence. I make content about women's rugby, body positivity, and sound-off the occasional fuck-the-haters monologue.

Dell (a.k.a. TheGymBreaux) makes thirst traps designed to look like workout advice. In every video, he wears skin-tight leggings that leave absolutely nothing to the imagination and a crop top. Every damn muscle he has is thick, defined, and glorious.

I've been attracted to an array of men in my life. Rail thin? Hot. Big boys? Hell yeah. But this man who looks like he's carved from stone, waiting for the world to be placed on his shoulders so he can see how many reps he can squat? *Oh yeah.* Mama likes.

He's known for his instructional workout videos, where he'll set up the camera to film his ass while he lunges—his *huge*, delicious ass on display. And he'll say things like, "Let's turn that pancake into a pound cake." Or, "We're gonna get some gnarly pumps in today, guys." Or he'll sing, "It's *peachin' season, and all of y'all be eatin'*" and then proceeds to have the camera zoom in to show just how deep his ass can eat Spandex before starting his tutorial.

Sadly, he doesn't wear the borderline see-through leggings during our sessions. He's all professional and shit—a white polo with his company's logo stitched on and regular pants that leave everything to the imagination.

But it's fine. It's good. He's been a perfect personal trainer to me, and I'm the strongest and fastest I've ever been because of it. And since he obviously didn't remember me from that day at Pride four years ago, I clearly wasn't anything special to him. I can read the fucking signs when someone doesn't like me.

Usually.

There is one exception.

After my warm-up, Dell has me doing a circuit with the agility ladder, burpees, and alternating wave lunges with the big ropes. When I get to my third round on the ladder, he catches me slacking.

"You're getting sloppy," he shouts over the ever-present country music. "Stay tight. Every movement should mean something." When I correct myself and focus on each foot placement and how my core should be engaged, he cheers. "There you go! Keep it up."

Dell puts me through a weight-lifting circuit before telling me to hop on the stationary bike. He plays with the resistance settings as sweat trickles between my breasts and I start my ride.

"You ladies find a coach yet?" he asks, increasing the resistance.

"Not yet," I huff. "There's someone I think might be great at it, but... I don't know."

"Who?"

"It's probably a bad idea." When I don't continue, Dell eyes me and increases the resistance to its most difficult setting. "Okay," I grunt. "It's because I've kinda had a thing for him for a long time."

"Oh," he sings, then mercifully lowers the intensity. "What? Don't think you can handle seeing your crush all the time?"

I see you all the time.

"He's just... we used to be so close. And now he avoids me like I'm the plague. I don't know what I did."

"Are you sure it was you?"

"I don't know what else it could have been. Maybe I gave

Friendzone vibes too strong back in the day, and now he can't see me as anything else."

"Oh, he's an old friend?"

"Yeah."

"He still likes you."

"What? What do you mean, *still*?"

"Did he want to hang out with you a lot? Did you guys spend time talking one-on-one often? Did you talk about deep stuff? Have you met each other's families?"

I'm silent for a moment as I think back. "Yes." All those tournaments and rugby parties we went to. We'd socialize with our teams, but we'd always gravitate toward each other and block out everyone else. Most of it was drunken fun, harmless to the untrained eye, but sometimes there were moments I could barely resist him. There was something so easy about him. So tender and kind on the inside. But our paths never aligned and I could never quite figure out if he wanted me in the same way.

"He still likes you," Dell says, matter-of-factly.

"Well, how the hell am I supposed to get him to talk to me again? I feel so awkward around him now. When it comes to him, I have no game."

"That's rather out of character for you."

"Tell me about it."

"Alright," Dell smirks, turning off the bike. "You've convinced me. I'll be your flirt coach."

Chapter 6
Flirt Coach

Dell

Here's the thing about me: sometimes I dive in head-first without checking how deep, clean, or safe the water is. But that's how I go through life, and it's worked out for the most part. I don't usually second-guess myself.

But with Robyn staring at me like I'm out of my mind, I do.

I remember so distinctly when I first saw her at Philly's Pride parade. The second she walked into my gym two years ago, I recognized her. I swallowed my pride and pretended it was our first meeting. I've been trying to make a professional name for myself since I opened my gym seven years ago, when I was twenty-six.

Once she came back into my life, I thought I could sweep our chance encounter under the rug and ignore that tiny suspended moment of my life where I was nothing more than a man who wanted to kiss a woman in the street. I wanted to listen to her speak and know everything about her. I wanted to know how she likes her eggs cooked and what kind of music she likes. I wanted to know what she tastes like.

Instead, I've ignored my instincts, praying that my attraction to her would fizzle out—but no. I have a big, fat crush on my pretty client. My pretty, Olympian client whose teammates have hired me at her recommendation.

There's no real rule against personal trainers dating clients. Hell, I know plenty of peers who have. I've done it myself too, many times. Nothing was ever serious, not that I do serious anymore, anyway. But I started getting a reputation that I fuck all my clients, which led to me being labeled as unprofessional by some, and, one by one, I lost the clients I messed around with. I decided that's not what I wanted for this new part of my life. I wanted to get away from all of that.

Therefore, for the last three years, I've had a strict No Dating Clients rule in an attempt to stay professional and rebuild my name.

So, that secret crush I have on Robyn Cassidy? It's gonna stay that way.

And yet, I've just offered her lessons in flirting.

These head-first instincts only work if everything else in my life follows suit. Now, I'm mixing two ingredients that should not go together: Robyn, my forbidden fruit, and assisting her with *her* crush.

What the fuck am I doing?

Oh well. I don't often second-guess myself; let's not start now. When I commit, I commit.

"Flirt coach?" she asks through labored breath as I increase the resistance again. "What does that mean?"

I shrug off my internal war and dive in. "It means I want to help you get the guy."

She eyes me speculatively. "Why would you do that?"

"Because we're friends. But now that I think about it, how is someone with millions of followers not able to get a date?"

"Trust me, if I was into women, I'd be married by now."

I chuckle thinking about the ladies in her comments. "That's true."

"Netflix reached out to me a few weeks ago about auditioning for some new queer reality dating show."

"Seriously? What was it called?"

"*Lesbian Lock-Up.* The show where contestants are

locked in a simulated prison, and compete for the affection of the star. But here's the twist: there are ten civilians and ten real prisoners. It's like *The Bachelorette* meets *Orange Is the New Black*."

"Get the fuck outta here," I laugh. "How is any of that legal?"

"I have no idea, but I'm gonna watch that show if it ever comes out."

"There could be a spin-off: *Breaking Out*. The show where the only way the bachelorette and her prisoner girlfriend can escape is with the help of the women whose hearts have been broken along the way."

Robyn laughs, "Like *The Amazing Race* meets *Shawshank Redemption*."

"Alright, hop off." Turning on my heel, I head for the weight rack. Robyn follows and grabs the weightlifting belt. "So, is that a yes?" I ask, sliding her plates onto the bar. "Can I be your flirt and dating coach?"

"What about your No Dating Clients rule?"

Alright, so I may have told her about my rule at some point over the years. I found telling my clients about this rule helped keep me in check, especially with her.

"This wouldn't be considered dating. I'm coaching you. It's different."

She stares at me.

"Would it be helpful if we put a time limit on this?" I ask. "Like, let's say we stop this after a month. A clean break."

She fastens the belt around her waist, but her eyes never drift away—like she's studying the inner workings of my mind. "But we're still friends? You're still my trainer? I really don't want to find a new one."

"Of course."

"Promise you won't make fun of me," she says, and it's not a question. It's a contractual term. She looks so worried, and I can't tell if it's because she thinks I would actually make fun of her or if she thinks she looks desperate. Maybe it's something else entirely. Regardless, I don't like it when she worries.

I slide the last plate on and level with her, all humor gone. "I promise. On BooBoo Kitty and Chester's life."

Robyn's hand flies to her chest and she gasps, her hazel eyes wide. She knows how much my cats mean to me. "Oh my god. That's like signing your name in blood."

"I'm that serious. I want you to be comfortable being yourself. I will not make fun of you. I'm here to help. Saturday night work for you?" Fuck, I sound too eager.

When she smiles like she is now, I'm transported back to the day we met. To the blurring of our surroundings and her strong features shining through. Her heated cheeks and her caught-off-guard smile.

So what if I am eager? I *want* to help her. I want her to be happy. Friends help friends like this all the time, don't they?

"Yeah," she nods. "Saturday night works."

"Good. I'll pick you up at seven-thirty. Now squat. Three sets of eight."

"I think you put too much weight on."

"Oh yeah? Show me how wrong I am."

Chapter 7

Dating Lesson No. 1

Robyn

Tossing the eighth dress into the heap on my bed, I howl, falling on top of it all in nothing but my skivvies and sweat. I have no idea how to dress for this dating lesson with Dell tonight. We're going to dinner at a trendy restaurant, but I don't know if I should wear something casual because we're just friends, or something sexy because this is a date... thing.

Ugh.

What have I done? Why did I agree to let Dell be my flirt coach? What good could possibly come of this? I guess the ability to get Isaiah to notice me as more than a friend. That is the goal, after all. It's the dream. But achieving that with the help of my other crush?

He's really taking personal training to a whole new level.

We've seen each other outside of training sessions a couple of times. Once, we ran into each other at the grocery store. Another time at a hockey game. But other than that, we've never hung out and for good reason. How am I supposed to keep it together when I don't have anything like working out to distract me from... him?

I have to redirect my thoughts and focus on Isaiah. I need to learn how not to be a total fucking weirdo around him.

When he left to play rugby professionally in London, we lost our near-daily connection. Our communication suffered, partly because he was busy trying to make a name for himself, and partly because I was wrapped up in my own stuff with school and rugby. From there, it only got worse. The more time passed, the more awkward it felt acting like the close friends we once were, and the harder it was to pick up where we left off. My more-than-friends feelings only caused more uncertainty. I've been a festering pit of nervousness about our relationship ever since.

A buzzing from my phone completely derails my thoughts, and I reach for it to see a text from my friend Angie, Isaiah's older sister. It's a picture of her infant twins wearing USA Valor onesies, and I instantly smile. My thumbs fly over the keyboard to reply.

> They don't even need to try out. They're on the team! I'm the captain, I can say that.

The dots come and go for a minute before a video call from Angie pops up.

"Hey, mama," I smile, and Angie's plump, heart-shaped face fills the screen.

"Are you naked?"

"Kinda," I say, showing her my strapless bra and then panning back to my face.

"Hot. I was trying to type, but texting is nearly impossible with two babies these days."

"You and Raf have your hands full."

"Oh god, you have no idea. Anyway," Angie drawls, "I need you to send me your new address so I can mail you a wedding invitation."

"Yes!"

"Of course, you'll have a plus one," she smirks, her comment obviously fishing for a reaction.

I roll my eyes, but my gut drops. She has no idea about my feelings for her brother. I've been hanging around Angie and her family for years, but I've never told her about this. It's not that I don't think she would approve. She's the matriarch of her family, and honestly, I think she'd be happy for us if we worked out. I'm just scared to make the effort—to put myself out there and be real with Isaiah. To finally tip the scales would be a huge change. But then there's the very real possibility that it would crash and burn, and the friendship Isaiah and I have (if you can even call it that) would crumble.

"I'll work on that plus one," I sigh.

"Are you laying on a pile of clothes?"

"Oh, yeah. I have a thing tonight and I don't know what to wear."

"What kind of thing?"

"Like a... date?"

"I don't love that you're unsure if it's a date or not."

"Yeah, me neither."

"Okay, where are you going? What's his name? What's the vibe? Do you need a playlist? I'll send you one. I'm also sending you a couple new dark romance book recs. There's this one about a dude falling in love with his home security system, only to find out it's monitored and voiced by a real man and not artificial intelligence."

I laugh, "Top of the reading list it goes."

"So who's the guy?"

"His name is Dell, and we're going to dinner at Nero's." Before my next words come out, Ang has already sent me a playlist called *Sexy Getting Ready Mix*.

"Thanks, girl."

"You're welcome! Now give me a fashion show."

· · · · • • • • · · ·

An hour later, I'm wearing a black, fitted thin-strap dress and heels, with gold earrings and red lips. It's a look I'm comfortable in, but as Angie put it, I look like I invented the phrase "good boy." And I think that's going to help me tonight. I need to feel powerful and in control of myself. I need to guard against Dell's charm and figure out how to flirt with Isaiah.

As I walk up to the restaurant, I check my phone and find the group chat blowing up.

> Serwaa: Good luck tonight Birdie!

> Khaos: $100 says it ends with a kiss

> Skirt: Wait, I thought this was a practice date?

> Serwaa: It is, but have you SEEN this man?

> Serwaa: <Video of Dell in a thirst trap>

> Casshole: He makes our glutes look tiny

> Khaos: I don't understand why you need flirting help, Birdie. Just show guys your tits and they'll be all over you! <two melon emojis>

> Casshole: <eye roll emoji> Khaos, that's how YOU get girls

> Khaos: And it works every time!

> Serwaa: Keep your tits in Birdie

I start to type my reply, but I'm greeted by a familiar, low voice. "Hi."

When I look up, I'm momentarily paralyzed. *Fuck, he looks good.* His long blonde hair is down, which he never does, and he's wearing a black, short-sleeve dress shirt with tiny white dots. His colorful tattoos with bold, clean lines only serve to increase my body temperature to an unbearable heat. Unable to stop my eyes or close my mouth, I take in his black jeans and well-worn… cowboy boots? Interesting. The silver bracelet he's wearing pops against his exposed, tattooed forearms. Rugged and chic. What a delicious combo. I don't know what I was expecting. It's not like he was going to wear gym clothes or his work attire. But this… this is fascinating.

"Hhhhhi," I breathe.

"You look beautiful, Robyn," he says, leaning in close and placing a kiss on my cheek. Oh god, he smells like mint. And oh god, Dell Breaux just kissed me! It was chaste, and some would say friendly—European, even.

Oh no. I should reciprocate! That's what Europeans do!

But I've waited too long, and right as he pulls away, I flinch and graze his lips with mine.

"Oh shit," I huff out. "I'm sorry." I rear back instantly, but I overdo it and fumble over my own heels. Dell reaches forward and grabs my waist to steady me before I make an even bigger ass of myself on the sidewalk.

"Okay," he drawls. His eyes are wide, and the corners of his lips turn up. "This is not you."

I push his hands off me. "I know," I squeak. "See, this is what happens when I try to flirt—" I cut myself off before I accidentally add 'with someone I like.'

"Take a deep breath," he orders, drawing in a long inhale and waiting for me to follow. Our eyes lock into each other as I obey. Wow. In the low, early evening sunlight, his dark chocolate eyes have a halo of gold I've never noticed before. So *pretty.*

We exhale.

"You are not a clumsy person. You are an agile athlete and a beautiful woman and *you* are going to do great tonight."

"Okay," I huff and give myself a little shake to reset.

"Are you hungry?"

"Always."

"Good," he smiles, then wraps his arm around my shoulder and leads me toward the restaurant doors.

"Oh god, it's busy here."

"I know," he smiles, his thumb dragging back and forth across my bare upper back. He cuts through the waiting line of people and leads me to the hostess stand. "Reservation for Dell."

"Like the computers?" the young woman asks.

"Yes," he chuckles. "Also, a small valley."

"A what?"

"A dell is a small valley," he clarifies.

"No, Adele is a singer."

"Yes, she is. But my name is Dell."

"Do you know Adele?"

"No, but if I sing *Rolling in the Deep*, will you seat us at our table?"

The hostess finally looks at her tablet, then back at him with a glint of mischief. I can tell she doesn't think he'll do it. Her eyes narrow. "Yes."

"*We coulda had it—*" he sings unabashedly before her eyes widen, and she scurries from around the podium with two menus.

"Okay! Okay! Excellent job. Right this way."

"I can keep going."

"Not necessary," she trembles.

"Are you sure?" I ask as she sets our menus down at a table set for two near the windows. "I can perform backup vocals. I was in my high school's musical rendition of *Silence of the Lambs*."

Dell pulls out my chair, and I sit. "Robyn here has many talents."

"I'm sure," the hostess stutters. "Your server will be right with you. Enjoy your meal."

Dell laughs to himself as he sits in his chair. "She couldn't get out of here fast enough. *Silence of the Lambs*, huh?

How'd that go?"

"The review in our school newspaper read: *Not everything can or should be a musical.*"

"I'm going to need to see footage someday."

"Nothing would make me more uncomfortable," I wince.

"And how are you feeling now?"

"A little nervous."

"You gotta look past my rugged good looks if we're gonna get anywhere."

I snort. "I'll try," I say honestly.

"I want you to act normal." I level him with a stare before he adds, "Er, as normal as you can. Like we don't know each other, and this is our first date."

"Okay. But the thing is, you're supposed to be coaching me to flirt with someone I actually know pretty well. It wouldn't be a blind date."

"Oh, that's right," he muses, falling back in his chair and crossing his arms, his biceps bulging. He sits back up. "Well then, think of this as a real date with yours truly. You know him, and you know me."

Before I can reply, our server comes to take our drink order, and we a bottle of wine to share.

"So how's the summer rugby season shaping up?" Dell asks casually as we skim our menus.

"It's hard to tell. We haven't had a game yet, just practices. But the whole team is unsure how we're supposed to move forward without Laura."

Dell lays his menu down and stares at me. "Why did you get into rugby?"

It's not an uncommon question when you play rugby. Back when I played softball and soccer, no one ever asked me how I got into those. But when you play a weird sport, you get this question a lot.

"I started playing my freshman year of college when I didn't make my school's softball team. Turns out, I'm a lot better at rugby. I don't think I've told you this, but my parents are both Olympians."

"Really?"

"Yeah. Dad met Mom at the Olympic games in Atlanta. He was a soccer player. She was a synchronized swimmer. And, well, I was sort of conceived there."

His eyes round. "What?"

"No joke."

"That's some high-octane genetics."

"You could say that," I chuckle softly. "Anyway, she was from Minnesota, and Dad lived in California. When she found out she was pregnant, they got married right away and he moved to Minneapolis."

"Are they still together?"

"Oh yeah. My dad is obsessed with my mom. And my mom is obsessed with maintaining her Olympic figure."

"Ah. Is she one of those almond moms? You know, knows the exact amount of almonds in a serving size? Focuses more on weight than well-being?"

"Ohhhh yeah. By the time I was twelve, she was keeping a weekly chart of my caloric intake. They're both pretty extreme. I get pressure from both of them about *making their mistake worth it*," I say, air quotes emphasizing my point.

Dell cocks his head. "Wait. What do you mean?"

"Like, it's up to me to make sure their mistake of getting pregnant pays off. That I'm the best. That I'm an Olympian, too."

"Jesus," he grumbles.

"They like to play it off as a joke, but they've said it so many times that I truly think they mean it. And I'm gonna shut up now because that was too much information and too deep for a date. I'm sorry."

"No, don't apologize. I like getting to know more about you."

"Pinot noir," our server says as she reapproaches our table. I'm thankful for the interruption because I really should not have gone that deep, that fast. It's just so effortless to talk to him, and my nerves are through the roof. Did I put on deodorant? I think so. Did I brush my teeth? Shit, why did we order red wine? Now I'm going to have stained teeth all night.

"Are you ready to order?" our server asks.

"Yes," I say, fumbling with the menu. "I'll have the branzino and cauliflower. Can I also have a side of the buttery whipped potatoes?"

"Of course," she says. "And for you, sir?"

"We'll start with the tuna tartare, and I'll have the pork sausage and herb pasta." When our server walks away, Dell turns his full attention back to me.

"How was that?" I ask, trying to hold back my desperation.

"How was what?"

"My order. Was it too much? Should I have ordered a salad?"

The gaping look he gives me only adds to my nervousness. "Who are you right now?"

I take a fortifying drink of my wine. "I don't know. Should I order something more... delicate? More feminine?"

"Robyn, take a deep breath." I do. "I would never expect you, an Olympic athlete, to order a damn salad for dinner. If your date thinks you should be eating something smaller, then they're a trash human, got it? And it wouldn't matter if you were an athlete or a librarian, lean or fat, you should order what you want."

I take another deep breath to calm down. "You're right. I know that. Not really sure what has come over me."

"I was gonna say, based on your social media content, I'd never think you would be worried about something like your food order. Didn't you recently post something about how the whole point of living is warm carbs?"

"I did," I say fondly. "And dessert."

"So why are you doubting yourself?"

"Because," I sigh. "I don't know. This guy... he's seen me at my best and my worst. I mean, really, he's seen me in some of my worst moments, physically. In college, there was more than one occasion he saw me with a bloody tampon up my nostril, covered head to toe in mud, and sunburnt to a crisp. I just... I wonder if I need to replace that image for him."

Dell's quiet for a long moment. "You shouldn't be changing a goddamn thing about you, Robyn."

My heart flutters, and I choke up—caught between feelings for two men, unable to decipher where to place my attention. But Dell's words seep into my brain and flow straight to my heart.

Suddenly, I'm fighting back memories. "Then why do guys always treat me like a bro?" I sigh and roll the stem of my wine glass, watching it swirl. "I wear feminine clothing because I want to. I wear jewelry and perfume, and I style myself in a way I love. I know I dress on trend, but it doesn't seem to matter to guys. I've always been their secret hookup, or the girlfriend they don't tell their friends about. Either way, it always ends quickly."

I finally look up at Dell, and he's watching me with soft eyes. "So yeah, maybe I'm flailing. I've clearly been doing something wrong. Can you blame me for trying to reinvent myself?"

"I don't blame you. But with absolute certainty, I can say those guys didn't know their ass from their head. It would break my heart if you changed yourself because of someone else. So I'm going to tell you again," he says, reaching to take my hand in his and brushing his thumb over my knuckles. "Do not change yourself. A good partner is someone who wants you to feel full, happy, and desired."

I know what he's saying is true, and I know in my heart of hearts that changing myself isn't going to magically bring all the boys to the yard. But maybe there's a part of me that I'm not showing off enough. That's what I want to find out.

"You speak like you've experienced that."

"I had that for a time. Once."

That piques my interest. "Who?"

He takes a sip of his wine, sets it down gently, and clears his throat. "I can trust you?"

"Of course."

"I had an ex-boyfriend, Travis, who I dated during my senior year of high school and then again during college for a bit until I was about twenty-four. I had a ring for him and everything."

I had no idea he had a serious partner before. The only things I've seen him take seriously are his business and his brand. He may post silly thirst traps, but he does so with a purpose.

"Anyway," he continues, twisting the wine glass around with one hand while still holding my hand with the other. "Things got kinda rocky when Travis started going out with some new work friends. He was drinking more than I'd ever seen. Staying out all night. Ignoring me. Then I caught him making out with another guy at my cousin's wedding. In a bathroom stall."

My own heart aches for him. What a hard thing to have to go through.

"We fought all night. All week," he says. "I was tired of being gaslit. I was tired of his bullshit. And when I said enough was enough, he threatened to..." He trails off, looking around, then back at me. With a lowered voice, he continues, "He threatened to upload a couple of videos we made."

"Like... *those* kinds of videos?"

He nods. "Like videos I thought would only stay between

him and me. And he did. He blurred his own face, but not mine. But I can be just as stubborn as him. I decided to make an OnlyFans account, create solo content, and let his uploads light my fire. I don't half-ass anything, and I sure as shit don't let others steamroll me."

"Oh my," I whisper. "Not that I want to look—"

"Don't lie to yourself," he smirks.

"—but do you still make that content?"

"Not in a couple of years, no. I deleted my account. Switched to good, old-fashioned thirst traps, the way our Lord intended. Y'know, that wholesome stuff."

"And where does personal training fall into this?"

"I went to school for kinesiology and business. Always knew I wanted to go into something that kept me in the gym. There's a lot of clarity and control there for me. And I enjoy helping people."

Suddenly, I'm reminded that he's helping me right now.

We're not on a real date.

He likes to help people. He just said that. He doesn't like me. He doesn't remember me from the sidewalk four years ago, and he certainly doesn't want—*no.* I need to stop.

"Tuna tartare," our server says, throwing me out of my selfish pity party and placing the dish between us.

"Thank you," he says softly. He turns his gaze back to me and squeezes my hand gently as the server walks away. But something changes inside of him, I can tell. All his confidence vanishes, and a rare downturn of his mouth forms. "Does knowing what you know now change the way you see me?"

"No," I say urgently. "I know a thing or two about giving the middle finger to haters," I remind him. "You did the same thing. And I don't think sex work is shameful."

Our hands stay locked together as our appetizer sits untouched between us. There's more in his eyes, though.

"What's wrong?"

He takes a long inhale and I'm on pins and needles when he finally speaks again. "The real reason I don't date my clients is because I used to—a lot. It was never anything serious. Just hooking up and a casual lunch here and there. But it got to a point where I started getting a reputation in the local training community that I was unprofessional."

"Oh."

"Hence the rule, which has kept me in check for three years now."

What a tortured soul. I never knew this side of him. Our training sessions are centered around playful banter and gossip, but this side... he hides it well. You'd never know this carefree gym bro cares deeply. He protects himself.

"Do you want to tell me more?"

A slow grin creeps across his handsome face before he sips his wine. "No," he says simply, his tone low and even; his confidence returned. "I'd like to sit here and listen to you talk. I like watching the candlelight flicker in your eyes." His gaze drags low as my body temperature spikes. "And I'd like to watch your chest flush when you catch me appreciating your body. Just. Like. That."

Chapter 8
Dessert

Robyn

Of course we ordered dessert. How could we not, when he explicitly told me to be myself? He knows how I live for a sweet treat. Our server came around with the dessert cart, and when the wildflower honey crème brûlée caught my eye, I didn't fight it. That sweet, custardy goodness sang to me.

"Enjoy," our server says, placing two spoons and walking away.

I'm about to tap into the thin, torched-sugar crust when Dell stands up and moves his chair right next to me. When he sits again, his long leg brushes against mine. He leans in close. "Would you feel comfortable showing more affection at this point?" he murmurs, and my downstairs region clenches.

There's only one word that flashes in my head like a billboard at night. "Yes."

Wordlessly, he takes the spoon from my hand and breaks the sheet of crispy, burnt sugar, then drags a delicate scoop. With one arm resting on my chair back and the other elbow propped on the table, Dell grins lazily and whispers, "Open for me."

What kind of dizzying liminal space am I in? Because I'm simultaneously floating in this aura we've created and burning from his attention. His minty fragrance mingles with the honey and vanilla of the crème brûlée, and suddenly, I'm swept away—lost entirely to him and the gentle taste of sweet custard and crispy sugar melting in my mouth.

"You're gorgeous, you know that?"

Can he hear my heart pounding against my chest? Can he feel the vibrations from my body causing the entire restaurant to reverberate? He's too close to me, yet not close enough.

He feeds me another spoonful and laughs softly. "Now might be a good time to say something similar back to me."

"Oh," I say breathlessly. "Y–you have a nice... face. It's a good face."

He takes a bite of the crème brûlée and smiles. "Watch out, Shakespeare."

"I mean, I..." My eyes travel from where he's licking his bottom lip to his surprisingly long lashes. "I could get lost in your eyes. I want to fall into them like Alice in Wonderland."

Dell looks pleasantly taken aback. "There you go. You sure know how to make a boy twirl his hair."

Throwing caution to the wind, I tuck a long strand of hair behind his ear. My fingers gently comb through his silky mane until I catch myself playing with the ends. I've never touched his hair before—and now, the idea of stopping feels wrong.

"I like your fingers in my hair," he hums.

"I like you," I whisper without thinking.

Dell's eyes snap back to me as something invisible shifts between us. He clears his throat and pulls away only a few inches, but those inches feel like a mile. "You're really good at this, Robyn. Flirting, that is. Let's, um..." He swallows and looks around for our server. "Let's get the check and move on to the next phase of our date."

"There's another phase?"

· · • • • • • • · ·

Ten minutes later, the two of us are walking under the streetlights when he takes my hand in his. The warm summer night air is nothing compared to the heat of his palm. "You really did great at dinner, Robyn."

"I don't know," I grouse. "It felt more like flailing."

"Well, if that's flailing, keep doing it." He smirks down at me and squeezes my hand a little tighter. "It was very charming."

I have to remind myself that *he's my dating coach. My flirt coach. The man I pay to keep my body in top-performing shape.*

"Are you going to tell me where we're going now?" I ask. "I'm not sure how much farther I can walk in these heels."

"I know. It's not much farther. Have you ever been to ChaCha's?"

Lightning strikes through my body at his question. "I love ChaCha's! We're going dancing?"

"We are," he grins effortlessly. I wiggle in delight like a dog that's just found her favorite toy. "I thought you might enjoy that."

"You ain't ready for this," I taunt, letting go of his hand and stopping on the sidewalk to pop, lock, and drop it.

His chuckle is loud and carries down the old street. "Come on. Let's see how you are in a club setting."

When we walk into ChaCha's, I'm immediately thrown into all the memories I've made here over the years with my teammates. We usually end up here after wins, for birthday parties, and breakup blowouts. I've never had much luck here with guys, though. I'm not sure what Dell has in store for me, but I'm excited.

Thankfully, ChaCha's isn't the hottest or newest club in the city, so there's no line outside. This place is slept on, I swear. The best music, affordable drinks, and queer-friendly.

When the beat of the music becomes my own heart's

rhythm, Dell hands me a margarita and takes a sip of his own. I'm gonna ace this part of the date. Before I can say anything, he's holding my hand again and pulling me to the dance floor.

"Alright, girl. Show me what you got."

Chapter 9
Secret Security

Isaiah

My knuckles rap on the partially opened door to find Jeremy typing away at his computer. He's one of the bar owners I work for. It's a tiny office above his Irish bar downtown, and it's filled with holiday decorations, boxes of liquor, and clean rags. It's one of five bars my company, Alliance Security, works for. Instead of bars hiring and managing their own security, they hire us to take care of everything. It also gives the neighboring bars a sense of community, knowing one security team is keeping an eye out for the same riff raff from place to place.

Jeremy looks up at me as I make my way in and sit across from him. "Hey, you're looking better, man," he says.

"Yeah. Almost have my full range of motion back in my shoulder."

"And your neck?" he asks.

"Eh, I'm still at about seventy percent there." I've been going to personal training for nine weeks at this point.

"It'll come. Hey, I wanted to talk about renewing our contract with you, but I was hoping we could cut a deal."

Settling further into my chair, I take a sip of coffee. It's nearly 10:00 p.m., but I'm more than halfway through my shift. "What did you have in mind?"

"I was hoping I could get a better price if I signed a two-year contract with you instead of one."

Jeremy did recommend another bar owner hire me just last week, and that contract is almost buttoned up, which would make them our sixth customer. I'm sure I could make something work for Flanagan's Pub.

"How about ten percent off?" I offer.

"Done," he smiles, then leans over to shake my hand.

"I'll send you the email with the updated contract Monday. Other than that, is everything good?"

"Yeah," he nods. "Thanks again, Isaiah."

"You're welcome," I reply and stand up. "Call me if you need anything."

"Will do."

As I leave Flanagan's and head to my SUV, I quickly check my personal phone to see if Dell messaged me back. But my last text to him lingers unanswered from 7:25 p.m.

> How r u so far ahead of me? I'm only on ch 3

My second and third sessions with Dell went as well as could be expected. He was mostly focused on finding the right exercises for me. As we found our rhythm, we'd talk about sports and *Twisted Sisters* in the moments between sets. But after our third session, I was nervous to tell him I was actually going to see a live Q&A in Newark with Kate and Tiffany from the podcast. I felt like if I told him about it, I would definitely ask him to go with me and that probably wouldn't be appropriate.

But when I showed up to the Q&A that night, Dell was already there, surprise and happiness radiating off him like rays of sunshine when he saw me. All night we sat next to each other. I didn't have to explain myself to him about anything. The podcast, the minute details of the show—all of it he understood. When our conversations drifted in other areas, I found myself curious about what makes him tick. I wanted to dig deeper.

He checked on my pain levels throughout the evening to make sure I was comfortable, and even went so far as stuffing his hoodie under my arm to create a better resting position. Which was really fucking nice and it did help.

We talked each other's ears off about the podcast after the Q&A, too. Not just at the event, but after. We got a couple beers at a nearby bar and exchanged numbers. It's been a constant flow of communication between us ever since.

We started texting about the show, and we binged the crap out of it. That turned into talking about our favorite crimes, which turned into true crime documentary recommendations, which turned into live-texting as we watched and reading true crime books.

Now there's a mild compulsion to text each other about anything and everything. Like last week:

> Dell: How was the concert last night?

> Isaiah: Ended up not going

> Dell: This is the part where you elaborate, jackass.

> Isaiah: Raf and Ang came down with a stomach bug, and so Dad and I watched the twins so they could sleep.

> Dell: Awwww. What kind of tricks can they do?

> Isaiah: They can roll over.

> Dell: Sweet! You know I was a wrestler in high school and college? I could teach them a thing or two.

> Isaiah: <laughing emoji> Why does that not surprise me?

> Dell: Now you're picturing me in a tight wrestling singlet, aren't you? <wink emoji>

> Isaiah: I was not.

I was.

Dell has been growing on me these last couple of months. Well, *burrowing* into me is more accurate. He seems to take my gruffness as a personal challenge to scrub away. As much as I tell myself it irritates me, the truth is, I look forward to seeing him every Monday afternoon for our training session. I look forward to his daily messages and his boyish charm. He makes me feel good even when he's pushing me. And I know he's supposed to watch my body, but it feels different sometimes. He doesn't miss a single move I make. From the second I walk in the door to the moment I leave, his full attention is on me, and I'm starting to think maybe he's watching me with the same down bad interest I have.

Because I am.

I'm down bad for Dell Breaux.

What started as a single butterfly I tried to ignore has blossomed into an entire garden of them. With every text and every smile, I found my trust for him growing, and in turn, my infatuation.

But now, I stare at his last message from tonight about our book, and there's no reply. He usually responds quickly in the evenings, so it's a little out of the ordinary. I guess it is Saturday. People usually have plans, especially in the summer.

Then I check on my other compulsion—my Robyn. She hasn't posted anything today, so I do a cursory filter of her comments on the last eight or nine posts and report the harassing comments from my burner account. I'm sick and tired of these marriage proposals in her comment section.

No one proposes to my girl but me. I'll make damn sure of it.

When I get to my last stop for the night, a dance club on Market Street, I check in with my employee Omar, who's working the door, to make sure everything is good with him. Omar is one of my best employees, and I love him because he's clueless when it comes to famous people. Not that Philly is crawling with hot celebs, but I've seen him turn away professional athletes. He's hauled out high-powered lawyers and politicians. The man does not play.

Omar can identify any member of Philly or New Jersey's crime families, though. That's helpful.

He tells me it's shaping up to be a busy night and he only has a few spots left before the club reaches capacity.

When[1] I get inside, I perform a sweep of the perimeter before checking in with my bouncer who's posted up near the DJ. But before I get to him, I stop dead in my tracks. Through the red and purple strobe lights reflecting off the mirrors and crowd of bodies, I spot the two people who consume my soul.

Robyn. Dell. Here. Together?

No, that can't be right. Maybe they just met. I know Robyn comes here often with her friends, and I'm always working when she does. I usually know when she'll be here ahead of time, and I'll work ChaCha's all night until she leaves.

And, okay, maybe I will follow her to make sure she gets home safely. I always make sure I blend in. She doesn't know I work for this club or the other bars. She doesn't know I routinely have people kicked out for even touching her. All it takes is one word to my security team, and that fucker is gone.

When Robyn is here, I make myself scarce and watch

from a safe distance. I want her to have fun, but I want to protect her.

But why is Dell here? How did they meet? They're drinking the same drink, and he's looking at her like she's...

She's *mine*, is what she is.

Dell covers his mouth, watching Robyn in fascination as she does the jerk on the dancefloor—well, *tries*. She's wearing heels so it's really awkward. Around them, everyone else is grinding and body-rolling, but not her. She dances to the beat of her own drum. She dances for herself. It's not always pretty; in fact, it hardly ever is. I think most men find it intimidating, which is why I *love it*. Women will compliment her and join in, but the men stay far away, except for those rare few who manage to step up. But like I said, the second they touch her, they're fucking gone.

Downing the rest of his drink, Dell sets his plastic cup on a nearby ledge and does the same for her empty. When he comes back to her, his large hands steady her bare shoulders, and he fails to fight back his smile. Every fiber of my being wants to launch myself at him for touching her, but there's an unexplained force holding me back.

Her brow furrows for a second as he leans in to say something in her ear. The music is blaring, so it's the only way she's going to hear him. When she pulls away, realization dawns on her face, and she nods happily before turning her back into his chest.

No, *no, no.*

She's tall, but even in heels Dell is about three inches taller. His body cradles hers as they begin to grind against one another. His hands slowly slide down her silky dress, where he grips her swaying hips, and—*oh god.* Fifteen feet away from me, the two most beautiful people in the world are basically fucking with their clothes on.

There are too many emotions coursing through my body. If someone tried to talk to me right now, I'd bite their head off just so they'd shut up. I can't tell if I'm mad at him, or her, or both of them. If the blood rushing to my dick could fucking cool it, maybe I could think straight.

Fuck me, they're hot together. Dell looks like a sexy urban cowboy with those damn boots and dark jeans. Robyn is wearing her signature sleek look that makes me want to kiss her feet. Only now, she's wearing a tattooed man around her like a jacket.

Once again, Dell leans down to say something in her ear and even through the dark room and strobe lights, his devilish smirk sends a jolt to my cock. One of his hands snakes up to her neck, stroking her jawline while she arches into him deeper. Her eyes close like she's surrendering herself, and I still can't move a muscle except the one that ticks in my jaw and throbs in my pants.

When the song transitions into the next one, Dell whispers in her ear and points to the bar. She nods.

---

1. *Somebody's Watching Me Remix* by Rockwell & Syzz

Chapter 10

Show Me What You Got

Dell

"Okay, it's established, you can dance[1] and carry a conversation during dinner," I say to Robyn as we stand at a high top. I leave out the part that her normal dancing would probably scare most men away. It made me smile, though. She just needed a little redirection. But once her body was pressed against mine, I regretted suggesting it. I couldn't go another song without getting a full-on erection.

"Maybe you need to work on how you approach men," I suggest. "Let me see you pick up a guy."

"But," she hesitates, "I'm not picking him up. I already know him."

"True, but this is more about having confidence. Are you attracted to confidence?"

"Of course."

"Everyone is. And a woman who knows what she wants and isn't afraid to ask for it? You'll have him right where you want him."

"Okay," she exhales. "I can do this."

"I'll be right here, watching you."

Robyn takes one more deep breath before striding over to three guys at the bar. Ballsy. I know at least one of them was watching her grind on me with hungry eyes, so her chances should be good.

Right before she gets to them, her hands flex a couple of times. She's a little too far away for me to hear, but I don't need to—she's nervous as hell. She starts to hunch and hold her arms close. Her feet can't stay planted, and her chest is caving in.

Girl, what?

Thankfully, she catches my eye, so I gesture for her to correct her shoulders and stand taller. To take up space. She's already taller than two of them; there's no hiding that.

That's when shorter guy number one places a hand on her side and leans in to say something in her ear. His hand placement is... fine, I guess. I don't love it. Robyn doesn't seem to mind, though, because she's brimming with excitement, giving me a not-so-subtle double thumbs up as she walks by.

Just then, there's a hand on my waist. "Hey," a voice shouts over the music. My head snaps to find a cute guy dressed in a pink mesh crop top and matching skirt. "You wanna dance?"

"Oh, no thanks. I'm here with someone."

His sculpted eyebrow lifts, and he tilts his chin. "That girl?"

When I turn to where he's pointing, I find Robyn facing the stranger and grinding on him. "Yeah."

He gives me a look that says, *I don't think you're seeing what I'm seeing.*

"Thank you for offering."

"Find me if you change your mind," he says and saunters off. My attention refocuses on Robyn and the man dancing with her who is now aggressively grabbing her elbows and trying to kiss her!

Fuck!

Thankfully, she backs away from the almost-kiss and shakes her head.

Good. Kind of.

Now that my body is on high alert, my surroundings completely blur. I don't know what song is playing because my sole focus is Robyn and her safety. I don't give a fuck about her flirting lessons. Why did I think it was a good idea to let her hit on another man?

My mind whirls as I watch Douche Canoe's hands slide too low along her beautiful hips, and he aggressively grinds himself against her. It's way more than dancing and I'm more than done with this guy. She's completely tensed up before I'm bounding toward them. Just before I'm withing arms-reach, a burly security dude is hauling the guy away.

Wait. I know that burly security dude.

"Isaiah?" I shout over the din of the club. Robyn's hand is in mine in an instant, and as badly as I want to follow Isaiah, I remember what's really important right now. "Are you okay?" I ask Robyn, hauling her into me and closing my arms around her.

Her only answer is a nod against my chest.

"Come with me," I say. "Let's go find somewhere quiet to talk."

There's a small patio out back, and as soon as we step out, the cool summer evening washes over us.

"Please tell me the truth. Are you okay?"

"Do you know Isaiah?"

"Yeah," I say, furrowing my brow.

"How?"

"He's my client."

"Oh," she drawls. "Oh!"

"How do you know him?"

"He's literally the reason we're here right now. He's... he's the guy I'm trying to get."

No, no, no. This can't be happening. Isaiah is *my* little crush. We had established a timeline for his sessions—three months—and then he'd be on his own and I could finally ask him out. That Big Rugby Daddy teddy bear is supposed to be mine.

"I'm so embarrassed," Robyn says, pushing her hands into

her face.

"Of Isaiah?"

"No, of course not. Of this whole situation. I knew he worked in security around here, but I didn't know it was here. I'm embarrassed that I made a scene."

"Hey, no," I say, bending at the knees. I move her hands away from her face and look into her sad hazel eyes. "You didn't make a scene. None of that was your fault, do you hear me?"

She nods once, but the urge to comfort her doesn't diminish. Hugging her close, her arms constrict around my middle. And maybe, selfishly, I want to use her as comfort for myself.

"Let's take you home, hun."

The ride to her place is quiet. Normally, I'd be geeked to show off my fancy car to someone like Robyn, but it feels wrong here. I hold her hand in her lap between shifting gears and hope like hell I haven't ruined anything. It's impossible not to feel like I have, though. It would be selfish of me to take him away from her.

With a resigned heart, I swallow my pride. I'm going to take the hit and back out.

Robyn wants Isaiah.

Isaiah would be crazy not to date her.

Tonight was about helping Robyn gain confidence so she could make her move, but somewhere in the evening, I lost the plot. I tried to become the main character in a love story that's not mine.

---

1. *Dip It Low* by Ofenbach & Fabich

Chapter 11
Bubble Butt

Isaiah

It's half past ten when my alarm goes off, but I've been awake for the last hour thanks to some texts from Robyn. I should have expected as much.

> Hey. I didn't realize you worked at ChaCha's.

> Can we talk?

I haven't responded yet, and I don't know if I'm going to. She's going to tell me how she and Dell are a thing, or how pissed she is that I ruined her night, and I can't take that.

Because I'm a fucking coward.

So, instead of texting her back, I've been doing what I do best: stalking her online and letting her presence comfort me.

But as I scroll through her comment section, I find an account handle I've never paid attention to before, but it has a verified icon next to it. It's on a video of Robyn explaining that body mass index doesn't matter. She's going around to all her teammates asking what their BMI is as they work out in the gym together.

@TheGymBreaux: <Bullhorn emoji> Say it louder for the cheap seats in the back!! <Clapping hands emoji>

Instantly, I click on that handle because that's not a common enough last name to go unnoticed.

Holy mother of god.

It's Dell... and he has a huge social media presence. Two point six million followers. How the fuck did I not know he was internet famous?

Suddenly, my queer little heart stutters when I find a rainbow flag emoji in his bio.

Your favorite bi personal trainer <rainbow flag emoji> <muscle arm emoji>
Sign up for my Bubble Butt Booty Camp!

Oh my god, he's queer too. He's queer! He's always been flirtatious with me, but I assumed that was just his personality. As much as we've talked and grown a friendship, I've never been able to suss out his sexual orientation. I had inklings and hopes, but nothing confirmed. Not until now.

I take a deep breath to calm my racing heart, but it's useless when I open the first video. It's a version of Dell I've never seen. Sure, that same silly, cocksure persona is there, but he's wearing the tightest, thinnest gray leggings I've ever seen. Sweat soaks through, creating dark creases under his voluptuous backside. His quads are bulging—as is every blessed muscle on his body—as he hangs from a pull-up bar to demonstrate what he calls a "flying lunge."

Dear god, his package is so incredibly visible in those leggings.

As soon as the video ends, I watch the next one. And the next one. And about forty more. He really likes to focus on glutes. Loves to show people how to get a bubble butt just like his. All of it with that smile I've come to crave. All of it with that wink—like he knows exactly what he's doing.

Bricked up under the sheets, I surrender to his image.

The phone drops from my hand as I stroke myself, thinking about that delicious peach he's rocking. What I wouldn't give to take a bite of it. To hear him grunt as I sink into it.

Dell—at my mercy—squeezing my cock and begging me for more.

"Zay," he'd sigh. "I've wanted you for so long. Ughh, yes. Just like that."

"Do you need me?"

"Yes," he'd groan as I pump into him harder. "Only you, Zay. You treat me like a fucking queen."

I understand it's my brain fabricating his words and not him, but fuuuck me, that's what I want to hear. To know I'm appreciated. To know he needs me.

My balls tighten to my body as I approach my climax, but before I do, sexy dream Dell flips me over, pinning me to the bed. He kisses me and our facial hair scratches each other. His sweaty, god-like body takes control over me, and I willingly submit. Lost to his moans, his tongue opens me, and he takes what he wants.

"Daddy," I whisper aloud.

"I love you, Zay," he pants into my mouth and I fucking lose it. Every muscle in my body constricts as hot stream after stream shoots out on my chest and I arch my back. "I love you," he says again. "So good for me."

Dream Dell fades away as I regain consciousness and let out a conflicting grunt. I miss him already.

No. I should be focused on Robyn. She's been the object of all my desires for years. Dell has stayed at bay as a crush that's recently formed. He can't be here taking up my fantasies, too. That's my future wife's domain.

There's a buzzing from my phone, which momentarily distracts me from my internal war. I pick it up to find an email notification. When I see it's from my old college teammate, Kermit—or Kurt, if we're going by the name his parents gave him—I quickly sit, wipe my jizz with a tissue, and toss it into the trash before reading the email.

Hey IceMan, he starts, using my rugby nickname that's followed me ever since I took my shirt off to play a winter pickup game my freshman year of college. I knew it was a mistake after the first five minutes, but I was too stubborn to admit I was freezing. As a result, my nipples almost popped off, and I was covered in scratches from the snow and ice.

That's when my chest hair really filled out. My body was like, "Alright, we're not doing that again. Protect him!"

Good times.

> *Hey IceMan,*
> *I think it's time we pull the trigger on that training program. We've been talking about it for years now and I'm in a place financially that I can make this move.*
> *Let me know what you're thinking.*
> *Cheers,*
> *Kermit*

Kermit and I have been tossing around the idea of starting an East Coast training program for rugby teams that need temporary, dedicated support. Whether that means conditioning or coaching, we want to help teams build on what they have. Think of us as rugby team consultants, if you will. We would come into teams, identify areas that need support, and help them repair and build.

It started out as an idea when we'd been drinking years ago, but the more we thought about it, the more we loved it.

Now, I'm not so sure. I like my job with Alliance Security, but it would be nice not to work nights anymore. The harsh reminder that I can no longer play full-contact rugby comes roaring in like a bulldozer once again. Being back around rugby, running this training program, could scratch that itch.

But there's also—no. *Don't even think about it. I'll jinx it.*

Ughh, but it's impossible not to. The head coach job with the USA Valor has been at the forefront of my mind for the last couple weeks. Thanks to the internet sleuthing on my burner account, I saw Robyn's post about her team needing a new head coach. I've never applied to something faster in my life. I reached out to my old coach with the London Hornets and received a glowing recommendation letter along with a phone call from him telling me I'd be a fool to pass up this opportunity. I've been through two rounds of interviews so far and have been studying the team harder than ever.

Being head coach of a professional team is the dream of most retired players. With so few opportunities in the United States, it's a big fucking deal. The sting of never being able to play rugby again would certainly ease if I was offered this position.

The job won't pay very much, in fact, significantly less than what I'm currently making as the manager of a security company, but it'll be worth it to be near her again. Near her in a way that will feel safe. I won't be able to touch her the way I've dreamed of, but I'll be closer than ever and able to watch her. I'll be part of her life again.

I considered reaching out to Robyn to see if she would put in a good word for me, but thought better of it, wanting to earn this position on my own merit. Plus, I'd feel so shitty asking for something like this when I've been actively avoiding her for years.

After leaving London and playing professional rugby, I moved back to Philadelphia. I could have called her up and hung out the way we used to—Lord knows she was trying to get my attention. But by that time, she was cemented in my brain as my person, my future. I dedicated myself to rugby, to my dreams, *for her*. I had our future planned, and chilling with her as just friends felt entirely wrong. But when this coaching opportunity came up it created the perfect reason for me to be around her again in a way that fits in with my plan. Our plans.

So as much as I love the idea of working with Kermit on the training program, the opportunity to be head coach of the USA Valor is too tempting.

> *Hey Kermit,*
> *Can I get back to you in a couple weeks? I have some irons in the fire and I'm trying to see what happens. If nothing comes of it, I'm fucking ready.*
> *Cheers,*
> *IceMan (Cumeth)*

Alright, so some people just call me Cumeth.

Ruggers are a disturbing bunch.

The message is sent and I climb out of bed, throwing on a pair of discarded gym shorts. I head downstairs to get a pot of coffee brewing before I shower and start my day. But when I get to the main floor, I'm greeted by Rugger and Yogi, my brother's two giant Great Pyrenees dogs.

I groan but scratch their enormous heads. "Why are you here?"

Yogi gently holds my wrist in his mouth and pulls me toward the kitchen as Rugger follows.

"You know I'm not livestock, right?" I grumble. Jonah rifling through my cupboards when I enter the kitchen. I repeat the same question to him. "Why are you here?"

He doesn't even look at me as he continues his search. "I'm out of cereal at my place. Where's yours?"

"I don't eat cereal."

"What? Everyone eats cereal."

"Wrong," I mutter, grabbing the ground coffee bag and filling the machine. "You do, because you're a man-child."

Giving up, he shuts the cupboard and peeks over to watch me fill the coffee maker. "How much are you making?"

"Enough for me."

"Can I have some?"

"No."

"Why not?"

"Because you don't live here and are capable of buying cereal and coffee on your own."

"Can't a guy simply want to spend some quality time with his oldest brother?"

"If he can give some warning."

"Where's the fun in that?"

I sigh deeply and level him with a stare. "I assume you've already eaten my leftover chicken parm?"

"I'm a growing boy," he smiles.

I push off the counter to head for my shower. "I hate you."

"Hey, can you give me a ride to Dad's tonight for family dinner?"

That has me stopping in my tracks to turn back around. "Why? What happened to your car?"

He fiddles with his fingernails. "It, um..."

"Jonah," I growl.

"I gave it to Shirly—to borrow!" he adds quickly.

"The drug addict that hangs around your block at all hours of the day and night?"

Jonah shrugs. "She said she had a job interview."

"So let her take the bus!"

"She said she would give it back next week," he says, as if that's reasonable.

"Next week?" I bellow. "Why would she— It's one—" I grunt, then take a deep breath. "She's never going to give you that car back, bro."

"You barely know her. She's really nice."

"She sells crack, and from the looks of it, she's her best

customer."

"That doesn't mean she's a liar."

I shake my head and sigh. "Just wait until Angie hears about this," I threaten, giving up and heading back upstairs to shower. Hopefully, the fear of our older sister will knock some sense into him.

"No! Don't tell her!"

Chapter 12
Family Dinner

Isaiah

Jonah and I arrived at Dad's house thirty minutes late. When I arrived at my brother's place later that day, he and his two roommates were in the middle of building bunk beds for his dogs and were covered in sawdust. When I told him they don't need bunk beds, they need a barn, he gave me this look of realization that sent regret tumbling through my body.

Nothing good can come from Jonah's brain.

Our childhood home is in a suburb of Philly, and it's way too small for a family of six. Mom died in a car accident when I was eight, and our family never really recovered from her death. Angie definitely took over as our mother figure at only ten years old, while Dad faded into a shadow of himself. It wasn't until about a year ago—to the shock of us all—that Dad started going to therapy and grief counseling.

It's been an incredible transformation, but I wish we could have seen this version of him a lot sooner.

I'm not like my older sister, who is so free with her emotions. It makes her a great children's therapist and friend. While her inclination is to coax feelings from people, mine is to hide them. Growing up the way we did, all I wanted was for my mom to still be alive and for my dad to be proud of me. As an adult, I realized what I was trying to do was be the man of the house—as outdated as that idea is—since my dad wasn't mentally there for us. I never saw my dad show emotion outside of Mom's death bed and funeral. He always hid away, and that's what I thought I had to do with my emotions, too.

Thanks to Angie's relentless need to see what's going on in everyone's brain, it's a little easier for me to open up now, but not much. I know that makes me come off surly a lot of the time, but at this point, being reserved is my comfort zone.

We didn't know until recently that our mom wrote journals for each one of us kids which encompassed her pregnancy through our first year of life. I'm a little ashamed to say I haven't opened it yet. Dad gave them to us about a year ago, but I've been too afraid to read what's inside.

I'll get there someday.

Now that we're all out of the house, Dad's been calling us a lot more to come over for the smallest things. His loneliness is the reason we're all here, and why my sisters have established a mandatory family dinner every Sunday night.

And, okay, I guess it's nice to see everyone or whatever.

"Fuck yeah, enchiladas!" Jonah hollers as we step in through the back door to the unmistakable aroma of our childhood.

"Language, Jonah," Dad chides, holding his granddaughter to his chest. Zofia is unfazed as she takes a handful of Dad's salt-and-pepper mustache.

"She's six months old," Jonah drawls, helping Dad remove her death grip from his facial hair and taking her.

"Doesn't matter," Dad replies. "You should start watching what you say from now on. They're sponges."

"Who made dinner tonight?" I ask, bracing myself for the answer.

"I did," Rafael smiles, coming into the kitchen from the living room. He's in a dark floral summer button-up, and as always, his smooth terracotta skin and styled hair are flawless.

My whole body relaxes knowing we're eating well tonight. "Gracias," I say, giving him a tight hug.

Rafael and his younger brother Joaquín have been in our lives since we were kids. Their moms, Ana and Christina, were the adult mother figures in our lives, auxiliary to Angie. They live just a few neighborhoods over, and our families have been intermingled for decades. And now, with Raf and Ang getting married soon, we'll be even tighter.

"Hey, bro," Dane says, coming up next to me, holding our nephew Dominico.

I take a step back for a moment to study my brother. Dane usually wears dark clothes when he's not in his veterinarian scrubs or rugby kit. But tonight, he's opted for a band tee and ripped black jeans, complete with classic black Converse. Odd—he hasn't gone full punk since high school. He keeps a few lingering stylistic choices, like the small black gauges in his ears, but this is like he stepped back in time.

"Are you wearing eyeliner?"

"So?"

"Nothing. You just haven't worn it in a long time."

"It's coming back," he mutters.

"I don't think it is."

"What do you know about makeup?"

"Not much. It just looks like you're ready to get *Agony Nectar* back together." He bristles at the name of our family band we formed as teenagers, and I chuckle. "Are we going on tour?"

"Shut up."

"Just say the word, and I'll take my bass out of storage."

With the hand not holding our nephew, Dane tries to gently rub his eyeliner away. At the same moment, my eye catches Joaquín coming through the door.

"Hey, I didn't know Joaquín was going to be here today," I say. "Maybe he wants to get the band back together, too." I wave to him. "Joaquín!"

"Jesus," Dane mutters.

"Hey, guys," Joaquín beams, setting a plastic-wrapped bowl of salsa down and pushing back his long, shiny black curls.

"This is a surprise," I say, patting him on the back as we hug.

"Yeah, I'm here this week working on some of the houses."

Joaquín and Rafael run Jimenez Brothers Properties together, and Joaquín travels between here and Washington D.C. often to check on their various rental properties.

He lets go of me and goes in for a hug with Dane and Dominico—or Nico, as we've recently nicknamed him. "I heard you guys started a new family dinner tradition, so I thought I'd crash it."

"Dane wants to get *Agony Nectar* back together," I smirk.

The guys pull away from each other, and Joaquín looks like he just heard the juiciest bit of gossip. "Tell me more."

"We're not," Dane says.

But Joaquín rakes his gaze over my punk-rock brother. "We clearly are."

"Dinner!" Rafael hollers from the dining table.

I take a seat between Joaquín and Angie, who's at the end with Rafael so they can each access the kids in their highchairs. Rafael says grace for everyone, and we dig in.

"Where's Ivy?" I ask the whole table.

"She's at a birth right now," Dad replies.

"She's always gone."

Dad shrugs before serving himself. "Yeah. It's the nature of being a midwife, though. Always on-call."

"And where are Ana and Christina? They're usually here."

"They're visiting our family in Mexico," Joaquín answers.

"That reminds me," Angie chimes in over all the conversations happening. "We have an announcement about the wedding, everyone!"

The table quiets down but Dane finishes his side conversation with Jonah. "You only took that class in college because the professor was hot."

"She was," Jonah smirks.

"Jonah," Angie cuts in.

"What?"

"Stop talking. Thank you." Angie relaxes and takes Raf's hand. "We found a venue in Guanajuato and put a deposit down."

"That's great, bunny," Dad smiles.

"Jonah, this is your first reminder to make sure your passport is current."

"I don't think I have a passport."

"Yes, you do," Raf sighs. "You went to Ireland with the team two years ago."

"Do you know where you put it?" she asks, but Jonah's face goes blank, and she groans.

"I'll make sure he has one," Dad says.

Angie's expression is a curious one. "Thanks, Dad."

"Whatever you need, bunny."

Then she looks at me. "And yours is up to date, Zay?"

"Yeah."

"It better be," Dad says. "If you're going to be the USA Valor's head coach, you're gonna need—"

"Dad!" I hiss.

"Wait, what?" several people ask at once.

So much for trying to keep Dad in the loop. I'm not telling him anything ever again.

"Nothing's official," I seethe. "I don't even know if I have the job yet. I probably won't get it."

"Of course you will," Raf says with a pinch between his brows. "You'd make an excellent head coach."

"Whoa, whoa, back up," Dane says. "What about Robyn?"

Sweat forms under my arms. "What about her?"

"Oh, I don't know," Dane drawls. "Maybe it's the fact that you're in love with her?"

I need new friends who are not my family.

"I'm not in love with her," I lie.

"Does the Pope shit in the woods?" Jonah asks rhetorically.

"I think you mean 'bear,'" I say.

"No, I think he means 'hat,'" Raf replies. "He meant to say: Does the Pope wear a funny hat?"

"No," Dane says. "The phrase is: Does a bear shit in the woods?"

Jonah puts his hands up to quiet the noise. "Irregardless—"

"That's not a word," Angie and I remind him in unison.

"The point is, if you get this job, you're going to be around Robyn a lot," he smirks and points his fork at me. "And as it is, you're afraid to be around her."

"I am not."

"Who wants to hear about the time Isaiah met Robyn?" Rafael booms over everyone. At that, I get up from the table and book it downstairs to the basement, but not before I hear Raf start, "It was his sophomore year..."

Chapter 13
Certified Freak

Isaiah

Spring. Sophomore Year.

This is exactly how I like to spend my Saturdays: coming off a win against Penn Valley on their own turf, and drinking Pabst Blue Ribbon from a keg at a house off campus. Penn isn't too far from Brightwood, my college in New Jersey, so our club teams regularly play each other. Plus, it's nice to see my sister and Rafael since they attend Penn.

Raf played one hell of a game and has a bag of ice strapped to his shoulder. He's holding a beer in one hand and taking a puff from a joint that's being passed around.

We traveled with our women's team today, the Lady Killers, so there are four rugby teams filling this house and backyard. Some people have already left to go back, but there are still about forty people here.

"IceMan," my vet, Gimli, says, throwing an arm around me. He's nicknamed Gimli because, well, he looks like Gimli from *Lord of the Rings*. "I need you to sing 'Titties.'"

Gimli picked me as his rookie when I joined the team freshman year, and even though I'm technically a veteran now, I'll always be his rookie. And rookies do as they're told. Not that I need much convincing. I know every rugby drinking song by heart.

"Coming right up." I clear my throat. "Me me me me me

me meeee," I sing as loud as I can, pretending to warm up my vocals as I stand in a sea of ruggers.

Every single person shuts the fuck up. It's like, rugby law: you hear the tune, and you sing along.

I've sung this song a few times solo now, so I'm confident even while five beers deep. "Gimme gimme gimme gimme number one. When I see titties, I wanna have some fun! 'Cuz they're round—"

"Oh yeah!" the crowd barks.

"And they're firm—"

"Oh yeah!"

"When I see titties—"

"Oh yeah!"

"I wanna sperm!"

"Oh yeah!"

Ruggers everywhere proceed to dip their hands in their beer and fling the droplets over everyone's heads while slowly turning three hundred and sixty degrees, singing, "Titties titties titties!" on repeat.

Nine more rounds are performed. Everyone has spun their last spin, flicked the beer from their cups, and waited with bated breath to see if I fucked up the lyrics—to which I'm happy to announce, I did not.

Everyone drinks the remainder of their beer, and the din of the crowd starts back up. Except a tall girl with arresting hazel eyes steps forward and stands in the middle, where a small space is clear—right in front of me.

She holds her cup in one hand and pours more beer from a pitcher with the other, setting the pitcher down before hollering, "Hold on. I know at least half of us ladies love to sing about titties, but I think it's time the underrepresented straights have a turn."

I laugh because I can see her point. Women's rugby teams are stacked with lesbians.

Without any further ado, this girl launches into a song

I've never heard. It's a version of the titties song.

"Gimme gimme gimme gimme number one! When I see penis I wanna have some fun! 'Cuz they're long—"

All the ladies shout, "Oh yeah!"

"And they're thick—"

"Oh yeah!"

"When I see penis—"

"Oh yeah!"

"I wanna lick!"

"Oh yeah!"

All our guys start laughing because, one, this song is hilarious we're all immature, and two, the fucking balls on this girl are commendable. She's owning it. She has dried mud all over her legs, a black eye forming from the game earlier, and a sunburn across her cheeks.

And she's fucking fearless.

Her team is laughing right along with us, but soon everyone has joined in.

When the drunken chorus ends and the cups have been raised, there's a small ovation of cheers for this woman.

"Well done," I nod, softly clinking my plastic cup against hers.

"Thank you," she smiles brightly.

Rafael pushes past a couple of players and nudges her shoulder with a laugh. "You've been working on that one, haven't you?"

"I've been saving it," she admits. "Been waiting for the right moment to bring it out."

"Birdie, this is my buddy IceMan," Raf beams, throwing his arm around my shoulders.

I hold out my hand, and she shakes it. "Christian name is Isaiah."

"Birdie. Robyn in the real world."

Just then, my sister Angie stumbles over to us. "Penis, penis, penis," she sings, then hiccups before continuing,

"Penis, penis, penis, penis!" Her giggling makes them laugh, but I'm cringing.

"This is my social," Raf says. "And here you are, drunker than me."

"Can we go to Taco Bell?" she pleads, fisting his shirt.

Raf rolls his eyes. "Of course we can go to Taco Bell."

"Woo!" Angie cheers, throwing her fists high in the air. "T-Bell run! Who's sober—" she hiccups, "—enough to drive?"

Angie has already booked it to another group of people looking for a DD when Rafael pats me on the back. "No, no. Allow me to take care of your inebriated sister," he chuckles.

"Hey, I'm just a visitor. She's your responsibility at school."

"Yeah, yeah." Raf gives me a playful shove and leaves, trying to find his best friend.

"So, you're Angie's brother?" Robyn asks, and I nod. "And you go to Brightwood, obviously. How long have you been playing?"

"I'm a sophomore, and I've been with the team since freshman year. I played in high school with Raf, actually. How about you?"

"This is my first year playing. I started back in the fall. I'm a freshman."

"Well, you fit right in with the rugby community," I chuckle.

"Oh, you mean the community of fucking weirdos? Thanks," she smiles and holds her beer up. "It's a badge of honor."

"We are a strange bunch, aren't we?"

"I think you have to be in order to play this sport."

This has me curious. "What makes you weird?"

"Oh, besides singing to a crowd of people about dicks?" I huff a laugh and nod. "Let's see... When I eat extra spicy food, I like the way it hurts my gums, and I'll stick toothpicks between my teeth for added pain." Before I can ask a follow-up question, she keeps going. "I love the smell of my own body odor. In my hometown in Minnesota, I'm the reigning Mayonnaise Queen. I won that title in a Midwest Salad-eating competition."

"Salad?"

"Yeah. You know, like a hearty salad tossed in a lot of mayo?"

"Oh my god," I chuckle.

"I write Disney villain fanfiction. My two biggest fears include seaweed touching my feet and balloons. I think Owl City is the best band. I cry watching videos of hedgehogs, and I think I would perish if I got to hold one in real life. My favorite feeling in the world comes from scrunching up an empty bag of popcorn when it's still steaming," she says, her eyes rolling to the back of her head.

There's a long pause as this girl in front of me, I don't know... pretends she's holding a hot crumpled bag of popcorn?

"Okay," I drawl. "You're weird."

She bows dramatically, waving her hand delicately before saying, "Thank you."

Outside, we find a quiet place to chat and spend the rest of the social in our own little bubble. She's easy to talk to, and she gets me. When I told her about my favorite bands, she knew who I was talking about. We talked about our favorite rugby songs and verses. We laughed about the shock on people's faces when they hear rugby lingo for the first time, like ruck and hooker. About the professors who take us aside to gravely ask if everything is okay at home because we're covered in bruises most of the year.

She fucking gets me.

"Cumeth!" my teammate barks from the car idling in the driveway. "Let's go, dude!"

"Is he okay to drive?" she asks.

"Yeah, Woody's always the DD. He doesn't drink."

"Good," she exhales. "Can I get your number? We'll probably be seeing more of each other, I assume," she smiles.

"Oh. Y-yeah," I say, pulling my phone out as we exchange information. "Let me know when you're coming up to play against us."

"I will," she beams, then to my surprise, stands on her tiptoes and throws her arms around my neck. Instinctively, I hug her back, leaning down slightly. It's nice. But it's the way ruggers are—we're affectionate people. "Text me when you get home so I know you got there safe?"

"Sure," I nod, and we break apart. "Maybe go put some ice on that black eye," I tease.

A car horn blares over whatever she tries to say next.

"Nice to meet you, Robyn!" I call back with a wave as I jog to the car.

When we pull onto the road, I check my phone to see she's already texted me.

> Nice to meet you too <smiley face> <rugby ball emoji>

The rest of the ride back to New Jersey goes by faster than I imagine because Robyn and I end up texting the whole way. When I tell her I'm home safe, we spend another two hours texting until we both pass out.

Reality comes in like a freight train when my Sunday morning alarm goes off. And like every Sunday for the past year and a half, I get up, shower, dress, and pick up my girlfriend Jessica for church.

Chapter 14

Bad Kisser

Dell

"Two medium cold brews for Dell," the barista calls, and I give them a nod before thanking them and heading into work down the block. I'm hoping this coffee brings back some sense of normalcy between Robyn and me this Monday morning. Something to root me back into what we were before our "dating lesson" Saturday night. Before I fucked it up with my selfishness.

What the hell came over me? It was my idea to help her in the first place. She should be able to trust me, as both her friend and personal trainer, not to cross any boundaries. But there I was, watching her lick dessert off a spoon mere inches away from me as my heart punched its way out of my chest. I need to get a grip on this ridiculous crush I have on her.

But as soon as she walks into my studio gym, looking like her usual barely-awake self, my hindbrain kicks in.

She's so gorgeous. I wonder what she looks like when she wakes up in bed—*no. Bad. Bad Dell. Look alive.*

"Good morning, sunshine," I smile, offering her coffee.

She grunts, and it's like music to my ears. I love that this normally chipper and vibrant woman acts like a bear reluctantly stepping out of hibernation for the first time. She kind of reminds me of Isaiah in that regard.

See, I remind myself. *They're perfect for each other. Get the fuck out of their way.*

Her cold brew is drained in seconds, and we start our

session. It's ten more minutes before Robyn's responses turn into actual words. I'm grateful for the normalcy, but there's a niggling question I want to ask, and I can't tell if it would be unprofessional or not. Do I address our date night? Or can I play this off as a friendly question? Is it immature to not talk about what happened?

Goddammit, I'm thirty-three years old and a business owner—why am I spinning with uncertainty? I should call my gram; she would know what to do.

Through our whole session, I war with myself while encouraging and pushing her. But there's something she's keeping close to her chest, I just know it. I can feel it. Maybe I'm projecting.

"Good job today," I say as she dramatically drops to the floor.

"Thanks," she exhales. "Can you stretch me?"

"Of course."

She lays on her back, and I bend her right leg until it's nearly to her armpit. I'm on my knees, leaning my body weight against her. It's impossible not to look her right in the eyes when we're positioned like this—not to take myself out of the mindset of a personal trainer helping his client and just see a man atop a woman as she spreads her legs for him.

But there it is again—in her eyes. There's something she needs to get off her chest.

"How do you feel about what happened Saturday night?" I blurt.

Robyn takes a deep breath, and we switch legs. "Everything was just... so unexpected."

Is she talking about me? Could she feel that connection too? Jesus H. Christ, someone give me a blinking neon sign inside my brain that reads NO MORE DATING CLIENTS.

"Between you—I mean," she stutters, her eyes wide. "What I learned from you, that is. And seeing Isaiah and that… that guy I was dancing with," she groans, pushing her palms into her eyes. "All of it. I didn't want to kiss him."

"Yeah, that was painfully obvious. I'm glad you pushed him away before that happened. I was on my way to pull him off before Isaiah did." I bring her leg back down, and then both come up, her legs spread wide as I lean against them.

She huffs a humorless laugh. "Yeah, well, two more seconds and he would have discovered how bad I am at kissing and ran for the hills."

Record scratch.

"I'm sorry, what? You're bad at… kissing?"

She rolls her eyes. "Don't make a thing of it."

My eyes narrow on her. "You're twenty-eight years old, Robyn. There's no way you're bad at kissing."

"Then explain that to all the guys I've hooked up with."

Every thought I had until this moment vanishes, and it takes significant effort to temper my growl. "What. Happened?"

"Calm down. It wasn't any one thing in particular. It just happened enough that I caught on to it." Without breaking eye contact, I bring her legs back down, and she sits up with crossed legs. "Guys just," she hesitates, her head turned down as her fingertips play with the end of her shoelace. "They never want to kiss me for long, or at all. They just wanna fuck and dip out."

The way her voice shrank has my chest constricting. "What kind of jerks are you pulling, Robyn? Fuck."

She groans. "I know. I don't have the best track record. But c'mon," she sighs, finally looking at me again. "If they're all like that, it stands to reason I'm bad at kissing."

That blinking neon sign must be down for maintenance because the next thing I say is the wrong thing. "Kiss me."

"What?" she shrieks.

"You heard me. I wanna know."

"Dell! I will not subject you to that."

"Robyn," I say firmly. "Think of this as part of the flirt coach package. If you're not confident in the way you kiss, then I'm going to make sure you are."

"You're out of your mind," she huffs.

"Not at all. I'm a dedicated personal trainer and flirt coach. Now kiss me."

Her eyes flick to my mouth and her chest rises and fall in a different way than when she was working out. She's nervous to pull the trigger, so I sweeten the pot even though it kills me to do so. "Pretend I'm him. Kiss me the way you want to kiss Isaiah." Her breath catches as her gaze floats back up to mine. That's when I lean in a hair's breadth away, her eyes closing, and I whisper, "Do you want this?"

"Yes," she says softly before I skim her full lips with mine.

Our first real kiss is chaste, but it ignites my body in flames. It's tender and demure. But then she opens her mouth a little more and invites me in. When I slip my tongue against hers, I'm suddenly very aware that I'm on all fours and she's cross-legged. Not the ideal kissing position, if you ask me.

I need my hands.

Without a word, I brace my core and grab onto her waist. Her hands immediately come around my neck as she lets out a little squeak when I pull her forward, and I sit back. The way she's straddling my legs has her higher than me, but I have better access. My hands find their place on the back of her head and waist as our kiss becomes frantic and scorching.

She tastes like minty toothpaste and the morning coffee I brought her.

She kisses the way I knew she would from the moment I saw her on the sidewalk four years ago. She kisses like the woman who is unknowingly going to break my heart.

I'm going to savor this and burn it into my memory because it's all I'm ever going to get.

Our lips push and pull against each other as her fingers dig into my pulled-back bun and she grips it. Shivers race down my spine and my cock jolts. But right when her tongue dives back in to dance with mine, her hips give a slow little thrust that has me *very* aware of my growing erection. All at once, I'm bolting away and standing up to turn and tuck myself back in as discreetly as possible.

I clear my throat before turning back around and offering her a hand to stand up. "You're uhh... you're a very good kisser." I stammer like a fool, barely able to make eye contact. "No notes."

Her brows pinch. "Are you sure?"

Grabbing a medicine ball next to me, I place it in front of my crotch. "Do not change a thing," I say before coughing and nodding toward the door. "Off you go. Great session today."

"Are you okay?"

"Super duper!" I say, making myself cringe. "I'll see you soon!"

"Okay," she drawls and too slowly walks to the door. Before she leaves, she turns around. "You're sure I'm not a bad kisser? Because you're kind of... acting strange."

"You're a very good kisser," I practically scream. "Please take my word for it! Nothing is wrong with you, and everything is wrong with those other guys, okay?"

Finally, a small smile creeps across her face. "Okay." Mercifully, she leaves before I book it to my office to calm my boner before my next client arrives.

My next client! If I want to keep my clientele, then I need to stop acting unprofessionally. I've been so good at keeping my dick in my pants for the last three years. My reputation is slowly getting back to where I want it.

But damn it all to hell, deep down, I'd kiss her again if I had the chance.

As I reach my office, my phone buzzes. It's an incoming call from my older sister Brook. *Oooh, yes, the Boner Killer 2000.*

"Good morning," I say, sitting down in my chair. Like me, Brook is a morning person. At this hour, she has likely already gone on a five-mile run, showered, and made breakfast for her husband, Steven, and their five-year-old son, Liam.

She's Type A to a T. Even when we're on vacation, she's the one organizing everything. I think it's calming to her. Everything in her life is scheduled and planned. She even has allowances for chaos—no joke. I think that's why she's such a good mom.

"Good morning, Dill Weed," she chirps in her southern accent. I purposefully lost my accent when I left Kentucky. "I know you got a client in three minutes, so I'll keep this brief." See, she even knows my schedule. "I need a headcount for Gram's ninetieth birthday party. You're coming, right?"

"Of course. Remind me when that is again," I wince.

She groans. "It's next month at Castle Gardens. I need to make sure I get the right ballroom." When a chuckle escapes me, she balks. "Don't mock me!"

"You are literally the General Manager and run that venue. You can make anything happen, and you're worried about headcount at this point?"

"Don't get in the way of my planning," she hisses. "Gram deserves a flawless birthday party."

"I'm not saying she doesn't. Put your quad espresso down, Jitterbug. I'll be there."

"No plus one?"

Inwardly groaning, I lean back in my chair and toss my head. "Have I ever?"

"Why did you pause?" I can practically see her eyes narrowing.

I sigh.

"Dell, tell me what's going on."

"There's this woman... and this man..."

"Dell!"

"I know. They're both clients of mine." Brook lets loose a giggle that has me cocking an eyebrow. "What? I'm in peril, and you're laughing at me?"

"You're so fucked."

I think about the way my kiss with Robyn electrified my body and the way I feel when Isaiah so rarely smiles for me, and I close my eyes. "I know."

Chapter 15
Territorial

Isaiah

At exactly 1:56 p.m., I pull open the door to Personal Best Training and my already anxious heart explodes into a cold sweat. Approximately two million questions have been swirling around since I saw Dell and Robyn together at the club a couple nights ago. Questions I desperately want answers to, but am petrified to ask.

I'm scared to know the answers, too.

"Hey Zay," Dell grins while finishing a few pull-ups and dropping to the ground. But when he saunters over to me, his smile fades and he crosses his arms over his chest. "Do you have somewhere to be after our session today?"

"Um, no. Today's my day off."

"Okay," he nods and takes a deep breath. "I think we should talk about Robyn before we get started."

The cold sweat intensifies. "I agree."

We take a seat across from each other on parallel weight benches, and I watch his hands rub against his thick khaki-clad thighs and squeeze his knees.

Before he can say anything, I beat him to the punch. "Are you dating her?"

With a forlorn look he shakes his head, "No. I don't date my clients."

"She's your client?"

He curses under his breath and sighs, "Yeah."

"What's wrong with her? What did she injure? I didn't know she was injured," I say, failing to keep my composure.

"Whoa, back up. She's not injured like you. I've been her personal trainer for years."

Waves of relief wash over me, but there's a stinging poke in my chest at the same time. Am I relieved to know they're not together or relieved Dell is single? Goddammit. One question answered and five more pop up. "Then what was going on Saturday night?"

He leans over and braces his elbows on his knees before looking at me. "How much did you see?"

"Everything," I say through clenched teeth.

"Everything at ChaCha's?"

Suddenly I'm cursing myself for being so naive to not realize there might have been more before or after that. "Was there more?"

He swallows. "We went to dinner before that, and I drove her home after the club, but nothing happened, Zay. Nothing was ever going to happen because I was just helping her out like a wingman."

"Why?"

"I don't want to say too much, but," he pauses. "She's not exactly confident in dating. And, as her friend, I offered to help her."

Relief and confusion battle it out while I try to piece together my next question. "What are you talking about? Next to my older sister, Robyn is the most confident person I've ever met."

"'Fraid not," he shakes his head slowly—*knowingly*—and it makes my blood boil that Dell knows this about her and I do not.

"Are you gonna see her again? Outside of work, that is."

Dell's line of sight trails to some unfocused location on the floor between us, and he strokes his full lips with the tip of his thumb. He's taking entirely too long to answer my simple question, but he finally looks back up at me. "There's nothing wrong with two friends hanging out."

"Friends don't grind on each other the way you two were,"
I say firmly.

"I was showing her how to dance on a date."

"Her dancing is perfect the way it is."

"You two," he mutters, shaking his head. "Fine," he says
resolutely. "I won't dance with her anymore. I assume
you're acting like this because you like her?"

Understatement, I think to myself. "She's mine," I say instead.

"Yeah," he says, dejection etched all over his handsome
face. I can't tell if I'm pleased at pushing him away from her,
or uncomfortable for making him sad.

Dell isn't the first man I've chased out of Robyn's life.
He's well on his way to becoming the seventh, though. But
something deep inside tells me I cannot cut him out. Not
from her life and not from mine.

"Then can I ask... why aren't you with her now?"

"It's not time."

His thick eyebrows furrow. "What does that mean?"

I can't tell him. I can't admit the truth because all that
will do is expose my cowardice and insecurity. It's better to
keep it locked away.

"I just need to have my ducks in a row first."

"Oh god," he mutters. "You're one of *those* people. I should
have known. What's wrong with diving face-first into a
depth unknown, huh?"

"That sounds horrific."

"That sounds exhilarating!"

"That sounds like trouble."

"Live a little, Zay. You're a goddamn rugger; you play one
of the most blood-thirsty sports, and you can't live on the
edge a little bit?"

I don't tell him Robyn is anything but a lighthearted decision. She deserves the world on a silver platter, and I'm
going to do everything in my power to give her that.

"Rugby is calculated," I correct. "I don't need to seek out any more adrenaline outside of it."

For a long moment we're silent. Dell's expression softens and he tilts his head. "Have you been thinking about what life looks like after retirement?"

I nod. "Been thinking about it a lot lately."

"How does it feel?"

"Unnatural," I reply with a despondent tone.

Just then my phone vibrates. I pull it out to give a cursory glance, but all of my attention zeros in on the email.

"Are you gonna miss it?" Dell asks. "Rugby?"

"No," I say, unable to tear my eyes from my phone. "Because I'm the new head coach for the USA Valor."

Chapter 16

New Coach

Robyn

"Alright, settle down, everyone," Coach Bob announces as we all stand on the field after practice, panting from a hard fifteen minutes of touch rugby. "I have some exciting news."

"Are we getting the rainbow kits?" Khaos beams.

"No," Bob sighs. "That's not what I'm here to talk about."

"It's June, Bob! Honestly, it's homophobic for the Valor brand to not give us rainbow jerseys."

"I'll take it up with the board again," he grumbles. "In the meantime," he emphasizes, trying to get us all to focus, "the search is officially over. Please welcome your new head coach... Isaiah Johanssen."

All at once, the air vanishes from my lungs, and I can't feel my face. Isaiah walks onto the field with Coach Laura—well, former Head Coach Laura—and his eyes lock right into mine. He's wearing a team athletic polo, which does nothing to hide his broad, muscular shoulders and thick arms. Isaiah has always had a prop's body—which is to say, he clearly works out but clearly likes to eat. Big and strong, he's a boulder of a man. The kind of man that could toss a five-foot-ten rugby player like me around like a rag doll. The kind of man that bear hugs were named for.

Why does he look so at peace? Why is he not squirming away like he's done around me for the last few years? What is happening right now?

Serwaa leans in to whisper, "Babe, did you know about

this?"

"No," I whisper back. Serwaa knows about my long-standing feelings for him. She and I became fast friends when we joined the team the same year, and within just a few months of meeting, we had told each other our whole life stories. She's never met Isaiah, but oh boy, has she seen pictures and heard me talk about him.

"Oh my god," she drawls.

"Ladies and gentlethems," Laura says, "I'd like you to meet your new head coach, Isaiah. Coach Johanssen here played rugby in high school and college, played Premier League for the London Hornets for three years, and has been playing Division 1 with Philadelphia up until this last spring. He's gone through a rigorous interview process and background check. Needless to say, I'm very pleased with this placement. Give it up for Coach Johanssen!"

Like a sheep, I clap along with the rest of the team, but I'm so rocked to my core that I can't hear it.

He looks damn good. I mean, he always does, but he's so polished today. Even his dark beard is shiny and well-groomed.

"Hello, everyone," he waves.

Laura continues, "We've been watching you all from the press box, and I've been running him through your positions, though," she says with a smile, eyeing him, "he already knew all your names and positions, so that was helpful."

Of course he does. Isaiah takes rugby seriously when he needs to. I may have met him as a carefree college rugger singing about titties, but he's driven and educated. Oh god, he's going to make an excellent coach.

My coach... fuck. There's no way I can pursue him now. This isn't some club team where there are no restrictions around players and coaches dating. This is his job. This is *my* job. Even a whisper of something brewing between us could dissolve brand deals and ignite media backlash. If we were together, we'd both lose our jobs.

Why didn't he tell me he was applying?

"I know practice is almost over," Laura says, pulling me out of my spiral. "But I'd like you all to take some time to get to know him. We'll leave you to it." She leaves with Coach Bob and everyone swarms Isaiah.

Serwaa is the first to speak up. "You're friends with Birdie, aren't you?" she asks knowingly, and my heart rate speeds up. I pinch her butt in response, but she swats at me.

"Yes," he says. "Robyn and I met in college. We've been friends for a long time."

"How many siblings do you have?" Khaos asks next, and I'm grateful for the redirection.

"Um," his brows furrow. "Four..."

"What's the order?"

"Why does that matter?"

"Oh, it matters," Khaos replies, folding her arms over her chest.

"I'm the second born."

"But what's the order?" she repeats.

Isaiah looks to me for clarity, and I have to giggle. It's not that he's confused about what the order is; he's confused about why we're even asking. I give him a shrug.

"I have an older sister, Angie, then me, then my brother Dane, Jonah, and little sister Ivy."

"Ohhh," a few players hum.

Casshole nods her head. "Older sister, nice."

"His brothers also play for Philly's D1 team," I add.

"Thanks," he says softly before another question pops up that leaves him even more confused. "Do y'all wanna know about my credentials?" Isaiah asks instead.

"We were just told," Serwaa says. "Now we need to know the real shit."

"How do you feel about cats?" Skirt asks.

He crosses his arms. "What?"

"Zay," I start, but correct myself. "I mean, Coach Johanssen," I wince. That feels weird to say. "Just answer the questions. We're a relentless bunch."

He sighs and shrugs. "Yeah. Cats are cool."

"What's your sign?" Khaos asks.

"I don't know sign language."

"No, your astrological sign."

He doesn't say anything and looks back at me again.

"Tell them when your birthday is, Coach," I laugh.

"January 12th."

"A Capricorn?" Khaos balks and pretends to faint against me.

"That's a good thing," I beam, shaking her shoulders. "That means he's determined and hardworking. He's organized and honest."

"Sensitive," Serwaa adds.

"Loyal."

"Finally," Cass grumbles. "I won't be the only one anymore."

"Do you have a partner? Or kids?" Skirt asks from the ground as she takes off her pink boots.

"No and no."

My heart skips a beat at his answer. He's going to find someone else now.

I would love to be the reason he answered 'yes' to that, but it's not going to happen—I lost my chance with him. If there was ever a sign telling me he wasn't interested, then this was it. Because Isaiah would have never taken this job if he wanted me. He wouldn't have risked something between us if his feelings were mutual.

Dell's voice slices through the fog. *He still likes you.*

Ha. Clearly, he did not know what he was talking about. I should have listened to my gut and given up on Isaiah. For the last six years, we've rarely seen each other, as much as I've tried. Granted, he was across the Atlantic Ocean for three of those years. When he came back, he was different. I know suffering from that shoulder injury cost him his spot with the Hornets, and I wish I could have been with him to help him through what was probably a dark time. Instead, our friendship suffered those three years. We were both focused on our rugby careers. It makes sense that the friendship we formed in college faded because of that. I just expected we'd pick back up when he got back here.

There were a few times I was able to corner him at rugby events, and while the words we spoke were those of friends, his body language was unfamiliar. He was jittery and flushed and kept pulling at the back of his neck. He barely spoke, and I was too tongue-tied to say anything meaningful.

It hurt to know our friendship was reduced to that, but now that he's here and he's my coach, maybe we can have a fresh start and rebuild.

The team peppers him with questions for the next fifteen minutes, and by the time practice is over and everyone heads to their cars, I've mustered enough courage to speak my mind.

"Zay," I call, running over to him before he opens his car door. "Can we talk?"

"Of course," he says, and that calm confidence is back. Where has that been hiding all these years? That's the old Isaiah I remember and fell for. Not the cagey, hiding-in-the-shadows man I've come to know.

"Why didn't you tell me you were applying?"

"I wanted to earn this on my own merit."

Unable to stop myself, I let the thoughts tumble out. "How's your shoulder and neck? Angie told me all about it."

At that, he rotates his shoulder. "I can't play anymore, but it's a lot better." He swallows. "Dell's been helping a lot."

Guilt digs its sharp claws into my gut at the mention of our mutual... friend? "So, you quit your security job?"

"Yeah. I'm finishing up this week. I already hired someone to replace me."

"Listen," I sigh, doing my best to calm my nerves. "About Saturday night—"

"It's okay."

"No. Why didn't you tell me you worked there? I would have liked to see you. I go there a lot."

"I know."

Suddenly, my throat constricts slightly and an unexpected sting forms behind my eyes. *I can do this; I can speak my mind.* "Why have you been avoiding me?" I ask, unable to fight the tremble in my voice. "What have I done to you?"

"Nothing," he replies quickly. "I—I'm sorry. I just wanted you to be happy and safe."

"Safe? Why wouldn't I be safe? And I'd be a lot happier if we could be the kind of friends we used to be."

Isaiah pulls at the back of his neck. "A lot has changed since college, hasn't it?"

I nod.

"Can we start over?"

A clean slate sounds amazing. Maybe if we do this, I can get my friend back. Maybe if we do this, I can go back to a time when Isaiah was just a friend and no more—before my feelings ran deeper and my desires rampant. I can hope, can't I? It's all I have now that he's my coach. There's no trading to a different team because rugby isn't like other professional sports. There aren't multiple teams to get drafted to. Short of moving to another country to play, I'm stuck here with Isaiah Johanssen as my coach.

It's time to start fresh.

"Yeah, we can start over," I smile, and weirdly enough, a peaceful weight covers me. The corner of his mouth curls up, and suddenly I can see twenty-year-old Isaiah, the day

I met him.

A small, surprised grunt escapes him when I launch my-self into his arms for a long-overdue hug.

"I missed you, Zay."

His responding squeeze is delayed, but it blankets me in comfort. I've missed his strong arms. I've missed his scent, but it's a little different now. Is that coconut and almond? Rosemary?

Shamelessly, I take an exaggerated inhale. "Why do you smell so good?"

His chest shakes as he chuckles, and he pulls away to shoot his baby blues into mine. "It's my beard oil."

"I'm obsessed," I groan.

"Easy, killer," he smiles, and we break apart.

I missed this. I missed us. I can live with being just friends if it means he's himself with me again. A smiling Isaiah was always my favorite. If being my coach is the only way I could have this version of him again, then I'll take it. The comfort of his friendship outweighs my struggle.

For now.

Chapter 17
Strange Feelings
Robyn

Fall. Sophomore Year.

"Yes, Icyyyy!" I scream as Isaiah makes an excellent pass to his flanker while getting tackled.

"You know you're supposed to be rooting for our own men's team, right?" Angie asks.

"You know, most people, when they move on to grad school, stop coming around the games," I say sarcastically.

"What? It's not like I have class on Saturdays. Saturday's a rugby day," she says matter-of-factly, then shrugs. "And I wanted to see my baby brother."

Today, we're in New Jersey at Brightwood, where Isaiah's team is currently winning against my men's team, Penn Valley. The leaves have started to turn into deep oranges and dusty browns, and the temperature has dropped to an ideal level for playing. My game ended an hour ago against the Brightwood women's team, and we smoked them. Maybe it had something to do with my boost in pride when Isaiah was cheering for me from the sidelines. Family and friends have watched me play before, but it felt different today. I find myself playing my hardest, smartest games when he's watching me. Something inside itches to impress him.

"Uh-huh," I tease. "It has nothing to do with him?" I tilt my head toward the field, where Holloway is making a breakaway.

Ang snorts. "No. He's just my fuck buddy."

I haven't seen Angie since she graduated, but I have seen Isaiah. Over the summer, both of us attended a few different sevens tournaments together. I spent the rest of my summer training with my dad, attending camps, or working as a maid at a local hotel. Despite the fame and glory my parents received as Olympic athletes, we don't have a ton of money. I still had to work whenever I could.

Since meeting four months ago, Isaiah and I message each other often. Most of our conversations are about rugby, but sometimes they're about more.

Isaiah: Hey. What r u doin?

Robyn: About to leave work and then train with my dad.

Isaiah: How many hotel rooms did you clean today?

Robyn: 15 <sad face> My feet hurt. I wasn't made for manual labor.

Isaiah: Says the rugby player.

Robyn: I'm meant for playing rugby and laying on a beach with a coconut cocktail in hand. Not this: <selfie wearing a hotel housekeeper's smock and a frown>

Isaiah: LOL u will be back to college before u kno it, and then u can hang up ur smock for good.

Sometimes our conversations were about less. And in between hedgehog memes and rugby gifs, sometimes we went deeper.

I've learned a lot about him and met the rest of his siblings. He told me about how his mom died when he was eight and how Angie essentially raised him. I told him about my controlling parents and how envious I was of his huge family. He also told me about his girlfriend, Jessica. They seem cute together. I guess she has other things to do on Saturdays, though, because I haven't met her yet.

"Good hands, Zay!" Angie bellows while clapping aggressively for her brother, who just made an assisted try.

"He's getting better."

"I know. All he does is talk about rugby. His entire wardrobe consists of rugby clothes or band tees. If he's not playing or at his landscaping job, he's working out, eating, or watching rugby. It's pretty intense."

"Think he's gonna make a career out of it?"

Angie sighs. "I told him it was dumb to rely on his body like this, but I don't know if it's sinking in."

"Well, at least he's a good student, right? He'll have a degree to fall back on."

"Thankfully, yes. Between his love of music and rugby, I've been sweating bullets thinking he'll choose a career in either." I know what she means. While she hopes nothing but the best for him, finding success in either of those industries is tough.

After Brightwood beats Penn Valley 29 to 14, we all head to the social, this time held at Isaiah's off-campus house he shares with three other teammates. After we eat, Isaiah and I take turns leading the choir of ruggers in rousing verses of *The Marrying Kind*, followed by *I Used to Work in Chicago*. When everyone's good and toasted and the keg stands start, Isaiah's hand catches my eye.

"What happened here?" I ask, bringing his hand closer to inspect.

"Got stepped on in the second half."

"It looks awful. Can you flex?"

He flexes his biceps instead.

"Stop it," I laugh, but he concedes and attempts to make a fist before wincing.

"Go wash your hands, and I'll get you some ice."

With a placating smile, he ambles to the closest bathroom, and I fill a baggie of ice. When I get to the open bathroom door, he's gently drying his hands at the sink. Stepping in behind him, I catch his smile in the toothpaste-splattered mirror.

"Here," I say, taking his swollen hand and placing the bag over it. He takes a seat against the counter, and suddenly heat flashes through my body as I stand between my friend's legs with his hand in mine. His big, rough hand, with its blunt fingernails and angry red cleat marks.

I should let go of his hand. I should. It's so close to my chest, and a really stupid part of me wants him to shut the door, grab my waist, and kiss the living daylights out of me.

Where is this coming from? Why am I envisioning this? He's my friend, and he's in a relationship.

There's laughter and boisterous voices from down the hall, but the loudest thing of all is the sound of Isaiah swallowing.

When I risk flicking my eyes to him, this strange feeling between us intensifies, and I blurt the first thing that comes to mind. "Where's Jessica? When am I going to meet her?"

Something changes in his stare. "She's studying. She doesn't really come to my games. It's not really her scene. Plus..." he trails off like he doesn't know if he should say it.

"What?"

He rolls his eyes and sighs, "It's nothing. It's dumb."

"Well, now you're just dangling a carrot."

"She can get kinda jealous."

"Of... you spending time with your team?"

His free hand tugs at the back of his neck. "No. She, uhh, there's just certain friends of mine she doesn't love," he says, placing a peculiar emphasis on the words *friends*.

"I'm sorry. I'd still like to meet her one day. Maybe the three of us can get a bite to eat outside of the rugby scene so she's more comfortable," I say truthfully, because I do want to meet her. She's my good friend's girlfriend—why wouldn't I? Whatever bizarre little spark just flickered between us is most definitely one-sided and doesn't mean anything.

I'm probably just ovulating.

A sad sort of smile tugs at his lips, and his hand gently squeezes mine. "Maybe."

"Cumeth! There you are," one of his teammates huffs, slapping the frame of the door. "I thought you'd like to know your sister is doing keg stands in a dress."

Laughter bubbles up at the image of Angie upside down, showing her panties to everyone, but Isaiah scrubs his face with his uninjured hand and groans.

When his teammate disappears, Isaiah shakes his head and smiles, but neither of us makes a move to leave. This lingering moment between us feels so forbidden in the hottest and guiltiest of ways. I *know* we should get out of this small bathroom where I'm standing closer than I should, but he's looking at me with his piercing blue eyes like he doesn't have a girlfriend, and is anything outside of here all that important anyway?

"You okay?" he asks, his eyes flicking down to my neck. "Your shoulders are bunched up."

Now that he said something, I do feel stiff and achy. I try to release the tension but it's locked in. "It's fine," I shrug. "Just sore from the game."

"I'd say. It was a scrum-heavy game you played. Here..." He turns and removes a jar of Tiger Balm out from the drawer. "Want some?"

"I love that stuff," I smile, taking it from him and unscrewing the lid.

"I know."

It dawns on me then that I need to take my shirt off in order to apply this. Ruggers are notorious for being half-naked at any given time, popping our shirts off and having our shorts pulled down by opposing players, et cetera. Now, I'm acutely aware that this situation is different, but it shouldn't be.

"Would you like me to leave?" he asks, sensing my trepidation.

I don't, but saying I do would be admitting something is inherently strange between us, and I can't allow that. "No, it's fine. Um..." I step away from his legs and turn around before lifting my shirt over my head and exposing my black sports bra. Before I take the open balm from him, I flash a reassuring smile, though I'm not sure if it's for him or for me.

Scooping a couple fingers in the jar, I bring the potent pain-relief gel to my shoulders and rub it in. I'm angled halfway between him and the shower, unsure where I should be looking. When I try to rub it where it's needed most, just below my neck but a little out of reach, he says, "Here, let me help."

"Oh. Th-thanks."

I hold the jar out for him to take a swipe, and he stands closer before massaging it into my skin. "Down here?" he asks, his voice a little lower, a little strained.

I swallow. "Yeah, just under the fabric of..." Suddenly using the words 'sports bra' feels like the naughtiest thing I could ever say, so I don't. Thankfully he knows what I mean, and he slides his warm hand down my spine and kneads into my traps.

Why the fuck am I so aroused right now? I hooked up with a guy two weeks ago and it wasn't nearly this hot or erotic. What the hell is wrong with me?

"That breakaway you had in the last five minutes was incredible," he says, rubbing in tight, firm circles. "You played great today."

A bubbling spirit forms in my belly and I smile. "Thank you. You played great, too. I'm always impressed with how hard you launch into scrums."

The Tiger Balm is fully massaged in at this point and we both know it. But instead of taking his hand away, he slowly swipes his full palm across my shoulder blade and down my bicep. *Jesus Christ, I'm going to have to wash my compression shorts for two different reasons now.*

"Did I miss anywhere?" he asks.

My lips? I think to myself, but settle on saying, "I think you got it. Thank you." I swipe my shirt from the counter and put it back on, already missing the feel of his hands on me.

God, it's warm in here. I should change the subject. "It's too bad men and women can't play against each other. I'd give you a run for your money."

"Oh, would you?" he chuckles, but there's a dangerous

undercurrent. "I'd like to see you try."

"Are you challenging me?"

"It wouldn't be a fair competition."

"Why, 'cuz your hand is busted up?"

"Because I'm bigger, better, and stronger than you, Robyn."

"OH! So now you're wrong *and* you're challenging me?"

Isaiah throws his head back and laughs. "You are so stubborn."

"I'm confident, there's a difference. Now c'mon," I say, dragging him by the elbow out of the bathroom and heading for the backyard, determination taking control. "Try and tackle me."

"What are we supposed to do, play one-on-one?" he asks. We make our way through a sea of ruggers and step outside into the crisp autumn evening. "That's not a thing." The sun is still high enough to cast a warm early-evening glow.

"Girls versus guys," I tell him. I shout over to a couple of my teammates to join us, and a couple of his join, too. "Three-on-three should do it. Now don't hold back."

He sighs and shakes his head in amusement. "I am going to *severely* hold back."

I find a ball and with a foot tap, the pickup game starts. I regret challenging him within ten seconds because *holy fucking shit he is a lot bigger than me.* It's one thing when you're standing next to him chatting and sipping on a beer. It's another when a man that size is rushing toward you. I'm a tall, broad girl, and opposing players almost never intimidate me, but this is *different.*

How is he this fast, too? Props aren't supposed to be this fast!

My teammate offloads the ball to me before she's wrapped up by one of the guys, but Isaiah sees the pass coming and is tackling me to the ground the second I catch it. "Oh fuck!" I scream, and my hip hits the ground.

Somehow he manages to move his hands from my legs to cradle my head and shoulder before I go all the way down. It's an incredibly sweet gesture, but I'm still determined to beat him.

"Stop taking it easy on me!" I yell, and attempt to shimmy my way out of his hold. "Sir, he's not releasing!" I shout to the non-existent referee.

Ah well, rules be damned.

My teammate strides up behind me, and I'm able to make just enough room to pass the ball under my legs. When she strips the ball and runs off, I'm left there in the patchy grass, laughing uncontrollably while Isaiah pins me to the ground.

"Do you want to keep going?" he chuckles. "Because I'm only using about ten percent of my abilities."

"You're a liar!" I groan. He responds by trying to turn me over, but I manage to wiggle just enough and hook my leg between his and gator-roll him.

"What the fuck?" he bellows.

"I'm stronger than I look!" The sentiment is short-lived. We end up wrestling each other, fighting for dominance, but it's a losing battle for me. Neither of us can control our laughter, but he's not nearly as affected as I am.

The next thing I know, I'm on my back with my arms above my head, and his face is an inch away from mine. We're both hysterical, and tears are streaming down my face as he sits his full weight on my hips. With wild eyes and grass stuck in his beard, he's barely able to say, "I. Win."

"Fine!" I giggle while struggling to release from his grip. "You win." Isaiah lets go and rolls off before laying next to me, both of us catching our breath as the laughter slowly settles. When I turn to look at him, he's already staring back at me. "How's your hand?"

He lifts it to show the red marks from his earlier game. "Hurts like hell."

"C'mon. Let's get you some more ice, Icy." I stand, offering my hand to him as we abandon our teammates who have called the game off, too.

When we get inside and reapply a new bag of ice, I realize there are a lot less people here than there used to be. I carpooled here with three of my teammates and they're all here, drunk as a skunk, including Josette, who drove us here! I'm underage and I've had a few beers already, so there's no way I'm driving back to school.

Isaiah has the same realization, and when I look at him, he smiles. "You can stay here for the night."

Angie runs up to us, her hair disheveled and eyes glassy. "Can I spend the night? I may have drank too much."

"Oh, you *may* have?" he asks sarcastically. "Alright. Everyone's staying."

Angie and I grab hands and jump up and down. "Sleepover!"

· · · • · ♦ · • · · ·

Everyone's gone by midnight when Isaiah sets up the couches for us with blankets and the few pillows he could find, but when I claim my spot for the night, he shakes his head and pulls me away.

"Where are we going?"

He leads us upstairs, and the silence in the house is met with creaking from each step and a sudden pounding in my chest. *What the fuck is happening? Is he...? Are we gonna...?*

He opens the first door on the right, and I tremble with uncertainty and delight and a heightened awareness that he has a girlfriend and I'm his friend—*only* his friend. But as the door opens all the way, I spot Angie asleep in the bed.

"You're gonna sleep in my room with her," he whispers. "You both have water and granola bars on the nightstand. I'm gonna sleep downstairs."

Relief and disappointment wash over me all at once. "You don't have to do that."

Isaiah's face is solemn but sure. "Yes, I do."

I know why. He knows why. Then why does it feel so wrong for him to leave me? Why does doing the right thing, the gentlemanly thing, feel so dishonest?

"I left a clean shirt and some sweats for you to wear," he nods to his bed where they're neatly folded. "But if that doesn't work for you, you can wear anything you find." I'm now painfully aware that he's not moving an inch from his place just outside the threshold while I'm inside his bedroom. *Isaiah Johanssen's* bedroom.

"Thank you, Zay."

The small curl to the corner of his mouth is sweet. He nods and steps away. "Goodnight, then."

"Goodnight."

I think about Isaiah's hands on me as I slip into his clothes and inhale the scent of detergent and traces of Old Spice. I think about Isaiah pinning me to the ground when I slip into his bed and rest my head on the same pillow he uses every night. I think about Isaiah kissing me when I fall asleep and dream of him holding me.

Chapter 18
First Practice
Isaiah

"Ready?" Bob asks as we leave our shared office inside the USA Valor training facility and take the field together.

"Ready," I say confidently. Because I am. I'm secure in my coaching abilities because I've had great coaches I'll be emulating.

But what gives me true security is knowing Robyn will be under my care. I'll be able to keep a closer eye on her and hear more about her personal life through team chatter. I've been watching from afar for so long, hiding from her. Now that I'm here in the open around her, I need to be more careful. But it's all worth it to be able to hear the way she talks with her teammates— it's precious intel I never had exposure to before.

Yes, it fucking guts me not to be with her still, but it'll all be worth it in the end. What I'm doing is building our foundation. Thoughts of her swim in my mind late at night, and I've always wanted to be closer, to know more about her daily life and her feelings.

Blowing my whistle, the players halt their warm-up and jog toward us. Taking a deep breath, I channel my former coaches and keep a stern demeanor.

"Afternoon, everyone. Hope you're all warmed up and ready. My expectations are that you warm up before I step foot on the field. Conditioning is also your responsibility off the pitch when we're not practicing. I'm here for skillset and strategy, and it's your responsibility to be at your peak performance. Is that understood?"

Everyone nods in various degrees, but that's not what I want.

"I said, is that understood?"

"Yes, Coach," everyone says in some way or another. Robyn throws me a studious glance.

"Good. We're going to start by splitting up. Coach Bob here will take the backs, and I'll take the forwards. Scrummy," I say to Khaos, our scrum half, whose position straddles the line between a back and a forward. "Start with the backs and join us in twenty minutes. Then we're going to reconvene for some touch. Let's go," I nod and take off jogging to the try line.

I opted for wearing rugby shorts and a new Valor T-shirt along with my trusty boots and rugby socks. Some coaches prefer to stay in business casual for practices, but that didn't feel right. I plan to lead by example as much as my healing body allows. I may also be showing off. I once heard Robyn say in a video how much she loved thick thighs, so I... may have thrown on my shortest ones.

"Today we're working in pods. Robyn," I nod. "As the hooker, I want you glued to your props the whole time. In a scrum, and in phases through every play."

"Actually, Coach," Cass says, stepping forward. "We've been working on a rotating system where—"

"That's not what we're working on today," I cut in. "Cass, Turk, and Robyn, you're one pod. Khaos, Skirt, and Abs, you're pod two. Toni, Mo, you'll be filling in the weak side." I address the B-side players and assign them pods as well.

All the forwards give Robyn a curious glance, but she just claps her hands and gestures forward. "You heard him. Let's get into position."

Robyn is team captain, so I understand everyone following her orders, but this is my team, too. Establishing myself and gaining their trust is what I need to do. These side glances to Robyn shouldn't be happening.

It takes longer than I thought it would for them to get the hang of this new pod system of play. It's something my old coach from the Hornets taught us, and it worked beautifully. My team got the hang of it quickly, but the girls keep stopping to ask questions, and it's slowing everything down.

"Cass!" I call. "Stay with your pod!"

She's visibly frustrated as she gets up from a friendly tackle. "How am I supposed to be when I'm down and they're halfway across the pitch?"

"That's what you need to figure out with them. They are your pod!" I blow the whistle. "Again!"

By the second ruck in the next phase, the pods falter, followed by a knock-on.

That's it. We need to reset.

I blow my whistle again. "Sprint to the try line and back."

Like a bullet, everyone takes off for the other end of the field. When they get back to me, I notice a few of them still have disgruntled faces—they're still holding onto their frustration from not understanding the new system. I blow my whistle again, and they sprint twice more until everyone is back on the fifty meter line with me and too tired to be upset.

"Let's try this again." This time, I join an opposing B-side pod, hoping to lead by example. Unfortunately, within one phase, there's a gap so large I'm able to slip right through it and offload to a flanker to score.

The rest of my plans for practice are completely derailed because no one is catching on to this style of play, and if they do, they lose the rhythm shortly after. Am I not coaching professional athletes here? Robyn is clearly trying her hardest, and part of me feels awful for being so callous around her, but I can't give her special treatment. As much as I want to, I cannot wrap my arms around her and tell her it's going to be okay, that she'll get it soon. I have to be strong and steadfast for her and everyone else.

Practice comes to an end, and Robyn leads them through their cool-down stretching while I talk to Bob.

"Is this normal for them? Learning something new like this?"

"Laura had a special way with them," he explains, crossing his arms as we stand side by side, watching the players stretch out their hamstrings. "It's like she spoke their language."

"We all speak rugby," I shrug. "If I was able to learn it in ten minutes, why can't they?"

"Maybe it's the new coach feeling. No one has settled in yet." Bob pats me on the shoulder as the players finish stretching and dissolve back to the locker room. "We'll try again Thursday."

Rooted in place, I watch player after player shoot Robyn unenthused looks, each one exchanging some kind of silent language. She lingers behind with Serwaa, and I think she's going to come over to talk to me. Instead, she grabs a few balls from the ground and follows Serwaa to the twenty-two meter line, assisting her friend with kicking practice.

I want to stay and talk to her, but the way she glances over at me is something I've never seen from her. Like she doesn't understand something. She doesn't look at me for long before she catches Serwaa's kick and sends it back to her. Over and over again, the pair of them repeat this until their disgruntled demeanors turn into laughter. And while I'm relieved to see her back to her most natural self, I'm equally as hurt with myself for causing her frustration.

How the fuck do I fix this? My hand itches to pull my phone out of my pocket and call Angie. No, she doesn't have experience coaching any sport, but she always has a way of knowing just what I need.

"Hey," my sister answers while I walk off the field and head toward my car.

"Hey. Um…" Suddenly I feel stupid for calling.

"How was your first practice?"

I want to lie and tell her it was great. But it's her. "It could have been better."

"Why? What's wrong?"

"They just didn't get what I was trying to teach them. I don't really understand why."

"Have you—wait, no," she says, stopping herself. "Are you calling for a solution or just to talk?"

"Um, do you have a solution to make them get it?"

"You're literally the expert. I'm here if you wanna talk about it, but," she sighs. "Have you even cracked Mom's baby journal for you?"

Her question throws me off guard. Why is she bringing up the journals our mom kept for each of us during her pregnancies? What does that have to do with what's happening now?

"Not yet," I mumble as guilt bites at me. "How does that have anything to do with rugby?"

"I don't know. But I seem to find answers whenever I read it."

"Yeah, but for like, mom stuff, right?"

"No, not just for mom stuff. For life stuff. Just page through it sometime. I think it'll surprise you."

Rolling my eyes, I open my car door and flop inside. "Yeah, okay," I say noncommittally.

"You'll find a solution for your team soon enough. Be kinder to yourself, okay? Oh shoot, I gotta go. Zo just grabbed Razzle's tail and is trying to eat it. Bye!"

The call ends abruptly, and I chuckle at the image of my niece reaching for their elderly blind cat with her bizarrely strong baby grip.

From my car, I watch Robyn and Serwaa on the field still kicking away. Every time Serwaa makes a good kick, Robyn's hyping her up and making loud whooping sounds I can hear all the way in the parking lot. She's in her element here—helping her teammate after practice like this. She deserves the title of captain.

Now I have to figure out how to be deserving of the title Coach.

Chapter 19

Game Tape & Thirst Traps

Robyn

Only two weeks after Isaiah's first practice with us, we're in Dublin for our first official game of the summer season. We're not like other professional sports teams that get to play within their own country. Rugby is still too obscure in the United States to form a large network of pro teams.

So here we all are, the evening before, watching game tape in our hotel's conference room after dinner.

We've been practicing Isaiah's new pod system, and I'll admit we finally got it last practice. But then he was giving us more new plays, which is great, but it's hard to miss his annoyance when we take too long to get it. When he gets like that, I can't tell if he's upset with us or himself.

Keeping an upbeat attitude and reassuring the team has been my main priority lately. I mean, smiling is my default anyway, so it's natural. but it seems I'm working harder than ever to keep their spirits up. It's impossible not to miss our last coach, and I don't expect Isaiah to be like her, but getting my teammates to see the real him has been difficult. They can't see the version of him I've always known. Hell, it's hard for me to find that version now. Aside from our little talk a couple weeks ago in the parking lot, I haven't seen the old him in forever.

For my team's sake, I'm determined to find that man again.

But it's hard when he's standing right in front of us, critiquing and scrutinizing detail after detail of our last game.

"Cass," he says, pointing to her on the projected image. "This would have been an ideal time for you to set your lineout farther back. Especially if you're not going to have the hands to get it out to the backs."

"But look," I smile, gesturing to our jumper. "Toni got the ball here, and even though the play didn't go according to plan, she still made a good choice by going down for the maul. And look how fast Khaos was able to strip it and get it out to the back line!"

Isaiah huffs. "But then the backs weren't ready. Look at that flat line. We need to get steeper."

I don't have to look around me to know my teammates are giving me *the look* again. The look that says *how are you seriously on this guy's side?*

Play after play, Isaiah dissects each and every movement, throw, tackle, and pace. There's not a single compliment in sight, even though there's plenty to rave about.

When the second game tape ends, we all let out a collective breath as our coach turns off the projector. The urge to corner him and ask what his end goal is roars inside me as everyone solemnly funnels out of the conference room. But as I watch him quietly talk to Bob in the hall, nodding and planning, I hold my tongue.

He has a plan. I know he does. This has to be some kind of front he's putting on for a certain purpose. He's always been grumpy—granted, towards others and not so much toward me—but he's also kind and gentle. What was I expecting? That he would be the exact same silly rugger singing inappropriate songs at the top of his lungs? No one would take him seriously at this level.

He's just leaning into a more serious coaching style, as

he should be. We're not a college team anymore. We're the goddamn USA Valor.

Unlocking the door to my hotel room, I set my sight on the light pink pajamas I set out on the bed before I came down for our meeting. Little hearts are patterned all over them and it makes me smile how damn cute they are. And for some reason, I think of Isaiah wearing them and I smile. Serious, grumpy, Isaiah Johanssen, wearing pink satin pajama shorts and a matching top...

And it clicks.

If he's going to stay this stern, this steely and critical, then I'm going to be the ray of fucking sunshine to balance him out for everyone else.

Why didn't I think of this before? It's the classic good cop, bad cop dynamic.

Damn, I'm smart.

I peel off my clothes, but before I step into my adorable pajamas that I will forever associate with Isaiah, I realize Serwaa isn't here with me. Everyone shares a room with one other teammate when we travel and she's always my room partner.

That's when I peer at my phone to see a text from her.

> **Serwaa:** Come to Khaos and Skirt's room for some tarot reading!

> **Robyn:** Tell Khaos to read my cards on the plane tomorrow. I'm gonna take a shower and pass out.

> **Serwaa:** Kk. I'll be back in the room in 30 mins. Get yourself off nice and good with Roger before I get back <wink emoji>

I let out a full cackle thinking about the girthy blue dildo we all travel with. Every time we fly, one person must put the silicone monster in their carry-on so the TSA can see it on their monitors when we go through security. It's been a tradition for years, and no one knows why or where the name comes from.

It was my turn today. I like to look the TSA agent directly in the eye right after they realize what they're looking at and I'll wink for good measure.

Robyn: LMAO <salute emoji> Roger is in good hands <eggplant emoji> <yes hands emoji>

Before I step into the shower, I check my phone to find a new text from Dell and my heart rate picks up before I realize it's simply a reminder text to send him my workout video from yesterday. Oops. I shoot it off to him and remove my makeup. Right before I hop in the shower, he replies.

Dell: Yes! Look how much more you're lifting now that you corrected your stance! Do you feel that difference? And I like the way you modified your resistance bands for that row. However, it looks like you were going easy with the cross-climbers. Remember to engage your core before you start. Other than that, I think this looks great and you're definitely ready to add more weight to your squats. WoO!

Once again I find myself chuckling at my phone screen.

Robyn: Thanks <painted nails emoji> <weightlifter emoji>

Dell: <Video of him demonstrating proper technique for cross-climbers>

Settling my hip against the counter, I grin watching his instructional video / thirst trap. This one was posted a couple months ago, and he's wearing only lavender leggings so tight it looks like paint. And—*oh my god*—did he stroke himself before filming this? Jesus Christ!

"It's your GymBreaux, Dell, and today I wanna show you the proper way to do a cross-climber. First, make sure the yoga ball you choose isn't too high." With his hands on the floor, he places his feet on top of the yellow ball in a plank position.

"Now let your stomach relax; let it drop, don't worry," he winks. "It's just you and me here, no one is going to see. Now suck it in and keep your core tight. You want to make sure you're one solid muscle before twisting and tucking that knee to your opposite elbow." The camera angle switches from capturing his chest and abs to side view, where every ridge of muscle is gloriously on display. The curve of his ass into his monstrous thighs creates a valley I want to glue my hands to and squeeze.

I wonder if I've commented on this video already. When I open up the section, of course it's filled with the victims of his trap.

@*JaredHollow69* Why is this video 4 hours long? <popcorn emoji>

@*YuleLogBoyz* Weird way to propose, but yes

@*KrisKris* <laughing emoji> am i only one focused on the leggings?

@*RicARTo* I have nothing appropriate to say <biting lip emoji>

@*DeevonDee* <five blushing emojis> Sir

@*Et_tu_Brutus* those pants have hit max capacity

@WhatKindOfNameIsJeff <wide eyes emoji> Jesus of Nazareth

Looks like I haven't commented yet, so I do what I always do—comment like I don't know he's blatantly thirst trapping me.

@RobynCassidy Ohhh! Thank you. This was helpful! Can I add weights to my ankles to increase the difficulty?

I chuckle to myself as I post the comment and immediately get a text back from Dell.

> Dell: Good luck tomorrow. You're gonna kick some Irish ass! I want you plowing over them so fast they ricochet off you!!!

> Dell: Also, I'd like praise for using the word ricochet

As I type out *good boy*, I immediately rethink and erase it.

> Robyn: <medal emoji> <proud face emoji> Look at you using big boy words!

> Dell: That's a French-ass word, Robyn!!

> Robyn: Did you just google if that was a french word before you sent me that last text?

> Dell: *scoff* You know I'm French! Well, my dad's family is Louisiana French! And... <eyes only emoji> Ok fine i googled it.

Robyn: I'm still very proud of you.

Dell: <Big smile emoji>

Why can't Isaiah coach more like Dell does? It's hard not to compare the two of them, even though they're opposite in so many ways. As if reading my mind, Dell texts back and I ignore my steaming shower.

Dell: How are you feeling about Isaiah as your new coach?

And just like that, Dell switches from his ridiculously fun self to his caring mode. From personal trainer goofball to concerned friend in a split second. My heart warms at the simple change.

Robyn: It's not easy to be honest. I'm struggling to come to terms with the fact that he and I won't be a thing… ever.

Dell: Don't say that. It's not like you're going to play forever (no offense, you know the body can't play a sport that intense for long). Things could change <shrug emoji>

Robyn: But is it wise to wait even longer when I'm not sure, in fact I'm fairly certain, his feelings aren't mutual?

Dell's texting dots show up and disappear a few times, but I can't wait and send him another text before he replies.

Robyn: I don't think it is. I'm just going to focus on supporting him and the team for the time being.

Dell: Does that mean you want to end my flirt

coaching?

Oh. I didn't consider that. I guess we should, shouldn't we? We only agreed to do this for a month, and there are still a couple weeks left. Building the confidence to get Zay to notice me as more than a friend was the whole purpose, but there's no point in doing that now.

My mind whirls back to our kiss in the gym and how fucking right it felt. How I melted into Dell and lost my mind. How that rod between his legs searched for me and I wanted it pinning me to the floor of that gym.

Chewing on my lip, I hesitate before sending my reply.

Robyn: Maybe you could help me a little more? Get me ready for the dating pool? I don't have the best track record with men <wince emoji>

When he doesn't respond right away, I worry that he might be rethinking the whole thing. Am I asking for too much? But I desperately want to know how far I can take this without officially crossing a professional line with him. *Shit.* We kind of have already, haven't we? He has a rule about not dating his clients, but he said what we were doing wasn't the same.

Dell: I can do that. Maybe let's keep it a little quieter so Isaiah doesn't suspect anything?

Yes!

Robyn: Sure! I don't see why he would care tho. He's my coach and not interested… but that's fine with me! <three smiley face emojis>

Dell: I'll come up with a game plan for us when you get back. Now go get some sleep!!

Robyn: <salute emoji>

Finally setting my phone down, I step into the shower. The mirror and glass door are already fogged up as I inhale deeply. Hot water cascades down my body and drenches my long hair. Taking a washcloth, I pump body wash and lather up, gently scrubbing off the long day of travel. I give my trap a good squeeze, wishing someone was here to massage away the stiffness, and I sink into the idea of Dell doing it. Or maybe my sexy coach enters my room unannounced, slipping into the shower behind me and digging his thumbs into my shoulders until my chest heaves.

My thoughts are crowded with both Isaiah and Dell washing me. Roaming hands brush against my aching breasts and between my legs—constantly moving, never lingering long enough. Their imposing bodies cage me between them as they kiss and nip down my neck.

Yes. More.

My fingers find the apex of my thighs, and I regretfully wish that damn blue team dildo was in here with me. Not that I've used Roger. Oh god, have other people used it? No. There's no way the whole team is sharing a sex toy. This is not *The Sisterhood of the Traveling Dildo.*

Focus, sexy dream Dell whispers in a husky voice.

Ope. I bite my lip to keep from smiling. *Yes sir.*

Leaning against the shower wall, I imagine Isaiah is behind me, his brawny arm wrapped under my chest as he applies pressure to my clit. Dell cups my breast and the other is engulfed by his mouth, pulling and sucking, like he's taking his own pleasure from it. His other hand finds my pussy and he sinks two fingers deep inside.

The need to wrap my legs around him and grind overpowers me, but I stay planted—my arousal building like a storm with every convulsion of my inner walls. Frenzied fingers take control and I'm only seconds away.

Come for us, Robyn, Isaiah rumbles in my ear. *Come on our fingers.*

With one more delicious tweak to my nipple, my body releases the impending wave as my fingers sweep me over the crest.

Falling into a heap on the shower floor, I succumb to the high and relish in it.

Fuck.

I wonder how many more of those I can get in before Serwaa comes back.

Chapter 20
Tough Loss

Isaiah

Pulling into my dad's driveway, I notice Jonah's old Jeep is parked, and my jaw drops for two reasons. First he's not late and second, he got his vehicle back from his druggie neighbor without a scratch on it. I mean, without any more scratches on it. Shaking my head, I step out of my SUV and head to the front door.

The wheels of our plane hit the tarmac less than two hours ago, but I decided to come to family dinner instead of going home right away. I'm exhausted and cranky from our loss yesterday.

I thought my players had the new pod system down, but after only four phases, they were second-guessing themselves and bungled everything we worked for. Even after I reminded them how it's supposed to play out after the second half, they lost it again and reverted back to their old systems.

Bob and I spent most of the flight back brainstorming how we're going to get this through to them. We came up with some ideas, and I emailed the whole team a detailed breakdown of what I'm looking for. We'll see if that registers when I see them again on Tuesday for practice.

Even with a plan in place, I can't shake the unsettling feeling tightening in my body. So as I step inside my childhood home, I beeline for the only reason I'm here today and pick up my niece and nephew from the floor.

"Um, excuse me," Angie balks from her spot on the rug.

"They were trying to crawl."

Squishing their pudgy bodies close to mine, I inhale their sweet baby scent and relax the smallest bit. "I'm angry. Let me have this," I mutter.

Zofia grips a small tuft of chest hair peeking through the top of my dress shirt and Nico holds on to my beard for dear life. It hurts like hell but the endorphins overpower it.

"You okay, son?" Dad asks, walking into the living room with a long neck beer in hand. "That was a tough loss."

"Yeah, was your goal to have them create massive gaps in the D-line?" Dane asks from his spot on the couch.

"No," I growl, squeezing the twins a little tighter. "We were trying something new. Remember pod play when I was with the Hornets?"

"Yeah," he says, and Jonah and Rafael nod, too.

"We ended up taking that and using it in college when you were in England. Worked great," Jonah says.

"Yeah well, it's not working so great now. My team can't seem to grasp it long enough to keep it up. I don't get it."

"Who are you trying to emulate?" Dane asks.

"I'm trying to be like Coach Porter." The guys all nod because they either played for him in college like me, or they know of his coaching abilities because he's a rugby legend. I'm not the first or the last player he's had go into professional rugby.

"That's who I would wanna be like as a coach," Dane shrugs.

"Maybe you just need more time," Dad says.

"There's only two more games this season," I say. "I want us to head into the fall with some wins under our belt."

"You'll get there," Angie says in a way only a big sister can.

Nico wriggles, and I take his cue to set both of them back down.

"Where's Ivy?" I ask.

"She's been at a delivery all day," Angie replies. "She's been burning the candle at both ends. This is her third delivery this week. That reminds me," she says, her eyes lighting up as she leans over to place a hand on Raf's knee. "We should get her a massage appointment with Marco as a little treat."

"Make me one while you're at it?" her fiancé asks with a twinkle in his eye.

"Me too!" Jonah cheers.

"We're not paying for everyone's massages," Angie chides. "Book him yourself."

Marco is married to my sister's best friend, Cora. Cora is also married to another man, Jay. It's a throuple situation. I think they call it a polycule. I guess everyone's in love with everyone.

For a moment, the idea takes root in my brain. What if... Could I do that? It would certainly make things easier. Robyn and Dell? Jealousy rears its ugly head when I think of them together. It *is* jealousy, isn't it? Or is the idea of them together... super fucking hot?

"Sorry we're late!" Rafael's moms, Christina and Ana, holler as they walk in the front door. My vision zeroes in on the old Tupperware dish in Ana's hands that I know they only use to transport homemade churros. Suddenly all thoughts are lost, and my stomach growls for sweet, fried, cinnamon goodness.

"Fuck yeah, churros!" Jonah bellows, jumping from his seat and running for them.

"Language, Jonah!" several people say in unison.

"Ninguno para ti," Ana admonishes. "Los churros son para la gente que no dice groserìas delante de mis nietos." *None for you. Churros are for people who don't swear in front of my grandchildren.*

Crestfallen, Jonah whines. "¡Me detendré! ¿Por favor?" *I'll stop! Please?*

Ana slaps his hand from opening the lid and returns to English. "You need to prove yourself." She turns her body away from my brother and offers me to open it. "That was a hard loss, Isaiah. Go ahead, you get the first pick."

Smugly, I pluck one out and deliberately make eye contact with Jonah while I savor it. "*Mmm*. Still warm."

"Fu—" Jonah begins, before correcting himself. "Fudge."

Dane comes up next to me and takes one for himself. "No, it's not fudge," he teases, opening the dip inside the container and dunking his churro. "It's chocolate sauce."

I'm beginning to love these family dinners.

Chapter 21

Meddling

Dell

When Isaiah walks through my door Monday evening for his session, a tendril of guilt wraps around my heart and tugs. I have two plans mapped out, and they're either both going to work or both will fail. It's about to get messy, and friendships are going to change one way or the other. Because here's the thing: Robyn deserves to be happy, and I think I know just how to push Isaiah's buttons to make that happen.

Chester hops down from his window perch next to BooBoo to greet his man. Weaving between his legs, Isaiah is forced to stop and acknowledge my attention-hungry cat.

"Hey, pal," Zay coos, picking up the orange furball and walking over to me. "You clearly don't give him enough attention."

"All I do is love him," I reply, taking the big loaf from him. Chester climbs up my back and sits on my shoulder like a parrot. "He's obviously my son because he gets his lovability from me. I'm very lovable, Zay. You should give me more attention," I say with a wink.

Heat rises in his adorable round cheeks before he lowers his head. "You're hard to miss."

"What was that?" I taunt.

"You're hard to miss. You, um..." he pulls at the back of his neck. "You have quite the following on social media."

"Oh," I beam. "You finally found it, huh? Don't be shy, Big

Daddy. Tell me, are you watching for workout tips or for less respectable reasons?"

Right when I think he's about to turn away and ignore me, he looks me directly in the eye. "Why can't it be both?" He flashes me the faintest grin and saunters off to our warm-up area.

"I do declare," I drawl, fanning myself like I'm Blanche from *The Golden Girls*. "Did you hear that, Ches? I think Isaiah made a pass at me."

When he doesn't confirm nor deny it, I lean into my plan.

Grabbing the resistance band connected to a post, Isaiah sets up for his bilateral external rotations. His back is to me as he faces the wall.

God, his dark, hair-dusted legs are so thick and tightly muscled, and his back... What I wouldn't give to see him shirtless right now. I wonder if he has more tattoos than the team crest on his thigh and the black and blue partial sleeve.

No, think of Robyn.

His first few reps are smooth, and though his right shoulder dips a little from his injury, all in all, he's made good progress. When I think he has the cadence down perfectly and he's essentially trapped, I take a step closer and lean in.

"How's the new job?"

"Good," he breathes.

"Yeah? It must be hard having feelings for one of your players."

Mid-rep, he falters but catches himself quickly. "Yeah. It's kind of hard."

"I don't know how you do it. Being around her that much and not being able to do anything about it. She's so pretty, isn't she?"

"She is," he nods.

"But not as pretty as me, right?"

The pale skin of his neck turns pink. "You, uh, you're both

pretty."

Needing to see his face, I step back and lean against the wall in front of him. I cross my arms and wave my head around like I'm fluffing my hair, even though it's tied up in a bun. "It's the gorgeous long hair and muscles, I know."

Isaiah fails to stifle a nervous laugh, and Chester takes the opportunity to leap off my shoulder and join his boyfriend on the window perch.

"How is it that a man like you didn't make a move on her sooner? You know, before you became her coach. You've known her for a long time, right?"

"Since college."

"It's a shame," I *tsk*. A shock of nerves prickles under my skin, but I tamp them down and stick to my plan. "You know, I think I've had a change of heart. You wouldn't mind if I asked her out, would you?"

His eyes go wide and he stops his set. "What?"

It's high time someone makes a fucking move between the three of us.

"I thought you said you don't date your clients."

"Rules were made to be broken," I lie, hoping that thought niggles its way into the caveman part of his brain—all the while hoping that I can keep believing it myself.

When Isaiah's mouth gapes like a fish, I take my time scanning his burly body from head to toe. Even with a deer-in-the-headlights look about him, he has such handsome features. His ocean-blue eyes are striking against his pale, but slightly tanned skin, and his lush beard is almost as shiny as his inky brunette hair. He's wearing old rugby shorts and a T-shirt that's tight around his biceps and chest but skims his round belly. I wonder if he has hair on his stomach, too. My cock thickens at the thought.

Fuck, I love bears.

"But," he swallows, his voice shaky, "You said you were just her wingman. Just helping her out."

Where did that possessiveness go from the last time we talked? I distinctly remember him saying, "She's mine," followed by growling. *Hmm.* Does my big bear have a submissive side to him? Interesting...

"I changed my mind. I think I'll take her out again," I say lightly, pushing off the wall and gesturing for him to lie down on the padded table for his neck flexor sets. When he tentatively sits, I continue, any trace of a smile gone. I replace it with a stern, slow voice. "And this time, we won't be interrupted by security, will we?"

Visibly shaken, he nods in a way that confirms my earlier suspicion. He likes being put in his place, told what to do, even at the expense of his own desires. Maybe... this is exactly what he desires.

He's not security at the club anymore, but he still most likely has connections. If he's really a good boy, he's going to do as I say. But I have a feeling he doesn't need to know when I'm taking her because he's going to show up regardless.

It's time to see just how desperate Isaiah Johanssen is.

Chapter 22

Sidetraxxx

Dell

Pulling up to Robyn's townhouse Friday night, I take in my surroundings. Last time I was here, I brought her home from the club and we were both in some kind of intertwined emotional mess. I didn't pay attention to just how nice her place was. These townhouses can't be more than a year old.

I check my outfit in the reflection of her large windows on the small porch. Dark jeans, dressy cowboy boots, and a white short sleeve dress shirt finished with my ever-present gold chain, watch, and a few rings. I mean, come on, how else will people know I'm bisexual without the rings?

When she opens her door, warm interior light covers me as I stand on her front porch. "Hi," she smiles.

"Lord have mercy," I reply with a slight head shake, taking in her outfit. It's the dress she was wearing the day I met her four years ago—the day I pretend to not remember. It's a short, pink dress with the straps tied into bows at the shoulders. The square-cut neckline accentuates her toned chest and I find myself fighting the urge to untie one of the bows. She's pulled her hair back in a bun, just like mine, but hers is actually styled.

Soooo pretty.

Oh shit, I'm just staring at her. I shake myself out of it. "Sorry. These are for you," I say, offering the bouquet of calla lilies I bought this morning for her. "You're stunning."

Taking them in surprise, she gives them a whiff and gestures for me to come inside. "Thank you. You look really nice, too. Did you know these were my favorite?"

"Are they?" I ask honestly as we walk to her modern kitchen. The whole place is beautifully bright with an open concept. The living room is sunken just off the kitchen. There are gorgeous white marble counters, an island the size of a queen bed, and a natural wood dining table just next to it.

Most of the walls are pale green with white trim and there's so much of her here. Pictures of her and her team, her family. There are rugby cleats by the back door sitting next to high heels and running shoes.

Rugby doesn't pay much, so this must be from that influencer money. Good for her.

"No, I swear I didn't know these were your favorites. I just picked out the most striking bouquet. They remind me of you."

"Why's that?" she asks, opening a cupboard and pulling out a vase as I find a pair of shears to start cutting and arranging the flowers for her.

"They're elegant and strong. They demand you take notice. Long, lovely lines and gentle curves."

"Are you really serious, or are you just saying that because you're trying to show me what to expect from a date? Because I gotta say, no man has ever said something like that to me."

My brows pinch together as I drop the clippings into the trash. "I'm serious, Robyn."

"The most I've received from men in the past was take out."

"That's because you were dating boys, darlin'." I arrange the last few stems until it's finished, then look her deep in the eyes when I say, "And I'm USDA-certified grade A man."

Heat kisses her cheeks before she smiles. "I know."

A few minutes later, after opening her door and guiding

her into her seat, I take my own. She looks over at me as if she's just now registering the car I drive.

"I know I was in here before, but I guess I wasn't pay attention." She glides her hand over everything she can touch. "What kind of car is this?"

"Audi R8."

"Daaamn, Dell," she drawls and then studies me. "Excuse my nosiness, but you're either in crazy debt or you're making way better money than me. Here I was thinking I'm killin' it with my brand new Jeep," she giggles, gesturing to her mint-green hard top parked next to us.

I know it's shallow of me, but pride bubbles up in my chest and mixes with a little bit of guilt. "I'm doing alright. Making content and owning my own business has treated me well." Pulling at my neck, I admit the rest. "And my family kinda has money."

"What kind of money?" She shakes her head. "Sorry, that was way too invasive. Do not answer that."

"It's okay," I say and pull out onto the street. "My parents and sister run a fifth-generation whiskey distillery in Kentucky, just outside of Lexington."

"What's it called? My dad loves whiskey."

"Castle Whiskey."

Realization dawns on her. "What? That's a really famous whiskey, isn't it? I think I just saw Matthew McConaughey in an ad for it!"

I laugh, "Yes, that's the one."

"Jesus," she mutters.

"But I swear, almost everything I own I paid for myself. I did get seed money from Gram for my business, which she would not let me pay back, but other than that, everything is me."

"Do they know about your OnlyFans?"

I nod. "They knew when and why I started it and when it ended. My family is very... progressive, let's say. They didn't love that I did it, but they were supportive as long as I was happy.

"My dad lived in Louisiana. Came from nothin' and met my mom in college. After school, they got married and ran the business together. Kinda," I chuckle. "Gram's still kicking and acts like the face of the company."

"Aww. Are you close with them?"

"Very. Gram is my best friend."

"That's so cute."

"Her ninetieth birthday is coming up and we're having a huge surprise party for her."

"Do they ever come here to visit? I'd love to meet them."

Glancing over, her smile is radiant even in the darkness of my car, and an ache forms in my chest. I haven't introduced anyone new to them since Travis. After what he did to me, I didn't want them getting attached to anyone because I didn't want to get attached to anyone again. Even in the sea of clients and random hookups throughout the years, I haven't had a steady significant other since then. I haven't seriously considered being with someone until... now. *Now?*

The image of Robyn meeting my family plays like a movie in my head. She would give my parents a hug and then after her, Isaiah. *God, wouldn't that be the dream?*

I reach over and lace my fingers between hers, then guide her hand to hold the stick as I down shift. "I'd love for you to meet them." Remembering why we're doing this, I add, "What are Zay's parents like?"

"Oh. Well, his dad, Neal, is nice, but I think his relationship with him has been a little off. His mom died when he was eight."

"Oh shit. I didn't know that."

"Yeah. Zay didn't tell me any of this though. I heard it from his older sister, Angie."

"He doesn't like to talk about it?"

"Not really. He will if you bring it up, but he doesn't get deep about it."

When there's a lull in our conversation, our fingers gently stroke each other. Just that tiny movement has my blood stirring and my heartbeat galloping. Temptation sings, urging me to drop her as a client just so I can have her. But there's more to consider. It's not just us.

"What do you like about Isaiah?"

She sighs, "I thought we weren't focusing on him anymore. This is a dating lesson for a to-be-determined man."

As much as I want this to be a real date between us and not a practice date for some to-be-determined man—as much I want to blur the lines of this dating coach situation—I try not to let on. I simply smile at her. "Just tell me."

Her head lolls back and she thinks it over before smiling to herself. "I like the connection we have in rugby. It's like, even if we didn't have anything else, we'd still have that. He's also kind and gentle. He really listens to me. He just... makes me feel good. I know that sounds insignificant, but it's really that simple."

"He is like that," I hum back at her, then train my eyes back on the road. "He's also fine as hell."

"Dell," she drawls in an amused but surprised tone. "Do you have a thing for him?"

"How can I not? Don't you just want him to pick you up and spin you around?"

Her honeyed laugh is like warm tea on cold night. "You might have a better chance with him than I do."

"He's queer though, right? I'm usually pretty spot-on with these things."

"Yeah. He told me back in college that he was bi. Though to my knowledge he's only had one significant other. A girlfriend in college."

"Interesting..."

"Why?" she asks, her voice low and probing as we pull up

to Sidetraxxx, a nightclub in the Gayborhood I've been to several times.

"No reason," I trill and hop out, tossing the keys to the valet as he hands me a ticket.

Robyn eyes me curiously as she takes my hand to step out. "What do you have planned?"

"Follow my lead."

When[1] we enter the club, music and people overwhelm the senses in the best way. Nothing is said between us as I lead her to the bar and order our drinks with our hands intertwined.

That's when I spot him. Isaiah stands behind a crowd of people along the perimeter of the club, eyes locked on us. She hasn't spotted him, and she has no idea I taunted him so he'd follow us here. After Robyn takes her first sip, I lean in to whisper in her ear, "Show me what you've learned on the dance floor, darlin'."

When she leans back and looks up at me, her eyes sharpen and her smile expands. "Alright," she says, and pulls me through the crowd. "But first you need to dance like *me* before I dance like you."

I chuckle, "Oh, you mean dance like people don't have cameras on their phones?"

"So what? Free yourself!" she hollers, swinging her arms and spinning around. "Let the music speak to your body!"

I can't say no to her, especially when she's like this. Playful. Joyful. Completely unbothered by those around us as she coaxes me to dive in headfirst.

We're dancing separately, but together. My legs are wide as I squat, thrusting my hips in an upward motion. My head bobs along to the beat as she turns her back to me, spreads her legs wide, and bends all the way over. Her barely-covered backside is only inches away from me when I place my hand on her hip and she gives me a little twerk.

Before I can settle her against me, she's up and turned

around—throwing her hands in the air and jumping like a fish out of water.

Unable to hold back my laughter, I join in and match her energy. Our drinks spill everywhere, but I don't care. Not when the prettiest woman I've ever seen is shining brighter than the strobe lights and looking only at me. Not when she's doing the Dougie during a Dua Lipa song. And not when she's bent in half doing the Bernie Lean.

This girl lets it all go. She sheds every bad thought she's ever had and flings it across the dance floor.

When the song changes, she takes a deep breath and shimmies her way into my arms.

"Atta girl," I murmur in her ear, and she grinds against my thigh, her hands seeking purchase on my hips and mine on hers. "That's it." With her eyes on mine, I slide one hand up her back and press her closer to me so we're chest-to-chest. The desire to rip this dress off and feel her skin against mine is a welcomed invasion.

I've been her personal trainer for two years, and I know her body, but I *need* to know it completely. I need to know what color her nipples are and if she shaves or leaves it thick down there. I need to know what her sweat tastes like and what she sounds like when I make her come.

The No Dating Clients rule was created because I was gaining an unsavory reputation. I never wanted anything serious with those people, but I needed to be serious about my business. But what if I'm now neglecting my heart? What if she's the one? What if they are?

When I look up from our fused bodies, I catch Isaiah watching us like a hawk from the corner. *You like to watch, Zay? Enjoy the show.*

Turning my focus back on Robyn, I lean in to whisper, "Show me again how bad you are at kissing." Her eyes light up and it's like she was just waiting for the invitation to cross the line. She pulls me down and closes the gap.

Our dancing comes to a halt. Her lips are so soft and full, opening for my tongue to reunite with hers. And it's like all the time spent between now and our last kiss was just some stupid waiting period. Why haven't we been kissing forever? I don't give a damn that my dick is pressing against her, because the subtle push she gives back is all the confirmation I need to know she wants this, too.

I open my eyes to find Isaiah exactly where he was before, torturing himself by watching me take what's his. Without breaking eye contact, I slide one hand to her firm ass and pull her closer while the other cups the back of her head. I'm pleasantly surprised when she slips her hands into my back pockets and squeezes, too. The little whimper she lets out is like gas on the fire burning inside me.

For a second, I pull away and press my forehead into hers. "God, you're bad at kissing." She giggles in response and a very simple part of me lights up with fireworks because I *just made Robyn Cassidy happy.* "I think we need to practice a lot more."

She places one of her hands on the back of my head while the other presses to my chest. "Whatever you say, Coach."

Oh, shit, I like it when she calls me that. My grin meets hers. "Speaking of coaches... Isaiah is here. Don't look now, but he's watching us." I don't miss the way her breath catches and she stiffens.

But before she says anything, a Black woman with long, thin box braids and a short dress punches her in the shoulder. "I love you, you slut! Dance with me!"

---

1. *Training Season - Chloé Caillet Mix* by Chloé Caillet & Dua Lipa

Chapter 23
Prey

Isaiah

When Serwaa jerks Robyn out of Dell's arms, I let out the breath I had lodged, watching them grind together and makeout like ravenous teenagers. Not that I have experience with being a ravenous teenager, but I get the concept.

Serwaa's been in the club for about an hour already. I saw her come in and get progressively drunker before she finally saw Robyn and pulled her away. But there's a war inside me—one that simultaneously wants him to *stop* touching her and *keep* touching her.

Dell stands there shocked at Robyn's abrupt removal and quickly turns his eyes on me, silently asking, *Do you know her?*

I give him a tight nod to reassure him she's safe in Serwaa's tipsy hands. That's when his demeanor switches back, his eyes going dark, and he stalks toward me as if to say, *Don't move a muscle.* My body freezes under his attention. Apparently I'm not the kind of prey that fights or flights. When it comes to Dell Breaux, I'm the kind prey that rolls over and begs for a merciful death.

Crowding me against the wall, my hunter cages me in, his thick arms on either side of mine and his warm, sweet breath ghosts over my ear. That little bit of dark blonde beard scratches so *good.* "You liked that, didn't you?" he whispers, and the timbre of his voice sends a bolt of pleasure down my spine and my balls tense up.

All I can do is nod.

"You wish you could dance with her like that, don't you?"

I nod again, embarrassed that he knows this about me, and that he can see right through the facade I've created over years. He's willfully rubbing my face in the fact that he can have her whenever and however he wants.

"Then show me," his deep, velvety voice purrs. "Be a good boy and dance with me." When I don't move out of pure paralysis from being in his presence, he slides a possessive hand down my side and grabs my ass.

Oh my god. He's hard. He's hard against me. Hard for me?

"That wasn't a question, Isaiah. Dance with <u>me</u>[1]."

I don't know who I am in this moment, but Dell somehow unglues me from the wall and places my shaking hands on his chest. I'm burning alive from his tenacious stare and the way his body rolls against mine. From the soles of my feet to the top of my head, I'm fully cooked, ready for any scrap of attention he'll throw my way.

I've never danced with a man. I've never had a man built like a Greek god look at me the way he is—like he wants to devour and punish me at the same time. He dances with me and holds me like he did with Robyn, and my dumb heart wants to punch its way out of my chest.

Where is Robyn? I think, and turn my head to search for her.

A firm grip jerks my chin back, and I'm staring back into his chocolatey eyes. "I didn't say you could look at her. You look at me."

I swallow and nod because I'm fucking lost. I'm down bad.

"You're not my client tonight, Isaiah. You're just mine."

---

1. *The Motto* by Ava Max & Tiësto

Chapter 24
Can't Look Away
Robyn

"**I**s Coach gay?" Serwaa asks, gaping at the two men grinding on each other ten feet away from us. Then her drunk brain catches up to her. "Wait… that's Isaiah. You *like* Isaiah!"

"Yes, I'm aware," I hiss. "And that other guy is my personal trainer!"

"That's Dell? Gurl. Dat ass."

"I know."

My heart is beating stronger than the bass thundering through my body, and my panties are drenched. I thought Dell was giving me another dating lesson. Or, was he? God, I don't know anymore. I'm in too deep and I can't see the surface. What is he doing?

Dell catches my eye over Isaiah's shoulder; smoldering, he shoots me a wink.

Is he… doing this on purpose? Trying to make me jealous? Trying to make Isaiah jealous?

Suddenly there's a hand at my back, and I turn to find two men next to us. "Can we dance with you?" one asks. Both of them are your typical Philly/New Jersey nightclub type. Black T-shirts, gold chains, short, sculpted beards and eyebrows, and slicked back hair.

The guy with his hand on my back gives me a smile. Serwaa is already dancing with her stranger. "I'm a lesbian!" she shouts at him, but continues dancing. "So don't get any ideas!"

I venture a glance back to Dell and he gives me the *Go ahead* nod and wink. What the fuck is his game plan here? I'm flummoxed.

Settling my back against the man, because facing him seems way too personal right now, I dance the sexy and slightly boring way Dell has instructed me. Or maybe it's just boring because I feel nothing for this dude behind me. I don't even like his cologne. It's too strong. It's nothing like Dell's minty scent or Isaiah's heavenly coconutty beard oil.

I can't look away from them.

That's when Dell turns Isaiah around, and my heart plummets when my old friend's eyes lock on mine and Dell whispers something in his ear.

········

Isaiah

"You want to be him right now, don't you?" his deep voice purrs.

"No."

"Don't lie to me, Isaiah. It turns me off."

Damn it. He's right. But if anyone else was taunting me, I wouldn't let on. Why do I have this need to obey him? "Yes," I huff.

"And the way you're grinding this juicy peach into me right now, tells me that's *exactly* what you want." I'm shivering at every slow and menacing word that drips from his mouth like honey. "You wanna hold her hips like he's holding them. You wanna smell her hair and feel her pulse against your lips as you kiss down her long... beautiful... neck. You wanna know what it's like to have your cock nestled between her ass and feel her want you back. Don't you?" Except that question doesn't sound like a question. It's a challenge. A dark, depraved taunt that has me wanting to throw away everything for her.

And for him.

Dell has one hand holding firm between the juncture of my thigh and groin while the other massages my chest. His hard body is pressed against my back, and a greedy little voice inside my head whines, *Breed me. Punish me.*

"Tell me to stop, Isaiah."

That is the last thing I want. "No."

I'm stuck between two worlds, two people. I want to kneel for this man as much as I want to hold Robyn, to protect her and love her.

All at once, my thoughts clear and we both stiffen as the man behind Robyn whispers in her ear and she turns a hard look on him. A very obvious No from her lips. He keeps saying things to her, but she's getting angrier by the second. Another No.

She pulls away from him and turns on her heel. The women's restroom isn't far away, and as she tries to make her way there, he follows her.

Dell and I launch ourselves, but before we can reach him, Robyn must sense him trailing her because she whirls around and decks him square in the nose. "Take a fucking hint, douche bag!" Blood drains from his face as he hunches over and his friend tries to intervene.

"Back the fuck up," I bark. Security is already on them. Omar and Grayson, my old employees, grab the bleeding asshole and his friend, hauling them away before my hands meet their faces.

"What happened? Are you okay?" Dell asks, holding her hand and checking for injuries.

Tears prick at her eyes. "Yeah. It just really hurts."

"Let me see," I say, taking her hand in mine. It's already starting to swell. *Shit.* "Dell, can you take her home and get some ice on it? I'm gonna go deal with security."

"I want a fucking name and address," he seethes.

"On it."

Chapter 25

I Remember You

Dell

"Give me your hand," I say while pulling out a bag of fruit from Robyn's freezer and wrapping it in a thin dish towel. She lets out an uncomfortable sigh when I place it on her hand. "Keep flexing your fingers with this on." I don't particularly feel like letting go of her hand in this moment... or ever. "What did he say to you? I saw him whisper in your ear."

"He kept asking me if I would come home with him. I said no, and didn't want to deal with him anymore, so I was trying to head to the bathroom where I could lose him and collect myself. But when he followed me, I panicked. As soon as I sensed him behind me, it was a fight or flight response. I shouldn't have hit him."

I can't believe she punched that guy. Don't get me wrong, he fucking deserved it, but I didn't see that coming. I saw *my* fist coming. I saw *my* boot up his ass.

"There's nothing wrong with protecting yourself. I'm sorry I put you in that situation."

"You couldn't have known," she shrugs. "But I forgot how much that hurts."

"Where'd you learn how to throw a punch like that by the way?"

She huffs a laugh, "Isaiah, actually. In college."

"You punched him?"

"No. We were at a rugby social at someone's house, and they had one of those punching bags that looks like a man's head and torso. I said *I wish I knew how to throw a punch*, and he taught me." She frowns—there's something deeper than the physical pain building inside her. I can feel it bumping up against my own guilt.

I cup her bare shoulders, and the faintest tremble settles over her body. I stroke my thumbs over her warm skin. "What do you need right now?"

"Nothing," she sighs.

"No. Tell me, darlin'."

She takes a long moment to close her eyes and swallow. "I just want to be held for a little while. I... I just want to be touched without the threat of sex," she whispers, her voice shaky.

"Oh, honey," I sigh and pull her into my chest, being mindful of her injured hand. Her head rests in the cradle of my neck and instantly her body relaxes into me.

"Thank you, Dell."

"Please don't thank me," I murmur into the top of her head. I brush my thumb along her nape of her neck. "I should have never..."

"What?"

"I'm sorry. It didn't really sink in until we were driving here that I used you like a pawn tonight. I knew he would be there, and I tried to make Isaiah jealous so he'd make a move for you. I got so caught up in him and you; I didn't think it through. I should have talked with you about it beforehand."

Robyn is quiet as her breath fans over my collarbone, but she doesn't let go of our embrace. "You knew he'd be there tonight?"

"Yes. I told him I was taking you out."

"For a dating lesson?" she asks tentatively.

I know where her mind is going. It's barreling toward the same inevitable destination mine is. The lines of professionalism are too blurry, and I'm too far gone for this girl to keep it locked up anymore.

"No. I didn't tell him it was a dating lesson. I should have never let you dance with someone else, and I don't want to be your dating coach. I just want you."

She doesn't respond right away and I'm thankful. I'm glad my declaration is being met with consideration. In silence, we stand in the middle of her kitchen listening to the drumming in our hearts and the cadence of our breathing—the warmth of our bodies soothing the nerves that shot through our bodies like gunfire.

This kind of disgusting behavior that Robyn has experienced at the clubs is unacceptable. First, that guy who tried kissing her when she didn't want it, then the second douchebag tonight who learned the hard way that no means no. And those were just the times I was with her. This woman in my arms deserves to let herself be free and silly—to wear what she wants and dance how she wants without creeps like them clouding her sunshine.

When Robyn's hand slides down my back and squeezes my waist, a little more of her warmth seeps in like good liquor and calms me.

She's okay. She's right here.

"Dell?"

"Yeah?"

"I don't know where to go from here."

"What do you mean?" I ask, her face still cradled into my neck.

"I like you. I have for a long time. And I'm really sorry if this complicates things."

My heart beats wildly and I can't breathe for a moment, but I tell her the truth. "I'm not sorry, Robyn." Gently, I remove her bobby pins and release her bun, finger-combing her long silky hair and massaging her head.

It's the truth. I'm not sorry this complicates things. I'm so tired of burying my feelings for her. For him. I'm the kind of man who dives in head-first and asks questions later. It has done nothing but gut me to ignore what my heart wants.

I haven't felt this kind of attraction to anyone since Travis. It's the kind of attraction that is so much deeper than their bodies. The kind that makes me yearn to make them laugh. To provide and care for them.

All the people I've slept with since Travis have meant nothing. Purely physical attraction. And when they got attached, I cut them loose. But these two? These two have figured out a secret code I wasn't even aware I had. A code that could unlock a certain part of me that's been hiding in the shadows for too long.

But there's something more pressing I need to tell her. Something that will show Robyn just how comfortable I am with our complicated reality, and just how long I've known that I want her.

"Can I admit something to you?" I ask.

"Of course."

"Let's go sit on the couch first."

Stepping into her sunken living room, we climb into her plush sectional, the streetlights gleaming through the front windows. When I have her settled on my lap, her back against the arm of the couch and her long legs spread over the cushions next to me, I admit the truth that I've kept from her.

"I remember you, Robyn. We met four years ago at Pride." Her hazel eyes search mine as her jaw drops the tiniest bit. "You were wearing this dress," I say, my fingertip tracing the bowtie strap over her shoulder. "And I thought you were the prettiest thing I had ever seen. I felt like I had been struck by lightning when you smiled back at me." A bemused smile adorns her face. "Yeah, like that. I invited you to a barbeque and you said you were on your way to see your boyfriend," I shrug.

"I remember."

"You do?"

"I didn't think *you* did! It's not every day you get shot through the heart with Cupid's arrow," she giggles. "But, I swear, I thought it was one-sided when we found each other again because you acted like you had never met me. So I thought, *There's no way he remembers*."

"As soon as you walked through my gym doors, I knew it was you."

Her eyes are as soft as her voice when she says, "Dell." She lifts her good hand to my face, rubbing against my stubble and then leans forward to press her forehead to mine. "Dell."

"Robyn," I whisper, nuzzling into her and finally letting my heart run like wild horses. I want to stay in this perfect moment where it's warm and indulgent. Where there is no bad, there are no rules. There is only our open truth holding us together as we block out the outside world.

"You have The Rule," she reminds me. "So the right thing would be for me to find a new trainer, wouldn't it?"

I nod solemnly.

"I don't want to do the right thing."

"Neither do I," I murmur. "What's worse, if we dated, someone's going to put you on blast when they find out I used to do OnlyFans. The media would devour you, and it could hurt your chances at the next Olympic games. Optics are everything, Robyn. I try my best to delete those 'hey aren't you Dixon Hand?' comments when they pop up in my videos, but with our combined fan base, there's no way we'd be able to hide. I thought by covering my body in tattoos and growing out my hair I could hide in plain sight, but they still find me. They still ask where my OF account went. I'm so sorry."

"No," her voice wobbles. "Don't be."

"Never have I regretted making that account like the way I do now. I'd take it all back for you if I could."

"I know."

For a while we sit there in silence, dragging curious fingers over shoulders and coiling hairs—both of us lost in each other and in our own heads. I just can't see how this will work.

"Maybe," I say, "just for tonight, we could forget everything and just be us."

"What are you saying?"

"I don't wanna *say* anything." The inch that separated our mouths disappears, and our soft kiss takes over. Slowly, her hand travels from my cheek to the back of my head, and I momentarily forget everything.

I pull back. "Wait. No. You said you just wanted to be held... without the threat of sex. Not that this will lead to sex, but—"

She shuts me up with another kiss that has me short-circuiting. "Let me make it very clear: I want you, Dell. I want you to touch me and make me come. Right now."

"Okay," I manage to reply before she's fusing to my lips again and repositioning herself to straddle me. Soft cushions cradle my head as it falls back. She takes charge and I eagerly succumb. *God, she tastes good.* Electricity thrums through my body and warms my blood, sending it below my belt where it's wanting most.

Even as a pleasure Dom, I enjoy this side of things, too. Here, below her, at her mercy. She pushes her hips into me as our tongues dance. My hands slide from her hips to her impeccably sculpted backside. *The backside I helped build,* I think, a surge of trainer pride making me smile.

When her fingers dig through the underside of my hair tie and grip, a deep moan pours out of me like water. I think I could makeout with her for hours on end. I want her beautiful lipstick covering my face and her scent imprinted on my skin.

Tentatively lowering my right hand to her bare thigh, I slip it under her dress. Before I can ask, she senses my trepidation and whispers, "You can touch me anywhere you'd like."

My answering purr makes her smile against my lips and that's when I discover Robyn Cassidy is wearing a thong.

Kill me.

God must have heard that last thought because there's a sudden jostling noise at the front door, and Isaiah is bounding through it.

Chapter 26
Watch

Isaiah

As soon as I'm through the door, Robyn leaps off the couch—no, *off Dell.*

"How did you get in here?" she asks, straightening her dress. "Did I leave it unlocked?"

I clear my throat, but it's useless. "Yeah," I lie.

"Wait, how do you know where I live? You've never been to my new place."

"That's not important." I round the couch and pick up her injured hand. "Are you okay?" Judging by the fact that it's freezing cold and doesn't look too swollen, I can assume the answer.

"Yeah," she nods. A line forms between her eyebrows, then she looks down at Dell. "I'm sorry," she says to him.

He throws an arm around the back of the couch and looks between us. "What's going on with you two?"

"I could ask the same thing."

"I could ask the same thing!" Robyn shouts and the three of us are motionless, waiting for someone—*anyone*—to make the first move.

I look down at Dell. "You first. Tell me the truth."

He smirks. "I thought I told you. Rules were made to be broken." He grabs Robyn's good hand and pulls her on top of him. "And if you're such a rule-follower, then watching us wouldn't be breaking any rules, would it, Coach?"

Oh fuck[1]. He has me right where he wants me: with my back against the wall. I might as well be wearing handcuffs, a blindfold, and a gag by the way I'm rendered completely useless.

Dell gently tucks a lock of hair behind her ear, his gaze on hers. "Draw the blinds and sit in that chair, Isaiah," he commands, like I'm nothing more than an errand boy. My heart plummets into my stomach, but like the sheep I am for him, I obey.

He's going to make me watch. He's going to touch and kiss and take her right in front of me because he can.

Because he can. And I can't.

Sitting in the chair catty-corner to them and placing my hands on my thighs, I wipe the sweat from my palms on my jeans.

"Is this okay?" Dell asks her, his voice lower than a whisper.

Robyn chances a look at me and then back to him and nods. "Yes."

"Good. Just tell me to stop if you need to. Now, where were we before we were so rudely interrupted? Oh, yes," he grins devilishly, drawing the skirt of her dress up and exposing the ivory skin of her ass. He toys with the waistband of her black panties. "I believe you said I could touch you anywhere."

He kisses her, their mouth connecting like magnets, like they were always meant to be this way, and he groans. Peeks of tongue quickly find their place inside the other's mouth as their kissing grows into a storm of passion. Wet lips glisten and hands grope while my dick stands at full attention, but I don't dare touch it. I don't deserve to.

In a flash, she gasps as Dell bands an arm around her and pins her back down on the cushions, the top of her head closest to me. He kneels between her legs, slowly slides his hands up her strong thighs, and drags her panties down. He flashes me a satisfied smile, like he knows he's already won. When he inhales the panties like they're cookies fresh from the oven, jealousy, arousal, and a kernel of unexplainable joy collide in a maelstrom behind my chest.

An embarrassing whimper escapes my lips, but he ignores me.

"Completely bare?" he asks in awe, then groans. "Show me that pretty pussy, darlin'. Open up."

Darling? He calls her darling?

Placing one leg on the back of the couch and the other foot on the floor, she spreads her legs, and he bites his lower lip in admiration. "Good girl. God, you're beautiful." He swipes a finger between her legs, causing her back to arch. "And you're soaking wet for me," he says with a pained expression.

"Yes," she whines.

"Does this pussy ache?" he asks, his corded forearm flexing. Why why *why* are his forearms so fucking sexy? "Does it ache for someone who can actually take care of you?" He zeros in on me. "Someone who knows how special you are and can treat you like a queen?"

"Yes. It aches," she whimpers and cants her hips up, searching for more.

"Don't worry," he grins and settles between her thighs, his pointed gaze back on mine. "I... won't keep you waiting."

And with that, the imaginary gun pointed at my head fires.

"Yes," Robyn moans, her hands flying to her breasts as Dell finally shuts up and dives in. His big hands dig into her inner thighs, his rings reflecting sparkles of low light. "Dell," she sighs.

"That's right," he grunts. "Who makes you feel good?"

"You do," she breathes, pinching a nipple through the bodice of her dress.

Why am I here? Why am I torturing myself like this? I could leave. I could stand up, walk out, and put a new plan into action. I could get rid of Dell like I got rid of all those other guys over the years. Silently. With threats so real.

But… I won't.

Because it's Dell, and I'm his whether he knows it or not.

When his hungry chestnut eyes find mine again, I think he does know I'm his.

Robyn cries, "Right there! Yes, yes, please don't stop. *Ungh*, you feel so good."

Dell's focus is solely on her now as he inserts a finger. Or two maybe? I don't know. I can't see from this angle. What I can see is Robyn writhing and her hands flying down to his head to lock him in.

"Yes," he says, his voice muffled. "Use me. Ride my face. *Hmmm*," he growls, his hand pistoning inside her. "Do you like the way my beard scratches your pretty little cunt?"

Robyn whimpers and nods.

Dell latches on to her clit and sucks hard, pulling her flesh into his mouth so strongly that her hips lift. He releases her but keeps stroking inside her. He sucks again and releases, repeating the pattern over and over until she's coming hard and fast, but he doesn't stop. He doesn't let her orgasm fade—he just keeps it rolling into the next one.

Loud, lewd sounds emanate from between her legs, and I can't tell what I want more: to be her, under his attention, his mouth wrapped around my cock and making me lose control. Or to be him, giving her mind-blowing pleasure I've only dreamed of.

Or is this exactly what I want? To be put in my place and scolded? For someone to discover my secrets and expose them. To shame me for it.

My whole body shivers at the thought, and my fingertips brutally dig into my thighs.

Definitely the third one. Well, mostly the third one.

Dell lifts his head from her wet pussy but continues to stroke her. "I'm so sorry he can't do this for you, Robyn. He's not fucking man enough to have you. To taste you. To watch you come apart for him and to hear you scream his name." He dives back down for a ravenous taste. "Why don't you come for me again and let him know who you *really* belong to?"

"Yes!" she cries when he reapplies his tongue. Those muscles he works so hard for dance, and his entire arm seems to vibrate as she bucks her hips uncontrollably. Screaming. Whimpering. Completely falling apart for him. "Dell! Dell! Yes, oh god. I'm coming! *Ahh!*"

I suddenly catch myself before falling over the edge with her and push my hand down on my balls to stop myself from coming. No, I chide myself. Do not *embarrass yourself more than you already have.*

"Dell," she sighs, her body relaxing into the cushions and her hands cupping his face. "Oh my god. That was amazing."

He hums a smug grin into her pussy and gives her a sweet kiss. "I love the way you come." He shifts his weight and positions himself over her, his fingers still between her thighs, and he kisses her softly on the mouth. "Stay right here. I'm not even close to being done with you."

She nods blissfully and he stands, indicating for me to follow him. Wordlessly, I obey and he crowds me until my back is quite literally against the wall. Our hard dicks press against each other through the fabric of our pants and all I want to do is drop to my knees and beg for his forgiveness and mercy.

A warm, calloused hand grips the side of my face as he leans in and whispers, "Open." My mouth listens and before I can ask myself what he's doing, Dell is shoving his tongue against mine, feeding me Robyn's cum. Her earthy, beautiful cum I've yearned for.

I groan, but all too quick, the precipice I was teetering on breaks away and I lose control, spurting hot, wet jets into my own pants.

Goddammit.

Knowing exactly what he did, Dell backs away, and the loss of his body heat is the ultimate punishment. All humor gone, he looks at the door and then back to me. "Go home, Zay."

---

1. *Scream Drive Faster* by LAUREL

Chapter 27
Good Cop Bad Cop

A few days later, I'm sitting in the locker room before practice, smiling at my phone like an idiot. Dell's flirtatious texts have been a welcome distraction from overthinking about seeing Isaiah again today.

Dell: Come kiss me again

Robyn: You certainly made my workout yesterday worth it <biting lip emoji>

And girl, did he. After our morning session yesterday, we were so worked up from keeping it professional that as soon as my time was up, he had me pinned to the floor with my hands above my head and was kissing me senseless. It only lasted a couple minutes because he had another client coming, but I've been living off that and Friday night's memory like it's my only energy source.

"What's happening?" I asked after Isaiah left my place with his tail between his legs.

The couch dipped as Dell laid down by my side and kissed me. "I'm showing him how hard it's going to be if he loses you for good. He's in love with you, Robyn, and don't tell me he isn't. I'm gonna make him step up."

"What about you? You want him too."

"I want you both," he said simply, tracing his fingertip along the curve of my lips. "I'm not going to deny it anymore. Neither are you, and neither is he."

"What about your rule?"

"That's a bad, bad rule that no longer applies to either of you. Don't you wanna be a little bad with me?" he said smoothly.

I did. I *really* did.

"We can be bad in secret," he murmured, and his words crept in like sweet sin. "You're bad at kissing," he said, and I felt his grin against mine. "You're bad at dancing." Another kiss. "You're bad at keeping your legs closed for big, strong, personal trainers." Kiss. He crept down my body leaving kisses in his wake, and I showed him just how bad I am again and again.

When I tried to reciprocate, he denied me, which kind of stung because *fuck me* do I want to see what he's packing. We spent the rest of the night cuddled on the couch and kissing slowly, unable to get up from our secret little bubble. I forgave him for using me like a pawn at the club, not because of the world-altering orgasms he gave me, but because I saw his vision for us; I saw his big, meddlesome heart.

We woke up in our rumpled clothes and he made me an omelet the size of my head, which is exactly the size I like, before dipping out for an early client appointment.

Serwaa called me that afternoon to try and piece together what happened Friday night since she was two sheets to the wind. Unable to keep anything from her, I told her what happened. Everything. About the punch, which she didn't remember. About Dell and Isaiah at my place. About the tangle we have found ourselves in.

I'm not really sure what we are right now or what this means for our professional relationships, but I kind of don't care. I want more of them.

I want to see Isaiah squirm under Dell's command again. God, that was hot. Exhilarating. With Isaiah watching us from his chair, I was floating in pleasure and power. I wanted to make him jealous just as bad as Dell did. I loved hearing Dell put him in his place. I loved every whimper coming from Zay as I rode my trainer's face.

Having Dell dominate us like that could have gotten me off all by itself—his words alone had me clenching.

Like I am right now... oh god, *cool it, Robyn.*

"Ooooh, Birdie's smiling at her phone," Skirt teases. I find her shimmying toward me with a mischievous glint in her eyes.

"Shut up," I smile, turning off my phone before she tries to wrestle it from my hands.

"Remember Birdie," Khaos says, rolling her socks up, "any nudes you take must be approved by the rugby coven before sending."

"Yes, I'm very aware of the rules. Our phones are blown up daily with pictures of your naked body. How could I forget?"

Casshole speaks next. "Can there be a rule that no nudes should be sent to the coven if you're in an established relationship? I'm looking at you, Khaos."

She gasps. "Fine," she mutters. "But what if I get my tiddies tattooed? Would you want pictures then?"

"Of course we would," I say and everyone nods. "That's expected."

"Y'all are sending nudes to each other?" Skirt asks, her eyes round.

"Oh, sorry!" Khaos chirps. "We forgot to add you when you joined the team. Do you want in the coven? You *will* receive unsolicited nudes at any time of the day and night."

"Your membership will also include you to the list of handlers for Roger when we travel."

"Roger is... the team dildo, right?" Skirt asks.

"Yup!" Khaos smiles.

She nods. "I consent."

"Sweet," Khaos drawls and types on her phone. "You're

added, rookie. Welcome to the rugby coven, Skirt."

"Alright team," I announce and head toward the door. "Let's go!"

I lead everyone through a fifteen-minute warm up before our coaches take the field. And there he is again, wearing black rugby shorts and a white and blue Valor T-shirt, looking like a snack with his meaty thighs out like that.

How dare he.

I expect Zay to ignore me or at the very least treat me indifferently, but when he gets closer, he gives me an un-expected and pointed smirk.

Oh shit. So we're just telling everybody that you watched me get off, huh?

When he turns his focus to the rest of the team, I exhale and try to calm my nerves. I'm being dramatic.

"Backs with Coach Bob," he calls. "Forwards and scrum-my, you're with me."

Be his sunshine, I tell myself. *You're the good cop.*

I have to repeat this mantra to myself several times through practice because Isaiah is back to his demanding ways, barking orders and growling at everyone's mistakes. Mistakes that I find fair, considering he's giving us new lineout drills we've never done before.

"C'mon, we got this, ladies," I clap, trying to keep our energy high and positive. "We're almost there. We're so close, I know it."

"Cass and Mo," Zay bellows. "If I see you lift Toni too soon one more time, everyone on this team has suicides and burpees coming their way! Get it right."

Both of their jaws tick before they let out a combined huff.

"It's okay, guys," I cheer. "We're going to nail this one."

Turk stands on the sideline, ball at the ready with Isaiah next to her. "Forty! Baja! Tango! Matchbox!" She calls out as Toni sprints from my side into Mo and Casshole's front pod and waits for Mo's tap. She's lifted into the air from her knees right as Turk throws the ball down the imaginary tunnel and into Toni's hands. Yes! In a flash, the ball is thrown to Khaos, and I follow her until we hear the whistle blown a second later.

"That's what I'm talkin' about!" I whoop, skipping back to the group.

"Finally," Isaiah sighs. "Let's run it again."

Again we run it, and again he shows no emotion outside of his perpetual scowl. Who is this man? Where's my friend Zay who used to cheer for me from the sidelines and recap the great plays with me? I'm ten times the player I was in college, and he was so supportive of me then. Where did that man go?

The weight of our upcoming home game this weekend looms over everyone and grows more ominous as practice goes on, especially with our coach barking at us. I'm trying my best to counteract his grumpiness, but I can sense pressure building in everyone.

The locker room is somber when we get back in and the coaches are gone. No more talk of the coven. No smiles. Just sweat and eerie silence.

Like a knife, Serwaa's voice cuts through the quiet. "You need to talk to him, Birdie."

"Yeah," Casshole mutters.

I don't have to ask what they mean because every face staring at me has the same serious expression. I know they're not happy with him. They don't know he's capable of being kind and genuine like I do. He needs to step up, and I need to push him.

I don't care that he watched Dell eat me out in front of him a few nights ago. If anything, it makes me more determined to speak my mind. If Dell can force him to face his fears head on, then I can muster the courage to tell Isaiah how the team perceives him.

I peel off my compression shorts and wrap a towel around my body and swallow. "I'll take care of it."

· · · · ● · ● · · · ·

Fresh from the shower and dressed, I make my way to my car, ready to call Isaiah, when I see his SUV still here. Walking up to his window, I catch him scrolling Instagram. My Instagram.

I tap on the window and he jumps out of his skin, turning off his phone. Bemused, I smile as he rolls down his window. "Hey," he blushes.

"Hey," I reply and point to his discarded phone in the passenger seat. "If you wanted beauty tips, you could have just asked me."

He clears his throat. "I'll keep that in mind."

"We need to talk, Zay."

"Um, I'm actually on my way to meet my brothers for a drink."

"Cool. I'll join you."

He jerks his head back slightly. "Really?"

"I'm not trying to talk about what happened Friday night. Although, we do need to talk about that. No, I need to talk to you about your coaching style."

A crease forms between his eyebrows. "Okay," he drawls.

"Good. Tell me where you're going and I'll meet you."

"Flanagan's Pub."

"See you there," I smile. When I get to my Jeep, a notification pops up on my phone. It's a text from Dell.

Dell: Can you move your Monday session next week to later in the day? I have a scheduling conflict.

Robyn: I don't have to wake up before the sun?! Of course I will!

Dell: I promise to make your sacrifice worth it <wink emoji>

Chapter 28
It's Not Working

Isaiah

"Two pitchers of Guinness," our server says, setting them down with a thud followed by five clean pint glasses. "Anything else?"

"No," I say.

"Thank you so much!" Robyn smiles, and carefully pours herself a glass. She's sitting across from me and when our server turns away, she leans a little closer. "Who orders pitchers of Guinness? This isn't the proper way to serve it." She shakes her head.

"We wanted the same thing," I shrug, taking a glass. "And I know my brothers. This is what we drink at an Irish bar. And since when are you that picky about beer?" I huff. "I seem to remember you doing keg stands in college."

She lowers her head to watch the light brown cascade of nitrogen give way to black. "That was different," she smiles. "I'm a classy lady now."

"Says the woman who recently punched a man in a night-club." I grin. "You broke his nose by the way. Good hit. Cheers."

Her eyes narrow, but she smiles and clinks my glass before we both tap the bottom of the pint on the wooden table and drink.

The creamy foam of the beer sticks to her upper lip and she darts her tongue out to wipe it away. "Since you brought up Friday night, can we talk about what happened before your brothers get here?"

Is there a pile of sand I can stick my head into around here? Be cool. "Yeah."

"Are you okay?"

That's her first question? If I'm okay? The fact that she thinks of my feelings first pulls at my heartstrings.

"I shouldn't have been there, but..." I pause, studying her reactions. "Watching you two together was... incredible." A tiny smile plays at the corner of her mouth.

"Dell kind of pushed some buttons... said some things."

"He did, but I don't know. I deserved it. And I liked it."

"I liked it too," she smiles. "Maybe next time—"

"Robyn, you know there can't be a next time. Not right now at least. I'm not going anywhere, though."

"But you *do* have feelings for me?"

It's one thing for Dell to force me to admit my feelings while using lust and shame to control me. It's another thing to freely admit them in the light of day, of my own volition. It's so much harder. My plan for us is not shaping up the way I intended, but I never factored in Dell either. But she knows now, and she wants me to be honest.

So I won't lie to her. For the first time ever, and with the amp in my heart turned to eleven, I admit it. "I do have feelings for you."

The sharp inhale and twinkle in her eye are like a reward for my honesty. What's even better is when she places her hand over mine. The urge to skip like a child with our hands clasped tight erupts from the small gesture.

"Birdie!" a low voice sings, and in a flash we retract our hands. Rafael walks through the door, bright afternoon sunshine pours into the windowless bar before the door closes behind him. Robyn and I are both in clean athletic wear, mine now a little damp from anxiety sweat. Rafael in comparison, strides in looking like the picture of a businessman about to relax as he unfastens the top two button of his dress shirt. "I didn't know you were gonna be here," he says, leaning in and giving her a tight hug. "Good to see you."

"You too," she smiles, her demeanor shifting from our heart-to-heart. I blow out a deep breath at the quick change in conversation. I've never been more thankful to see Rafael. "Your soon-to-be brother-in-law ordered pitchers of Guinness."

"Pitchers?" he asks, sitting down next to her and taking a glass. "Uncultured swine."

"Alright," I grumble.

"How's Ang?" she asks Raf.

"Great," he says with a toothy grin. "She took a long maternity leave and she'll be going back to work in September. I think she's really looking forward to it."

"Is she home with the twins right now?"

"No, on Tuesday afternoons my moms watch the kids and she and Cora stir up mischief."

Robyn giggles. "Good for them."

"Are they still trying to buy that sixty-acre plot of land?" I ask him.

"Yes," he groans. "They keep talking about getting pigs. Cora drew up the plans." He shrugs and takes a drink.

"Are you talking about Angie?" Dane asks by way of greeting and then leans in to give Robyn a hug, too. "Hey, Birdie. Good to see you."

"You too! Didn't feel like changing out of your scrubs?"

"It's been a long day," Dane sighs, looking down at his black scrubs covered in animal hair. "Ignore me."

"Easy enough," I say.

"What brings you to our happy hour, Birdie?" Dane smiles. "And who the fuck ordered Guinness in a pitcher?"

Robyn and Rafael both point a finger at me.

"Figures," he mutters, but pours himself a beer anyway.

Robyn grins and then turns her head toward me. "I need to have a chat here with your brother about his coaching style." Oh thank God. I mean, I didn't think she would open our dirty laundry for my brothers to see, but I was sweating.

"What about it?" Rafael asks. Suddenly I don't love having an audience for this.

"Who are you trying to be?" she asks simply.

"What do you mean?"

"I mean, I've never seen this side of you before."

"Well, I've never been your coach before."

She *tsks*. "See, I don't buy that. In college, you used to watch me play and cheer me on. At the socials afterwards, we'd talk about the memorable plays I made and you were so encouraging. Where is *that* guy?"

"*That* guy wasn't a professional coach. I'm trying to be like our old coach, John Porter."

"The man's a legend," Dane nods, raising his glass. "Best coach I ever had, too."

"Same," Rafael adds.

"You guys went to different colleges," Robyn states. "How did you all have him as a coach?"

"U22," Rafael nods. "He was our head coach at UPenn, and in the summer we formed that traveling sevens team."

"Oh, that's right," she sighs.

"He's coached championship teams all around the world," I remind her. "And he was widely regarded as one of the best collegiate coaches before he retired last year."

Her answering exhale tells me this isn't going according to her plan. "I don't know then, Zay," she shrugs. "What you're doing isn't working. And I know you wanna see the Ws, and so do we, but it's not just about winning. You need to think of the players' images, too."

I take a long drink and she continues.

"Most of us will be trying to make the Olympic team again or play in The Rugby World Cup. If we lose, that's one thing. But if we look bad while playing, that's going to hurt our chances."

Robyn takes a drink of her beer and gives me a shrug. She stands and quickly covers her mouth to burp away from us. I try to hide my smile when I catch her cheeks flush red.

"Excuse me. But I'm serious, Isaiah. Something needs to change because the team is frustrated, and it's showing in our game. You have to do something different."

Shit. I think she's right. No, I know she's right. Even if she was wrong, the look on her face would make me burn the world down if that meant she'd be happy with me.

"I gotta go," she says, leaving her half-drank beer and giving a round of hugs. When she gets to me, she lingers a little longer. Or, okay, maybe I hold her a little longer.

"I'll try," I murmur into her hair. She replies with a sad little smile before heading for the front door.

Fuck. I'm going to lose her and our whole future if I don't turn this around. Because here's the thing: even if I did make her happy, if her teammates aren't, she won't be either.

When she swings open the front door of the bar, Jonah's right there, and he immediately picks her up.

"Birdie!" he screams. "I saw that stiff arm you practically shoved down that bitch's throat! Fudge yeah!"

"If you're not careful, Zay," Dane whispers, watching the same interaction I am, "Jonah will charm the literal pants off her."

An image of Robyn writhing on her couch with no panties on flashes before my eyes. "Shut up."

"Seriously, dude," Raf says. "What's your plan with her?"

Jonah sets her down and they catch up in the doorway. "I'm her coach and her friend," I shrug. "That's all I can be."

Robyn gives Jonah her phone, and he types something into it and hands it back. She gives a wave and walks out. Before my little brother can get to us, I take her half-drank pint and down it—and maybe I take a second to imagine her lips and tongue caressing the same glass just minutes before.

When Jonah finally joins us, he's beaming. "Well, it's official." He flops down on the stool across from me and grabs a new glass. "I'm in love with Robyn Cassidy. She's my soulmate."

"Do you have a death wish?" I ask.

Ignoring me, he guffaws. "Who orders Guinness in a pitcher?"

Chapter 29
The Best Laid Plans

Isaiah

Fall. Senior Year.

T he only thing sweeter than starting my senior year of college is seeing Robyn Cassidy sprinting across an empty rugby field and jumping in my arms[1].

"Icy!" she squeals as she koalas herself around my body and I chuckle. "I missed you!"

"I missed you, too." More than she realizes. We both spent the summer working and training our asses off—her back home in Minnesota, and me across different camps up and down the East Coast. Thankfully my landscaping job was pretty flexible and allowed me to miss a week here and there.

I've been a bundle of nerves all week knowing I'd see her today, knowing I'd be asking her the question I've been ruminating on for weeks now. Ever since I dumped Jessica, I've finally let myself face the truth: I'm in love with Robyn. Jess broke my heart, but the pain of losing her was no match for the spark that lit up at the thought of Robyn. In the wreckage of a love I thought was true, I found the promise of something more beautiful, something that felt like it had been waiting for me all along. With her in my arms, like she is now, everything clicks into place.

She smells like Tiger Balm—like camphor, menthol and

clove—and I smile. Some people hate that scent, but I love it on her. It's for pain relief and she only wears it because of rugby, and I'm lucky enough to see her like this. I'm lucky to be part of her inner circle and truly know her. I'm lucky enough to have once massaged it into her skin.

She hops down from our embrace and runs back to her team for warm-up. "I'll find you after our games. I have so much to tell you!" she cheers.

"Me too!" I wave back. Dane, who's now a sophomore at my college, is lacing up his boots next to me and snorts. "What?"

He looks down at the knots he's tying and sings, "*Robyn and Isaiah, kissin' in a tree...*"

I smack his head. "My hand slipped. Sorry."

"Ass."

Of course Robyn plays like the machine she is, plowing over people and even scoring two tries over my college women's team. She's definitely improved since I watched her last. If I thought she was fast before, it's nothing compared to now. She's like a gazelle.

She plays the full eighty and tears her scrum cap off as she walks off the pitch with an exhausted smile.

Our game follows hers, and even though the women's teams have already left the field to start the social, she stays back to watch and cheer. Not for her college men's team. Not even for mine. But for me.

She's the one.

I know it.

· · · • · • · · ·

"Good game, Zay," she smiles, handing me a beer after we enter the social at, once again, someone's grody off-campus house.

"You, too." We clink our plastic cups, and I take a fortifying sip and pray for courage. "Can I talk to you outside, actually?"

"Yeah. It's too crowded here anyway."

The late afternoon sun is still warm as we head to the backyard where there are a couple small groups of players talking and laughing.

"Sorry we couldn't see much of each other over the summer," I say as we both take a seat on a small grassy hill.

"I know, me too. My dad was on my ass all summer training me."

"I can't imagine what it would be like having two former Olympians as parents."

She sighs dramatically but doesn't say anything before taking a drink.

I stare at my beer and say it. "I broke up with Jessica."

"What?"

I nod. "A few weeks ago. I caught her cheating on me."

"What—how?"

"I don't think you knew this, but she and I never had sex. She was waiting for marriage," I say and venture a glance to see Robyn's eyebrows high. "Which, I was fine with. I'm not really one to have those strong urges with someone right away anyway. It takes time for me."

"Okay," she whispers.

"So you could imagine my surprise when I walked in on her having full, penetrative sex with the guy from her Bible study."

"No," she bellows.

"She cried to me about it later. Said she was broken. Begged me to help her and stay with her, but," I shake my head. "I couldn't. I didn't want to."

"You guys were together for like..."

"Three and a half years."

"Isaiah, I'm so sorry."

"I'm not," I smile. "I'm glad it ended."

"Well I'm sorry you went through that, but," she raises her cup to mine again, "cheers to seeing the positive, I guess."

"How was your summer?"

"What? Like we didn't text for most of it?" she teases.

"I know," I chuckle.

"Actually!" she beams, the lightbulb in her brain turning on. "I didn't tell you! Last weekend I was at my cousin's wedding as a bridesmaid, and I met the most incredible man! I've never experienced anything like it."

My heart crashes into a brick wall, but she continues.

"We met at the reception, and we had this instant connection. Apparently, his parents were friends with my mom in high school, but I've never met them! His name is Wyatt, and we talked all night and at one point," she pauses to giggle and push her hand against my shoulder. "At one point, he calls over to my cousin and shouts, 'I'm gonna marry this girl!' Can you believe that?"

No, I really can't. I want to crawl into a cave and die.

"The next thing I know, he's showing up the next day to pick me up on his motorcycle and drive me to meet his family."

"Robyn," I hiss. "You got on a motorcycle with a stranger?"

"He wasn't a stranger," she says and rolls her eyes. "We had spent the whole reception together the night before and our families know each other."

Suddenly I can't control my breathing. "Robyn, motorcycles are really dangerous."

Her eyes narrow. "I know. That's kind of the exciting part." She places a hand on my shoulder again, this time in a reassuring manner. "I was fine, Zay. He didn't try any stunts or drive too fast or anything."

"What did you say his name was?"

"Wyatt."

"Last name?"

"O'Connor..."

I nod casually. "Is he a student?"

"Yeah, he's a senior at Brandywine studying engineering."

"Well if he knows what's good for him, he'll stop riding a motorcycle." She looks at me like I'm a fuddy-duddy. I don't care. "Are you seeing him again?"

"Yeah," she blushes. "He's coming to visit me next weekend. I think he's going to ask me to be his girlfriend."

Fuck.

"Do you want to be?" The heart that once kept me alive is trampled with her happy little nod. I sigh because what else can I do? I lost my opportunity. I had the smallest fucking window to climb through and prove I could be more than a friend to her, and it closed before I even had the chance.

All I can do now is be what I've always been—her buddy. I'll be the guy she texts about rugby—the one who gets hedgehog gifs and pictures of her giant bruises after a match. The guy she sends new, made-up verses to old rugby drinking songs. And I'll pretend the friend-shaped space in my heart doesn't go deeper. I'll pretend. Because a life without Robyn Cassidy isn't much of a life.

"So what else is going on?" she asks, oblivious to the husk of a man next to her.

"I was invited to a training camp with the London Hornets next month," I say despondently. It's funny, I imagined myself telling her this exact thing today but with a much different attitude.

"ZAY!" she screams, throwing her beer on the ground and tackling me. "That's amazing!"

She may have just unknowingly broken my heart, but I can't sulk when she's this happy. "Yeah," I chuckle.

"Do you want to play pro after school?" she asks, and we shift ourselves back into a sitting position.

"I think I'm going to give it a shot," I admit.

"Good! God, that's incredible. I'm so jealous. How do you feel?"

"Nervous, honestly."

"I bet. But think about what an opportunity this is! You're going to do great. There isn't a better prop playing at the college level that I've seen. You're gonna crush it."

Her positivity is infectious and it soothes my wounds, like she's my own personal Tiger Balm. "Will you still talk to me when I'm famous?"

"That's the spirit!"

---

1. *Wait* by Alexi Murdoch

Chapter 30

Home Game

Robyn

"**W**elcome to the field your USA Valor!" The announcer booms through the stadium speakers and we all burst out of the tunnel like a confetti cannon. I wave my hands in the air to get the crowd pumped and I roar along with them.

South Africa took the field first and was on the pitch waiting for us. It feels good to be on home soil for today's game. I'm rested, my lipstick and braids are on point, and I think I've done a bang-up job infusing my team with the energetic attitude we all need.

I'm ready to kick some ass.

After this match, we have a three-week break before our final game of the summer, and a small group of us are going on a girls' trip to the Outer Banks. The team has been going for the last nine years for bonding as well as some much needed relaxation.

But right now, all of that is forgotten as we set up in a flat line for kick off. I spot Isaiah and Coach Bob on the sidelines. In crisp slacks and a dress shirt, Zay's looking sharp and sophisticated, like a man with a plan. I noticed a slight change in his coaching style after I confronted him at the bar. He certainly growled less, despite our continued confusion during phase play. I hope it clicks today. I want to make him proud.

Suddenly my eyes catch on someone sitting in the stands right above our coaches.

Dell's here. Butterflies erupt in my belly and my mind shifts to the sweet and salacious moments we've shared. *Focus!*

Serwaa lines up and dropkicks the ball to begin the game and we all charge toward South Africa in a flat line. One of South Africa's backs catches the ball and sprints toward her goal line. Before that can happen, I wrap up around her waist and haul her down, making the first tackle of the game.

The crowd lights up in cheers, and several of my teammates do the same as I quickly stand and sprint for the next phase.

That's the last positive thing I hear before the other team gets the ball out of the ruck and down to the edge of the field where their winger makes a breakaway through our line and scores a try—not even five minutes into the game.

I can hear Isaiah bellowing, "That was your tackle, Skirt! Come on! Get there!"

After that, it's a domino effect of negativity that I'm trying uselessly to counteract. Casshole is chirping at Khaos for not getting the ball to the back line sooner. Skirt is chirping at Serwaa for not being deep enough in the offensive line. Isaiah is barking at everyone.

My encouraging words are not meeting anyone's ears.

In the second half, Toni is able to exploit a gap and score our one try and Serwaa kicks to make the conversion. When I chance a look over to our coaches, Isaiah simply has his arms folded then gives a perfunctory clap. "Set it up, Valor!"

That's it? South Africa is kicking our asses and we finally make a good play, and that's all we get from him? Why isn't he getting it? We need him to cheer us on. Where is my supportive friend?

"Let's do it again, ladies!" I shout, jogging back to midfield. I shake Toni's shoulders and cheer, "Great job!" But all she does is let out a huff in response.

God, I hate when games go like this. Once the team starts feeling down, it can be next to impossible to lift everyone up again.

Needless to say, we lose 33–7.

Dejected and laden with feelings of failure, we march back into the tunnel and head for the locker room. Just before I file in, there's a high-pitch whistle, and I turn to find my personal trainer leaning against the opposite wall with a smile, blue jeans, and white Valor T-shirt. He gestures for me to hold my head up high.

I could cry this very instant from that reminder alone, but I need to keep myself together because I know what's about to happen.

"I'm still trying to wrap my head around what happened out there," Isaiah says once we're all sitting in the locker room. "So I'm gonna take a back seat for a minute, and you all are gonna tell me what went wrong in your eyes."

When no one says anything, I speak up. "I think a lot of us were in a negative head space once they had that first breakaway."

Isaiah nods. "I'd say I agree."

Serwaa speaks next. "But I think the forwards had a good handle on their pods. That seemed to work most of the time."

"What does that even matter when you're biting each other's heads off?" he bellows.

"That's fuckin' rich," Casshole mutters next to me, and I close my eyes and sigh.

"Excuse me?" Isaiah asks. "If you're going to say something, Cass, say it with your whole fucking chest."

"I said *that's rich* coming from you, Coach," she scoffs. "All you do is find the negative and push our faces in it. Have you ever heard the phrase, '*What goes around comes around?*'"

"You're professional athletes! *You* are in charge of your mental game." Isaiah seems to realize he was too loud and he takes a deep breath. "I want you all to take these next coming weeks and find new ways to get in the right headspace when things start to go sideways. We can't afford to have the whole team spiraling just because we make a few bad moves. Is that understood?"

A dozen *Yeah*'s and solemn nods answer him before he turns on his heel and walks out.

Serwaa shakes her head and lifts off her jersey. "I thought you said you talked to him."

"I did. I mean, we saw some improvement this last week at practice, didn't we?"

"It's not enough and you know it, Birdie."

"Just give him some more time," I plead. "I know he's capable of being an amazing coach."

"He's right though," Casshole says. "We should be able to pull ourselves out of these black holes instead of pulling each other in. Khaos," Cass sighs, peeling off her sock, "I'm sorry for yelling at you like that. I know you were just trying to help."

"Thanks," they say with a sad smile. "I'm sorry, too."

I muster up a smile. "Let's all take his advice and with this time off, let's remember why we love each other and deserve to treat each other with nothing but respect and admiration on that fuckin' field, okay? Now can I get a group hug because I need one right now or I'm gonna lose it."

"Aww, Birdie," Serwaa coos, and everyone scrunches in for the stankiest group hug ever.

Chapter 31
A Little Praise

Dell

I saiah storms out of the locker room, and before I can talk myself out of it, I'm catching him off guard and blocking his path. "Is that really how you coach?" I hiss, and he jumps back.

"What are you doing here?"

"I'm a fan of women's rugby, obviously. Answer me. Because I could hear everything from where I was sitting today. Is that really how you coach?" I repeat.

He swallows. "What's wrong with the way I coach?"

"Dude, you can't coach women like that. Have you never coached women?"

"No. But it's not any different than coaching men."

"The fuck it isn't! I would never speak to my clients that way. Maybe you've played on or coached men's teams that responded well to militaristic orders. Fine. But your players need something different. They need positive reinforcement. They need to hear that you're proud of them before you can give them critique. You want them to respect you? Let them know that you're a safe place to ask questions."

His brows pinch together. "They can ask me questions."

"I don't know, Zay. Other than Robyn, no one on this team looked like they would come to you for advice. You need to get to know them on a personal level before anything else. Have you tried that?"

"Um, they... they asked me a lot of personal questions when I first joined the team."

"Okay," I smile. "See, that's because they wanted to know who you really are behind the curtain. Did you ask them similar questions?"

He looks at his feet. "No."

"Hey," I say softly and lift his thickly bearded chin. "Do you remember when you first started coming to your sessions and I asked you a million personal questions?"

"Yeah. You're pretty invasive."

"I know," I chuckle. "But then we found out we both love true crime, and our friendship built from there. *That's* what needs to happen with you and this team. You can do this. You just need to get to know them on a personal level."

For a moment, I get lost in Isaiah's beautiful blue eyes until he looks both ways down the empty corridor and back to me. Suddenly, I'm being squished by mighty arms. Would you look at that? This big grumpy bear just needed a little bit of praise.

"You can do this," I repeat softly, holding him close. "Think about how much it will mean to Robyn if you get to know her teammates the way she does?"

He nods against my neck.

"Who knows," I smirk. "She may be so happy that she'll kiss you."

Isaiah pulls back and scrubs a hand over his beard as heat rises in his cheeks. A couple players walk out of the locker room and head in the opposite direction.

"We have a social upstairs I need to get to," he says. Robyn then steps into the hallway. When she finds us, she stops in her tracks as if wondering whether she should follow her teammates or join us.

"Why don't you go," I nod. "If it's okay with you, I'm going to talk to her for a minute and then send her up." Isaiah looks pleasantly surprised that I even asked him, not that either of us are in charge of her, really.

"Okay," he says, walking over to her to say something

before heading for the stairwell.

She walks slowly over to me. "What did you say to him?"

"That if he didn't change his attitude, you were never going to kiss him," I tease.

"Dell!"

I chuckle and grab her hands, pulling her into an alcove nearby. "I know you have to go upstairs, but come here." I push her up against the wall and lean my forehead against hers. "You played great today." She smiles, and her fingers find my hips as I cradle her jaw and steal a hungry kiss from her lips. She still has the smell of the game on her and I kind of like it. "You looked so strong and commanding," I murmur into our kiss.

Robyn relaxes against me and lets out the cutest little whimper that I eagerly swallow down.

"What do I have to do to get you to tackle me in bed?" she quips, and I chuckle.

"You minx. I have a plan for the both of you."

"Does it involve you?"

Pausing our kiss, I push back the flyaways from her hair, but they pop right back up. "It does now. Don't worry, darlin'," I whisper. "He's ours."

Chapter 32
It's a Trap

Isaiah

After the game, I tried to take Dell's advice and get to know my players better at the social, but they weren't having it. They all seemed wary of me, and I guess I don't blame them. I have been asshole-ish. I've never felt the need to be friendly with a coach before, so this is new territory. Once everyone comes back from break, I'll set up a team bonding night. Maybe Robyn can help me figure out the best way to do that.

For now, I put Robyn and the team out of my mind to focus on what's right in front of me: my last personal training session with Dell. But when I open the door to his gym, there stands Robyn herself, with confusion painted all over her face. We both look at Dell.

"What's going on?" I ask.

Dell steps behind me and locks the door with a *snick* so loud I flinch. "No one is leaving here until we figure this out," he says definitively.

"Are we not doing my training session today?"

"Consider today a mental training. Now," he claps, "first thing's first: You can go ahead and check your ego at the door when you coach, Zay. Women don't respond well to it. They can smell it from a mile away."

"I don't have an ego."

"You're right," Robyn nods. "You don't. At least I've never known you to have one. Not until you became my coach. I *know* the real you, Isaiah, and even if I didn't, I would *know* the way you coach isn't you. You're putting on a front, and you don't come across like the authority figure you're trying to be. It just makes you look like an asshole."

"I'm not fucking... Ted Lasso, or whatever."

"No one is asking you to be," she sighs. "But I know there's a silly rugger inside you. I've seen you blissfully sing your heart out to your team song. I've watched you pummel rookies with joy at their first tries. You're capable of lifting players up. It's natural to you. At our last game, you did better, but you reverted back into asshole mode."

She's right. Of course she's right. I don't know what I was thinking pretending to be someone I'm not. Coaching the way I have has felt so fucking unnatural this whole time, but I thought it was me working through imposter syndrome. I just needed time to settle into my new role and figure out how to be Coach Porter 2.0.

Have I been wrong in my approach this whole time?

"You need to treat us like we're your teammates, not your subjects," Robyn says with a wan smile. "Treat us like we're your family. If Angie played, would you talk to her the way you do to us?"

"Never."

"Exactly. Zay, talk to me like you used to! We used to be the best of friends, remember?"

Dell crosses his arms and looks between us. "Yeah, whatever happened with you two?"

I sigh. "I'll tell you exactly what happened."

Chapter 33
You're Robyn to Me

Isaiah

Spring. Senior Year.

Ending my collegiate rugby career on a win should have my spirits soaring. Instead, thoughts of Robyn consume me. In one week, I'm graduating college and moving five time zones away to play in the Premier League for the London Hornets, and this may be the very last time I see her.

Everyone has been congratulating me since I found out a month ago, but it still hasn't sunk in yet that I'll be playing professional rugby. Me. Someone wants to *pay* me to play the sport I live and breathe, in a land where rugby is adored as much as soccer and cricket.

How is this my life?

And how is it that the day I found out I was going to be a professional rugby player and move across an ocean, Robyn Cassidy became single? *That* is some Shakespearean bullshit.

She still has another year left in school, but she's working to make the USA Valor women's team. She's been attending training camps wherever she can and making herself known, really making a name for herself.

There's no way I could ask her to be mine now. It's too late. Though both centered on rugby, our lives are going in different directions. Maybe we were only meant to be friends. Maybe the sound of her laughter will someday fade away and her smile, once a burning obsession in my mind, will be long forgotten. Maybe.

"Don't look so glum," she says, pushing my shoulder. Her hit catches me off guard and I fall over into a bush. "Oh no!" she giggles, and as she tries to catch me, she falls too. It's late and we've left the social, like we always seem to do when we're together, to find a quieter place to talk.

Awards were given out tonight for senior players, and the team sprang for having the social at a local bar instead of a rank house. It was as classy as college club rugby can be, which is to say, barely.

"Look, a park!" Robyn cheers, pointing behind the dimly lit parking lot of the bar. She grabs my hand and pulls me. "Let's go!" Why we're both running is beyond me, but I don't question it. She lets out a *harumph* when she lays on the ground and I take my spot next to her.

"This is nice," she sighs. Framed by streetlights and shadowed trees, the night sky embodies the possibilities ahead of me, but my heart aches despite it. Then there's a small hand that finds mine, and that same strained heart sputters. "I'm going to miss you," she whispers.

I squeeze her hand and swallow. "I'm going to miss you too, Robyn. A lot."

Her head turns to me. "Why is it you never call me by my nickname?"

"Birdie?"

"Yeah," she frowns. "Everyone in the rugby community does. Everyone in my family does. I don't think you ever have."

The moon illuminates her lovely features and I wish I could touch her the way light does, even just for a second. I wish that I could keep her hand in mine forever.

The pressure of truth builds on my tongue before its

sweet release. "Because you were never like everyone else. You're Birdie to them, but you've always been Robyn to me."

"Oh," is all she says. And maybe the old me would have tried to back track or add some kind of qualifier to make sure she knew I only meant it as a friend, but I don't now. I let the meaning sink in and her realization dawns.

Together we turn our faces back to the night sky and lay there quietly, sounds of the thumping bass from the nearby bar and the occasional car passing by filling the void. She doesn't let go of my hand.

"Zay?"

"Yeah?

"Can we make a marriage pact?"

"What?"

She turns her face back to mine and repeats herself. "Can we make a marriage pact? If we're both single by the time we're thirty-five... well, when I'm thirty-five and you're thirty-six, we get married," she smiles. "Even if we haven't spoken in years, we find each other again and get married."

Suddenly, my mind plays like a rugby match and the uprights of my life come into view as an enormous gap appears. Only a fool wouldn't take this opportunity. I'm not the fastest, but I'm taking this breakaway and barreling for the try line. It's going to be a long run, but victory will taste so sweet.

Newfound hope rebuilds my outlook on life, and I vow right then and there to stay single until Robyn Cassidy is walking down the aisle to me.

"It's a plan, Robyn."

Chapter 34
No Choice

Dell

"**I** forgot about that," Robyn gasps, her hands covering her mouth.

Then it clicks into place. The marriage pact, his old job in security, the way he jumped down those dudes' throats when they got close to her... it all comes together. Confronting this, I ask knowingly, "You've been cockblocking her for years, haven't you?"

He swallows and there it is again—shame. "Yes."

"Isaiah," she says, her hands moving from her mouth to her heart. "I don't know what to think. Have you stayed single, waiting for me?"

"You were it for me, Robyn. Until..." his eyes train on me, "until I fell for him, too."

My pulse picks up as my heart flutters. I remain in control but surely, they both can see me blush. "Now we're getting somewhere," I beam.

Robyn walks up to him and rests her hands on his arms. "Why did you stay away from me for so long? Even when you moved back here you made yourself scarce."

"I thought if you knew I was... trying to keep you single, that you'd hate me. And you'd especially hate me if you found out I've been watching you like I have. Taking that job as security was mostly to keep an eye on you when you went out. Taking this coaching job was along the same lines. I was able to stay involved in rugby after my injury and keep tabs on you. I was too afraid you'd see how I shaped my life around you and you'd freak. I thought it was safer to just wait it out."

She huffs a disbelieving laugh. "Until we were thirty-five?"

"Yeah."

"I can't believe you've been low-key stalking me for years."

I clear my throat. "Yeah, let's not gloss over that."

Robyn turns to me with an unapologetic look. "Is it wrong that I'm not that upset about it? It's actually kinda sweet in a fucked-up way."

I stifle a laugh. "Maybe cool it with the dark romance books."

She turns back to him and sighs. "Zay, I would have been with you since college if you would have just asked. If I just would have known."

"Our timelines never worked out. I was going to ask you out the day you told me you met Wyatt. By the time you were single again, I got the news that I was going to play for the Hornets. I couldn't ask you to come with me and give up your future rugby career. So, when you proposed that we make a marriage pact..."

"You took it to heart," she finishes in a whisper. My own heart breaks for these star-crossed friends to lovers.

He nods and places his hands on her hips gently, like he's afraid she'll book it out of here any moment. "And I took the head coaching job because I wanted to be closer to you."

"Zay," she whispers mournfully.

"I'm really sorry, Robyn," he says and takes a step back, releasing her. "I'm sorry I put us in this position, but... I am your coach."

"But," she whines, "no one has to know."

"It isn't right."

I tsk. "Says the man who's been stalking her." Two sets of eyes find mine and an idea takes root. "You know what I think?" I grin, stepping closer to them, my arms still folded across my chest. "I think you should kiss her."

"Dell," he pleads. "You know I can't."

"I'm not asking you to. I'm telling you. You've spent years in your head about this. Wouldn't it feel nice to have someone take the pressure off and give you the permission you've been craving?" Leaning in, I catch the slightest tremble in his breathing before I whisper in his ear, "All you have to do is obey. Nothing that happens here will be your decision. Would you like that? Would you like to be my good boy?"

"Yes." He huffs his reply so fast, like relieves him just to say the word.

"Good. If it all becomes too much, you need to tell me to stop. Is that understood?" He nods, and I look at Robyn who nods as well. "Wonderful!" I jog over to the window where Chester and BooBoo Kitty are cuddled together, and I'm suddenly extremely grateful for these windows being one-way because I'm itching at the idea of having both of them naked and panting for me without onlookers.

Now's not the time to try out my exhibition kink, but it is time to lock the cats in my office. "I'm sorry, guys," I wince, setting them down on my desk and giving them each a quick peck. "Daddy doesn't want to scar your innocent little heads. Ignore all the sounds you're about to hear."

On my way back, I dim the lights, and Isaiah's hands flex as I approach. The pair of them haven't moved an inch, waiting for me.

This is going to be fun.

Wordlessly, I take both of their hands and lead them to the closest wall, pushing Robyn's back against it. Already my dick twitches. "You two have never kissed before?"

"No," they say in unison, and I bite my lip.

"But you've wanted to. God, this is hot, okay," I nod and whisper in Zay's ear. "Try not to come in your pants this time." He gives me a side eye and growls. I smirk, "No, no.

Save the throaty moans for her."

"Please Zay," Robyn begs, skimming her hands up his chest. He leans closer and rests an arm above her head, the other pulling her hips to his.

"Go on. Kiss her like you've always wanted to."

He hesitates, and I'm convinced he's going to back away, but finally he leans all the way in, and brushes his lips to hers. His dark beard presses against her pale skin, and her strong jaw meets his. Her fingers dig into his T-shirt, and she pulls him as close as possible. Twin sighs are released. Their kiss grows hungrier and the energy shifts between them. It's like I'm witnessing a chemistry experiment go exceptionally, terrifically right. Their heads bob as tongues search for more and soft moans only encourage more ravenous behavior.

"Isn't she terrible at kissing?" I tease, but neither of them seem to care that I'm here.

"No," he says seriously, panting and unaware of my little inside joke with Robyn. With every roll of their tongues and nip of their lips, they grow more esurient. Soon her hands are slicing through the strands of hair at the back of his head and he's bracketing her face.

Damn. I want in.

"C'mere," I say, gently guiding Robyn away from the wall, but they refuse to fully detach. "Don't mind me," I chuckle. Kneeling behind her, I remove her gym shoes, socks, and leggings. I chuckle to myself because these two can't seem to register that I'm stripping them. When I take off her tank top and sports bra, it's only then that Isaiah really understands what's happening, and he pulls his mouth away from hers long enough to take in her naked beauty.

"Fuck," he breathes, trying to slide his hand over her small breast where her light-pink nipple perks.

I smack his hand away. "Not so fast." I turn to him and remove his clothes, too. When I'm kneeling before him and taking liberties with his ridiculously muscular rugby quads, he chokes in realization.

"I—I can't. I can't... with her."

"I know you can't. Because you made a bad decision, Isaiah." I stand up between them and look down on him while only being an inch taller. After I remove his shirt, he stands there buck naked and completely, gloriously vulnerable. "Which is why I will be making the decisions from here. You chose to make her miserable in wanting you. You also chose to make yourself miserable in wanting her. You chose to stalk her and cockblock her. And now that you've had your taste, you're going sit over there on that weight bench, and you're going to watch me fuck her."

Robyn's breath shudders behind me as Isaiah's pupils dilate.

"Off you go," I tell him, and of course he listens. Of course.

I turn my back on him and guide her down to the mats where I push a medicine ball out of the way. "You can tell me to stop, too."

She props herself up on her elbows. "I know. I want this."

Reaching into my back pocket, I pull out my wallet and plant a kiss on her soft lips, lips that now taste like Isaiah. The condom falls to the mat beside her, and my shirt follows. I'm not in the mood to be one of those Doms that keeps their clothes on as a power move. I want to feel Robyn's skin against mine. I want Isaiah to lose his ever-loving mind with desire.

I want to teach him how to please her.

Coach him.

Train him.

Removing the rest of my clothes and laying her all the way down, my lips trail across her neck and down her chest. While her chest itself is large and built, her breasts are small, with just enough lovely, soft tissue to press my lips against and indulge in. And indulge I do. Why did I ever think my No Dating Clients rule should apply to them? This is so much better. They are the real deal.

"Tell her how good she's doing, Isaiah," I say without looking over to him, pulling a stiff peak into my mouth and flicking my tongue across it.

"You're... you're doing great," he stammers.

"More," I growl, hiking her bare leg around my waist. "Our girl likes to be praised, don't you, darlin'?"

"Yes," she breathes.

"You're... so... beautiful," he says with some grit to his voice. "You deserve to feel good. You deserve to be worshiped."

"I agree," I rasp, rubbing my hard-on against the tantalizing warmth of her cunt. "Tell me, Robyn, how do you like to be pleasured?"

"Um," she hesitates.

"Do you like it hard? Spanking? Do you wanna feel used?"

She shakes her head. "I like it to be gentle, and soft." The way she says it momentarily breaks me; like she's afraid of what that means or to even ask for it. There's a sudden bite of anger that flashes like a splash of water in a hot pan at the thought of her being reluctant to speak her truth. I never want her to feel like that when she's with us.

Anger whirls with confusion, too. I don't know why her answer surprises me, but I pull away from her chest and search her worried eyes. "Of course you do," I smile, smoothing my hand over her head, cradling it. "You're this big, strong athlete. Of course you crave softness."

I think of what she wears off the field and outside of the gym. She's sleek and feminine. I think about all the hurtful things people say about her on social media—saying she has a masculine body, outright calling her a man—and it fucking clicks. "You wanna be treated like a princess, don't you?"

Nodding, she bites her lip, and my cock stirs against her

heat.

"Oh darlin', I'm your man. Relax and let me take care of you."

Releasing her leg, I lower down her toned body and swipe a flat tongue against her wet center. That kiss with Isaiah must have revved her up. Me too. Humming against her, I settle in and languidly feast. I pull on her sensitive lips and push my tongue inside to get a better taste—to memorize her arousal. Her warm scent fills my senses and I freefall into a hedonistic haze.

God, how I've wanted this. I've been watching her workout for two years now, pretending I could keep my infatuation under wraps. But I've dreamed of tasting her. Pleasuring her that night after the bar only made my thirst more insatiable. There's a push and pull of two equal measures happening in my brain all at once: a boyish glee that can't believe I'm really doing this—that she's really letting me do this—and a dominating, egotistical male satisfaction that knows I am going to make this woman see stars.

"That's it," Isaiah says. "Let him take care of you."

I venture to look up at him and slide a finger inside her. "Touch yourself, Isaiah. Just your tip." Straight and cut, his cock is so damn beautiful from here. Dark tight curls dust his groin and just like his beard, it's well groomed.

In a flash, he grips his crown and pulls, like he was just waiting for me to give him permission. His shoulders sag and the muscles in his legs relax.

Adding a second finger, I locate that rough little patch on her inner wall and she bucks into my palm. "Yes, princess. Give in to me. Listen to your body and don't fight it. None of us should be doing what we're doing, but it feels so good to be bad, doesn't it?"

"*Mhm*," she whimpers.

"Your coach is watching us, Robyn. He's stroking himself because he can't touch you. Doesn't that make you want him even more?"

"Yes," she cries, and I furiously rub her G-spot.

"Look at him," I growl, and she obeys. "Look how pathetic he is. All he can do is sit there, massaging his tip and pretend he's me. Or maybe he's pretending he's you. Who do you wish you were, Isaiah?"

"Both," he whimpers. "I want to be both of you."

At that, Robyn's channel tightens around my fingers, and I bend over to suck her hardened clit, coaxing her magnificent orgasm and swallowing it.

"Good girl," he praises. "Good. Oh, that's so, so good, Robyn. Give it all to him."

She chokes out a few more sobs before sinking into the mat and smiling, totally blissed out.

Before she opens her eyes, I'm sheathing myself in latex and positioning myself at her glistening center. My tip drags against her wet, swollen clit.

"Oh my god," she whispers, finally looking down at where our sexes kiss. I'd like a fucking gold medal for having the restraint of a saint. Well, a saint that fucks. Is there a patron saint of restraint? Or would it be the patron saint of fucking? Either way, I'd like to submit my application, because surely *no one* has been this close to fucking Robyn Cassidy and not lost their goddamn minds in a lusty selfish fog.

"*Unghh,*" I groan, rolling my lip under my teeth.

"Please, Dell," she whines, thrusting her hips forward and begging to swallow my aching length. "Please..."

I'm lost. "Baby. Fuck. Fuck, you're so sexy."

"Take it," a low, murky voice says near me. *Oh shit.* I almost forgot Isaiah was watching. That's how entranced her bare, perfect pussy has me. "Take it for me too."

"Oh god!" she screams as I thrust into her tight, wet heat. And at that, I officially revoke my application for the patron saint of restraint.

Slow down, Dell, I remind myself. *Gentle. She likes it gentle.*

Collapsing on her, our foreheads touch, and my hands grip underneath her shoulder blades. "Robyn." My mind disintegrates into nothing more than fizz and I'm reduced to animalistic urges. There's a soft, deep voice rumbling from nearby, and I vaguely clock words of praise. The only thing tying me to reality is remembering that voice is my cute and grumpy Isaiah. But how can I think about anything other than this goddess of a woman below me, writhing and screaming for me, hooking her strong legs around me and pushing her heels against my ass?

Ass. Suddenly I need to see hers.

With a grunt and nothing short of a miracle, I pull out of her and find a yellow yoga ball within arm's reach. Rolling it in front of her, I lift her gently into the position I want. With her stomach on the ball, she presents her glorious backside with the cutest little tuft of blonde peach fuzz over her tail bone.

Aww.

"Yes," she groans as I thrust into her again. My chest is pressed against her back when I peek up at Isaiah.

"More. Tell her how beautiful she is."

"You are," he groans, stroking the head of his dick. "I dream about you, Robyn. I dream about kissing you under the stars. I dream about you, Dell, fucking me like you're fucking her."

"Yeah? Where am I fucking you?"

"Here. In my bed. In the back of a car. In a pool. On our honeymoon."

Honeymoon?

"Oh fuck, that's hot," Robyn moans.

"Yeah? You like that idea of me fucking him?"

"Yes... Yes sir." Suddenly my entire body halts, and I have to focus on not coming. "What's wrong?"

"Nothing, darlin'. Just... Please don't call me that if you want me to keep it gentle and slow."

She catches my meaning and giggles, "Oh."

"Oh, is right," I say, wrapping an arm around her and pressing my fingertips against that budding juncture of her legs. She lets out a breathy gasp. "You can thrust yourself against me here," I offer, flattening my finger for her to rock against with the help of the yoga ball. She gives me a surprised little *oh* when she realizes it won't take much work for her to ride my finger.

My eyes roll back in my brain when I resume my pumping, and I realize with every thrust against my finger that presses into the yoga ball, she's clenching and pulling my cock along with her. "Yeeeeeees, princess. Oh fuck, that's good."

Isaiah grunts. "Be a good girl and take his dick."

My forehead finds her shoulder. "Yeah," I grunt back. "What he said."

Hooking my finger suddenly creates a perfect little scoop for her clit to grind into, and again her tight pussy constricts as she screams. I love that she doesn't shy away from letting me know just how much pleasure I'm giving her.

There's a chorus of curses and *oh gods* thrown everywhere and I can no longer hold back either. "Fucking come, Zay!" I bellow. "Come with us!"

"Yes!" he rasps. At the same time, Robyn milks my cock for all it's worth and my balls try to climb up inside my body, only to release and drop moments later.

With a blurry mind, I push the ball away and lay her back down, kissing her languid lips and pliant body. "So good for me," I whisper. "Don't move, princess." And without thinking more of it, I crawl over to Isaiah who is sitting limply on the weight bench, his head rolled back and eyes closed. Without warning, I grab his gorgeous, spent cock and lick him clean. His answering gasp alerts me to his spectacularly surprised eyes, and I revel in him watching me lick every drop of cum off his body.

"It feels good to listen to me, doesn't it?" I grin.

All he can do is nod, pupils blown wide.

"Come on, you two." I lean down to pick up Robyn in a bridal carry. "We're taking a shower."

"I'm two hundred pounds, Dell," she lazily giggles, but wraps her arms around my neck. "Put me down!"

"Don't insult me like that." And just to prove my point, I let go of her back and carry her with just one arm under her legs, the other grabbing Isaiah's hand to drag him along.

"I forgot there was a shower here," he says as we walk into the small bathroom behind my office. It's just big enough for a sink and a couple stalls, but beyond the tile wall is a shower big enough for the three of us.

After discarding my condom, I turn on the water and let it warm up. Robyn relieves herself and then joins us in the warm spray. There are no washcloths or loofahs here, so my hands will have to make do for now.

"How do you feel?" I ask her while pumping the mint-scented body wash from the wall dispenser into my hand. As it lathers in my palms, she rests against Isaiah and allows me to cover her body in suds and massage her tight muscles.

A contented sigh escapes. "Wonderful."

"And you, Isaiah?"

One of his hands finds mine while skimming her back and he stops it—squeezes it. "I feel amazing and awful," he says slowly. "Thank you."

My brows furrow. "Why do you feel awful?"

"Because I've been a coward. You were right," he says, nestling Robyn into his chest further. "I made myself and her miserable. And there's still no way out of this."

"Well," I sigh, rubbing body wash into his shoulders, my own body pressing Robyn between us. "You two have a little break between now and your next game, right?"

"Yeah," they say.

"I leave Wednesday for my week-long girls' trip to the Outer Banks."

"And I leave Thursday for my grandma's surprise birthday weekend back home in Kentucky," I say. My next words itch to come out as the idea of the three of us becoming more takes root. Couldn't we? I've never considered polyamory before, but the longer I think about it, the more it makes sense for us. "Why don't we take this time to think about us and if we could work as a throuple."

A brush of surprise paints their faces as my statement is thrown out into the wild—into real life.

"Wouldn't we have to hide?" she asks. Looking up at me, she continues, "You said you were afraid that if people found out we were together, it could hurt my image if your OnlyFans account resurfaced."

My gut drops as the impending doom cloud settles over us. "That's... definitely something we all need to consider."

The three of us stand there in silence for a moment processing and gently rubbing slippery circles against one another. "Okay," Zay says, pulling myself and Robyn into a hug.

"What are you going to do while we're gone?" Robyn asks him.

"I don't know. See if Ang and Raf need help with the twins I guess."

All at once a delicious little idea pops up. "Why don't you come with me to Kentucky? You can meet my family." This would be the perfect opportunity for the two of us to deepen our connection. Maybe we won't work as a throuple, but I want to give us the strongest chance of it working, and that means more time exploring each other.

"You want me to meet your family?"

"Of course I do," I shrug, like this hasn't been a huge

fucking deal for me in the past. There has been no one in my life since Travis. When that man cheated and uploaded revenge porn, he did a lot more than burn our relationship. He burned me and my desire for that kind of close relationship—he burned my trust in others. No one has ever been able to hold my heart again. Not until now. The unexplainable urge to take care of these two and finally open my heart again is profound, and it feels too good not to chase it.

So of course I want them to meet my family. Why is he questioning that?

"Unless, wait. Are you not out? Shit. I didn't even think about that."

"No, that's not it. I mean, I am out. I just—I've never been in a relationship, or, almost-relationship with another man. And," he lets out a ragged breath that has me on edge. He swallows. "I think there's something you two should know."

Robyn pulls her head off his chest to study him, and I'm suddenly very aware of my heartbeat in my ears.

A fresh red color creeps across his face, and it's not from the heat of the shower. "I... I'm a virgin."

...*Buffering*...

"Can someone please say something?" he begs when neither of us say a word.

"Let me get this straight," I blink. "I cuckolded you twice, and you're a virgin?"

"Yes."

"But, Jessica..." Robyn trails off, and he sighs.

"Remember? Before she cheated on me, she was waiting for marriage. Ergo, I was waiting. Then I fell for my rugby friend, Robyn," he smiles sadly, and cups her jaw. "Became a little obsessed—"

"Understatement," I add under my breath.

"—and well, a while ago, after Jessica, Angie helped me realize I was demisexual. So like, I don't usually form sexual attraction for someone unless I have strong romantic feelings for them."

"Oh my god," I say in awe. "It's like a perfect storm."

"And there was no one before Jessica?"

"No."

"Dibs."

Robyn smacks my chest. "You can't call dibs on his virginity."

"I can."

"It's his decision!"

Isaiah holds Robyn a little tighter, and the smallest curl forms at the corner of his mouth. "Yeah, it's my decision."

A low rumble flows from my chest. "*Mmm*, then come home to Kentucky with me and let me plead my case."

He can't hide that smile now. I've got him.

Chapter 35
New Beau

"**A**re you sure it's okay that I come on this trip?" I ask nervously as we grab our luggage from baggage claim.

"Stop asking me that," Dell chuckles, his long golden hair flipping over his shoulder as he hauls his bag off the conveyor belt. It's the *only* conveyor belt and honestly, I'm surprised this itty-bitty airport even has one.

"Everyone knows you're coming," he reassures, throwing his arm around me as we walk to the doors for both arrivals and departures. "If you turn back now, Gram will be very upset."

"She would?"

He nods solemnly. "She's very old and very frail, Isaiah. This might be her last birthday. You wouldn't take away her joy of knowing I found someone special, would you?"

Oh. "Of course not."

He leans in and presses a little kiss to my temple and my insides flip. "Good."

As soon as we step outside into the muggy late afternoon air, a silver Mercedes-Benz G-Wagon screeches to halt in front of us. A tall, thin woman with a long, perfectly curled blonde ponytail comes out in a huff. "Get in," she barks, flinging her arms around Dell and then me in rapid succession. "You must be Isaiah," she says robotically, lifting both of our suitcases and throwing them haphazardly into the open trunk. "You're very handsome." It's then that I can pick up her southern accent.

"Zay, this is my sister, Brook. What's wrong with you?" Dell asks her in a bemused tone as we both hop in. "And where is Dad? I thought he was picking us up."

The gas pedal is floored before we even click our seatbelts. "The Lockhart's cows got out and everyone's trying to corral them."

Dell laughs from the back seat and I turn to him. "Who are the Lockhart's?"

"Our neighbors. They have a small dairy farm about a mile down the road from us. How many cows got out?"

"All of them."

"Jesus Christ. How do you feel about wranglin' some cows, bud?"

"There's a first time for everything."

Dell smiles and brushes his bottom lip with the pad of his thumb, glancing out of the window as farmland whizzes past. Soulful chestnut eyes flick back to mine. "There is."

Thirty minutes later, I'm painfully aware of the difference between cowboys and city folk like myself. The funny thing is, I never really thought of myself as a city guy since I grew up in the suburbs, but compared to Dell and his family, yeah, I'm a city boy.

He's out there chasing cows and throwing lassos, while I've been put in charge of standing by the property line fence. About every ten minutes, someone rides over to me with a wrangled cow or two, and it's my job to walk them over to the enormous barn where Mrs. Lockhart then takes them. She's nice, albeit a little annoyed at today's fiasco.

As I walk a young heifer to the barn (after learning the difference between a cow and heifer) I gaze out on the pasture and spot Dell galloping along. Where he found a cowboy hat between the airport and now, I have no clue, but I don't dwell on it because *damn*. He's so... poised and confident. I mean he's always confident, but there's something about him riding a horse that's doing something to me. The way his ass lifts up along with the horse's trot; the way he's gripping the horn of the saddle; the way I can hear him laugh from all the way over here. I want him to ride me like that.

Did I have a thing for cowboys before today? I don't think so. Do I now? Definitely.

"Last two," Dell calls, breaking me out of a sexy mind reel. He hops down from his white and brown mare and his dad follows suit. With that signature smile and knowing eyes, Dell hands me the reigns of his horse as we all walk to the stables.

"Hell of a way to meet you today, Isaiah," his dad laughs, and I can finally register just how much Dell looks like his dad. He has the same dark blonde hair, cut shorter and barely peeking out from under his cowboy hat. "Thanks for helping out. I'm Reed, by the way," he says, outstretching his hand. I shake it firmly.

"Nice to finally meet you. And it's not a problem. How often does this happen?"

Dell and his dad share an amused look. "Too often."

"Look who we found," a low voice croons. I turn to find quite possibly the tallest man I've ever seen, leading a calf by makeshift reins with a child riding on top. "This girl was eating her way through the neighbor's garden," he smiles.

"Hey hey," Dell beams, momentarily letting go of his cow to hug this giant with dark brown skin and an easy grin. "Steven, great to see you, man." Ah. His brother-in-law that he told me about on the plane ride here. He played basketball in college where he met Dell's sister, Brook, and now he coaches at the University of Kentucky.

Then Dell hugs the small child with medium-dark skin sitting on top of the calf.

"Hi, Uncle Dell."

"Hi, Liam! You're getting so big now."

"Yeah," he says, ducking his head and reaching for his father to pick him up.

"Aww, it's okay, buddy," Steven says.

We get to the stables with the last of the round up, and Mrs. Lockhart thanks us profusely before we head back down the road in Brook's G-Wagon. When she slows down and pulls up to a gate to press a code into it, a wave of realization crashes over me.

Holy fucking shit. Dell's family is rich. I'm not talking upper middle class—I'm talking *wealthy*.

Stepping out of the SUV, I gape as Dell chats up with his family, and we walk the pebbled stone path up to a goddamn palatial estate. I don't know anything about architecture, but it looks like a cross between old English style and… I don't know… Italian style? There's ivy crawling over the brick facade and one of the many chimneys. Is this place a million square feet or something? From my experience working in landscaping in college, I have a rough idea of how much they'd have to shell out to just maintain this vast manicured lawn and garden.

As we approach the mansion, there's a chorus of howling from beyond. Dell's dad pushes open the enormous, arching double wood doors with decorative glass and we step onto a white and black checkered floor. Marble? Of course it's marble. Just beyond the wide hallway and through another set of glass doors, there's an inground pool with expensive lawn furniture symmetrically placed. Just past that is a freakin' fountain.

"You're home!" a cheerful voice greets us over the howls. A slender woman with big, nearly white-blonde hair goes right for Dell. His mom, Mary Ellen. Definitely. Then there's a stampede of basset hounds rounding the corner, their stubby little legs tripping over their own ears and rolls of floppy skin flying in the air.

"And you must be Isaiah," Mary Ellen beams, ignoring the

dogs who are actively trying to knock us over. That same smile of his that I've come to adore is on her face too, and the warmth of her welcome is sweet. She brings me in for a fierce hug that nearly chokes me. "Good, strong name. I like you already."

I chuckle, "Thanks."

Mercifully, she releases me before any more blood is restricted to my brain. I bend down to pet the slobbering, velvet love bugs, six in all.

Man, herds of cows *and* dogs? My brother Dane would be in heaven here.

Dell already has one of them lifted to his chest and the dog licks his face. "I missed you too, Mabel. Oh, such a good girl."

"And who is this one?" I ask, the dog at my feet flopping to their back for belly rubs.

"That's Ruby. She likes to eat rocks."

"She's getting better," Mary Ellen says defensively, then eyes all of us from head to toe. "Y'all are filthy and I'm not talking about the dogs. Go'n upstairs and clean yourselves up before dinner." She takes Liam's hand. "Come with me, little man. I can see dirt under your fingernails."

They take the grand, winding stairs first and Liam, who is apparently a lot more comfortable with his grandma says, "One of the calves was eating the green beans in the garden."

"Well, that little girl has good taste. Boys," she says, turning to find us following her up the stairs. "Y'all are in the south wing for this visit. Dell, the walls in your old bedroom are being refinished. Is that okay?"

"Yeah, Mom. Thanks."

"And your bags are already in there for you."

"Thank you, Mrs. Breaux."

Finally reaching our bedroom, nay, suite, Dell closes the door with a grin.

I cross my arms. "Were you going to tell me you were loaded?"

"My family is loaded," he shrugs.

"Can I ask how? Do you guys have a blood diamond mine or something?"

He chuckles while steering me into the ensuite bathroom. "Whiskey is our family business."

"What brand?" I ask as he pulls off my black Henley that's now covered in dust and animal hair.

"Castle Whiskey," he says casually.

"Castle Whiskey?" I exclaim. "I have a bottle at home! Why didn't you tell me?"

"Because I wanted to see this exact look on your face when you found out."

"We flew here in coach!"

"Yeah," he says, craning his neck. "We're not doing that on the way back."

I huff out a sigh as he strips off the rest of our clothes and pushes me into yet another warm shower—a huge, stone shower with a glass door that makes absolutely no sound when it moves. That's how you *really* know people are rich.

But this time my brain isn't lost in a sexy post-jerk haze—it's focused on the way he washes his body. Without showing off, he cleans himself like a man who's comfortable and at peace.

Sudsy dirt and airplane grime trickle into the drain as we rinse off, and Dell reminds me to relax. Again.

Freshly showered, he's looking so goddamn good in his jeans that hug his round ass and thighs like a second skin. He's wearing a simple black T-shirt with his company logo on it, but it's the belt and boots that are doing it for me.

When we're ready, we make our way downstairs through the grandiose foyer, down another wide hallway lined with huge pieces of art and sculptures of horses, where almost everyone's gathered, cocktails in hand, sitting in a parlor of sorts.

A freakin' *parlor* covered in lazy basset hounds lounging on couches and rugs and in front of a huge fireplace.

"Do you drink whiskey, Isaiah?" Reed asks, taking a crystal tumbler from the shelf.

I clear my throat, "I do."

"Here," he grins with ease, handing me a glass of it poured over one large cube of clear ice. "This is our small batch Kentucky straight bourbon whiskey."

"Thank you."

"Tell me what you taste," he urges.

"Reed," Mary Ellen chides.

"Now hold on," he drawls. "Let the man talk."

I sniff the familiar whiskey and take a sip. "Lemon. Vanilla. Caramel. Citrus."

His brows furrow. "No pepper?"

"Oh, here we go," Steven chuckles from his spot on the tufted leather sofa that looks like it costs more than every piece of furniture I own combined.

Reed harrumphs, "There should be notes of bl—"

"—black pepper," everyone answers.

"Exactly!"

I shake my head. "Sorry, I'm not picking that up. But y'know, I'm not very good at this kind of thing."

Liam shuffles over to tug on Reed's shirt and whispers, "Papa, dinner's ready."

"Say it louder so everyone can hear ya!" But Liam tucks himself behind his grandfather's legs. Someone is painfully shy.

"Alright," Reed smiles, picking up Liam in his arms to stride into the dining room next door. "You know, our son hasn't brought home anyone in years, Isaiah."

"Dad," Dell warns.

"You must be pretty special," he teases, and heat floods my face.

Thankfully I have a moment to collect myself when we all sit and Mary Ellen leads us in grace. But that moment is short-lived.

"Lord bless this meal that it may nourish our bodies and give us strength to honor your loving name. Thank you for this beautiful family you have blessed us with and for Dell's new beau, Isaiah. May you bless their life together."

Dell's entire body shakes in silent laughter next to me.

"In your name we pray, Amen."

"Amen," everyone repeats.

"So what do you do, Isaiah?" Mary Ellen beams, taking slices of brisket from a large platter in front of her as the nose of a basset pokes over the tabletop.

"I coach women's professional rugby. And I used to play, too."

"Oh," she drawls. "I didn't know you used to be a woman. Or transitioned, rather."

"No," I chuckle. "I used to play *men's* professional rugby."

"Oh, well that's nice, too. Brisket?"

I offer her my plate. "Please."

"Our Steven here is also a head coach. Men's basketball at the University of Kentucky. Very proud of him. Guess coaching runs in the family now," she cheers.

"Liam, how's the wife and kids?" Dell asks from beside me, pointing his fork to his five-year-old nephew with a sweet potato stuck to it.

He buries his head into Brook's arm next to him, unable to respond. She gives a sympathetic shrug. "He's really into musical instruments right now."

"Oh yeah?" I ask, taking my plate back from Mary Ellen and adding some cornbread to it. "Do you know what an electric bass guitar is?" He nods excitedly. "That's the instrument I play."

"Oh yeah?" Dell asks beside me.

"I can play the piano," Liam says, surprising everyone.

"And the drums and the wookawawee."

"Ukulele," Steven clarifies. "He's working on that one."

"You can play all of those instruments?" I ask, genuinely impressed.

"Yeah! Can I show you? Can you come over to my house?"

"Sure," I laugh. "I'd love that. You must be a really good musician like my brother, Jonah. He can play all the instruments."

Liam's eyes nearly pop out of his head. "He can?"

"*Mhm*. He has the ear for it."

"I have *two* ears!"

Suddenly there's a strong, warm hand wrapping around my knee and I turn to find Dell's dark brown eyes gleaming. The conversation around us breaks off into various tangents, and he leans into me. "I've been trying to get that boy to talk to me like that for years."

"Really?"

"You should feel proud."

"How can I not be?" I smirk. "I'm your new beau, remember?" He laughs quietly to himself, and before he can lean back into his chair, I add one more thing. "Also, I love how your accent comes back when you're around them. Think you could turn it up a notch for me later?"

He leans back, pops a sweet potato in his mouth, and gives me a wink.

Chapter 36
Surprise

"**G**ood mornin,'" a low, raspy voice murmurs near my chest. Near my chest? My eyes open and Dell's face is pressed between my pecs as my whole body koalas him.

"Sorry," I say and clear my throat. "How long have I been holding you like that?"

"Just the last half hour. I'm starting to get sweaty, but I like it," he says and nuzzles his nose through my chest hair.

After dinner, Steven, Brook and Liam went back to their home a few miles away, and we watched a movie with his parents. I couldn't tell you what the movie was about because Dell was holding my hand the whole time and laying his head in my lap. When I started stroking his hair, he purred like a big, muscly kitten and fell asleep. When the movie ended, I led his sleepy butt to our bedroom and we both passed out.

"Your parents are so nice," I say, lifting my leg off of him and shifting so we're eye to eye. Under the covers, I find his toes and touch mine to them. "It's not every day you hear about such progressive southern parents."

"Yeah. They used to be a lot more closed-minded. But when I became a teen and started kissing boys and gettin' in fights for just... having crushes, that's when things started to change. My mom told me years later that the church elders came to my parents and said I needed to go to conversion camp. And they considered it."

"They did?"

He nods. "But my mom knew someone from childhood, a friend of hers, who went to one as a teen. I guess she called him up and they talked for a long time. He told her how he'd never send his own children there. Said it messed him up for a long time."

"I've heard the horror stories."

"Yeah. Well, he got through to her and she got through to my dad. I guess when the elders asked if they were going to send me to the conversion camp, my mother said 'There's nothing wrong with our son or who he loves. And if there is, then I'm going straight to hell with him and I'll see y'all there.'"

"Did she really?"

"Yep. Marched right out of that church and never looked back. That's why I got this tattoo," he says, shifting his arm to better show me the old school American heart tattoo with a banner across that says *Mom*. "She's the fucking best."

"But they're still religious?"

He sighs, like what I said it's quite that simple, and he's trying to find the right words. "They believe in a God who loves all people. They believe in nature and science. They believe we were given brains and we're supposed to use them and not blindly follow a book that was written by men."

"And how do they feel about throuples?"

He shrugs. "I don't really care."

My head rears back. "You just told me how much you love your mom and how you got a tattoo for her on your arm, but you don't care?"

"Don't get me wrong, I do love her, but it's my life. I have never and will never live it according to someone else's standard for happiness."

"Your youngest sibling energy is strong."

He chuckles. "You wanna go work out and swim in the

pool?" He rolls over to check the time on his phone. "We have a few hours 'fore we have t'start gettin' ready for the—oh my god!"

"What is it?"

He twists back around, eyes locked on his phone screen. "Robyn just got picked up as the face of Adidas."

"Holy shit! Call her!"

When she picks up, she's sobbing.

"Adidas, Robyn? Are you serious?" Dell exclaims as both of us sit up. "That's huge!"

"I know," she cries. "I just found out ten minutes ago."

"This is incredible," I smile. "I'm so proud of you!"

"They want me to fly to New York in a couple weeks for a photoshoot and everything!"

"Of course they do because you're a fuckin' knockout, darlin'!"

"Wow, that accent got a lot thicker since you've been gone," she laughs. "S'cute."

Then someone in the background with Robyn yells, "Mimosas for everyone!"

"Okay, we'll let you go," Dell smiles. "Sounds like you're celebrating hard today."

"I can't believe it," she squeals.

"I can," I grin. "You earned it, Robyn. Enjoy it."

"Thanks, guys. I miss you."

My eyes find Dells before I say, "We miss you, too."

When the call ends, Dell leaps out of bed and with a grunt, throws a tight fist high in the air. "That's our girl! C'mon, Zay. We gotta pump some iron in the gym before I get any more wound up. Whoo!"

• • • • • • • • • •

"Dell," I drawl, stepping out of an F-150 we borrowed from his dad. "What is this place?"

"This is Castle Gardens. It's like a public park and event center."

"Let me guess, your family owns it?"

He just smiles and takes my hand. "Castle Senior Center is just down the way there. Gram likes to go there and volunteer."

"Volunteer? She's ninety. What does she do?" I ask as we step into the beautiful grand entryway. This place is exactly what you'd get if you put old money whiskey style with lush gardens. The chandelier above our heads is the size of a compact car, dotted with dim lights.

"About ten years ago, I taught her Zumba, and she fell in love with it. Now she teaches it at the senior center."

"Currently? I thought you said she was frail and didn't know how many more birthdays she had."

Following a few other people, we step through the first set of doors into a damn ballroom with wide, expansive windows that overlook rolling hills of curated gardens and trails. More fountains. More sculptures.

"Do we ever *really* know how many more birthdays someone will have?"

"She's super healthy, isn't she?"

"Very. She walks five miles a day and drinks beet juice every morning. She's constantly sticking her fingers in corporate purchasing's business. And she's been known to travel to our competitors' whiskey tasting rooms to dissuade patrons and promote Castle Whiskey."

"Oh my god."

"She's fuckin' awesome."

"There you are," Brook says out of breath, coming to stand next to us with determination, an ear piece, and a clipboard in hand. She touches the button in her ear. "I got them. Isaiah, no thanks to my brother, but I didn't plan for you. Do you have any dietary restrictions? I need to tell the catering staff immediately."

It's then that I remember Dell telling me she's the General Manager here. I'm about to say no, but he cuts me off. "Brook, are you okay?"

"No," she hisses. "Everything is running smoothly and I just *know* something is going wrong. Something big. *What are your dietary restrictions, Isaiah?*"

Again, Dell cuts me off. "He's a vegan. He's also allergic to tree nuts."

Brook's eyes blow and her jaw unhinges. "Oh my god," she gasps and turns on her heel, running toward the door with her hand attached to her ear. "I have a code green! I need all hands..." her voice trails off as she hightails it out of the ballroom.

"I'm not a vegan."

"I know, but trust me when I say, it's better that she has something like this to worry about. She derives great fulfillment in situations like this. Honestly, she won't enjoy the party if she isn't organizing or fixing something."

"Yeah, but now I have to eat a vegan meal."

He chuckles and brings me into a quick hug. "I'll switch plates with you."

Dell introduces me to all of his aunts, uncles, and cousins, all of whom are incredibly nice, and I can't tell if they're *actually* kind or that *southern* kind where they're nice to your face but secretly judging you. I'd like to believe it's the former. Especially since most of them seem to take sincere interest in Dell's work. I watch as one-by-one they flex their arms and thighs for him to evaluate and ask him for advice on how to get rounder shoulders and better mobility.

It all makes me kind of miss having a big extended family like this. My mom's sister lives in Poland, and I've only met her a handful of times. My dad's brother and his kids live in Calgary, and we almost never see them. We didn't have much money growing up, so going away for vacations and visiting family didn't really happen. I guess I'm fortunate to have such a large immediate family.

An image of the baby journal my mom kept for me flashes in my mind. *I know,* I think to myself. *I need to read it.*

"She's coming!" Brook softly cheers, dimming the lights to get everyone's attention. The room settles, and when the doors open, Dell's grandma stands there next to his mom, holding her hand over her mouth when everyone yells *Surprise!*

There's laughter and giggles as everyone greets her with hugs and kisses on the cheek. When it's Dell's turn to hug her, she grabs him tight. "You knew, didn't you, Gram?"

"I love her, but your sister is about as subtle as a cactus chair."

His smile is so real and genuine when he pulls away from the short woman with a straight white bob and fashionable glasses. "Gram, I'd like you to meet Isaiah."

"Oh, I've heard so much about you," she beams, bringing me into a hug.

"You have?"

"Of course. My Dell here called me up a while ago and told me all about his client he was fancy for."

I stand up to look him in the eyes. "Did you?"

He shrugs. "She's my best friend; I can't keep secrets from her."

"I heard you like true crime, Isaiah. I've got some books for you back home, so make sure you stop by before y'all head back, okay?"

"Yes ma'am."

"Good. Now I gotta go mingle. But hey," she says, placing her hand on Dell's arm, "help me convince your sister to pass out ouija boards as party favors at my funeral."

He seems unfazed by the casual way she mentions her own death. "Brook's planning that?"

She cocks her eyebrow. "You know she is."

"I'll see to it," he grins effortlessly, and she kisses him on the cheek before heading off. "Joanna Castle is gonna be running this family from the grave."

"I can see why she's your best friend."

We grab a couple lemonades and walk over to a set of comfortable armchairs and have a seat in front of the windows overlooking the gardens.

"Does she know about your content?"

There's a slight curve to his mouth when he takes a sip. "Yep. All of it. She watches every workout video and then calls me about 'em. Suggests better angles. She's somethin' else."

The next couple of hours fly by as we talk with his family and flip through old photos. Trips they've taken. Horses they've ridden. Standing in front of buildings they've acquired and two-story high Christmas trees decked out with glittering ornaments and crystal.

When couples start to leave, Steven comes up to us with a nudge to Dell's arm. "Bunch of us are headed to The Front Porch. My parents are taking Liam for the night. You guys in?"

"What's that?" I ask.

"Bar down the way," Dell nods and looks to me for an answer.

"Sure, why not?"

Chapter 37

Instincts

Dell

The Front Porch has been around since the mid-seventies. Like everything else in Kentucky, it's decorated with whiskey barrels, college basketball posters, and Derby memorabilia while bluegrass music plays over the sound system. On Saturday nights they usually have local live bands. It's almost a guarantee I can run into at least one old friend from school when I'm back here.

But my eyes aren't searching for anyone I used to know as we take a seat under the large, covered porch with beers in hand. How can I focus on anything other than Isaiah's shy little smile he's had plastered to his face since we landed? That grumpy bastard persona may have intrigued me to pry him open and see how he operates, but it's this softer side of Isaiah Johanssen, the side that smiles and stands close by me when we're talking to people, that has me falling head over heels.

As much as I want to dive right in for the first time in a long time, I have to remember we are not a thing yet. We might never be. Maybe I could be with just him? But where would that leave his obvious obsession with Robyn? Let's be honest, where would that leave my own obsession with her? And Zay and I being together without her? That would break her heart. We'd all be broken.

"I can't believe Robyn's gonna be the face of Adidas," Isaiah says wistfully. "Cheers to her." *Clink.*

"It certainly doesn't make our decision any easier."

He catches my meaning and sighs, "I know."

"So, Isaiah," my cousin says, taking a seat next to him. "Did I ever tell you about the time Dell got kicked out of the Scouts for setting fire to the whole camp?"

"Considering I've only known you for a few hours, no, you have not told me that story. Proceed."

I roll my eyes. "No one died."

My cousin regales him how it was all my fault, even though he was my accomplice. When he starts on the second story about how we used to sell used horseshoes claiming they were from unicorns and therefore had magical powers, I take my opportunity to bow out. "I'm gonna go see a man about horse and then bring back a pitcher." I catch Isaiah's gaze. "Y'alright for a few minutes?"

When he looks up at me with that winsome smile, a momentary paralysis takes over. There's something about him listening to my crazy cousin with rapt attention, chuckling along with the stories, that has me seeing a future. I can see him at family gatherings with my cousins holding his shoulder so they can lean in to tell him something stupid. I can see our Thanksgiving football game turning into touch rugby as Isaiah and Robyn teach everyone the rules.

I see them fitting into my family like a puzzle piece I never knew was missing. I thought the picture was complete. My career, my brand, my family: it was enough. But now that I have them in my life, I can see the gaping hole right in the middle that I've been overlooking for years. I can't anymore.

How can I ignore the feeling of freefalling when Isaiah's dark blue eyes shine for me?

"Yeah," Isaiah says, unaware of my pounding heartbeat. "I'll be alright."

Walking [1]back through the neon-lit bar, I'm vaguely aware of a couple hands waving my way as my head floats with bewitching thoughts of Isaiah. When I get to the small empty bathroom and take my spot at one of the two urinals, I relax more into the thought of him.

Lost in my own mind, I don't pay attention to the door opening, but when I hear the sound of it locking, the hairs on the back of my neck stand erect.

"Hi, Delly."

Fuck.

I don't have to look over my shoulder to know that's the voice of my ex almost-fiancé. "Hi, Travis."

Travis Howard. The red-bearded man who once fiercely held my heart but could never hold his liquor, nor his temper.

My sweet thoughts of Isaiah are replaced by our memories. Good ones. Like driving down old country roads and hollering our favorite lyrics. Like playing poker with our friends. Like swimming naked in the creek in the middle of night.

I zip up my pants and turn to find his green eyes, and the bad memories show up louder. Like him kissing another man. Like glassy eyes and incoherent jealousy. Like truck windows being smashed and revenge porn.

"So you're just gonna show up here and not tell me," he says with a cheshire cat grin that once allured me, but now scratches my heart like nails on a chalkboard.

"Yeah, Travis. That's kinda how this works when we're from the same hometown. I'm gon' show up every now an' again."

"Why'd you block me?"

My brows pinch together because is he serious right now? "'Cuz you're a piece of shit, and I don't want to hear from you."

All at once there's hands punching at the bathroom door. "Travis unlock the fuckin' door!" Steven bellows from the other side.

"I just wanna talk."

I roll my eyes. "No, you don't. You wanna start shit."

My brother-in-law hammers at the door, and when I try to step around Travis to unlock it, he blocks me. With only an inch separating us, I step back and blink. "Move," I growl.

"No. Come on, let's get a drink and catch up."

"I'm here with someone. Now move," I warn as Steven relentlessly pounds at the door. Suddenly I'm all too aware of being locked in a bathroom with my ex as my family makes a scene outside. My thoughts race with what Isaiah could be thinking if he knew what was going on. This is a bad look. I have to get out of here now.

My last drop of southern gentleman evaporates and is replaced with blind rage. "Travis, get the fuck outta my way or I'll make you!"

Before I'm done speaking, he's gluing himself to the wall. With a huff, I unlock it, and Steven comes barreling in with my cousins and Isaiah behind them.

"No," my cousin Luke barks as he forms a family blockade at the doorway. "You've done enough damage!"

"I just wanna talk to him!"

I grab Isaiah's hand, who I'm glad looks confused more than anything, and a gap opens for us to leave.

But Travis says something that stops me in my tracks. "I—I want my ring back," he stammers, like he's grasping at straws just to talk to me.

"Your ring?" I laugh humorlessly, turning to face him once again and holding Isaiah's hand behind my back. "We were never engaged! Why? So you can sell it for the money since you can't keep a job? What? Did cash flow dry up when that little video you made of us stopped going viral?"

"You bought it for me, Dell," he says through clenched teeth.

"Well, have fun lookin' for it at the bottom of the Kentucky River," my cousin sneers. "I watched him throw it in."

"What? That was mine!"

"Shoulda thought about that when you cheated on me." I quickly turn on my heel and place my hand on Isaiah's lower back. "C'mon, baby. We're gettin' outta here."

"Baby?" Travis booms, but we ditch him through the crowd of my family who's holding him back.

I'm vibrating when we get to the truck and Isaiah puts me in the passenger's seat. I know I tried to put on an unaffected front, but Travis can get under my skin faster than a fox in a henhouse.

There are no words spoken or sounds from the radio. Isaiah drives quietly while I'm caught up in visions of my crumbling life from seven years ago, when Travis not only broke my heart, but changed the trajectory of my life. The sun has just begun to set when we turn into my family's property through the gates. When the truck comes to a stop, Isaiah turns to me and holds my hand. "What do you need right now?"

I need to clear my head and drop this mental weight.

"I need to swim," I say despondently.

"Okay," he whispers, and gives my hand one more squeeze before turning off the truck and taking me inside. When he tries to take the stairs to our room, I ignore it and pull him toward the back terrace.

"Oh," he says as I strip everything off, leaving my clothes in a trail heading for the pool. As soon as I'm close enough, my chin trembles and my breath shakes before I dive in. Cool water closes in on me—the pressure holding me like a weighted blanket. The rough walls of the pool grate against my fingertips when I get to the end and resurface. I exhale Travis, flip to my back and float there, inhaling the soothing country air I've missed—the aromas of bee balm and yuccas from our gardens faintly wafting over the scent of salt water.

It's then that I feel him next to me and finally open my eyes again. "Hey," I say softly, reaching for him. He's simply floating alongside me, waiting, watching. He pulls me by the elbow, and I slowly crash against his naked body. This time, it's my turn to koala him.

"It's okay," he says softly in the shell of my ear. "It's okay."

Isaiah holds me like a child because that's exactly what I feel like right now. My emotions are too big and too loud. They're consuming me like a swarm of locusts or a flesh-eating bacteria. Why does this happen every time I see him? I'm the one who broke up with him! He's the one who broke my heart and tried his hand at revenge, yet I'm the one torn to shreds. I just want to get to a point when seeing him doesn't hurt so bad.

"I'm sorry you had to see that."

"There's nothing to apologize for. Do you wanna talk about it?"

I sigh, but keep my face buried in him. "So that's Travis."

"I gathered."

"My ex-boyfriend-almost-fiancé who cheated on me at my cousin's wedding amongst other places and uploaded revenge porn of me."

"Dell," he sighs, rubbing my back gently.

"It's fine. I'm really over it. But it's like, every time I see him the hurt comes back. I think I'd visit home more if I knew I wouldn't run into him."

"Do you want me to kill him?"

"Please."

"Okay," he coos, brushing wet strands of hair behind my ear. I can hear his smile. "I'll kill him for you."

"Thank you."

"Do you think I'd go to prison here or back in Pennsylvania?"

"Probably here."

"Okay. I could make a decent life in prison, I think. I could put my makeshift tattoo skills to good use."

I think of his inner forearm and rear back. "Is that what

that is?" I ask, grabbing his arm. "What is this supposed to be?"

"That's Floyd Pepper, bassist from Dr. Teeth and the Electric Mayhem. You know, the band on The Muppets Show."

"It looks like a bruise."

He smiles, "That it does."

"You're not going to do very well in prison."

He sighs dramatically, "Probably not."

"Maybe it's best you don't kill my ex-boyfriend."

He boops me on the nose. "Another day, then."

I realize my heart rate has returned to normal and my tunnel vision has opened up.

"So, you know about my solo content on OnlyFans, right?"

He nods. "I found it after doing a deep dive on you."

"I used to have a lot more. But even though I deleted my account, there are still videos that pop up every now and again. I had never planned on making content like that, but Travis," I sigh. "He told me if I didn't take him back after he cheated on me, that he would upload our video." I shrug. "I called his bluff, but was prepared for him to really do it. And he did. So, like the rational and not at all bull-headed young twenty-somethin' I was, I got in front of it and made my own content. All he did was fuel my fire."

"I'm sorry."

"Y'know, I never used to be. I didn't think about what it would mean for future me or my romantic relationships, because after him, I didn't think I'd ever trust someone with my heart again."

"Then why do you trust me?"

For a few long moments I float there, wrapped in arms so big they make an ox like me feel small, searching for an answer in his eyes—his eyes which are more brilliant than the sparkling pool holding us together. More brilliant than the sunset behind him.

"I dunno. I'm just runnin' on instinct with you."

Isaiah's answering smile is too sweet to leave alone, so I kiss him and savor every second. Innocent and promising, it stretches on for a lifetime, into a future I didn't know could exist for me.

---

1. I Remember Everything by Zach Bryan ft. Kacey Muskgraves

Chapter 38

Sunrise Picnic

Isaiah

With pruny skin, damp hair, and a *Twisted Sisters True Crime* episode in our ears, we went to bed early as determination overpowered me. Dell Breaux was mine to take care of.

I resolved that in the morning, I would wake up and make him breakfast before he even stirred. Instead, I woke to an empty bed before the sun was even up.

He isn't in the bathroom and his boots are gone. His phone is gone. Maybe he's working out?

Throwing on some jeans and an olive-green T-shirt, I slip on my shoes and head downstairs. The entire house is quiet, but there's soft clanking coming from the kitchen. Rounding the corner, the smell of fresh coffee greets me and I catch Dell placing something in a basket on the counter.

"Hey," I whisper, scaring him, but he chuckles. "What are you doing?"

Wearing almost the same thing I am, jeans and a white tee, he pulls at the back of his neck. "Fixin' a picnic. Would you like to watch the sunrise with me?"

I swallow the sudden lump in my throat, will my heart to calm down, and nod[1].

We hop in the truck, and he drives us down a dirt lane on their property that's lined with trees. After traversing down a hill, Dell parks the truck at a clearing near a lil-lypad-covered pond and sets everything up. A blanket, a couple of pillows, napkins, and a basket full of fruit, bagels with cream cheese, some hard-boiled eggs, and a thermos of coffee. Right as he pours our coffees into metal mugs, the first burst of sunlight flashes over the rolling hills in the distance. It catches on the agricultural board-on-board fences that define property lines and Kentucky as a whole. It catches on barns, and slowly illuminates the green pastures in new light.

Taking a sip of black coffee, I smile and lean back into his chest, his legs bracketing mine. "I don't think I've ever seen the sunrise like this. It's beautiful."

"I've never seen a sunrise with someone *as* beautiful."

The butterflies fluttering through my stomach must have some kind of contract with the temperature controls of my blood, because suddenly my cheeks are on fire. "That's not really a word I've been called much."

"Then I'll make sure you hear it every day."

Oh god, I'm going to say it aren't I? No. I can't. Is it too soon? It's definitely too soon. But I've known him for months and this need for him pounds like a drum inside me. I need him like I need to breathe. I need him like I need Robyn. I want to take care of him and listen to him—listen to the things that scare him and—

"I love you, Isaiah."

Did he just... "What?" I ask, setting down my mug and whipping around to look him in the eyes.

"I love you," he repeats confidently. "Aww," he smiles, touching the back of his fingers to my cheeks. "You're so cute when you blush."

"I love you too," I whisper, suddenly unsure of what to do with my hands as my heart thumps wildly in my ears.

Thankfully he knows what to do with my hands and he guides them to his shoulders as I straddle his lap. "Yeah?"

"Yeah."

Dell cups the back of my head and whispers, "Say it

again."

I kiss him. "I love you, Dell."

"Again," he says through another kiss.

"I love you."

Taking me with him, Dell lays back and I cover his body with mine, getting lost in his coffee kisses and unruly mane, in his faint minty scent and the grassy fields beyond. My hands search for the warm skin of his hard stomach and skim up his chest to dig in. But I need more.

Lifting his shirt off and tossing it aside, I bite my lip before planting more kisses along his neck. "Make love to me."

"Are you sure?" he pants. "You said... *oh god*, that feels good," he says distractedly when I lick up his neck and bite his earlobe. "You, you said you needed a deep emotional connection."

I grind my stiff length against him to drive home the point. "I fucking love you, Dell. I'd say that's pretty deep." His answering moan tells me I have him, but when he flips me over with the ease of a former wrestler, I realize *he* has me.

And I want him to.

"You're definitely sure?"

I reach around and pluck my wallet from my back pocket and present him with a condom and a lube packet. "Yes."

He eyes the lube. "How long have you been carrying that?"

"Since I left for the airport," I smile. "I have more in my suitcase. A Costco-sized bottle."

He falls against me, his chest rumbling in deep laughter that infects me.

"What?" I ask. "You don't think that's enough? We can get more."

"I love you," he chuckles, peeling off my shirt. He takes a deep breath and sifts his fingers through my chest chair.

His laughter dies but the adoration in his eyes remains. "I love your body."

"I don't exactly have a professional athlete's body anymore."

"I know," he says. "I like this one. I like some cushion for the pushin'."

My thumbs graze his trim waist above his belt. "I love your body, too. It shows how hard you work for it. You probably don't need me to tell you that. You have hundreds of people in your comment section doing it."

"Yeah, but it means nothing when they say those things, and it means everything when you do."

Our lips find each other again. Our hips grind and our bodies sing. Somewhere in our tangle of arms and legs we manage to remove our shoes and jeans, but before we can think of removing socks, his tongue finds the base of my shaft and drags along the underside to my tip, and I die of pleasure.

"Baby," I whimper. I hold back Dell's hair so I can better watch him. Slick heat circles my crown as my cock disappears between his gorgeous, perfect lips. With his eyes closed and his hand circling my length, he hums his own pleasure with mine. Saliva drips down and Dell smears it with each stroke, coating me as my toes curl and my balls tighten. "God, that feels good," I drawl.

With a hand still working me, he pops his head off for only a moment. "I love your cock. Fuck, it's perfect," he says before sending kisses along its side and down to my balls and the crease at my thigh. He pulls my tip between his fingers. "So thick and dripping for me. Tell me, Isaiah... did you jerk off to any of my videos?"

I don't pretend to hide it. "Yes."

"Which ones?"

"Your workout videos. In those... *unghh*... those leggings... that crop top."

"Would you like for me to give you a private lesson in that outfit one day?"

"Yes," I reply way too fast.

"Is the sexy, swole gym teacher a fantasy of yours?"

"If it's you, it is."

Pleased with my answer, he descends down my shaft again, and his chuckle adds to the already mind-blowing pleasure. Then he's spreading my legs wider, parting them at my center and diving his face in my—*oh fuck!*

"You don't have to," I huff.

Dell swipes his tongue across my tight hole. "Oh, I disagree. I *need to.*"

"Oh no," I whine. "Why does that feel so good?"

"Because it's me." He rubs his face in deeper while pushing my balls up for better access. "Do you wanna take my cock, baby?"

"I do."

"Good." Dell licks his finger and presses the tip to my back entrance. "Because there's a lot more where this came from."

I'm relieved I showered right before we left the house because for the next twenty minutes, my pleasure rises along with the sun as Dell prepares me. He feasts until I'm a squirming mess, blabbering and begging for him to take my goddamn virginity already.

He's already opened me up with his fingers, but once the condom is on and he's kneeling over me, lube spread liberally over the both of us, his tip requests access and I realize *that* is so much more than his fingers.

"Hey, hey," he soothes. "It's going to be okay. I'll go slow. And if it doesn't fit, we can try again another time."

"No, I know. I want to. You're just—"

"I know. But you're doing so well for me, Isaiah. You opened on my fingers perfectly." Dell leans down, his chest against mine, and kisses me so deeply I forget about what we're trying to do until there's a tight blinding pressure below. "That's it, baby. You're doin' it. Try to push me out and it'll go in easier, I promise. *Unghh*, yes. Yes."

"It's too much."

He stills, allowing me to accept his size. "I'm all the way in, baby."

My entire body shivers as a cold sweat takes over. "You swear?"

"I swear," he smiles and kisses me more. "You have me. I knew you could do it."

The tenderness and praise from this man is sending me into a frenzy of emotions I can't make sense of, but I know that I like it.

I like it a lot.

I like his cock dragging in and out of me like he's testing the waters. I like that even with a cool morning breeze I can still feel the heat of his body. I like that he's kissing me through every unhurried thrust. I like the way he's slowly losing his mind and whispering nonsense into my temple. I like the way he licks the sweat off my neck.

He likes the way I wrap my legs around his waist and urge him to go faster—to go deeper. He likes the way I claw at his broad back and dig my fingers into his ass. He likes the way I force my hand between our stomachs to grab my cock and stroke it. He likes the way I moan his name for all of nature to hear.

"I'm so close, Dell."

"Me too," he rasps and sits up, smacking my hand away and stroking my dick hard and fast. My knee is way up, and he watches where we're joined like he's committing it to memory. I hold my other leg and with both knees up, his rock-hard length hits against my prostate mercilessly until I'm falling over the edge.

"Yes, baby," he growls. "Come for me just like that." Hot pulses of cum shoot out, covering my chest and his hand as he jerks me. His pumping speeds up until he's falling too, his thrusts faltering as he spills his release inside me.

A drop of his sweat falls from his forehead, landing on mine, and he collapses over me. "Tell me again," he exhales, and I kiss him for being so damn good to me.

"I love you."

"I love you, too."

Dell pulls out after we lay there for a while, breathing in each other's bodies and calming our racing heartbeats. The condom is discarded and pulls me into his arms, kissing my forehead as we lay on our sides.

"How do you feel?" he asks.

I sigh blissfully. "Really good. Like I waited until the exact right time to do this." There's a strange pause, and I open my eyes to catch him with a tear slipping down his cheek. "What's wrong?"

"I'm just really happy I could do this for you. *Be* this for you."

"Baby," I whisper, holding him tighter. "You were amazing. I could not have asked for a better first time."

He sniffles. "All I wanna do is make you happy."

My own tear spring free. "I feel the same way." I close my eyes for a slow, gentle kiss. "You and her."

Dell nods against my lips. "And her."

"I was thinking..."

"Yeah?"

"Could we take a picture?" I ask and immediately regret it because it's so stupid.

"Of course, baby." He reaches above our heads for his phone and opens the front-facing camera. "Say cheese."

Chuckling, I close my eyes as he plants a kiss on my cheek and snaps a few pictures.

"Like that?" He asks, showing me the cutest fucking couple I've ever seen on his screen.

"Yeah," I smile.

"Let's send it to her." He shoots it off in a text to Robyn. Immediately the image has a little heart at the corner and a text follows below it.

> Robyn: Aww. What are you guys doing?

> Dell: I called dibs, didn't I?

I pinch his nipple and he laughs, "What?"

> Robyn: Really?! Omg!

But before Dell can text back, she's calling and he swipes open the video.

"Oh," she smiles her head in a pillow. "I didn't realize you were texting me from the scene itself."

"Zay needed evidence that this wasn't a dream."

All three of us chuckle and Robyn beams, "How did it happen?"

"He packed us a picnic and we watched the sunrise."

"You make it sound like I was planning this," Dell says. "You're the one who showed up with lube."

I shrug.

"Shut up," Robyn beams. "That's so romantic! My first time was on my high school boyfriend's bunk bed. No top sheet, one sad pillow, two condoms. Of course I didn't come, and it was over in less than a minute."

Dell winces. "Ooof, that's bad."

"You guys look so happy. I miss you."

"We miss you, too," I mumble into Dell's chest and then look back at the screen. "How's your trip?"

"Great. Been at the beach mostly. I'm glad we're on the phone now, because... well, I've been talking to the girls about you, Zay."

I tense. "What about?"

She swallows. "They were wondering if you'd like to come

visit us while we're on our trip. We realized we used to make this trip with Laura when she was our coach. I think it would give you a good chance to get to know everyone."

"Really?"

"Yeah," she smiles.

"I'd really like that." Dell squeezes me a little tighter.

"Great!"

"When is our flight back to Philly?" I ask him.

"Tomorrow. Why don't I just change your ticket to fly into Norfolk?"

"And I'll pick you up," Robyn adds.

"Are you sure?" I ask... both of them, I guess.

"Absolutely."

"Yes!"

"Okay, but I don't want to overstay my welcome. Maybe just for a night. Is there even a bed for me? Should I get a hotel room?"

"There's an extra bed," she says. "Just bring yourself."

Dell smirks. "And I'll make sure you're in first class."

I gasp, remembering my shock from a couple days ago. "Robyn, did you know Dell's family is loaded?"

---

1. *This Could Be Good* by Morningsiders

Chapter 39
Ocean-Side Rugby
Robyn

Turns out I didn't have to drive all the way to Norfolk because Dell paid for Isaiah to fly right into the Outer Banks in a freakin' seaplane. He practically flew into the yard of our vacation rental.

Rich people.

As soon as I see him, I have to remind myself not to launch into his arms or show any public displays of affection.

He's my coach.

Coach.

Head. Coach.

No touchy.

Maybe if I say it enough times it will sink in.

"Hey!" I wave because I have no idea what to do with my arms. He scoops me up from my middle with one arm, squeezing me.

"Missed you," he whispers over the sounds of waves crashing next to us. And holy moly does that alone have me weak in the knees. I know he's seen me get off a couple times now, and he held me in the shower at Dell's studio gym, but there's something so new and thrilling about Isaiah openly being sweet to me that has me dying a perfect death. It's both the old him and the new him, meeting me right here with our hair whipping in the ocean air.

Sooner than I'd like, he sets me down. "Was that okay?" he asks, and we head for the wooden stairs to the house.

"Yeah, I think so. Friends hug like that, right?"

He nods.

"Are you hungry? We were just about to clean up from lunch."

"I could eat."

Sliding the glass door open, there's a chorus of heys and welcomes from everyone. After spending the past few days here, everyone is relaxed and truly excited for Isaiah to join us. At the beginning, when I brought up the idea of him coming for a visit, I was met groaning. Thankfully Serwaa always has my back and made them realize we would have done this with Coach Laura. It really didn't take much to get everyone on board, and as the days went on, everyone was getting antsy for his arrival. Mostly because we have a plan and we need him.

"Is this everyone? Just the six of you?" he asks, eating the last bite of his sandwich, and looking out on the deck to where my teammates are lounging with mocktails and cocktails. I've already set him up in his bedroom in the basement. No one else wanted it because the rest of the bedrooms are upstairs and we wanted to be close to each other. That, and the basement bedroom just wasn't as pretty as the other ones.

"Yeah, that's everyone. It's mostly just the players without kids."

Khaos comes to the slider wearing a bikini top and shorts with a shit eating grin and an empty margarita glass. "Did you ask him yet?"

"Ask me what?"

I wince, "Would you be willing to help us with a social media trend?"

"That depends. What is it?"

"Just keep in mind, this will help the image of USA Valor." Isaiah just looks at me. "Have you seen the 'my boyfriend does my makeup' trend?"

"No," he says flatly.

"Well, I think you pretty much get what that means. But we were thinking you, Coach Isaiah Johanssen, could do our makeup and we'd film it. It would be the 'our coach does our makeup' trend."

"Please?" Khaos begs with the hardest puppy dog eyes I've ever seen.

"It'll be really funny!" I add.

"Do I have to wear makeup?"

"No," Khaos and I both say.

"Unless—" she starts.

"As long as I don't have to wear makeup, I'll do it."

"Woo!" she cheers, shoving her margarita glass high in the air and turning on her heel to tell everyone outside. "We got 'em!"

· · · · • · • • · · ·

"Do you carry this much equipment with you wherever you go?" Isaiah asks me as I turn on my ring light which blinds us in the bathroom.

"Of course. I'm a content creator. Okay, so I've already shot the intro, so all we need to do now is film you applying makeup. Camera rolling," I say, placing my clear travel makeup case in front of him.

His eyebrows pinch. "All of this? You use all of this?"

"Just pick out what you think will do the job," I smile, knowing that probably makes him more confused.

Muttering something, he fingers through everything. He picks up a tube and reads, "What's a high spreadability silicone primer?"

I shrug playfully. "Use it and find out."

"I'm gonna look like an idiot doing this."

"Oh," I chuckle, "I think we're gonna be the ones looking dumb, not you."

"That's reassuring." Isaiah opens a matte finishing powder and grunts before pressing *his fingers* in it. "Here's goes nothing."

His index and middle finger glide over my cheek, and I can barely suppress my laughter. "What?" he asks, moving his fingers over my forehead.

"Nothing."

"You're making a face."

"No I'm not. You're doing great, Coach."

"You know, when I took this job, I didn't realize I'd be the team's makeup artist."

"You're a man of many talents."

Isaiah finishes with the powder and grabs for a stick. He reads it, "Berry Me in Sunshine cream blush? Whatever."

With an unsure hand, he swipes it across my cheek and applies way too much, then tries to correct it, but the blush ends up everywhere.

"What's the point of this video anyway?"

"Well it's a trend," I say. "It will bring attention to our team. But it's also about showing people they can be both feminine and masculine to whatever degree that means. For instance, I love makeup and it makes me feel powerful. That's why I wear lipstick and mascara on the field."

"Oh shit," he whispers to himself. "I forgot about mascara."

"Some of the players today will only have you do their skincare because they don't wear any makeup. We want to show fans and youth players they don't have to give up anything about themselves to play the sport they want to play, or to look the way they want to look."

"So, this isn't just about how bad I am at makeup-ing."

"Not at all. Well, a little bit. It *is* funny. I've never seen someone apply concealer over their eyeshadow before," I giggle.

"Sh—shoot," he corrects, and tries to remove the concealer with his thumb.

The whole time Zay poorly applies my makeup, I'm stuck in a liminal space where we can't talk about us or Dell because the camera is on. And there's something a little naughty and pleasant about keeping it all locked up and pretending we're just friends again. Alright, it's also a little torturous. I do want to feel his big naked body against mine again and the way his chest hair feels against my skin.

Suddenly there's eyeliner being poked in my cornea. "Oh f—crap," he says, bringing me out of the memory of the post-orgasm shower we shared. "Okay, I'm calling it. That's as good as it gets, Robyn."

I turn around to face the mirror and burst out laughing. "I look like a clown who just performed in a hurricane!"

"Well I call that a win. I was going for drag queen in a flash flood."

"My turn," a gremlin-like voice growls out of nowhere, causing both of us to jump out of our skin.

"Khaos!" I scream. "Cheese and rice that scared me."

She hands her makeup bag to Isaiah. "I'm going for the goth princess look."

"Sure," he mutters. "We'll both pretend I know what that means."

"Sure you do, Coach," I smile and pat him on the shoulder. "Just make her into the ideal fan for Agony Nectar."

He gives me a look that says he's not amused, but I'm hustling out of the bathroom and giggling.

Before I'm out of ear shot, I hear Khaos ask, "What's Agony Nectar?"

· · · • · • · · ·

When each girl is done with their makeup or skincare, they join the rest of us on the expansive deck overlooking the ocean. There's a massive dark storm system coming in, but we're determined to soak up every last bit of sun before it comes our way.

Mo was the last one and sits next to me at the patio table with a grin and a damp face. She's wearing rugby shorts and a sports bra. That's pretty much her vacation, lounge, and work wear. Mo has the shortest haircut of all of us and a more masculine build like me. "You can tell he's trying," she says.

I smile and nod. "Too much?"

"No. It's good. What's too much is the amount of vitamin C serum he applied all over my face—*after* my moisturizer."

A cackle bursts out of me as Isaiah finally makes his way to join us.

"Alright, alright," Isaiah says, and walks over to the table where a well-worn rugby ball sits. "You've all had your fun. I think it's time you indulge me." He tosses the ball to Serwaa and takes off for the deck stairs to the beach below. "Come on. We're playing footy."

"It's about to rain!" she chortles.

"Then let's play fast," he calls over his shoulder as he's halfway down. Grabbing a baseball cap next to me, I'm already high-tailing it. My pulse picks up as I chase him over the sand and waves lick at my heels. Soon everyone has followed us, and we divide into small teams before giving the ball a foot tap and starting.

There's no tackling or scrums, there's no jumpers or real strategic play—it's just playful ruckus made harder by running through sand—and I've never seen Isaiah happier. He's laughing at Serwaa who keeps tucking her tits back into her bikini top, he's cheering for Skirt finding a breakaway, and he's falling over with a thud and a childish grin.

The storm clouds that were once ominous make good on their threat, and when the downpour begins, our game doesn't stop. Poorly-applied mascara runs from our faces faster than our legs can take us.

I missed[1] this Isaiah—the one at college rugby tournaments decked out in a speedo or a thrifted prom dress. The one who led the dirtiest verses in our drinking songs. The one who would do anything for his teammates simply because they were his teammates. The one covered in sand and pelted with rain, running toward me with determination in his eyes.

It's really him. Here's the man I played pickup rugby with all those years ago. Who pinned me to the ground and made me laugh harder than I ever had. Who rubbed Tiger Balm into my skin and gave me his bed to sleep in. He's right here. He's back.

When I wrap up around Isaiah and he tries to push through to the makeshift try zone, he grunts and laughs and shoves a gentle hand in my face to further smudge my makeup. There may be no real tackling, but I can't help it when my foot connects with the back of his knee, and I take him down.

"You ruined my makeup!" I squeal.

He grunts from the ground below me, "It's too late for that! Save me, Skirt!" he yells over the din of hard rain and laughter.

In a flash, she's on him, spraying us with kicked-up sand and picking the ball from his clutch. Losing her footing, Skirt immediately fumbles and falls to the ground before anyone can tackle her, but she's not getting up.

"You okay?" Isaiah asks. We both get up to find her laying there, laughing her ass off. Everyone around us is doing the same—wheezing and holding their sides as they roll in the wet sand. Khaos is wrapped around Toni. Mo is waving her arms and legs in the sand to make a beach angel. It's like everyone is laughing in the face of this dark afternoon storm, reveling in the beauty we can make on our own.

Isaiah's eyes find mine, and if I could bottle this moment and save it forever, I would. Whenever I'd need a little pick-me-up, I'd open it and take a long whiff. I'd dab the memory behind my ears and on my wrists and remember the way his rare smile heals something in my soul. I'd remember the scents of ocean and sunscreen; of heavy rain and the grippy texture of a leather rugby ball. I'd remember the way he's looking at me, like he's missed this version of us, too. Like even if our relationship right now is defined by, *we can't* and *think of your image*, we will still have this.

We will always have ocean-side rugby in the rain.

---

1. *The scarlett empress* by College

Chapter 40
Team Bonding
Robyn

The first crack of lightning has everyone booking it for the house and clamoring for the showers. By the time everyone makes it back to the spacious living room in their loungewear and wet hair, the late afternoon has turned into early evening, and darkness from the storm settles over everything.

I don't care that it's still warm outside, it's dark and rainy and I'm in the mood for a fire—albeit electric. Flipping the switch on the wall, the flames erupt in the fireplace and I sit down on one of the large chairs with a cup of tea.

"God, that was fun," Serwaa says as she enters the living room and sits next to me on the couch. "Getting the sand out of my hair, not so much."

Toni follows in, braiding her damp brunette hair to the side. "I feel like my whole body has been exfoliated."

"Coach still in the shower?" Serwaa asks.

"Yeah," I say. "He was waiting for everyone else to finish first."

"Well this is cute as shit," Mo says. She takes a seat next to Toni and cuddles into her. "Are we having sleepover girl talk?"

"Obviously," I smile, extending my leg to show off my billowing stretchy pants. "I'm wearing my conversation pants."

"There's a hole in the crotch," Serwaa deadpans.

"They're well-loved."

"Easier access for Roger," Toni teases in that

brighter-than-sunshine way of hers.

"Who has Roger right now?"

Skirt raises her hand as she strides into the room wearing, of course, a baby blue tennis skirt and matching top. "Me. Y'all don't... use it, right?"

Toni gasps. "Roger is a very private dildo. He/they don't like to disclose that kind of information."

Skirt simply studies all of us before finally saying, "Ew."

"Can we order pizza tonight?" Serwaa asks everyone. "My period started and I'm in need of warm, cheezy carbs."

"Oh my god, we're cycle-sisters," Khaos sings while entering the room and pulling out their phone. "I'll order for delivery."

A fresh and clean Isaiah finally joins us looking relaxed, and he takes the last open chair across the room from me.

"You good with pizza, Coach?" Toni asks without looking up from her phone.

"Great. Let me pay for it though, as a thank you for letting me crash your vacation."

"Not stopping you there," she smiles.

"Boy, it's really coming down out there," he muses.

"I love the rain," Skirt sighs, braiding her platinum blonde hair. "Reminds me of home."

"Where's that?" he asks[1].

"Seattle. My old team used to play in the rain all the time," she says with fondness. "Some of my favorite memories took place in the rain."

"Like what?" he asks, and my heart gives a little pitter-patter at him asking more questions.

"Like," she drawls, looking off into her mind. "When I was a little girl, maybe six or seven years old, I remember my dad carrying me on his shoulders as he ran through the rain to get to our minivan that was parked really far away." She pauses a moment, still thinking of the memory. "I have no idea where we were coming from, but I remember us laughing and holding onto him tight. I never want to forget that."

"That's cute," Serwaa smiles.

"What about you, Serwaa?" he asks. "What's a memory you never want to forget?"

My bestie looks off in her mind for a minute before humming through a smile. "I never want to forget the way my nana's house smelled back in Ghana. Like a medley of jollof rice, fufu, and light soup. To this day, whenever I miss her, I'll make it all myself just to feel like I'm there again."

My mouth waters at the thought and I groan. "I love your cooking." I could swim in that tomatoey chili pepper broth.

"Is she not around anymore?" he asks her.

"No. She died about five years ago. I still have family there, but no one's home smells the same."

"Sounds like a team potluck is in order," he says.

"What about you, Coach?" I ask. "What's a memory you never want to forget?"

Isaiah's dark blue eyes find mine for a brief moment before turning to the window beside him where raindrops cling. "I remember this one time when my mom was still alive, we were all packed into our bathroom because there was a tornado warning in effect. I was maybe eight. Yeah, eight, because she died soon after that. Anyway, all of us kids were in our pajamas and I remember being confused about the siren going off, so my mom sang to us. My dad joined in."

"Do you remember what song they sang?" I ask.

He thinks for a minute, his brow furrowing, but then he chuckles. "You know, I never realized how on-the-nose it was until now, but they were singing "My Favorite Things" from *The Sound of Music*."

"Your mom died when you were a kid?" Khaos asks. "I'm so sorry."

"Our family was... pretty broken for a while."

I'm a little stunned he's opening up like this. Sure, he showed me this side of him back in the day, but I quickly found out he doesn't do that for many people—almost no one, in fact. Even Angie has a hard time knowing what's going on in his brain sometimes. What did Dell do to him? Because the man before me—looking like he has no better place to be than here with all of us around a crackling fireplace and the white noise of summer rain—is showing himself.

His real self.

"She died in a car accident shortly after that. She was driving my baby sister Ivy back from a doctor's appointment when she was hit. Only Ivy survived."

There's a collective inhale and Serwaa says, "Jesus."

"Dad was... in a bad place for a long time. My older sister Angie basically raised us. Her and our friends' moms who lived close by."

"Hold up," Skirt says. "Do you mean multiple friends' moms from multiple homes, or someone who has two moms? Moms plural?"

"Lesbians?" Khaos gasps.

Isaiah nods. "Christina and Ana, yes."

Khaos clutches her heart and leans against Serwaa. "He was practically raised by lesbians!"

Isaiah chuckles. "They fed us, watched us. I know Spanish because of them."

"You know Spanish?" I ask. "I didn't know that."

"Sí, *hablo español. Más que simplemente pedir comida también.*"

Okay, suddenly my undercarriage tightens and I *need* to hear him speak Spanish quietly in my ear. I don't care what he says. He could tell me he has a hernia and needs to seek medical attention, but as long as it's murmured into the shell of my ear, I'll dissolve.

"You okay over there, Birdie?" Serwaa asks, pulling me

back to the conversation happening outside of my brain.

"Oh," I stammer. "Yeah. I'm just hungry is all."

She narrows her eyes on me. "Yeah, I bet you are."

"Anyone want a beer?" I ask, quickly making my way to the kitchen. Everyone chimes in and Serwaa joins me by the fridge.

"You doing okay?" she whispers as we stand in front of the open door, the artificial light and chilly air a welcome distraction.

I grab four beers. "I'm fine."

Serwaa looks over her shoulder to the living room and back at me. "Hey. I won't say anything if you want something to happen with him. Okay? I'll take it to my grave."

"I know."

"I understand why there's a rule against coaches dating players, but... you two have known each other so long."

"Serwaa, I kissed him," I blurt.

"You did?" she hisses. "When?"

"Last week."

"Wait, what about your trainer?"

"I kissed him, too. We all kissed. And a lot more happened." Serwaa's eyes widen. "We're all trying to figure out how to make us work. Like, the three of us. But I still don't know how we can. With the team, with the Olympics, with the brand deals," I shrug. "I'll be eaten alive."

"And Dell and Isaiah are... what to each other?"

"Deliriously happy and in love. Also trying to figure this out with me."

"Holy shit. I thought Dell was just helping you with flirting."

"He was. It turned into *way* more." I lean in closer. "Serwaa, he fucked me against a yoga ball in his gym while Isaiah watched."

Eyes dilating, my bestie bites her lip. "Fuck, that's hot," she whispers.

"I know."

"So, you and Isaiah haven't..." she trails off.

"No. Nothing more than kissing and some naked shower hugs."

"Is that a euphemism?"

I chuckle, "No. Literally."

"This is huge, Birdie! He likes you! You've been worried for years that he didn't."

Way more than she knows. I probably don't need to tell her about the obsessive way he's been watching me. Would that be a huge red flag to most people? Yes. But *oh god*, I love it.

I swallow and nod. "Oh, he likes me alright."

Serwaa glances over her shoulder again where Isaiah is talking to Mo about something we can't hear from in the kitchen. "He's doing really good with the team right now. I can feel everyone opening up to him."

"I know. I'm so happy you guys are seeing what I've always seen."

She looks back at me. "I think you need to go for it, babe. Sneak around if you have to. If you want to make it public, I'll be here fighting for you too. I'm with you."

With you—those two words carry a heavy weight in rugby. It might be the most common phrase heard on a pitch. When you're running the ball, you can know you're not alone when you hear "with you" hollered by a teammate who's close enough to ruck over you if need be, or is ready for you to offload the ball to them.

With you is support when you need it most.

Wrapping my arms around my best friend with beers still in hand, she returns the hug. "I love you," I whisper. "I'm always with you, too."

Serwaa and I make it back to the group in the living room and pass out the beers. Khaos is talking about the memory she never wants to forget: making brownies with her cousin and aunt and the way her uncle would sneak his finger in the batter.

"What about you, Robyn?" My coach asks before taking a sip of his beer.

I never want to forget the way he tastes. I never want to forget the moment our tables turned and he admitted he's been watching me—wanting me—all these years. But now's not the time to say those things aloud, huh?

Probably not.

"I want to remember laying on the living room floor surrounded by candy with my family after trick-or-treating. My mom has always harped on me for what I eat, ever since I could remember. But for some reason, Halloween was always an exception. She'd sit there with me, and we'd eat as much as we wanted. I'd give her all the disgusting candies like Almond Joy or plain Hersey's bars. I would sort and take inventory. Dad would try to steal a Twix or Reese's cup, which was a crime in my book—punishable by clawing and wrestling for it back." I release a deep sigh. "But on Halloween, my mom was fun, and I never want to forget those nights."

The look on all the girls' faces tells me they know all too well what it's like to have a mom like that. Everyone takes a sip of their beer.

"What about you, Toni?" I ask. "What memory do you want to hold onto forever?"

Toni sits up from their position cuddled against Mo. "My friend and I used to play this drinking game when we were younger, where we'd sing the lyrics to songs we mostly knew. If you screwed up the lyrics, you had to take a drink. So, the more you drank, the harder it was to sing the words correctly, and thus the circle of drunkenness continued," they laugh. "God, we were dumb. But I don't think I've ever laughed harder."

All at once, an idea pops up and begs me to release it.

"You know," I drawl, pressing the power button to the TV and grabbing my phone, "Coach here has some experience singing."

Every muscle in his face drops. "Robyn," he warns.

"That's right," I smile, tapping away until I find what I'm looking for. I mirror my phone screen to the TV and queue up the video. "Our coach once had a budding musical career in his family band, Agony Nectar."

"Wait!" Khaos gasps. She stands for a better look. "This is awesome."

"Guys," Isaiah pleads. "We weren't that good. Look, there's only seven hundred views in ten years! I wouldn't say—"

"We are so watching this," Toni beams. "Press play!"

The video is grainy, the way digital videos used to be, but young Isaiah is unmistakable. It's a cover of "In One Ear" by Cage the Elephant and these guys are dressed the part. Isaiah's hair is almost shoulder-length, and he's wearing a flannel long sleeve and tight jeans. Dane's in even tighter ones and sporting a plain black T-shirt. All I can see from Jonah is a yellow band tee of some kind, blonde hair flying every which way as he hammers away. And Joaquín's in an oversized zip-up hoodie with bright blue Converse.

"Where is this?" Serwaa asks.

"My basement," he sighs.

"And who's with you?"

"That's my brother Jonah on the drums. I'm on bass, my other brother Dane is singing, and our friend Joaquín is on electric guitar."

"I love this song!" Mo shouts over the volume.

Skirt shakes her head. "I've never heard it."

He groans, "How old are you?"

"Twenty-two."

"Oh god," he groans harder.

"Let's go, brother!" I cheer in my best Hulk Hogan voice. To encourage him more, I launch into the rock song I've heard a hundred times—specifically this version. When everyone joins in, I turn the volume up all the way. We're screaming the lyrics and dancing when I extend my hand to him. With a reluctant smile, he takes it in his and stands up, belting the tune and pretending to play his bass. He's lashing forward along with me as I throw up my devil's horns on my left hand.

I wish someone was recording this moment right now. A bunch of rugby players rocking out in a vacation home that looks like it was created by the set designer for a Nancy Meyers movie.

Agony Nectar can fuck, I'll give them that. They're not great, but skill has nothing on their magnetic presence. Isaiah is just as into it now as he looks then. I wonder when the last time he picked up his bass was. When was the last time he played with his brothers? When was the last time he let it all go like that?

Watching all us ancients rock out to a totally foreign song, Skirt peels with laughter on the couch. She takes over the remote and runs away from Isaiah when he tries to take it away from her. He gives up and lets her play song after song from his basement punk band.

When one of us messes up a lyric, Toni commands us to take a drink. By the time our pizza is delivered, we're deep into Agony Nectar's discography. I've listened to these songs so much that I haven't even finished my first beer. Skirt and Serwaa, on the other hand, know almost no lyrics and are drunkenly thanking the pizza delivery girl for being the kindest, most beautiful soul in the world and urging her to play rugby. Isaiah pays and apologizes for his players with a smile.

---

1. A *Real Hero* by College & Electric Youth

Chapter 41

Break Rules & Get Sexy

Isaiah

When midnight rolls around, I clean up the empty pizza boxes and cans as the girls either pass out in the living room or head back to their rooms for the night. Serwaa and Robyn are cuddled on one of the couches, having zonked out at least twenty minutes ago. Robyn looks so peaceful.

All I want to do is kiss her goodnight. Kiss her for giving me this chance to bond like this with my players. Kiss her for pushing me out of my comfort zone and reminding me that Good Time Isaiah is always right here, lurking under a scowl.

I cover the pair of them in a blanket and head for the basement stairs. Though, basement might be too negative of a word for what this level is. The whole floor is just as nice as the other two, with white carpeting and pastel furniture.

A sense of loneliness creeps in as I strip down to my boxer briefs and slide into the large, fluffy bed. I wonder if Dell is awake. I shouldn't call him this late. Maybe I'll just watch his videos. Popping in my wireless earbuds, I grab my phone from the nightstand to see that he texted me five minutes ago.

> I hope you're having a good time baby. Call me soon.

> I love you <kiss emoji>

Tapping his contact icon with a smile, I settle in as the phone trills.

"Hey baby," he says groggily.

"Did I wake you?"

"No," he says, probably lying. "I was just listening to the newest *Twisted Sisters* episode. How did everything go today?"

"It was... really great. I feel like I'm connecting with them."

"That's awesome. I knew you could do it."

"They made me do their makeup as some kind of trend."

Dell chuckles, "I know, I saw the video. You were so flustered and cute. It's going viral by the way. So is #AgonyNectar?"

"Great," I say with a roll to my eyes but smile nonetheless. "Then we played some beach rugby in the rain and, god Dell, I don't think I've had that much fun in a long time. It was nice to just... play with her, you know?"

"I know. I'm surprised she's not in bed with you."

I huff a little laugh, "You know we can't. Not here. Plus she's upstairs dead asleep with Serwaa nestled into her."

"Doesn't Serwaa have a girlfriend?"

"Yeah, but it's not like that. I learned her girlfriend's name is Dani, she lives in Denver, and she's chill. She understands what Robyn and Serwaa have is strictly platonic."

"Look at you. Learning about your players and their personal lives. Not being jealous and shit."

I chuckle, "Yeah, yeah. Hey, do you think we could listen to that new *Twisted Sisters* episode together? Just until I fall asleep?"

"Of course, baby. I'll go back to the beginning." The Share-

Play button appears and I tap it. The familiar voices of Katie and Tiffany and eerie background music fill my ears and soothes me; as much as real life stories of brutal murders can.

There's a soft knock on my bedroom door as it opens slowly, revealing Robyn's peaking head. "Zay?"

"Oh, shit," I whisper.

"What is it?" Dell asks through the earbuds.

"She just came in."

"Sorry," she says. "Are you on the phone?"

"Yeah, but it's Dell. Do you wanna talk to him?" She slips in and closes the door behind her as my heart rate picks up. "Someone wants to talk to you, baby," I tell him.

Robyn opens the covers and shimmies in, sidling up next to me and laying her head on my chest. Blood begins to rush to my groin at the thought of anything more happening between us, but I do my best to squash it and hand her an earbud. Dell pauses the podcast.

"Hey," she smiles.

"Hey, darlin'. How are you?"

She settles into me further and rubs her face against me like a cat. "Sleepy, but perfect now that I can touch him."

"Where are you touching him?" he asks.

"I'm laying on his chest, and he has his arm around me."

"*Mmm.* You're being very naughty sneaking into his room like that."

"It's nothing compared to the naughty things I've been thinking about all day."

"Robyn, please," I say. "I'm already fighting my dick for control here. You shouldn't even be in my room."

"No one saw me," she says coyly, playing with my chest hair.

"Yeah," Dell says. "No one saw her."

"Who's side are you on?" I ask him.

"The one who wants to break the rules and get sexy."

"Me. I'm the one," Robyn replies.

"Oh god," I groan, and my cock raises to attention as if to say *me too!*

"Do you want me to take away your choice again, Isaiah?" Before I can say anything, Robyn licks my nipple and tugs it between her teeth. *Oh fuck.*

"H-h-how much did you have to drink tonight?" I stammer.

"Just the two beers," she whispers, and she flicks her beautiful tongue across my beading nipple again.

"I'll give you one chance to bow out," Dell offers.

I know I want this, and I know it's wrong. I know there are players sleeping above us and the risk is high. But Robyn Cassidy is in my arms, and she's warm, and her hips are pushing into me. Her perfect mouth is on my chest. Why the hell am I waiting?

"I want this," I say.

"Good," Dell drawls. "I want you both to listen to me and do everything I say. What are you wearing, Zay?"

"Boxer briefs."

"Keep them on, but take off her clothes."

I make quick work taking off her soft, stretchy pants, along with her panties and T-shirt. "Jesus."

"Her tits are perfect, aren't they?" I can't form words right now, so I just whimper like a simp. "Sit against the headboard, Zay, and have her lay against your chest. Spread your legs wide and position her against you."

As I'm situating myself, Robyn asks, "Do you want us to switch to video?"

"No," Dell says quickly. "Video sex is not something I'm comfortable with anymore." *Oh, shit.* Of course he'd feel that way. My heart drops thinking of his vengeful ex and what he did to Dell; thinking of all the content he made as a result. "Don't worry," he says. "I still *very much* want to listen to this."

"Okay," Robyn pants, leaning into my chest, eager for the next command. "I'm ready."

"Good girl," he says. "Now, darlin', you may put your hands anywhere you'd like at any point. Zay, have you ever gotten a woman off before with your fingers?"

"Yes."

"Good. You both need to be quiet. Zay, I want you to gently, *gently*, stroke one finger through that sweet, heavenly slit between her legs." Robyn's hands find my thighs as I drag my fingertip against her bare entrance. "Tell me what you feel, baby."

"She's wet," I whisper. "And so soft."

"Use your other hand to play with her breasts. Tweak them and then dip into her pussy; really coat your finger." Robyn moans softly, lolling her head against my shoulder and caressing the hair on my thighs as I obey.

"Is he hard, Robyn? Can you feel him behind you?"

"Yes," she murmurs.

"Put your mouth against her ear," he commands me. "She needs to hear every breathy moan you make. Now find her clit and circle it."

"Oh," she gasps.

"*Shh shh shh*, princess. Be quiet. You don't want anyone to hear, do you?"

"No."

"No," he drawls in a teasing tone. "Because you don't want anyone to know how your coach is fucking you with his fingers. How you came into his room late at night with your desperate, wet pussy, and begged him to take care of you. No, that would be *very* bad."

With eyes closed, Robyn nods her head against my shoulder as if Dell can sense her agreement. I press my finger against her clit a little harder and watch her abdominals clench. She chases my touch, urging me for more.

"So needy," I whisper in her ear, and she whimpers in

response.

"Say it in Spanish," she begs.

"Did that get you going earlier?"

She nods.

"Tan necesitada," I whisper.

"Oh fuck, that's hot," Dell groans in our ears as Robyn shivers and goosebumps skitter across her sun-kissed skin.

"No tienes idea de lo que estoy diciendo. Pero no importa, ¿verdad?" / *You have no idea what I'm saying. But it doesn't matter, does it?*

Her chest caves in as she bites her lip, and I dig into her soft flesh a little more.

"Use both hands, Zay," Dell rasps. "Two fingers on her clit, and two fingers pumping inside her." Swallowing my fingers in a rush, her body accepts me, and I imagine it's my cock sinking deep into her. Writhing in my arms, her nails dig into the meat of my legs right over my old rugby team crest. I'm positive she's leaving dig marks that I would gladly tattoo there for the whole world to see—so that everyone knows who I belong to. I love how worked up she gets, and for the first time, she's getting worked up from *my* touch.

From my fingers.

From *me*.

"Go for the kill," Dell says in a dark, velvety tone. "Rub fast and don't give up." She turns her face into my neck, panting and near tears. Her legs try to close, but I hook mine over and pin them wide.

"Quédate así. Con tu coño en exhibición. Entonces, si alguien entrara aquí, lo vería todo. Verían mis dedos volviéndote loca." / *Stay just like this. With your cunt on display. So if anyone walked in here they'd see everything. They'd see my fingers making you crazy.*

Every muscle in her body tightens, and my fingers are trapped in her channel while the other ones keep their pressured rhythm, strumming across her clit in a frenzy. "I'm coming," she hisses.

"Shh," Dell soothes. "That's it, princess. Come as quietly as you can." She holds on to my thighs for dear life and chokes through her divine orgasm. My god, she's beautiful. Before she can take her first deep inhale, Dell is commanding me again. "Lay her down and clean up the mess you made, Coach."

"Of course," I whisper, and I quickly shift out from under her, then jerk the back of her knees closer to me. She takes in a surprised breath but keeps quiet. I realize then the bed is also quiet, and I send a little prayer to the vacation house gods for this mercy.

I'm already spreading her open and licking her cum when Dell asks, "Have you—"

"Yes," I grunt, cutting him off, and returning to the pussy of my dreams. Dell fed me her cum that first night after the club—after he ate her out. Her taste then was more than I could handle. But now her scent, her taste, is at full-strength as I drink straight from the source. I find myself grinding into the mattress, seeking more as I dip my tongue inside her and groan.

"Fuck, that sounds good," Dell sighs. "I can hear how wet she is. Is he doing a good job for you?"

Her fingers take root in my hair as she whispers, "Yes."

"Take your time, baby," he tells me. Or maybe that's for her. I don't know anymore. What I do know is I'm savoring this meal and listening to her muffled moans and the distinct sound of Dell jerking himself in my ear. "*Ughh*, that's right. Take all the time you need. You two make me so *hard*," he groans.

"Tell me what you're thinking about," she whispers.

"I'm thinking about my cock deep inside his ass. He's riding me while you sit on my face. I'm thinking about both of us taking your pussy at the same time."

She shutters in response, and plays with her small, stiff peaks, then she flexes around my fingers as I enter her again. This time I find her G-spot and pad its rough texture while sucking and releasing. Sucking for longer and releasing again. Again and again I repeat until I'm only breathing out of my nose, and her lips are permanently fused to my mouth, my tongue flicking and fingers pumping. When her legs clamp around my head, I think about all the training she's done over the years to be this strong. Every scrum and breakaway led her thighs here, spasming with my head happily locked between them, and grabbing the pillow to cover her face so she can groan through another orgasm.

After several long moments, she surfaces with delirious determination and adjusts her Airpod. "Make him fuck me, Dell. *Please.*"

"Do you want this to be your first time together? I'm asking both of you."

Truth be told, I always envisioned my first time with Robyn with her in a white gown, or a white bridal lingerie set. It's not that I thought we would wait until we were married, but with our marriage pact in place, well, it was a fantasy I replayed time and time again. But here she is, laying before me in a bed of white with the sounds of a rainstorm and waves crashing in the distance—and our lover in our ear.

"Yes," Robyn answers confidently.

"Yes," I smile.

"Do you want me here for this part?" he asks with the smallest tonal change. Like he's nervous. Like he really doesn't know that I want him to see every part of my life. On the other hand, this is me and Robyn we're talking about. Dell and I had our first time alone, maybe this is what we need, too.

My beautifully flushed friend looks at me from under hooded eyes, her dark lashes fanning over her cheeks as low lamp light blankets us. She searches for my answer, waiting for me.

"I'm torn," I tell him. "I don't want to turn you away but... I think I want this to be just us."

"Of course," he says.

"I love you, baby."

"I love you, too. Now, go make love to her like you've always wanted."

I rest my body against hers, and she gives me the biggest smile. "We'll call you in the morning," I say, getting lost in her hazel eyes.

"Goodnight," she whispers, and I tap the ear bud to end the call, then place both on the nightstand.

"I've dreamed of this," I whisper.

She lowers my boxer briefs, catching them with a toe and sliding them all the way off. "I know. Me too."

The warmth of her swollen, wet center against my shaft has me getting lost, but then I remember... "Let me get a condom."

She clutches my shoulders. "Wait. I have an IUD. My last test was clear six months ago, and I haven't been with anyone except Dell. I've never gone bare."

"You," I swallow thickly. "You want me to go bare?"

"Please. Only if you want to."

My hips settle against hers as I let the thought wash over me. "Yes." I lean down and press my lips to hers, realizing this is our first kiss since I've been here.

Her hand slips between us and she lines me up, my wide tip pushing between her smooth, slippery entrance. "Please, Isaiah," she begs softly against my mouth as her hips undulate for more.

There are moments in my life that I'll take with me to my dying breath, and sinking into Robyn Eleanor Cassidy for the first time will be at the top of that list. I want to remember the way heat shot up my spine and the way she lost her breath. The way her hands found my shoulders and slid into my hair. The way I had to muster the strength not to come instantaneously.

"Zay," she huffs as I pull out to the tip and enter her again.

"Robyn."

Her knees come up, and I hold one over my shoulder, still kissing her through it all— through every thrust and rock, through every slap of our skin and whisper-soft moan. "Eres mi todo, Robyn. Nunca voy a renunciar a ti." / *You're my everything, Robyn. I'm never going to give you up.*

I trail desperate kisses along her neck, careful not to leave any marks even though all I want to *do* is mark her. I want to mark her with Dell and tell everyone once and for all that she is taken—that she is loved so fucking fiercely that it intimidates them.

With her knee still pinned over my shoulder, I play with her breast. I tease and massage it while she scratches my scalp, my hair crimping in her grasp and a fresh wave of arousal crashes.

Like me, I know she's holding back in order to keep quiet, which is its own sweet torture. The breaking of rules between coach and player, the thrill of being heard mixed with blinding pleasure is all too much. This thing between us has been building for too long. I'm completely, irrevocably lost in lust and love and her.

Holy fucking shit—*her.*

"Look at you holding out," she teases, and a low laugh rolls out of me. I drop my hand between us to find her clit again, and she gasps when I play it. She might be my new favorite instrument. I sit up and watch her unravel again as my thumb and cock never relent. Her cunt flutters around me as she clutches her chest and rides out her third orgasm, all while trying her best to be silent.

Unable to wait for her to come down from her high, I lift by the shoulders so she's straddling me as I sit on my heels, knees wide. "Hold on tight," I warn, my voice low and gritty. With my arms bound around her, she wraps her long legs around me and I thrust hard. She latches onto my neck and hair, her breathing erratic and intoxicating. With each slam into her, arousal drips down my shaft and coats my sac. Rolling, riding, our entwined bodies sweat against each other in ecstasy.

"Oh my god," she cries softly. "You feel so good, Isaiah. This position—*shit*. I'm... I'm gonna..."

My balls are tight against my body and I'm hurdling fast toward my finish. "Me too, baby." Then the final rush of cum barrelling out has me clutching her to my chest.

"Yes," she chokes out, her pussy contracting around my length and she humps relentlessly, begging, begging, begging.

Eons later when my muscles relax and my mind returns, I open my eyes to find the most beautiful woman in the world in a state of bliss. Her limbs loosen, so I hold tighter and kiss her.

She sighs, and if I were a poet, I think I could write endlessly about it. Her sigh that calms. Her sigh like a song. Her sigh that calls to my very soul.

As we sit in the middle of the bed, our tongues are lazy and thankful, our lips swollen and soft. Dreamy kisses carry us through the next ten minutes as I make no attempt to pull out, allowing my softening cock to keep warm, nestled perfectly inside her.

Carefully, I lay her down, unable to stop kissing her, holding her, inhaling the scent that we made together.

With her hands slicing through my beard, she pulls her lips away slowly to say, "I wish I could stay here all night. But..."

"I know. I'd give anything to keep you right here in my arms and watch you wake up."

She gives me a lopsided grin. "Who knew Isaiah Johanssen was such a romantic?" With a quiet chuckle, I kiss her again. "Was that okay? For your first time with a woman?"

I kiss her temple. "With you, it was everything I wanted and more." She inhales deeply with a small curl to her lip and brushes the longer hair at the top of my head back. "How about you? Was I... um... did I...?"

She puts me out of my misery. "It was perfect. Between you and Dell, I've never come so many times in a row."

"I'll admit, I did a lot of research before this. Like, a lot. About what to do, feel, and listen for."

"I love a man that does research," she beams, but then her features drop when she realizes what she just said.

"Oh yeah?" I tease, fighting back a smile.

There's a long pause between us, and her hands slide down to my chest. "I want you, Zay. I want Dell. I know the risks if we get caught, and I'm okay with sneaking around because I *have* to have you both. It's killing me to pretend that I'm not—" she stops to swallow and collect herself. "—that I'm not madly in love with you. I want you to know that every single day. And if that has to be in secret, then so be it."

She loves me! She said it! Thunderous beating emanates from my chest once again as those three little words kick off their shoes and make themselves at home in my heart.

"I love you, too."

"Really?"

"Of course. I realized I loved you a week after Jessica and I broke up. I was scrolling through our old text messages, gif after gif of hedgehogs," I say, and she giggles. "And it hit me then, just how much my friend Robyn really meant to me."

Her smile fades. "You could lose your job, Zay."

"So could you. And you have a lot more on the line."

Robyn's eyes dart away and lose focus, her mind working.

"I know." She idly coils my chest hair. "No one can know, not even my parents. Especially not them." She finally looks back at me. "It's the optics. It's nothing against you or Dell. Well, maybe a little bit of Dell. They will not be pleased to know I'm dating a former porn star."

Suddenly I'm very aware that I—*a damn virgin*—made her come repeatedly like she did with a porn star. I'll be filing that tidbit of information away under the label Smug Male Satisfaction.

"Until we can figure out how to be open about us, we'll keep it all under wraps. Everything."

"Is there anyone you would trust to know about us now?" she asks.

I think I know why she's asking. "Do you wanna tell Serwaa?" She nods vigorously. "If you completely trust her, then go for it. I know how much she means to you."

"What about you?"

"*Hmm.* Honestly, I could trust my whole family," I say and then laugh, "They'd be fucking ecstatic to hear I finally made a move on you."

"Do they know about Dell?"

"No, not yet."

Robyn's toes curl around mine and her eyes hood. "Maybe we could go introduce him to your family."

"Like... the three of us?"

She shrugs. "Since you trust them not to say anything, would it be so wrong to be a normal... throuple... around them? There's nowhere else we could."

"You haven't met Dell's family yet," I chuckle. "But, yeah. Why don't you and Dell come over for Sunday dinner?"

"Yes! Are you going to warn them?"

"Absolutely not."

Her answering squeal is as soft and sweet as her lips on mine. "Okay, I'm gonna go back to my room now. If I stay in this bed any longer, I'm gonna get a UTI."

Chapter 42

The Family Johanssen

Dell

Robyn returned from her team vacation less than a week ago, and the three of us have been working out and hooking up every day since. There's been pillow talk and goodnight kisses, good morning texts and *I miss you* phone calls. There's been massaging of tight muscles and irresistible urges only quelled by the nearest flat surface. We have dinner most nights at Isaiah's place, once at Robyn's. But tonight is different.

"Quiz me again," I say as we pull into the driveway of Isaiah's childhood home. Robyn sits next to him in the passenger seat of his SUV, and I'm in the back panicking.

He laughs, like this is some joke! I'm about to meet my man's family for the first time and he's laughing. This is nothing like him meeting mine. Mine is so much smaller than his. He has four siblings, a dad, and a brother-in-law. And there are kids! And the lesbians who raised him!

"Do you have any antiperspirant in here?" I ask, dabbing my pits.

Zay puts the vehicle in park and opens the center console. He hands me an Old Spice. "Okay," he says, smirking back at me as I pray the aluminum not only stops my sweat, but calms me down. "What's the order?"

"Angie, you, Dane, Jonah, Ivy."

"Good. And who is Rafael?"

"Angie's fiancé. He's Mexican American. They have twins, Zo and Nico."

"Very good," he smiles. "There will be a stocky, masculine, white woman with short auburn hair, most likely wearing a gray T-shirt and cargo shorts. Who is that?"

"Christina," I answered confidently. "Married to Ana, who is Rafael's biological mom. She's Mexican."

"Okay, stop twisting your hands," he chides and places his hand over mine. "What's my dad's name?"

"Neal. He's an engineer but also does small engine repair on the side."

"Nailed it," he says and opens the door. "Let's go."

Before we can get to the back door, Robyn's quizzing me. "What are everyone's jobs?"

I list everyone off on my fingers as we walk. "Angie is a children's therapist. Rafael is in finance. Dane is a veterinarian. No one really knows what Jonah does, and Ivy is a midwife."

"Yes," she cheers as we come to the back door. "You got this. And you look very handsome."

I changed my outfit five times. "Thank you," I huff, smoothing my distressed brown Henley and jeans. Why did I wear jeans? It's so hot today.

"I've never seen you like this," Isaiah says with a disbelieving shake to his head. He's sporting a USA Valor T-shirt and shorts that make his hamstrings look good enough to eat. "They're going to love you. Just be your normal, charming, cocksure self. Come on, give me a pump," he says and shimmies his chest, gesturing for me to give my pectorals a little dance. I roll my eyes, but do it anyway.

They both smile and, okay, fine, that does make me feel better.

Robyn's wearing white linen shorts and a simple but sweet light-blue tank top. Her hair is up in a bun like me but, of course, hers is styled, and she's wearing gold drop earrings. God, she's pretty.

"They're all very nice, Dell," she soothes, her hands skimming my arms.

Suddenly the back door opens wide to reveal a grinning blonde man with shoulder-length hair, holding a baby on his hip. "What the fudge is this?"

"Jonah," Isaiah says with narrowed eyes. "You know Robyn."

"Of course, she's the love of my life."

Isaiah grabs her hand. "Finders keepers."

"You finally did it?" he gasps.

"He finally did it," she beams, and then grabs my trembling hand. "And this is Dell. He's our boyfriend."

Jonah's eyes pop out to assess me and then trace back to Isaiah and Robyn. "This hunk of man is your boyfriend?" Then he shakes his head like a cartoon character. "Wait, bro, you're gay?"

Isaiah pushes past him and drags us with him. "Kinda. Yeah."

His little brother, who's about my height, then cuts us off before we enter the kitchen and dining room and exclaims, "Did everyone know Isaiah is gay?"

"He's bi," a shorter, curvier version of Isaiah says without looking up from setting the table. Must be Angie.

"Hey girl," Robyn says simply.

Angie immediately looks over and clutches her chest. "Robyn! Why are you here?"

"She's dating Isaiah!" Jonah replies and then throws his head my way. "And this dude! Hey, how much can you bench, man?"

"I max at four oh five."

"Fudge!"

Angie barges over to give Robyn a fierce hug. "Don't lie to me," she cries. "Is this really happening?"

A tall man with smooth, deeply tan skin and black hair comes in with another baby in his arms. "What's going on? Robyn, what are you doing here?"

"Okay, family meeting!" Jonah shouts, running into the living room to gather everyone in the kitchen. Isaiah grips my hand a little tighter as confusion and chaos erupt before everyone is finally paying attention.

"Everyone," he announces calmly. He holds up his hand which is laced with Robyn's. "This is Robyn, as most of you know." Then he holds up my sweaty hand that's clutching him like a lifeline. "And this is Dell. The three of us are together."

My eyes lock on his dad's and I can see an older, somewhat slimmer, Isaiah in him. Inwardly, I smile knowing my boyfriend is going to age very fine indeed. But Neal has a pinch to his brow. "The three of you?"

Zay nods.

"Dad," Angie says. "Remember when I told you about my friends Cora, Marco, and Jay? How they're polyamorous? It's like that." Then she turns back to look at Isaiah. "Right?"

"Yeah."

"You're gay?" Jonah asks yet again.

Dane rolls his eyes, "He's bi. We've been over this, bro. This is not new information."

"Who else in this family queer?"

Neal raises a lazy hand. "I'm not."

Jonah clicks his tongue. "Eh, jury's still out." He hands the baby in his arms over to his dad and takes out his phone. "Maybe I should try dating men. I'm gonna download Grindr."

"Oh god," Rafael groans. He shifts the baby to his shoulder and rubs a gentle hand over their back. "What are you guys doing about the team? Is the Valor cool with the head coach and captain dating?"

"So, here's the thing..." Isaiah drawls, and everyone goes quiet. "No one can know outside of here."

"Gasp," Angie huffs.

He tucks Robyn into his chest, and I put an arm around

them both before he continues. "If anyone finds out, it's game over. Robyn will lose endorsements, maybe her position on the team, and I'll definitely lose my job."

"Jesus, son," Neal mutters, now pinching the bridge of his nose. The following silence makes my heart drop in my stomach like a ton of bricks. They don't even know my half of the story. Now's not a good time to tell them I used to jerk off for millions of viewers.

"Listen," he sighs. "I don't ask for much from you guys, mostly because I don't know how. But, we don't have anyone else we can be ourselves around. Not here. Until we can figure out how to be public about what we are, this is what we're left with." Isaiah swallows hard and I'm blown away at the vulnerability he's showing. "It would mean a lot to me if we had your support."

Slowly, there's a low chorus of assurances before Neal makes his way over to us, and my second-hand Old Spice fights for its life. He looks at me and then Robyn. And with a tilt of his lips, he wraps his arms around all three of us. "Of course you're welcome here. I won't say a word."

The largest sigh of relief whooshes out of me. He's not even my dad, this isn't even my family, but the acceptance tastes just as sweet.

"Oh, that's enough," the beautiful Mexican woman with a long, curled ponytail says. She pushes Neal out of the way and squeezes us. "Welcome to our family, Dell and Robyn. I hope you two are hungry. We're having tacos."

"That's my favorite food group," Robyn says.

"*Buena.* You will all go home with some." Ana grabs a plate and starts loading it up and asks Robyn, "Do you like spicy food?"

"Love it."

"*Perfecta.* Though, no one handles spice like Angie. She's a freak, that one."

Rafael leans in for a chip next to us and murmurs, "In

more ways than one."

His hand is promptly smacked by his mother. "Wait your turn. Ladies first, *mijo*."

Ana continues speaking to Robyn while she heaps food onto a plate, and Rafael takes me to the side. Isaiah hands me a beer, and I didn't even realize he had stepped away long enough to do that. "Thanks," I say.

"How did you guys meet?" Rafael asks. He shifts his daughter in his arms who is sucking her entire fist, drool dripping down her hand. "I obviously know about Robyn."

"You do?"

"Yeah, Angie and I went to college with her."

I look at Isaiah to make sure it's okay and he bobs his head. "I was his personal trainer."

At that very moment, Angie comes to join us. "You were? Oh, what scandal!" she sings, her eyes alight with zeal. "But wait." She places her hand on her brother's arm. "So, you're telling me, your career playing rugby ended, but your career in love had just begun?" Angie's daydreaming face is a sight to behold.

Isaiah's eyes sharpen on her. "You read too much romance."

"That's not a thing." When he doesn't reply, she turns her wide smile on me. "Do you want to join our book club? So far it's just me and Joaquín."

"I'd love to join."

"Really?" she asks

"Sure."

"We only read ro—"

"Smut," Isaiah interrupts.

Angie's lip hooks in a snarl. "Romance."

Zofia slaps her wet hand against Rafael's neck before he adds, "Last month they read about a minotaur with a breeding kink."

I chuckle, "That sounds fascinating. I'm in."

And it's the truth. Maybe I'm doing what I've always done and diving into something I know little about. But maybe I'm just listening to my instincts that are telling me these people are special and important. It's impossible to miss the love they have for each other through jabs and eye rolls, smacks on the hand, and genuine interest in each other's lives. It's the family I've been missing since I moved away. The same family, really—just bigger. Louder. Less acres of land and whiskey barrels, more tacos and tight quarters.

Seriously, this house is small. How were five kids raised here?

It's then that my eyes catch on the corner of a wall. There, scribbled in different colored pens and markers, are the heights of all the kids throughout the years. There's one very pronounced tick mark about one foot off the ground with several years of dates listed, one after the other. For someone, probably some*thing*, named Razzle Dazzle.

I extend my foot and grab Isaiah's attention. "Family pet?"

When he catches my meaning, he chuckles and nods. "The cat." Suddenly an image of the entire family holding a cat in place so they can measure it assaults me with silent giggles. "He's still around by the way. Angie has him."

"How old is he?"

"Who, Razz?" Rafael asks. "He's gotta be knockin' on twenty-one at this point."

There's a quick ringtone from Isaiah's pocket, and he pulls it out to scan the notification. It's a long text message that he opens up.

"Who is it?" I ask.

"My old teammate, Kermit. He just started the rugby training program we thought of together."

"It was your idea?"

"Both of ours. We had this idea to sort of act as consultants for teams that needed some dedicated focus in certain areas. Help them build."

"That's cool," I say. "So he's running the whole thing now?"

"Yeah," he says despondently.

"You okay?"

He nods. "It's just been an idea for so long. It's surreal to see it become a real thing. He already has two teams he's working with."

Eventually we all find our seats for dinner, but there's not enough room at the dining table, so we all scatter to any available spot. After two bites of steak tacos, I black out in a delicious haze and inhale several more rounds alongside Robyn, who meets me plate for plate. Are these homemade tortillas? They have to be.

When Isaiah finishes before us, he cleans up his plate and a few empty glasses before taking Nico from Angie's arms. She looks relieved when she can finally eat alone. Zay sets Nico on the ground and then takes Zo from Rafael's arms and does the same thing.

"Race 'em," Dane says from the couch, then pops off and joins his brother on the rug. They both stare down their niece and nephew.

"I have twenty bucks on Zo," Neal chuckles.

"Fifty on Nico!" Jonah hollers.

With matching grins, Zay and Dane start thumping the ground with their hands, cheering for the twins to crawl to them.

"Come on, Zo!" Robyn cheers, setting her plate down and clapping. The babies slowly make their way toward their ridiculous uncles, stopping when the occasional giggle overpowers their tiny muscles. When Nico reaches Uncle Dane, he lifts him in celebration.

Robyn gets up, lays next to Zo and speaks to her like an adult. "It's okay, girl. We're gonna train hard and beat him next time."

I watch on as my partners give Zo a pep talk, and I wonder if either of them want children. They're both so at ease with them. Isaiah is so uncharacteristically animated with his niece and nephew, and it's like he can't stop himself from squishing their little cheeks, arms, and feet. Then I remember several videos of Robyn at youth rugby events, laughing and teaching. I think about how sweet Isaiah was with my nephew Liam; asking him about music and instruments, finally getting him to really talk is no small feat, and Zay was able to do it so effortlessly.

Having children has never been something I was particularly interested in, but watching the two people I love play with them has me considering the possibility. Could we make a family someday? Do either of them want that?

"I had the same look in my eyes when I first saw Ana with her children," Christina says, sitting down next to me and nudging my shoulder. Well, her shoulder nudges just above my elbow. She's very short.

Slightly embarrassed, I clear my throat. "What's that?"

Christina nods to Isaiah and Robyn on the floor with the twins. "I knew I loved Ana, but once she finally introduced me to her kids and I saw the way she loved them, the way they made her laugh, I was done for."

"It's hard to see the future when there's so much we have to hide."

She taps my forearm in a comforting manner. "Your path will clear soon enough."

Isaiah catches my eye and he graces me with the smallest curve to his lips before standing and handing his niece to Ana. He gives me his hand. "Come with me." Isaiah leads Robyn and me up the narrow, creaky stairs to a small landing and opens the first door on the left.

"This was your bedroom?" Robyn gapes, stepping into an offensively green space.

"Who chose this color?" I chuckle.

He sighs, "That would be me. We had a thing for Mountain Dew back in the day."

"I'd say so."

There's not much in the way of artwork, but there are rugby team posters of the All Blacks and Springboks mingling with band posters of Cage the Elephant, Queen, and Green Day. There's even an Agony Nectar poster that looks like it was handmade.

"I shared this room with my brothers."

"All three of you slept in here?" Robyn asks.

"Believe it or not. When they annoyed me, I'd go sleep on the couch in the basement."

"Can we see it?" Robyn asks. "I have to see where the band began."

Jonah and Dane are already down there, letting the twins tinker with the drums. I take a seat on the old couch, and Robyn sits in my lap while Isaiah pulls his old bass from a well-worn case.

"I can't believe you all have musical abilities," Robyn muses.

"Our mom was gifted," Dane smiles. "She had some strong genes because we all got it."

"What about your dad?" I ask, and all three of them laugh.

"Can't carry a tune to save his life," Dane chuffs.

"He can't even hold a beat," Jonah adds, then cheers on Zo who's sitting in his lap and slapping a drum. "Yeah, girl! Nothin' like you!"

Holding Robyn close, we watch on as the Johanssen brothers fiddle with their instruments, making sure not to play too loud in front of the twins—who, by the way, have this entire family wrapped around their little pudgy fingers.

I wonder if Robyn is feeling the same warmth spread in her chest that I do right now.

She leans her head against mine as I sweep my hand over her arm while the other skims her firm, warm leg. I wonder if she's thinking the same thing as me. If she can see herself in this family, too. If she can see dinners and pickup rugby games in the backyard; birthday parties and babysitting.

But when her golden hazel eyes find mine, I know she sees me.

Something powerful and familiar breaks through the surface of my uncertain future and it begs me to release it. I whisper, just loud enough for her to hear, "I love you."

Her shapely eyebrows raise, and her lips part in a smile. She quickly looks around and back to me. "You just said that."

"I just said that."

"You love me," she repeats and it's not quite a question.

"I love you."

I've loved her for a long time and foolishly kept it bottled up. But here, on a casual summer Sunday in the childhood basement of our boyfriend, where we can be exactly ourselves and love out loud, I tell her the truth. It feels right and real and good.

Pink blooms across her cheeks and down her neck as she bites her lip. Lacing her hands behind my neck, she cradles it and whispers, "I love you, too."

Chapter 43
Worshipped

Dell

The takeaway container of taco fixin's taunts me from my lap as we drive down the Schuylkill Expressway to Isaiah's place. This has been the best cheat day ever. Maybe just one more bite...

Robyn's phone rings and after a cursory glance, she silences it.

"You don't wanna take that?" Isaiah asks.

"No," she sighs. "It's just my mom. She usually calls on Sunday nights, and it usually puts me in some kind of mood." She takes Zay's hand. "I'd rather not spoil everything that happened tonight."

"Did you have a good time?" he asks.

"I had the best time."

"Me too," I say from the back seat. "Robyn professed her love for me tonight."

She turns around and taps me on the knee. "You said it first!"

"Is that what was going on on the couch?" Zay chuckles, but then all three of us stop when another call comes in from Robyn's mother.

"Alright," she groans. "Two in a row means it's serious." She swipes open the call and taps speakerphone. "Hey, Mom."

"Hi, Birdie. Are you driving?"

She looks at Zay. "Yeah. What's going on?"

"Your photoshoot with Adidas is this week, right?"

"Thursday morning in New York."

"I'd like to be there."

Robyn looks back at me now, as if I contain the answers. "What? Why?"

"Well, your father and I were talking, and we think it would be in your best interest if you had someone there looking out for you."

"Mom, I already had our team lawyer look over the contract, and it's been signed."

"That's not what I mean. You need someone there to make sure you look your best."

A pause stretches out and Robyn purses her lips. "I'll have a makeup artist and hair stylist, mom. And they're giving me a wardrobe. That's kind of the whole point... *they're* styling me."

"I know that, sweetie. But you know, they don't know you like I do. They don't know your best angles."

Robyn lets out an exaggerated sigh and slumps into the seat back. "Mom—"

"No, you listen to me. This is your first big brand deal, and we've been working hard for this. Other brands are going to take notice, and you need to look your best. I would be mortified if Adidas didn't know how to capture your shoulders properly."

"Again with the shoulders?"

"Yes, of course with the shoulders! Listen, I'm sorry you took after your father in that regard—"

"Mom, you're a swimmer. You also have wide-set shoulders."

"Yes, but I know how to hide them, dear. *That* is why I need to be at the photoshoot with you. If this ad campaign is done right, you should be expanding your image not only to other athletic... stuff, but fragrance, makeup, and cars! If you want to be perched on a Cadillac one day, then you need to listen to me."

"I'm more of a Jeep girl."

"Robyn!"

"Fine, Mom. You can come."

"Wonderful," she chirps, her airy tone returning. "Send me the details, and I'll meet you there. Oh, this is so exciting! Bye, sweetie!"

"Bye," she mutters before the call ends.

"What the fuck was that?" I ask.

"That would be my mother, Diedra."

"She's, uhh…" I fumble, trying to come up with the right word.

"A pill? Yeah."

Isaiah brings her hand to his mouth and kisses it. "I forgot she was like that."

I'm suddenly reminded of what she told me on our first not-date date. "Didn't you say your parents joke about you needing to make their mistake worth it? The mistake of getting pregnant?"

"And ruining her Olympic career? Yeah," she snorts.

"Baby, I'm really sorry," I say, and I rub my hands over her arms. "First of all, your shoulders are a work of art, and if I were you, I'd be showing them off any chance I could."

She sighs, "Yeah but you're not a woman."

"Hey," Isaiah warns, about to launch into something, but she cuts him off.

"I just mean, you two are really big, definitely masculine men, and no one probably makes fun of you for having feminine or ambiguous features. I, on the other hand, have to constantly show off my femininity by decorating myself. And… I know, I know, I really, actually love makeup and dresses and jewelry, but I wish I could feel free enough to live in my masculine energy, too. To wear sweatpants and an old T-shirt once in a while. Outside of rugby. In public! Be able to post videos of myself like that and not have to explain myself.

"Instead, I have to relentlessly keep up my feminine side so that I can show women they can have it both ways. They can be athletes and wear the gown." She exhales and rubs Isaiah's hand with her thumb. "I just... I don't wanna have to think about what I look like so much. So, in a really fucked up way, my mom coming to the photoshoot takes away a little bit of that overthinking."

"I wish I could go with you," Isaiah says gently.

"Maybe I could," I say.

Robyn exhales, "No, it's too risky. Are you forgetting that a lot of people know who you are too?" She rolls her head to look out into the dark evening sky, the glow of red taillights flickering over her forlorn features. "It'll be fine, guys. I've been dealing with her my entire life. It's nothing I can't handle."

Deafening silence fills the vehicle as my mind whirs. How do I make this better? How do I make this woman see how beautiful she is no matter what she wears? How worthy she is of love? I momentarily get lost in the fact that I love her and she loves me and smile to myself. I'm in love so hard. I have a girlfriend! And a boyfriend!

A broken sob cuts through my love-sick puppy dog thoughts, and I catch her dabbing under her eyes. *Shoot.*

Isaiah's there first to soothe a hand over her thigh. "Oh no, hey hey hey."

"Baby," I plead, my hands squeezing her shoulders. "It'll be okay. Come here. Come back here with me."

Wordlessly and without putting up a fight, she unbuckles her seatbelt and deftly climbs between the front seats to straddle me in the back, her arms locking behind my neck as she nestles her face in the crook of my neck. She feels like a puzzle piece locking into place against me. Caressing my hands over her muscled back, I inhale slowly as she releases whatever it is that needs to be extricated.

"Don't listen to her," I murmur. "You're beautiful exactly

as you are. You'd be beautiful with bigger shoulders. You'd be beautiful with no shoulders. If you were just a head in a cryogenic chamber, we'd love you."

Her whimpering laugh slices through the tears, and I take the tiny victory. "Would you still take me dancing?"

"Of course we would."

"We'd bring you to every rugby game you wanted," Isaiah adds from the driver's seat. "I bet they'd give us primo parking and front-row seats."

"And we'd find one way or another to make you come."

"You guys are so stupid," she giggles through the diminishing tears and sniffles loudly. "Thank you."

"You're going to look amazing in your Adidas spread," Zay says, eyes peering into the rearview mirror. "Do you honestly think they'd make you look anything less than extraordinary?"

With a long, shuddering inhale, she waits a beat before answering. "No. I'm really, *really* excited for this."

"As you should be," I say. Her breathing returns to a normal speed, and she slowly pulls away from my neck to look me in the eyes. There's darkness all around us, but her everlasting sunshine breaks through it all. Even with self-esteem shrouded, her brightness calls to me.

Robyn pushes her chest close to my face and circles her hips against me. "Will you make me feel better?"

Oh. What a delightful little detour.

My eyes catch on Isaiah's hands flexing around the steering wheel before returning to Robyn. "Is that what you need right now, princess?"

"Please," she whines, tugging her lip between her teeth.

A better man might tell her to wait until we get home.

I am not a better man.

Thankfully, her white linen shorts have a wide leg, so I easily slip my hand between us and play with the seam of her panties. "This?" I tease, skimming the softest touch where she's warmest. "Is this what you want?"

Eyes hooding, she hisses, "Yes."

"Okay. Only because you're such a good girl for us, and you deserve anything you want."

There's a low groan from the front seat, and I catch Zay's dark blue eyes in the mirror again before I dip a finger under the stretchy material and touch her butter-soft skin. "Do you like knowing he's right there? Watching. Listening."

She nods, her eyes closing all the way.

"I know you do. He likes it too. He likes to be punished as much as he wants to fuck you. To fuck me." Before I even breach her slit, there's wetness catching on my finger. "Isn't that right, Isaiah?"

"Yes, Daddy."

A surge of electricity shoots down my spine, and my dick pulses. "Jesus Christ, dude! Warn a man before you call him that!"

There's a shared giggle that reverberates throughout the cabin of the car before I slide one finger inside her, immediately locating that sweet little bundle and rubbing it. Her laughter dies, replaced with a sudden gasp.

"What?" I smirk. "Is it not so funny when I tickle this little spot?"

Sharp nails dig behind my bun and lock in as I use my other hand to slide up her leg, swipe under her panties, and grip her backside. The muscles of her wet channel constrict as I apply a thumb to that perfect little button between her legs and play with it.

"Can you hear how wet she is from up there, Zay?"

"Yes." He's white-knuckling the steering wheel now. Knowing we turn him on like this is like sipping good whiskey and feeling its warmth radiate from your belly.

"That's because she's a good girl. That's because her body is fucking perfect. Isn't that right, darlin'?" When she doesn't reply, I pump inside her hard and lean in to press my face against hers. "Answer me," I growl, using a tone I don't even recognize.

"Yes," she shudders, but I don't stop my angry thrusting.

"Yes what?" I rasp.

"Yes... my body is perfect."

"That's right. You have millions of followers and, if given the chance, every single one of them would worship the ground you walk on. They'd kiss your heels, lick your boots, and beg you to simply look at them."

"But... only you," she croaks, completely unable to hold her pleasure at bay. "I only want you guys."

Isaiah's eyes find mine again as if both of our hearts beat in tandem—as if we share one mind—and the gravity of what she means catches up to us. I was trying to make her see how desirable she is by explaining how many people want her, love her. But the weight of what it all means settles between us. She has an enormous following—bigger than mine—and no matter what she thinks, she could give a wink to any one of her fans and they'd scoop her up like the rarest ice cream flavor and savor every bite.

That sudden realization has me wondering what her ring size is and making a mental note to talk to my financial advisor.

We're never letting her go.

Isaiah turns onto his street, and I know we're only minutes away from his place, so I kick up my rhythm to a sex toy-level of relentless vibration.

"Dell!" she cries, and I give myself an early award for turning her tears into something good. Her pussy throbs and spasms as she bucks against my hand, and the music we're making is better than anything we could find on the radio.

Zay pulls into his dank little garage from the back alley and kills the engine as Robyn rides out the last of her orgasm in my lap.

Without a word, he's shooting from his seat and whipping around to the back to open my door and haul Robyn out. Like a fucking caveman, he throws her over his shoulder and leaves me to follow him up to the townhouse, up three flights of stairs. Electricity flows in my veins from my rapidly beating heart. I'm worked up, hard as rock, and determined to make her see how beautiful she is no matter what she's wearing.

When Isaiah reaches his room, he throws her on the bed and tears his T-shirt over his head in one fell swoop.

Okay, that's hot.

I follow suit and join him on the bed where we hover over our flushed woman. As a team, we peel away her clothes as fast as humanly possible and descend on her breasts—each of us taking one in our mouth and lapping, sucking, tugging her light pink nipples until she's arching her back and searching for more.

"Go get yourself ready, Zay," I rasp. He knows exactly what I mean, and even though I know he wants to stay here and enjoy Robyn longer, he wants what's coming to him, too. I devour the pathetic little whimper he gives me before he's shoving off to the bathroom.

The more Robyn moans, the harder the bar between my legs tries to punch its way out of my jeans. It's like a heat-seeking missile that's begging to be launched.

Down boy—we're just getting started.

For the last week we've been warming her up to take us both, but it's been proving to be a longer process. Not only is she incredibly tight back there, but she's been scared to take anything more than one finger; and if she's not relaxed enough, it's definitely not going to happen.

She's competitive though, that's for damn sure. Even as we did our best to fruitlessly warm her up, she never wanted to give up. I realized if Isaiah or I didn't call it quits for the night, she wasn't either. So now I've learned to cut her off before she gets too worked up and frustrated with herself.

We'll get there someday, and if we don't, that's perfectly fine with me. Not everyone is meant to take a dick up their ass. Her pussy on the other hand is very, *very good* at taking two.

·•·•·•·•·

Robyn

In the next ten seconds, if I don't have a dick inside me one way or the other, I'm going to combust. Dell, however, has other plans that apparently involve swatting my hand away from unbuckling his belt.

"Please, Dell," I whine, not caring how desperate I sound.

"No," he says while flicking his devilish tongue across my nipple. "I like taking care of you."

Until now, I hadn't realized how his pleasure Dom ways can be both a blessing and a curse. He gives and gives and *gives* until we're incoherent messes waving a white flag—only then will he find his own release. I can't take it anymore. I need to please him like I need to breathe, and he has yet to let me suck him off. Him or Isaiah.

"I know you do," I moan. "But I want to."

Removing his mouth, he leans up to join me face-to-face while slipping his fingers between my legs and rolling us to our sides. "Baby, I can get off from this alone," he says, his eyes darkening and his meaning clear. He gently pinches my clit, still swollen and needy from my backseat climax, and I inhale sharply.

"This is what I love," he coos. "The sight of you coming apart for me is everything I want."

Daring to touch his stomach, I trace along where his warm skin meets denim. I try my best to collect my thoughts before speaking. "Yes, but... is that a hard limit for you?" When he doesn't answer, I search those pools of chestnut brown. "Because if it's not, then I'm begging you to let me. I'm telling you I *need it.*"

Closing his eyes, he takes a deep breath and stills his hand inside me. "No, it's not a hard limit."

Eagerly, I take the next logical step and surprise him by rolling him to his back, straddling his waist, and pinning his arms above his head. "Do you have any hesitations?" I ask sincerely.

The way his Adam's apple bobs has me on edge once again. *Shit.* Did I already push this too far? Thankfully, he smiles.

"No, I just... It's hard for me to give up control sometimes."

An energetic little devil perches on my shoulder and whispers to me before I relay it to the Greek god staring up at me. Slowly I say, "Then tell me to do this. Tell me to take off your pants and put my soft lips around your aching cock."

Tight hands grip both of my hips. "Fuuuck."

Like a snake, I slither forward and roll my body against his, cascading my breath over his jaw. "What if I called you Daddy?"

"Princess," he warns.

I don't know where this new-found seductress has manifested itself from, but she's fucking hot and I like her. "No one has ever taken care of me like you do. Wouldn't you like for me to thank you... Daddy?"

And that's it—he snaps.

"Goddammit," he hisses. "Yes. Take my pants off."

He doesn't have to tell me twice. I scoot down and unfasten him as quickly as possible before ripping his jeans, briefs, and socks away.

Just like the rest of him, Dell's length, with its slight up-curve and ruddy crown, is perfect. Dark blonde curls dust the base and short, manicured hairs lead to his navel.

How dare this man be so delicious? He's raw and rugged. When Isaiah told me about Dell riding a horse like a pro, I nearly came then and there.

I wonder if there's a cowboy hat laying around here some- where...

"Lick the tip."

Oh, that's right.

Fixing my eyes on his, he throws both arms behind his head and watches me with a hooded expression. Wetting my lips, I descend on him with a small o-shape, and gently suction his tip. When he exhales, I give a little flutter over his slit and his eyes roll back before giving me a sexy groan. "Yes, baby."

With his mind distracted, I pleasure him with my own agenda. I want this to be slow and torturous. I want to take my time and learn every inch of him. I want him to know how fucking good I am at this.

Removing my mouth from his crown, I replace it with gentle fingertips caressing in small circles while I run my nose along his velvety shaft and nuzzle him.

Hot, wet kisses are placed on every available inch of his groin, shaft, and taint before I lick a long stripe up the seam of his sac. The low, thunderous purring coming from the head of the bed has me surging with sexual power. I feel like I'm conducting some kind of sinful orchestra.

After a few more minutes of exploratory kisses, I slide a fist down his bulbous crown and back up, jerking him as gently as I can. With the other hand, I lift his testes and press my tongue firmly against his taint. I fight back a smile when his knees shoot up to either side and his hands fly down to grasp his thighs.

"Fuck, darlin'."

Suddenly a naked Isaiah comes back into the room, and witnessing his jaw drop is its own kind of satisfaction. "She gets to blow you?" he asks, quickly coming to my side and rubbing his hands all over Dell's abdomen and legs.

"Do you want to help her?"

"Yes, please."

"Then get down there and put that pretty little mouth to good use, Isaiah."

"Yes, Daddy."

Dell groans. "You two with this Daddy shit is gonna have me—*ughh!*" He grunts as Zay replaces my hand on his shaft with his own and immediately takes him down to the root. With both hands available, I now fondle his sac as my tongue explores.

Dell places a hand on the back of our lover's head and holds tight to the dark brunette strands. Isaiah's hair is about three inches in length, and I never noticed just how grippable it is until this very moment.

We're working in tandem to drive Dell up a wall, and I'm loving the team energy we're applying to this blowjob. Look at us go! Dell's losing his mind and starting to thrust, I'm turned the hell on and ready to ride someone (or two someones), and Isaiah is sucking dick like he's done it a hundred times.

He probably did a lot of research for this.

Nerd.

Sexy, beefy, no-longer-a-virgin jock nerd.

I'm wet.

Isaiah rips his head away to gasp, a long trail of saliva billowing in his departure before he swiftly lowers himself again—his hand leading the way down Dell's cock in forceful strokes.

"Yes," he croaks, his muscles tensing everywhere, his balls pulling in tight, right before warning, "I'm gonna come," and jerks Isaiah's head away just in time to hold his head in place and shoot rope after rope of cum all over his face. It lands in Zay's dark beard and across his nose, forehead, and cheeks. It lands across the biggest smile

Isaiah Johanssen has ever had.

Holy fucking shit.

In a flash Dell is sitting upright and pulling us with him. He frantically licks Isaiah's entire face, beard and all, while stroking my hip and backside as I straddle his quad, definitely leaving a wet spot. "You two did so well. Oh, my sweet, sweet," he pants, then switches to kiss me, "delicious... little pets."

Ooooooh I like that.

Something seems to unlock in him when I whimper between passionate kisses, because one moment I'm humping his thick tattooed leg, relaxing into his mouth, and the next he's off the bed, walking to Isaiah's closet and coming out with several silk ties.

He knots two of them together and without looking up, he asks, "How do you feel about bondage, Robyn?"

I can't look away from his big, strong hands as the fabric slices between his fingers. "Never done it. Sounds hot."

"Good. Lay face down on the bed. Tie her wrists to the bed frame, Zay. Leave a little slack for wiggle room."

A frisson of desire tickles inside my pussy and shoots up into my brain before I squeal and flip over, bouncing with glee. Dell has me raise my ass in the air, and he ties my ankles to each corner at the foot of the bed as Isaiah does the same for my wrists at the head.

"Mmm," a low, masculine growl rumbles, and Dell blindfolds me with one last tie. Then he's murmuring in the shell of my ear, "You're going to listen to me."

"Yes," I reply breathlessly.

"If you wanna tap out, just tell me, baby. *Stop* or *No* is all you need to say."

"Okay," I say, unable to hide my giddiness. I can't see them, but the bed dips on either side, and large hands are smoothing over my back and legs, then up to my neck and down my arms.

Dell speaks. "Do you know why you're tied up like this?"

"Because I called you Daddy?"

Isaiah's answering chuckle is the first thing I hear before Dell releases a playfully indignant sigh. "No, princess." Fingertips trace up the shallow dip in my spine to my upper back, sending a blanket of goosebumps over my skin. "It's because we want to worship your shoulders. We want them wide and on display for us. We want you to *feel* how much we love your body."

Oh.

"And you don't fucking hide it for anyone," he grits out, his voice like gravel.

I'm stunned for a moment as I lay here with my face in the sheets. He's right though. I know he is. I project this message to my fans that they don't need to hide themselves, that they should take up space and be proud of what their bodies are capable of, no matter how big or small. But we're all human aren't we? We all falter, and self-doubt creeps in and offers us the easy way of thinking—the harmful way of thinking.

And here I am with two watchful sets of eyes, waiting to slap that bullshit out of my head when it finds a weak spot to worm itself in.

"Do you understand me?" Dell asks again.

I swallow and nod. "I won't hide them for anyone."

There's a soft kiss to my shoulder blade. "Good girl."

There's a distinct bristle of a beard and pliant lips pressing against my skin on the other side, and four hands caress every muscle and curve of my body, every limb. Never would I have thought burning alive could be so pleasurable. Never would I have thought being commanded into body acceptance could be both erotic and tender.

I feel so loved.

With every graze of their hands and press of their lips, my pussy pulses in anticipation. I want to zip my legs together and grind against anything—a pillow, a thigh—hell, I could probably get off on nothing more than my crossed legs, but I'm stuck here, bound to each corner of the bed.

"You're so beautiful, baby," Isaiah whispers along my neck, his hands massaging my shoulders.

Dell trails his tongue along my lower spine before asking, "Are you forgetting how you struck me like lightning that first time we met on the street? Your glorious neck and strong shoulders were on display like the fucking goddess you are."

That moment has replayed in my mind like a highlight reel since it happened. I've been catcalled and objectified enough times by strange men that walking down the street looking as fine as I felt that day should have put me on high alert. But the way Dell did it—the way true electricity and magic sparked between us the moment we locked eyes, the way he looked as if he'd been struck in the heart by Cupid's arrow—I felt the opposite of objectified. I felt as though he could see into my soul and find himself already there. He saw his place amongst my flailing heart, right next to Isaiah.

"I remember," I say wistfully. "You took my breath away with how handsome you were."

"I think I could have married you on the spot."

How ridiculous, I think, but a girlish thrill races through my body, causing me to tuck my forehead deeper into the mattress, my smile a mile wide and my body temperature spiking.

"I think she likes that," Isaiah muses and nips at the juncture of my neck. His hands slide beneath and play with my breasts, sending another direct hit to my aching cunt. A hand slips between my legs and glides along the crease of my ass before dipping inside my wet center.

"Princess," Dell coos, and it's like I can hear his smirk. He presses two fingers between my lower lips and inserts. "Are you ready for your two, big boyfriends to cherish you?"

Truth be told I already feel like that, but my pussy is a greedy girl and she's screaming at me to let them in. I bite my lip even though I know they can't see it before whining, "Yes, Daddy."

Dell pumps his fingers into me faster, and I nearly choke. "You keep that up and I'm going to rip that IUD out."

"Jesus," Isaiah mutters. "I think *I* just got pregnant."

My sentiments exactly.

"Get under her, Zay."

Yes! Dom Dell is the fucking best.

With a bit of finagling, Isaiah shifts his body under mine as I starfish over him. I have just enough room to bend my arms a little. As soon as he's settled, that hot bar between his legs finds my cunt, and he coats his shaft in my arousal—the arousal that's been building since the car ride.

I love the way his chest hair feels against my soft skin. That tantalizing friction against my nipples only heightens my need. I love the way his belly gives way to me when I roll my hips against this.

Though Zay's hands are on my back, his cock dances along my opening—Dell must be guiding him. The smell of coconut beard oil and cum swirl into a heady combination right before Isaiah plants a searing kiss on me. Our tongues tangle, our teeth fight, all of it aiding the anticipation of that first—

"*Ughh,*" we both groan into each other as he sinks in with one fast thrust.

"Yes," our Dom rasps from behind us before his mouth fuses to where Zay's length meets my flesh. While I'm making out with Zay, Dell's down there making out with our sexes, and all the while a thick cock is pumping into me.

What did I do to deserve this kind of mind-blowing attention and skill? I should be paying for this!

Dell's hands spread me open wider and he growls between noisy tongue-lashings, "You two taste so good." Suddenly fingers make their presence known and slip in next to Isaiah's cock, stretching me. "That's it, baby."

"Robyn," the man beneath me moans, but it's more like awe-struck wonder. "Why are you so good to me?" he asks, completely unable to detach from each other's lips and skating his hands all over my back.

"Because I love you."

"I love you, too."

Dell lets out an audible breath. "You guys," he drawls in a cutesy tone. "That was beautiful." Then his tone shifts into something sinister, and there's a second blunt tip pressing at my entrance, demanding access. "Now show me how you take two beautiful cocks."

It's so fucking tight, but he pushes his through the mind-melting stretch. "Yes," I moan, and my breath catches as he forces his way in.

Isaiah's holding me so tight with one hand on my nape and the other digging into my waist—like if he lets go of me, everything will fall apart. "Fuck me," he bellows.

"I'm trying," Dell says huskily, but there's a strong undercurrent of strain. "Why does your cock have to be so goddamn thick and pretty, Isaiah? Why does your pussy have to be so fucking hungry, Robyn, *hmm*?" With another strenuous push, Dell sinks in all the way and I'm definitely stretched to my limit. "*Fuuuuck.*"

"So perfect," Dell sighs, his hands taking their place on my ass as he methodically pumps into me, finding a rhythm with Isaiah and making me feel so... damn... *good*. If I wasn't already blindfolded, my eyes would shut on their own. A tasty little earlobe finds its way between my teeth, and I nibble, causing Zay to shudder the same way I am.

"Let's have some fun," I whisper as softly as possible, and he nods instantly. "Call him Daddy."

His breathing changes for a brief moment like he's blown out a giggle, and with the next surge of their cocks, Isaiah lets out a pussy-clenching whimper, "Yes, Daddy."

Oh my god—there's just something about a big grumpy Isaiah shedding his facade and giving into his inner submissive that has me hurtling dangerously close toward an orgasm. Joy and arousal clamor for dominance in my belly at his words, and I bite my lip for the toe-curling, impending wrath.

"Fucking hell," Dell chokes out, and his hands grip me harder. He slams into me but between their holds on me, I barely move an inch. I'm locked in and I wouldn't dream of being anywhere else.

"Oh shit," Zay grunts. "It's too much. I'm gonna—"

"No, you're not," Dell barks. "I swear to god, Isaiah, if you come too soon I will make you watch for the rest of the week with your dick in a cage."

That unexpected mental image has me falling over the edge, my inner muscles seizing around them. "Don't stop!"

"Daddy wouldn't dream of it," Dell purrs, and every last one of my brain cells vanish in a haze.

"Not... fair," Isaiah painfully musters out.

Together, my pussy and I weep, and when my climax flashes, it's blinding, white-hot pleasure engulfs me. Words cannot be formed. Only animalistic noises erupt from our joined bodies.

When the smallest fraction of my brain reemerges, I realize they're both completely still. Before I can say anything, they're pulling out, and Zay is removing his body from underneath me. It seems coordinated, but I'm too lost in a fog of orgasmic bliss to hear anything.

The next thing I register are my ankles and wrists being untied, and I'm flipped on my back. With the blindfold still in place, I can only rely on my other senses for understanding, but I'm too lost in a sex-drunk cloud to care.

A yummy body with a fuzzy round belly settles on top of me, and pillow-soft whiskers nuzzle into my neck. Zay's cock plunges into me without warning—or maybe there was a warning, I don't know. I can't connect a single dot from my body to my brain, and I don't want to. All I want is the heavy weight of a man pressing in and holding me close.

A sharp inhale from the hot body above me whispers into my mouth, followed by a low grunt. "Yes. Oh, god, Dell."

"You're doing great, baby. Stay still and push—yes. Just like that. That's perfect."

With Isaiah sheathed inside me for safe keeping, Dell opens him up. No, I can't see it, but just imagining it has me building, building...

"Stop... clenching," Isaiah warns me with a tremble to his voice.

"She can't help it," Dell drawls, clearly amused by our state of arousal. "Can you, princess? And what would happen if I pushed..."

Isaiah releases a sudden gasp and his cock pulses inside of me.

"—that little spot."

Zay does his best to collect himself, but it's a losing battle. "Please, D-Dell. Please hurry. I need it."

"I love it when you beg. You're almost there, baby. Let's see... one more finger," he muses, sounding like some kind of villain scientist performing an experiment. "There he is. You think you're ready?"

"Yes!" Isaiah barks, his impatience palpable.

Dell only chuckles before Isaiah inhales sharply. "Make that ass swallow my cock, baby." With every inch pushed into him, Isaiah grows harder inside me. His coarse pubic hair scratches along my bare pussy, right where I was stretched, and I find myself chasing that beautiful scratch.

"Perfect," Dell hums. "Ready when you are, baby."

"Thank fuck," he says and resumes his impressive thrusting. But now, it's punctuated with the force of Dell behind him. Between the clapping of skin on skin, the tongue fucking my mouth is receiving, and the deft fingers that have just found their way to my clit, I'm back in my cloud and bucking mindlessly.

"Make her come one more time, and I'll reward you."

"Yes," Zay huffs, and he pounds into me harder and faster, adding more pressure to the steady strum against my engorged bundle of nerves with his fingers.

God, these men with their powerful thighs are relentless!

My knees fly up to his sides and I squeeze him as my—I don't know, millionth?—climax bursts. I have him so tightly bound to my body that his hand stills, but it doesn't stop me from grinding on it like a wild animal, completely at a loss of control of my own body.

I'm still getting second-hand blows from him via Dell's relentless hips when he commands, "Come for me, Zay. Come inside our girl."

It only takes him three more thrusts before Isaiah goes rigid and he's shooting inside of me, grunting like some feral beast and joining me in heaven.

"*Ohhhyeahhh*," Dell exhales. "That's so... fucking... beautiful." He grunts and his pumping falters. "Jesus H., your ass is perfect."

"*Mmm*," Isaiah groans, sinking his lips against mine once again and humming his happiness into me as Dell finally stills.

Finally taking a deep breath.

There's a new hand on my calf where it cradles Isaiah's waist. "You both did so good for me. I'm so proud of you."

His praising words wash over and swaddle me in my ethereal state.

I'm a good girl.

As we detach from one another, Dell leaves and returns with warm, wet washcloths to clean us, then comes back again with glasses of water and kisses. He gently inspects both of us to check for any tears or accidental bruising. Reluctantly, I dash to the bathroom to relieve myself before snuggling back in.

"How do you feel, darlin'?" Dell asks, sliding in behind me as Isaiah holds me to his chest. Zay's bed is not big enough for the three of us, but no one seems to care.

"Lovely," I reply dreamily, still floating high.

"Do you feel thoroughly worshiped?"

A lazy, satiated smile crosses my face. "Yes."

Dell kisses my shoulder. "Good. And you, baby?"

Zay leans over me to kiss Dell before murmuring, "Wrecked in the best way."

The scent of sweat and sex seep in like a drug, lulling me deeper into something perfect. "I love you guys. Good game."

To my amusement, both of them smile and tap each other's asses, then mine, and repeat the quintessential phrase of every good sport.

"Good game."

"Good game, buddy."

Chapter 44
Little Noodle

Isaiah

"**I** don't wanna go home," a sex-rumpled Robyn declares. "Can we have a sleepover?"

Dell taps her nose. "You have an 8:00 a.m. session with your sexy personal trainer, missy."

She groans, "I know. But this is so nice."

"It is," I smile.

"Fine," Dell concedes. "We'll all sleep in Isaiah's too-small bed when both of us have kings at home."

Robyn and I cheer like children.

Dell takes the opportunity to plug in our phones, set alarms, and ready the room for the night. Right before he gets back in bed, he plucks the hardback novel sitting on my nightstand under the lamplight. It's the true crime book we're currently buddy-reading, but he's more interested in the thinner book resting below it.

"What's this?" he asks.

"Oh," I hesitate, "That's my mom's baby journal she kept for me."

"The what?" Robyn asks, rearing back to look me in the eyes.

I swallow. "Apparently, my mom kept a journal for each of us kids while she was pregnant and through the first year of our lives."

"That's adorable."

"I haven't read any of it yet."

"Why not?" Dell asks.

I shrug. "I don't really know."

Robyn's busybody self lights up. "Can we read it now?"

"I don't see why not."

Dell's already sliding under the covers and leaning against the headboard with the journal in hand. Robyn and I follow suit, and the handwritten book is handed to me.

"Guess I'll start with the first page?"

My partners nod eagerly, and for some reason, their interest sparks my own. The hurdle of opening her words doesn't seem so high anymore[1].

"September 20th," I read aloud. "Hello, baby. It's been two weeks since I found out about you, and this is the first chance I got to buy a new journal. You haven't been with me long, but you're definitely making your presence known by sucking all my energy. It seems all you want me to do is sleep."

Robyn chuckles softly, and Dell wraps his arms around her before I continue.

"But it's okay, sweetie. I fall asleep happy knowing you're on your way. I can't wait for you to meet your big sister, Angela. She already carries around a baby doll everywhere she goes, and most of the time, the baby is upright. You'll be in good hands with us. Your father is downright beside himself with happiness. He can't wait to meet you either. You're already loved so much, baby. All my love, Mama."

"Oh my god," Robyn sniffles. "That's beautiful."

"Can you read more?" Dell asks.

Finding myself as eager as they are, I flip the page and begin again. "September 29th. For the last couple of days, I've had a melody playing in my head, and I think it's yours. I'll sing it for you soon once I figure it out. Your sister loves to dance, so you better take after me and not your father with your musical abilities. Angela and I will need all the help we can get against him. I haven't decided on your nickname yet, so I'm going to throw anything that pops into my head. I love you, Donut. Mama."

"Donut," Dell chuckles. "I like that."

"More," Robyn smiles brightly.

Skipping ahead, I land about halfway through and clear my throat before reading the date—just two days before my birthday. "January 9th. My sweet, sweet child. If I get any bigger, I'm going to explode. Please hurry up and meet us. I've become a menace, and I fear for your father. He's a strong man, but these mood swings would be hard for anyone to handle. I cried watching a commercial for laundry detergent today. Then again when I burned my grilled cheese at lunch. But your father said everything would be alright, and, bless his tone-deaf heart, tried his best to sing your melody. It didn't calm me down so much as it made me laugh. I love you so much, *Kluseczko*."

"What does that mean?" Robyn asks, but I have no idea.

Dell grabs his phone and leans over to read the spelling in the journal before typing it in. "Aww, it means 'little noodle' in Polish."

"Another?" Robyn asks.

"Alright, one more, then it's bedtime. You both need to be up early."

"Yes!"

I smile and flip near the end. This is so much more than I expected. I expected a little snippet of her life and mine, sure. What I didn't expect was really remembering her. Remembering her bright blonde hair and even brighter laugh. The way she sang and played piano like she was leading a tavern full of drunks through a ballad. The way she used to carry all of us—together—all over her body, as we giggled and shouted for her to run through the backyard. Then she'd make it as far as she could and yell for my dad to "Go on without me! Save yourself!" I remember her collapsing dramatically, and my father coming to her rescue, peeling child after child off of her with that hero presence he once had. He'd scoop her up and run away with her in his arms as we'd chase after them.

She was strong. She was loud. She was sunshine... and she made every last one of us better.

All at once, I feel as though I'm falling off a cliff, remembering just how broken our life was after she died—how drastically our lives changed. At some point, the pain became normal, expected even. It's like the curtains were drawn, shutting out the sun and all the levity that came with it.

It all catches up to me, emotion welling in my eyes before I clear my throat again. "December 25th. Merry Christmas, Isaiah. You spent the whole day toddling around, playing in tissue paper, and destroying the Christmas tree. We thought by hanging the ornaments up higher, you would stop, but no. You're a persistent little man and saw the next best thing—lights!"

My partners chuckle once again, and I can just imagine my mom, animated as ever, shaking her head with a smile on her face.

I continue reading. "When the whole tree fell over (for the first time today), your big blue eyes looked for us, and you simply said, 'Uh-oh!' And oh goodness, you were so eager to help us fix it. My heart soars to see you so determined. You didn't care that you made the mess, all you were focused on was moving forward and making everything better. I think I can learn a thing or two from you, Isaiah. I love you so much, my little Sugar Plum. Mama."

Quickly closing the journal, I place it on the shelf next to me and wipe silly tears from my eyes.

"Baby," Robyn says with a sad smile before wrapping me in a hug. "She sounds like the best mom." Her words sink deep into my soul, and more memories of her flood my mind faster than the tears fall.

"She was."

My face is buried in Robyn's, and then a large hand warms the skin at the back of my neck. Dell manages to pull both of us into his arms as I let it all out for the first time in a long time. Maybe a decade.

Now I remember why I don't like to think about her—because it hurts so goddamn much. It hurt when she died, but it hurt even worse when our family fell apart because of it.

"I miss her," I croak, nearly choking on the pain.

"I know," Dell whispers.

"It's good that you're thinking of her," Robyn says softly.

"You're a good son, Isaiah. Reading this was hard, but she left the journal for a reason, and you're honoring her by doing this."

"You think so?" I whisper through unsteady breathing, and I hate the feeling of being so unsure. I hate being out of control like this.

"Of course," he says, and his confidence brings me around—it collects and calms me. It reminds me there is steady ground just ahead. I just have to look up and find my lighthouse in them.

"Thank you for sharing this with us, baby," Robyn hums.

I finally lift my head from her shoulder and take one long inhale. "I love you both. Thank you."

"We're always here for you," Dell smiles sweetly and leans in for a kiss that relaxes every muscle in my body. *How does he do that?* "And we love you, too."

We hold each other for a long time after that, and I'm not sure if it's because they think I need it or if none of us are willing to break the safety of this emotional bubble we've created. But there's a question knocking around my head, begging to be released in the open.

Lamps have been switched off and we're cuddled into each other, but I can still see their relaxed features. Now's as good a time as any, I guess.

"Guys?"

"Yeah, baby?" Dell replies.

"How do you feel about kids? Like, your own," I clarify.

Robyn simply kisses my chest and murmurs, "I love kids. But I don't know if I want them. My whole career is based on my athletic abilities and my body is everything to me right now. But," she sighs, "maybe someday."

She's right. I could never ask her to change her plans, her career, just to have kids. I mean, ever since Zofia and Dominico were born, I've considered what my life could look like with children of my own. But this is our situation, not mine alone.

"Not gonna lie," Dell grins. "You two were giving me but-terflies when I watched you play with the babies today. But, I can work with *maybe someday.*"

"Me too," I smile. "It's your call if you ever wanna make it, Robyn. We're with you."

---

1. I Will Follow You into the Dark (Instr. Version) by The O'Neill Brothers Group

Chapter 45
Coach Johanssen 2.0
Robyn

As a pack, my team and I round the corner of the field for our last lap of warm-ups before practice officially begins. We have two weeks before our last game of the summer, and everyone is reenergized from our mid-season break, but I know there's an undercurrent of doubt. It's impossible to miss the hesitant looks from teammates who have been listening to our Outer Banks vacation stories with Isaiah. Toni, Skirt, Serwaa—everyone—has been gushing about how different he was when he finally let loose. But the players who weren't there aren't totally convinced, and I get it. It's hard to envision such a serious man letting go.

Visions of him letting it all go in front of me and Dell just two nights ago play in my mind: him reading his mom's thoughtful words and praises, releasing emotions that I can only assume have been building behind his walled-off heart.

That side of him may only be for the two of us, and it's okay if he wants to keep it that way. He has us now. He finally has a safe space with us.

As we finish up our last lap, Isaiah and Bob take the field to meet us on the fifty-yard line.

"Hi, everyone," our coach waves. "Circle up and stretch out if you need to."

Bob and Isaiah take a couple of spots between Casshole and Khaos, and for a moment, Zay locks in on me before taking a deep breath. Suddenly, I'm holding mine.

"I hope everyone had a nice break," he says, crossing his arms and widening his stance. "I know I got to know many of you over that time, and I'm glad I did. I think you got to know me a little better too."

"Hashtag Agony Nectar!" Khaos bellows, making everyone laugh, including those who weren't there. Seriously, that video they took of us rocking out in the living room went viral.

He chuckles along with us, and his Adam's apple bobs before taking another deep inhale. "Yes, long live Agony Nectar," he says with an eye roll. "But over the break, I did some reflecting myself and realized I haven't been coaching y'all the way I should have."

Oh, damn. So, he's just owning it, huh? He's just going to flay himself and show everyone?

Look at my brave Little Noodle!

Isaiah scans the circle of players in various stretching positions before saying, "I want to apologize. I need to do a better job at earning your trust, and I want to listen to you more. I was coaching you the way I preferred to be coached, but you're not me. I'm sorry, and I hope you can find it in your hearts to forgive me as we move forward."

Ever the stoic one, Casshole speaks first in a low voice. "Thanks, Coach."

"Yeah," Khaos adds. "Unexpected, but," they shrug dramatically and smile, "let's move forward."

With his shiny head and a mouthful of sunflower seeds, Bob speaks next. "Does anyone have any issues with the change?"

Toni raises her hand. "Are either of you concerned that a change in coaching style will set us back?"

"No," Zay says. "It may do just that, but I think it'll be worth it in the long run. We're gonna do our best against Wales in two weeks, but in the meantime, it's gonna be my mission to oil the machine you all have created."

Who is this man? He didn't tell me he was going to do any of this. Did something unlock in him? I want to tackle him to the ground and kiss him senseless. *Oh, the urge. It tingles so good...*

"Alright, let's get started," Bob claps, bringing me back to reality. "Backs with me, forwards with Coach Johanssen."

As practice unfolds, I sense Dell had a heavy hand in the alterations to Isaiah's coaching style, which immensely pleases me. As far as I can tell, three big changes have been made.

First, Isaiah is listening. Instead of coming in with brand-new plays, he asks us what has been working in the past and what hasn't. For the plays that haven't worked, he asks why we think so. We show him the wonky plays we could never seem to iron out, and only then, after listening to our ideas, does he suggest modifications.

Which then leads to change number two—he waits. Instead of us running a play as soon as we learn it or its modifications, he allows us the time to slow it down and walk it out. Each of us gets the chance to fully visualize and feel the cadence before going full-force.

The happy *Ohs* and *I get it nows* came fluttering in like a welcome breeze as practice went on.

The third change has been just as monumental.

"Yes, Cass!" he barks when she correctly offloads the ball to her right-side support, just before taking a simulated tackle. "That's it! Did everyone see Cass? That was perfect! Show them again."

Praise flows out of him like a river. Even when things are dragging and he's giving us the time to explore the plays, he's encouraging. He doesn't let out a disgruntled sigh when someone asks a repeat question. He doesn't pinch the skin between his brows when a phase doesn't work. He simply resets or gets in the mix to give another example.

"Okay, team," he announces, and there's mischief in his eyes. "We have ten minutes left, and we're gonna play a little game."

When we're all standing in the end zone, Zay hands the ball to Coach Bob and smirks. "Who knows the kick game?" Several of us groan, including me, but there's devious laughter coming from our coaches. This "game" is essentially cleverly disguised suicides with an every-player-for-themself rugby theme.

The ball is kicked, we all run to catch it, and the first one back with the ball wins that round. Tackling is heavily encouraged.

"Normally, there is only one rule in the kick game: the first player back with the ball wins and gets to finish their day while everyone else keeps going. But," he drawls, "I'm gonna sweeten the pot and say anyone who makes an assisted try also gets to be done for the day."

Before anyone can say anything, Coach Bob kicks the ball far, and we're off, racing down the field to be the first to catch it. I'm gunning for the ball when it bounces near the thirty-meter mark and, mercifully, takes a detour my way.

Mine!

Picking it up as fast as possible, I scramble to run back, but as soon as I turn, Isaiah tackles me. "What are you doing?" I squeak, taken aback by his hands-on involvement in this game. Due to his previous injuries, everyone knows he's off-limits for a proper tackle, but he can still join in the fun—just like he did on the beach.

He yanks the ball away from me, and there's not just mischief in his eyes anymore. There's the wild competition, and he grits out, "Winning."

He's dashing away before I can get to my knees, but Skirt gently slams into him and strips the ball away before sprinting for the try line with Toni hot on her tail, yelling,

"With you!"

Skirt checks her periphery once, and before Mo can get too close, Skirt passes the ball to Toni, who darts for the try line and scores. Round one is complete as Toni and Skirt give each other a double high-five and laugh through labored breathing.

As the "game" goes on, once again Isaiah surprises me by running every round, down and back. He scores his first try in round two with an assist, but he keeps running. I win round four, and he keeps running, playing, chasing—all with a sinister grin.

Standing in the end zone and cheering for my remaining teammates (and my secret Coach boyfriend), I can't help but see all of us on the beach again, playing in the rain, goofing around. I see his mom and dad running in their backyard with kids hanging off every limb.

I see Coach Isaiah Johanssen finding himself.

There are twenty-two players on the field today, and he runs every last kick.

Chapter 46

Photoshoot

Robyn

For the first time since the three of us decided to be in a secret relationship, we spent the night apart. I left for New York in my Jeep right after practice on Wednesday so I could spend the night in the city (thankfully on Adidas' dime, because *dang* that hotel was fancy). The guys called me on the drive, and we talked the whole way. The best part was finding snacks Isaiah had hidden for me in my center console.

Then, because he had been snooping—I mean, it's *Isaiah*—he mentioned my complete lack of emergency roadside gear and told me he'd be giving me flares and whatnot when I got back. I acted like he was weird, but I actually swooned a little.

He's so protective.

It's been raining all morning, but the gloomy weather can't keep me down. I want to keep the promise I made to my guys: I won't hide my shoulders. I'll be proud of them and show them off. The thing is, most days I am secure in my body. I am proud of what it can do and how I've built it, but there are just times when I can't love it. I can't even like it.

But today is not that day!

The driver Adidas sent for me tucks me under an umbrella, and all my belongings are brought inside the high-end highrise.

"Ms. Cassidy, welcome," a short, sophisticated Black man

with a sharp haircut and a pristine, all-black suit says. He holds out his hand, and I shake it way too eagerly.

"Thank you. Hello."

"My name is Xavier, your photographer Ingrid Harper-Tate's assistant."

"Oh yes," I beam, and for some reason I decide to hug him. "I remember emailing you."

"That's right," he says with an unsteady tone and a tense hold before I let go. "If you would, please follow me. All your belongings will be waiting for you in the studio."

"Oh, um, actually I'm supposed to wait for my..." I trail off, unsure if I should reveal that a professional rugby player is waiting for her mommy.

"Your agent Diedra? She's already here," Xavier says crisply, and gestures for me to follow him.

I want to roll my eyes, but I don't. *Sure. Let's go with 'agent.'*

Xavier takes us to the thirty-first floor, and when the doors open, the whole place comes into view. There are floor-to-ceiling windows giving us a three-hundred-and-sixty-degree view of the city, and evenly separated columns throughout the space. There are a few doors next to the elevator bank, which I assume are dressing rooms. A few work tables filled with shoes and accessories are near a large white backdrop.

Keep your shit together, Robyn. Act like you've done this before. I have done photo shoots for the team and stuff, but *nothing* of this magnitude.

A server immediately takes my drink order for a coconut water before Xavier takes me to meet Ingrid. I spot my mom's same tawny hair amongst the small crew, already talking to someone.

One more deep breath in, and here we go.

"Robyn," the woman I know as Ingrid Harper-Tate, based on my search history, trills, extending both arms out wide as people move out of her way. I think she's going in for a hug, but instead, she places her hands gently on my arms and gives me two air kisses on either side of my face. "I'm so happy you're here," she remarks in a posh British accent. There's a small curl to her deep purple lips. Her snow-white hair is pulled back in a sleek ponytail, and her smooth, ivory skin is flawless. She's wearing enormous black cargo pants that swallow her and a tailored black vest. I look around the room and notice everyone in the crew is wearing black.

"You already look splendid, my dear, so our team will barely need to touch you. Doesn't she look *gorgeous*, Marguerite?" she asks the woman next to us, spinning me around.

Void of any emotion, Marguerite replies, "Gorgeous," after looking me up and down.

I like these people; I don't care if they're fluffing me because it's working.

"Birdie," my mom coos, coming up to me and wrapping me in a hug. As much as our last call got to me, it is always nice to be wrapped in her arms. For all the annoying things she's capable of, there are far more good things about her. Her very real, very genuine hugs are one of them.

"Hi, Mom," I sigh, and my chin falls to her shoulder. *Oops. Forgot about the 'mom' thing already.*

"Oh, this is your mother?" Ingrid asks as we pull apart. "Oh yes, I most definitely see the resemblance now. Aren't they stunning, Marguerite?"

"Stunning."

I mean sure, we share the same hair color, eyes, and nose, but I tower over my mom by five inches and have about sixty pounds more muscle than she does.

My mother blushes and waves away the compliment. "You're too kind."

"Diedra," Ingrid says. "Have you been offered anything to drink yet? Oh, Xavier, please escort our guest here to the break area for some refreshments, won't you?"

"Of course," Xavier says with a smile, and leads my fidgeting mom across the room.

Ingrid arches an eyebrow and leans toward me. "Your mother was just telling us about your *shoulders*," she says, dramatically drawing out the last word as her eyes round, like she's trying to gather my reaction.

"I'm so sorry," I whisper. "She has this thing about how big they are."

"Do you?"

"Well, no, not really. This is just what I'm working with." I shrug and throw my hands out to the sides, accidentally smacking the server bringing my drink.

"I'm so sorry," I grimace. Thankfully the bottle is capped, and I'm able to catch it before it drops to the floor.

"It's okay, miss. Can I get you anything else?"

"No, I'm okay. Sorry again."

"Oh, don't worry about Esther," Ingrid says with a flick of her dainty wrist. "She plays roller derby, she can handle it. Now tell me, truly, Robyn. Do you have any reservations about your shoulders or any part of your body that I should be aware of today?"

The easy thing to tell her would be to avoid my shoulders looking so big, just like mom wants. But Dell's words ring back to me.

You don't hide your body for anyone.

He's right, I think to myself, determination locking into place. That whole evening flashes behind my eyes and the way each of them worshipped and reminded me just how incredible I am. And if I am, I need to act like it. I am *not* going to hide.

"No," I tell Ingrid, feeling resolute. "Feed your camera whatever you want."

"Splendid, dear. Now, how do you feel about nudity?"

Suddenly my mouth goes dry. "Uhh..."

"Oh, no, no, darling, I'm only joking. No, never. All right now, Marguerite will take you to your private dressing room, then Monica and Quillian will be in shortly after for makeup and hair. Any questions?"

Relieved nudity is definitely off the table, I exhale forcefully and shake my head. "No. Let's do this."

•••••••••••

Three hours and four outfit changes later, my stomach growls as I pose wearing next season's orange track suit and matching sports bra. Even with music playing in the background, the entire crew can hear it.

Are they going to feed me? Oh, god, I'm not cut out for this model life. Like a baby, I need to eat every couple hours, and I'm sorry, but the eggs benedict, strawberry smoothie, greek yogurt, and hashbrowns just weren't enough this morning.

Miraculously, as I turn into another pose, I catch several carts of food being wheeled in, and my tense cheeks relax. I don't care if that food isn't for me, *it will be.*

"Beautiful," Ingrid says from behind her lens as she crouches to capture an up-angle. Like a stage mom from one of those crazy children's pageant shows, my "agent" stands behind the crew but always in my line of sight, making sure I position myself the way she wants. I mostly ignore her, but throw her a bone once in a while.

Ingrid takes a few more clicks and looks at her camera screen. With a pleased nod, she stands. "So much to work with," she says to herself before addressing me. "You're a natural, Robyn. All right, take your... agent, and go have lunch before everyone else."

"Thank you," I exhale, my voice an octave too low. "Should I..." I trail off and gesture to my outfit.

"We're done with it, so you can keep it on if you'd like. It's yours by the way. Everything you wear here today is yours to take home."

"Ohmygod thank you," I giggle because, as I am proving, I'm a total professional and can keep my shit together.

When we sit at one of the tables with our food, she wastes no time and cuts to it. "Birdie, be careful how much you eat, you don't want to look bloated."

"Mom, I'm starving," I say around a mouthful of sandwich. There's no way I'm letting this woman make me feel bad for what I'm about to eat.

Placing her fork on the table, she shakes her head and reaches for her large purse on the ground. "Fine. At least I planned ahead and brought you a toothbrush." While she fiddles in her bag I get lost in my food.

Suddenly, her quiet but harsh tone comes out. "Robyn. Eleanor. Cassidy." Immediately my heart stops because she just pulled out my middle name, and that means business. She's looking at her phone with flames in her eyes and her jaw clenches. "Care to explain this?"

Taking her phone, I press play on the social media video but not before my gut drops. It's clearly footage from a Ring camera of a beautiful an familiar front porch.

The front porch of our rental vacation house in the Outer Banks.

The front porch where I stand with Isaiah, his suitcase sitting next to him.

The front porch where he looks around before pressing me against the post and kisses me.

It's a video from ChadSports, a creator I've seen before who reports on sports news. He's never been a fan of mine. I've never seen him speak nicely about any female athletes for that matter.

The video was posted forty-five minutes ago and there's over one hundred thousand likes. Eight thousand comments. Six thousand shares.

I can't breathe.

"Don't know who that man kissing *female* Olympic rugby player, Robyn Cassidy, is?" Chad asks. "That's Isaiah Johanssen. *Head Coach* Isaiah Johanssen for the women's USA Valor. Robyn's coach," he clarifies, and his condescending *gotcha* tone wraps around me like a blanket of thorns.

"Seems the two of them spent some alone time recently. And if you're wondering, can players and coaches date?" A screen grab of an email pops up behind his talking head and he continues, "The answer, directly from the offices of the USA Valor, say No."

Oh god, I'm fully dead.

"Since Coach Johanssen took over this summer, they've lost every game."

"That's not fair, it's only been two games!" I interrupt, like he can hear me.

"Clearly fucking your coach isn't gonna help put the points on the board, eh, Robyn?" he laughs. "I'll be posting more on this as it comes out, so follow me for more."

With violently shaking hands, I fumble with the phone and shut it off before I toss it on the table and run to my dressing room where my own phone awaits. My mom's voice is muffled through my panicked sprint, but before I get there, I notice everyone in the crew looking at their phones. Some of them have their mouths covered. People are leaning over to the person next to them and whispering. Eyes are tracking me.

Shit!

Whipping open the door, my phone lays on the vanity next to makeup brushes and hair styling tools and I grab it.

Twenty-eight missed calls. Seventy-one text messages. Thousands of notifications. Before I can even unlock it, a call from Dell comes in, and my knees buckle before hitting the floor.

"Dell," I exhale, my voice too high, but there's nothing I can do about it.

"Baby!" he shouts on an exhale. "Did you see what's happening?"

"Yes. What... How?"

"Zay has been called into the Valor offices, and he's on his way there right now."

"Oh god," I huff.

"Get up," Mom's hisses from behind. "Who are you talking to? You need to keep quiet about this, Birdie. Say nothing until we talk to your team's PR."

"Is that your mom?"

"Yes," I whisper.

"She's right, baby. Say nothing until a plan has been put in place."

Tears finally form and I choke on them. "I'm scared."

"How could you do this to us?" Mom asks, and I don't think I've ever seen such disgust on her face—not about me.

"But Mom, it's Isaiah," I plead, as if she remembers my good college friend who played for another school. I guess it's my fault she's looking at me like she has no idea what I'm talking about—it's not like I told her much about him. We've never really had that kind of relationship where I gushed about boys. My parents' focus was always on my athletic ability.

My dad's voice circles through my head.

What happened at practice?

There's a training camp in Colorado you should attend.

Your stiff arm is getting better.

Did you see France's flanker make that breakaway? That's how quick you need to be!

You need to make our mistake worth it.

"I don't care who he is," she says, her jaw so tight I can hear her teeth grind. "He's *just a man*. He's not fit to be your coach, and if the Valor have any ethics, whatsoever, they'll fire him immediately."

"But Mom—"

"No. You are not to speak to him."

"You cannot tell me who I can love, Mom. I'm a grown woman."

"Love?" she asks, her eyes wide as saucers. An unnerving stillness settles over her. "This isn't love, Birdie. This was just a little fling that will end the way all your relationships have ended. Quickly. Your focus is rugby. Your focus is your brand."

"I'm gonna kill your mom," Dell mutters in my ear, followed by the chime of a call on the other line—a call from the Director of Human Resources for the team.

Fuck.

"I have to go," I say to Dell, careful not to say his name in front of Mom. "HR is calling."

"I love you, darling. Call me as soon as you can."

"I will," I say with an exhale, hoping he knows why I can't say it back.

I switch over the call and somehow manage to stand up. The door to the dressing room is closed, so I switch to speakerphone. "Hello?"

"Robyn? This is Dan West with HR. I have Coach Johanssen in the office with me right now. Are you aware of the video footage of you and him circling the internet?"

I look at my mom and she nods curtly.

"Yes," I admit, and take a seat on the couch.

"How soon can you come into the facility to talk with us?"

"Uh, I'm in New York at the Adidas shoot," I say as my entire body trembles. "We still have three more hours to go."

There's a disgruntled sigh on his end before he says, "Then I'll make this fast. Isaiah, Robyn, effective immediately, you are both suspended with pay pending further investigation."

"What?" I ask. "But it was just a kiss!"

"I'm sorry, but this is the way it has to be. You will not have the ability to speak with the team's Public Relations until you are in good standing with the team again. I would advise you to hire your own. Do you have any questions?"

"What about the game next weekend?" I ask. "Am I allowed to attend?"

"You are both allowed to attend, but not as an active player or coach. Only if the investigation results in your favor may you participate once again."

"I'm so sorry, Robyn," Isaiah says, and without even seeing him, I know he's doing his best to remain strong, but he's falling apart too.

"Me, too."

· · · • • · • · · · ·

Plastering on a futile smile, I power through the rest of the photoshoot knowing full well that everyone here knows what happened. To my relief, no one brings it up to me, but that doesn't stop me from being a knotted, anxious mess. I have too many unanswered questions flying around in my brain.

I can't get out of here fast enough. All I want is to go home and run into the arms of the two people most capable of soothing my worries.

Taking my photoshoot makeup off is the least of my priorities, so I stuff everything in my bag and head for the elevators. Right when the doors open, my mom makes her way in next to me.

"I'm coming home with you," she says definitively as the doors close.

"Wh–why?"

"Because you're in no shape to drive like this."

She's not wrong, but even more unease settles in my gut at the thought of her taking up more of my time when I could be wrapped in a cocoon of Isaiah and Dell.

"I'll be fine, Mom. You need to catch your flight anyway."

"I will reschedule. Your father has already booked a ticket to Philly and will land tomorrow morning."

"What?"

When she looks at me, all traces of her disgust from earlier are gone, replaced with soft, soothing eyes, which throws me for a loop. I can't keep up with her mood swings. I can barely keep up with my own emotional load. She gently cups my shoulder. "You need us right now. You need a support system you can trust."

"I have that. With Isaiah and..." I stop myself from saying Dell's name. She still doesn't know about him, and I can't tell if it's a good idea or the worst to tell her yet. "Serwaa," I finish. It's not a lie. If I didn't have Isaiah and Dell, Serwaa would be the one to see me through hardship.

"I'm not taking no for an answer, Birdie. Just let me drive you home, and when your father gets there in the morning, we will all figure this out then." When I open my mouth to protest again, she cuts me off. "I know you think *he* knows you, but no one knows you like your parents. You know we have your best interest at heart," she smiles.

When the elevator doors open in the lobby, I immediately notice the rain has not let up. And there's something about the gloomy weather and the childhood comfort my mother is giving that has me agreeing. Whether it comes from reluctance or willingness... I can't tell.

"Okay," I sigh, shifting my bag over my shoulder and heading straight to the exit. Mom follows. "But can you promise me we won't talk on the drive? I need to be alone with my thoughts right now."

"Of course," she reassures, and I can't help but wonder where her change in mood is coming from. Did she really have a change of heart? Doubtful. Maybe she's simply trying to ease the tension. I don't know and honestly, I don't care right now. I want to hide away and delete my accounts. Delete my career. Delete.

As much as I want to turn my phone off completely, I have to give the guys an update, so I shoot off a text once Mom and I are underway. Before I can send my first message, Isaiah calls, but I send the call to voicemail.

Isaiah: Hey I was trying to call so we could talk while you drive. I know you're probably feeling a million things right now.

Robyn: How'd you know I was on the road?

Dell: Let's not pretend Isaiah doesn't track your location.

Isaiah: You are too!

Robyn: Sorry, I can't talk right now. Mom is driving me home <face palm emoji> and Dad's on his way too

Dell: Why? I really think we should all be together tonight.

Robyn: idk why. I'm so confused and scared right now… I have no idea what the right thing to do is. I didn't want to let her down. I don't want to let you guys down either.

Dell: It's ok darlin. Can we come over when you get home anyway?

Robyn: Idk if that's a good idea. She doesn't know about you yet. Should we just throw it in her face?

Robyn: God I want to. But at the same time, maybe we just need this time apart and regroup tomorrow.

Isaiah: I hate that idea.

Dell: Me too.

Robyn: Me three. But maybe I can take this time to butter her up (and my dad) before any plans are made. She was so mad when she found out.

Dell: Are you sure you don't want us there to help?

Robyn: I think it's best if I do this myself. I know how they operate.

Isaiah: Will you call us when you go to bed? I'd like to fall asleep with you in one way or another.

Robyn: Of course <hug emoji>

Dell: We're going to figure this out guys. Love always wins.

I hope with everything that I have that he's right—but

hope is not always enough to quell the dread.

Chapter 47

Aftermath

I saiah and I left Robyn's place after our text conversation last night. We were waiting for her to come home, but with her parents unexpectedly coming in with her, we left and went to my place. Without a second thought, I canceled all my appointments for the next day because there was no way in hell I was leaving either of their sides during this.

We decided we weren't going to talk about the blowup or look at any more social media for the night. We weren't going to answer any calls or texts unless they were from their team or her. What we needed was one more night, just a few more hours of ignorance.

Isaiah and I held each other all night in near silence, Chester and BooBoo laying atop our heads, trying to soothe our racing minds with their heated purrs. With Robyn sleeping on the phone next to us, we held each other hoping and praying that this wasn't the end, this wasn't goodbye. But how could I think it wasn't? A lot more was bound to be discovered, and with that, our chances of making it work seemed less likely.

I thought we had more time. I hoped, maybe naively, we had forever.

I didn't sleep a wink, and I don't think they did either. Somewhere in the night, the call disconnected.

When the sun breaks through, I leave Isaiah curled on his side with my pillow cradled into his chest and my sons snuggled behind his knees. I head downstairs to make a meal I'm sure will be tasteless.

But when I step on the main floor and enter my kitchen in nothing but a pair of Robyn's rugby shorts I stole from her, I'm struck by something. It's a crystal vase gleaming from its spot in my glass cupboard. It's a different vase than the one Robyn had the night I gave her the calla lilies, but my mind transports me to that fateful evening regardless.

"They look so elegant and strong," I had told her when she asked me why I bought them—why they reminded me of her. *"They demand you take notice."*

With my hand stuck on the refrigerator handle and my gaze locked on the vase, fresh determination takes a comfortable seat within me. "We're going to make it out of this," I tell myself. "And we're going to be stronger for it."

As I whip up a high-protein scramble, my mood shifts into something lighter with every passing idea, with every plan. I'm firing off text messages and emails as I'm setting the table with Cholula and utensils. I'm placing my bets and calling in favors because this is *not* happening to me again.

Right as I'm about to bound up the stairs to wake up Isaiah, he's making his way down in his boxer briefs.

"How much coffee did you make?" he grumbles as he rubs his eyes.

"A whole pot," I grin and kiss his temple. "Sit. It's time to make our plans."

He groans, flopping into his seat at the table. "Can't we just move away and live off the fat of the land?"

"Calm yourself, John Steinbeck. We'll call that Plan Z."

He studies me with heavy lids and a tilted head. "Why are you so chipper?"

"Eat," I say. "And I'll tell you what I'm thinking." Bringing two mugs and a coffee carafe to the table, I sit across from him. "First of all, we're going to come out of this. It's not going to be easy and it's going to hurt, but we're going to do this."

Isaiah looks skeptical when he glances into his fresh mug and back at me. "What did you put in here?"

"About sixty grand."

"What?"

"That's the retainer fee for my PR lady, Stephanie."

"Dell," he coughs. "Is that really necessary?"

"Yes! She works for my family. She's been dealing with my antics for years, making sure our family and company stay in good standing regardless of my OnlyFans content, etcetera. She's a total pro."

"Dell, I don't have that kind of money," Isaiah says quietly.

"That's fine because I'm paying."

"You are not. This is—"

"*Our* problem," I finish for him. "You two might be in the limelight right now, but I'm equal parts tied up in this."

"Yeah but," Isaiah starts, trying to find the words, "you don't have to be. I'd understand if you stepped away."

My eyes go wide. "If I left?" I shout. "Get a fucking CAT scan, dude, 'cause I'm worried you're losing brain mass."

"That's not really how CAT scans—"

"Whatever, you know what I mean," I say with a flick of my hand and then slam my index finger into the table. "I'm not giving up on us. I fucking love you two and *we* are going to make it through to the other side. Got it?" Now fully awake, he stares, but nods. "Good. Now eat your breakfast. We're going to Robyn's place after we eat."

"We are?"

"Yes. Stephanie is going to call me in the next hour, and I want our girl on the phone for this."

"What about her parents?"

"Well, I'm hoping she told them enough about us to help grease the wheels, but we don't have a lot of time to drag this out. The sooner we get ahead of this, the better. Plus, I'd rather we control the narrative than her parents, don't you?"

"Baby, this is..." he trails off while pushing his scramble around the plate. "Should we maybe take some time to think about this first before getting PR involved?"

What is he getting on about? "What's to think about? We need to protect her, right? We need to protect both of you. The sooner we can form a plan, the better."

"I just think... maybe there's another way we can go about this that doesn't involve a whole team."

"Isaiah," I say gravely, "You need to recognize that Robyn isn't some woman. She's well on her way to celebrity status. Hell, I don't even have the same following she does, but it was still necessary for me to hire a team to make me and my family look good. If you're going to be in this with us, you need to know this is how the game is played."

His eyes travel to his plate and he nods slowly.

"Is this about money?" I ask. "Because—"

"No. It's fine." When his ocean blues find mine again, there's an unreadable emotion tucked deep in there I can't decipher that causes my gut to tighten. "We'll figure this out," he says before taking a bite of his breakfast.

I get that he's uncomfortable. This mess we're in can't be swept under the rug, and we're in uncharted waters, but I know once we talk to Steph, he'll see the light on the other side calling us to a brighter future. One, hopefully, where we don't have to live in secret. He's not going to relax until that happens, so I'll make sure he's given every ounce of support I can muster. Both of them.

Chapter 48
Defense
Robyn

The sound of my bedroom door cracking open wakes me from a fitful sleep. There's no way I slept longer than a few hours.

"Birdie?" my mom says quietly before sitting on my bedside and placing a hand on my side. "It's time to get up. It's almost ten. I have breakfast waiting, and your dad just arrived. It's time to start making our plans."

They're not your plans, they're mine. They're Isaiah's and Dell's.

I told her everything about Dell last night. The OnlyFans account. The thirst traps. Him being my personal trainer and Isaiah's boyfriend, too. I tried to tell her all the good things, like how fun and hardworking he is, how kind and thoughtful... but she couldn't hear any of it. Dell was just another wrench thrown into my career, a career that she was desperately trying to piece together.

Opening one eye, I focus on her. "I'd like to wait for the guys since this involves them."

"Just..." she trails off while rubbing a soothing thumb over my shoulder. "Come downstairs and let's talk."

"Fine. I'll be right down."

With a soft tap, she gets up, and I press my palms into my eyes to rub away sleep when she leaves. When I fling my covers away and sit at the edge of the bed, the overwhelming sense of irrevocable and unwelcome change strangles me. Nothing will be the same once I leave my bedroom, and

I'm sorely tempted to stay in here forever.

But then I'd miss rugby. I'd miss out on the bone-deep exhaustion after a hard-fought victory. I'd miss out on the scrapes and bruises shown off like trophies. The smell of sunscreen and body odor all mingling together over a bed of grass.

I'd miss my teammates. I'd miss their smiles and their laughter. The stories from their day-to-day lives told over ankles being taped and submerged into ice baths.

I'd miss out on the career I have worked ruthlessly for. Playing at a professional level has cost me a lot, but given me more than I could have ever dreamed.

I wouldn't know Isaiah if it wasn't for rugby. I wouldn't have met Dell that fateful day at the Pride parade or become his client. These men were always supposed to be in my life. So how am I going to keep them without losing the sport that gives me everything?

Throwing on a sports bra, T-shirt, and athletic shorts, I head down the stairs to the main floor and immediately spot my dad. I haven't seen him since Christmas, but he's still the same towering presence he always was. He no longer maintains his Olympic figure like my mom, but with a small belly and broad shoulders, he still turns heads with just how imposing he is. With short dark brown hair that's a whole lot whiter than brunette, he looks the same, albeit a little tired from flying here last-minute. His green eyes fix on mine, and the fine lines around his eyes deepen when he smiles.

"Hey, Birdie," he says, coming to wrap me up in a bear hug. I want to believe he means well by being here, but I can't find it in me to relax. Stiffly, I hug him back. "We're gonna figure this out." He releases me, and he gestures for us to sit at my dining table just off the kitchen. "Your mom and I have been discussing this. You know we only want what's best for you, right?"

I stare down at the bowl of green apple slices and two boiled eggs atop a bed of fresh spinach. *Yup, my mom definitely made this breakfast.* "I believe you *think* that."

"What do you mean?" Mom asks.

A wave of rebellion licks at my heels. "I think you want what's best for me as long as it's furthering my career."

"Well of course, Birdie," she huffs. "You're carrying on the family legacy and we are your biggest supporters."

"My biggest supporters? *Hm.* Okay. So tell me what you two have been discussing. I can't wait to hear it." Stabbing two apple slices with a fork, I bite into the sour fruit and wait for them to speak.

Dad goes first. "First of all, we've spoken to a lawyer who comes highly recommended from a couple of my former teammates. We have a conference call with him at noon."

Mom settles her hands in her lap. "And we think it would be best for you to end things with Isaiah and Dell."

A sudden weakness tramples over my body, and a twinge of pain forms behind my jaw. "See, I knew it. I knew you were going to ask me to cut them out."

"It's for the best," Mom tries to soothe, but it only adds fire to my flames.

"Maybe for my career! But what about my personal life? When is it time for me to love and be loved?"

"We've never prevented you from having a relationship," she says.

"Up until now, no," I shrug. "But you've also never cared one way or the other because you've channeled all your love and attention for me into my athletic abilities and image."

Dad holds up his hand. "You're getting off topic—"

"I'm really not! My career, my image are directly in the line of fire right now thanks to the men I love and want to be with."

"And it wouldn't be if you just ended it with them, Birdie!" my dad booms, all niceties vanished, replaced with a flush of red across his face. A childish urge to shrivel away takes over my body. "Jesus Christ, how dense can you be about this? You obviously can't date your coach. And you obviously can't date a pornstar. Nothing is stopping you from dating someone normal! Someone who isn't going to derail your career!"

"Birdie," my mom says with intensity burning in her eyes. "If you fight this, I want you to really think about how the Valor will respond and how the media will treat you." When I don't reply, she continues. "There is a very real chance you could get fired if you stay with him—Isaiah. And let's say, by some miracle, you do keep your job, there's no way he is. You're too big of a player and he's too new. Now you're dating some disgraced former rugby coach."

I roll my eyes but she snaps at me. "No, you listen to me. And what of the other one? Dell. The image you've created of being America's sweetheart, the woman little girls aspire to be like, the athlete brands beg to represent them... now tarnished by dating someone who makes porn!"

"He doesn't do it anymore."

"It doesn't matter. You're going to be dragged through the mud by the media while he's praised. You're going to be painted as a whore, and he's going to be painted as a hero. He'll probably gain more followers while you lose a huge part of your fan base. Brands won't *associate* with someone like you. You *know* that's how this works."

For a moment, I think about all those young people I've met over the years, like that blue-haired fan at Pride who wanted nothing more than to start a rugby program at their school. They did. And I held up my bargain and visited them the next year. I'll never forget how they all lit up when I walked up with my teammates.

I would hate to lose that.

As much as it hurts, I know my mom has a point. What tears me up is the thought of the parents, whose kids look up to me, being disappointed in yet another disgraced role model.

Rugby player.

Role model.

Woman.

Why is it impossible to be all three? Why do I have to love two men who can give me everything my heart desires, but can crush my career without even trying? Why is everything so easy with them and so hard because of it?

Maybe... my parents are right. Maybe, once again, it's not the right time. The thought dangles in my consciousness because I'm too afraid to let it drop all the way down, too afraid to let it settle into place. I'm a fool one way or the other—if I break up with them, I lose out on the greatest love I've ever known, and if I stay with them, I lose out on my career.

Suddenly the sound of the front door being unlocked triggers my full attention. The door swings open and I'm greeted by the greatest love I've ever known—in the flesh. Every worry evaporates into thin air, and my feet carry me without another thought into their arms.

"Darlin'," Dell whispers into the crown of my head, his big arms wrapping around me as Isaiah joins in too. Tears well as their familiar scents fill my head. Dell's mint and Isaiah's faint coconut and almond beard oil comfort me.

"We're here," Isaiah says, and I suddenly realize how stupid it was to not see them when I got home from the photoshoot. I *needed* them, and based on the way they're holding me, they needed me, too.

My mother's displeased exhale fills the silence of our embrace, and I'm brought back to reality. Or maybe it's a different reality—because I know it's real here in their arms. But outside is a reality fraught with opinions from people who can make or break me.

"Can we talk now?" Dell asks as he pulls his head back and

wipes tears from my cheek.

My dad clears his throat. "We've already made our plans."

Dell furrows his eyebrows, stepping over to my parents who have made their way from the dining table to the living room. "Hi, Mr. Cassidy," he says seriously and extends his hand, which Dad does not take. "I—I'm sorry we're meeting under such poor circumstances." When my dad does nothing but stare at him, Dell offers a hand to my mom. "Mrs. Cassidy." She crosses her arms. Dell sighs, "Okay. Guess I have a lot to prove."

"There's nothing to prove," Mom says. "Because you're not staying in the picture. Neither of you are. All you need to know is that Birdie will be denying any involvement with the two of you. That kiss on the porch was a one-time thing."

Before my parents can say anything else, Dell's phone buzzes, and he pulls it from his pocket. He scans the screen and looks between me and Zay. "It's my PR lady. Robyn, is there somewhere we can talk to her privately?"

He hired a PR person? Shouldn't I be the one to do that?

"If you're talking to PR, then we need to be involved!" Mom huffs.

"No," I snap as I step closer and take each man's hand. "If there's a chance we can save our relationship, then I want to hear it."

Dad stares at me. "You know ending it with them is the only way to go. It's the only way to save what we've built."

"I don't know that for certain! Let me see what other options there are, and I will make that decision—*with them.* This is my life and my career, and while I appreciate your support, I need to learn how to navigate my own life." Adrenaline courses through my veins when I pull the guys with me and head downstairs to the lower level without another look back.

"You don't walk away from us like that young lady!" my

dad yells. And if there was any doubt that I'm making the right choice, it's washed away by my own father calling me young lady. Telling me I can't walk away from them... No professional would say that to their client. But of course, they don't see me as just their talent. They see me as their child they can mold.

Not anymore.

Chapter 49
Public Relations

Dell

A determined Robyn hauls us downstairs, and my heart races. Look at my queen taking charge! God, she's amazing.

Before my foot hits the last step, I'm swiping open the call as we make our way into her basement office. Like the rest of her place, the space is bright and furnished with white trim, white office furniture, and pale green walls.

"Hello, Stephanie," I say, closing the door behind me as Robyn takes a seat behind her desk. Zay and I stand.

"Dell Breaux," she sighs. "I just read your email and saw the deposit. You certainly keep me busy. What's going on?"

Isaiah and Robyn give me a signal to move forward. "Do you know who Robyn Cassidy is?"

"Of course I do. She and that coach of hers are blowing up right now. Why?"

"Well, she and that coach of hers... are mine. And they're sitting here with me."

"Dell, what are you getting at?"

"She's my girlfriend. He's my boyfriend. We're in a polyamorous relationship. I need you to work your magic. I want both of them to keep their jobs. And uh, if there's some way you can make it so everyone's real cool with her dating a former porn star, that'd be great."

Stephanie lets out a weird shuddering breath, and I know from experience she's closing her eyes and letting it all sink it. Truthfully, I think she gets off on the drama and stress.

She's kind of a freak like that.

"Can you take it on?" I ask.

"Of course I can," she chuffs. "Robyn?"

"Yeah?" she replies.

"First thing's first. Do not reply to anyone's comments online about this. In fact, I need you to be completely offline. You don't post anything until I approve it, is that clear?"

"Yes, ma'am."

"Isaiah, do you have a social media presence?"

"I'm more of a lurker."

"Perfect. Keep it that way."

"Oh, hey Steph," I grimace. "I forgot to add… I'm Robyn's personal trainer, and I was Isaiah's until very recently."

"Ohhhh," she says. "The plot thickens. Okay, I'll handle that later." She hums to herself and we wait.

Robyn fidgets with her fingernails, and I pray Steph has a way out of this. It nearly killed me speculating that Zay and I may have to break off. I know we didn't have any idea what was going to happen with us yesterday, but once my mind started reeling with the potential of us sticking through this, I latched on like a spider monkey.

Steph hums. "I'm looking online right now, and this story is *everywhere*. ESPN is talking about it."

"Oh god," Robyn mutters.

"Hang on a second," Steph says. "Dell? Did you know your ex is out here with his own video?"

A cold sweat breaks over my body. "What?"

"You need to see this." A moment later, the video link pops up in a text from her. With all feeling leaving my fingers, I press play.

There's a greenscreen picture of my account with Travis's ugly mug front and center. "Does someone want to explain to me why my ex-boyfriend, you may know him as The-GymBreaux, or by his OnlyFans name Dixon Hand, is also dating Robyn Cassidy's head coach and boyfriend, Isaiah Johanssen?"

Oh fuck.

"I just saw Dell a couple weeks ago and met Isaiah myself." The greenscreen cuts to a screenshot of the now infamous Ring camera porch kiss. "In fact, it was just a couple days before this happened. Looks like Robyn Cassidy has herself a cheater, too."

"Do *not* look at the comments, Dell," Stephanie cuts in when the video replays. I shut it off.

Shit. It's really happening. We're all exposed now. But the truth isn't known—there are too many dots to connect for anyone outside of our bubble to understand.

"This is not the time to spiral, guys," she says, as if reading my thoughts. "The more we know, the better prepared we can be. There is a bright side! I'm seeing a significant amount of Leave Robyn Alone energy. We can definitely play into that. Robyn, do you think we could gain the support of your teammates in favor of your relationship with Isaiah?"

"Um, probably. I can talk to my teammate Serwaa about helping."

"Work on that. Isaiah and Dell, I need you to email me all the details about the three of you and your relationship—how it happened and what you mean to each other. Send that to me by noon today and I'll call you an hour later with a statement."

"Shouldn't we wait for the Valor to conduct their investigation first?" Isaiah asks.

"No," she says. "We can't let them lead the way on this. To protect Robyn's image and hopefully save your jobs, we need to curate the narrative that this is true love. That people are rooting for you! Can you see it?" she asks, like she's envisioning a shooting star... and snorting cocaine. "I'm gonna get an award for this," Steph says quietly, like she's talking to herself.

"No." Isaiah stands back abruptly and throws his arms out. "Why would we go through all this trouble when…"

I narrow my eyes on him. "When what?"

His Adam's apple works before eyeing both of us. "When I should just step back."

What?!

"We can still play this off as a one-time kiss. We could," he shrugs. "we could just go back to the way things were."

"Isaiah," I warn.

"I'm serious. Things were safer when I wasn't in the picture. The best way to protect Robyn is to bow out."

"No, baby," I plead. "You can't mean that. We are a three-piece set."

He shakes his head. "It was better when I was on the outside looking in." Isaiah looks down at Robyn, whose chin is trembling like his. "I can do a better job at protecting you from afar."

"But what about my heart?" she whimpers.

Fists clenching, a tear slips down his reddened face. Isaiah's shiny eyes find mine. "He's gonna take it all."

"What? No! I need both of you."

"How fucking dare you," I say, my voice wavering. My blood roils with anger and heartbreak. How can he do this to her? How can he just step away like this? For two years she has been my client, and for two years l missed out on being deliriously in love with her, all because I thought my business and image were more important. I thought keeping *the* Robyn Cassidy as a client and all the clout it came with would be more important than what my heart wanted.

Why can't Isaiah see that life with her is worth any price? A life with me…

Emotion overwhelms me, but I push through a wavering voice, "And what about my heart, Zay?"

"I still love you," he whispers, his eyes pleading. "I know you love me, too. Please don't give up on me."

"Are you kidding?" I cry, and I have to press my palms into my eyes to physically hold back the flood. "Tell me, Isaiah. How do I love a man who breaks her heart like this?"

The words punch him in the chest, I know they do. I hate that they do, but I'm careening into the unknown and don't know which way to go. For the first time in my life, I'm diving head-first, but the thrill is gone. I'm diving because of the pain, and I can only hope the landing will kill me.

"My mom was right," Robyn softly cries. "I don't know what I was thinking. None of my relationships last. I was an idiot to think this one would."

I stand and pull her into my chest. "Baby, nooo. Don't say that. He's the reason why they didn't last. It has nothing to do with you, and everything to do with Isaiah's goddamn inability to fight for what he wants."

"But I *am* fighting for us," he pleads. "I just have to take a back seat."

"Until when?" she asks. "I retire? That could be seven years from now."

"I'm not gonna give up on either of you."

"Well, it sure as fuck feels like you are!" She digs her forehead deeper into my chest and cries while I stare daggers into him. If I could open my chest and let her crawl inside to protect her, I would.

"Get out, Isaiah," she whispers.

What happens next might be the most hurtful thing of all. With resignation painted across his face and a heaviness to his stride, Isaiah leaves without a word.

I'm still holding Robyn when the door shuts.

"Guys?" A voice cuts through from my phone on the desk. "I'm still here."

Chapter 50
Snap Out of It
Isaiah

It's been five days since I walked away from my whole world. Five days puttering around my home and wallowing in my own self disgust. Each passing moment feels like a lifetime thanks to the hurt burying me alive.

I'm doing this for them, I remind myself for the millionth time. But each time that thought surfaces, less of me believes it. Less of me understands it until there's just... less of me.

Angie tried coming by a few days ago when she couldn't get ahold of me on my phone. The only calls and emails I'm willing to take are from the team regarding next steps. So when I got the call yesterday that the Valor's investigation team was ready to speak to me later today, I buried myself deeper into the dark comfort of my bed.

With the blackout curtain drawn, I fall in and out of sleep. Every time I wake up, my body begs for me to stretch and walk around. I ignore it and pray that slumber, the forgiving beauty that she is, takes me again so I don't have to war with myself any longer.

A sudden shock of cool air breezes over my skin as my comforter is ripped away from my self-sabotaging pit.

"Get up." My eyes adjust to find Dane flinging the curtains open and coming to stand at the end of my bed with Rafael and Jonah next to him.

"Nice jammies," Raf says, clearly amused by my boxer briefs and the Bridgerton T-shirt I stole from Robyn that's too large for her but fits me.

"I want my keys back," I mutter. I turn into the pillow for more privacy, only to have Jonah take it away. I groan, "Leave me alone." Can't they see despondence and leave it be?

"No, bro. This is too big," Dane says seriously, ripping my pillow away. "How long have you been here?"

"Since yesterday morning."

Rafael, in his suit and tie, sits on the bed next to me, and I feel like human garbage laying here next to him. I glance at my alarm clock and see it's noon. Why are they here in the middle of the day? "We were worried about you," he says. "Angie told us the three of you broke up?"

I plant my face into the pillowless and blanketless mattress. "I broke off. They're still together. I think."

"Why would you do that?" Jonah asks. "You finally got your dream girl and that beefy bombshell and you break it off? What is wrong with you?"

"A LOT."

Raf nudges me. "Turn around. I don't wanna talk to your butt."

He should because I'm an ass.

Reluctantly I roll over and sit up against the headboard, feeling exposed with their eyes on me.

"Tell us what happened," Dane says, standing at the foot of my bed with his arms crossed.

"I put her in too much danger. I knew if I bowed out, we could still play this off as a single kiss, and neither of us would lose our jobs... hopefully," I shrug. "That is yet to be determined. We have a meeting with the team for the investigation today at three o'clock. I also put Dell in danger. Now I'm being dragged through the mud as a cheater, and Dell's past is coming back to hurt Robyn, too."

Dane scoffs. "You're so fucking dense."

"Fuck you. Get out of my house."

"I thought she was your dream girl," Jonah says. It's a simple statement; yet a new wave of hurt pinches my heart at my brother's words. If it were only that simple—to be able to keep my dream girl in my arms. The girl I wished for since college.

"She is."

She's the girl I had to protect at all costs, and that includes now. To protect her, my heart must pay the price. I can live with only the memory of her again if it means she'll be safe. And Dell has her. I know he'll take care of her and do his best to heal her broken heart; and she will heal his.

Maybe.

Maybe they'll heal so much they forget about me entirely. I deserve that for putting them through this. For thinking they could wait for me until our stars align once more.

"Is this your dream job?" Rafael asks, but I stop myself before answering automatically.

Is being head coach of a professional rugby team what I envisioned for my life? To some extent. I always knew it could be a possibility with my background, but if I'm honest with myself, being a coach was only a means to stay in rugby. It was my fallback when I could no longer play. It was the strongest connection I had to Robyn and if I ever lost that, what would I even be to her then?

Just some guy.

When I applied for this job, I never thought *This would be great for my career.* I thought, *I'll be closer to her.* I would have taken a job as a gas station clerk if it meant I saw her on a regular basis. It's the reason I worked that job in security—so I could keep a close eye on her and keep her safe. It's not like I'm using my degree in forensic science for any of this.

If it wasn't for Robyn, this job... means nothing.

Nothing.

She means everything.

They mean everything.

I refocus my stare on Raf. "No. This is not my dream job."

Dane bugs out his eyes and shakes his head. "Then resign, dumbass. You want the best chance at saving her career and getting her back? Quit."

"You think she would take me back?" I want to retract the words immediately for sounding so pathetic.

"Have you not been on social media in the last twenty-four hours?" Jonah asks.

"No, I've sorta been hibernating."

"You mean wallowing," Raf adds.

"Whatever. Why? What's going on?"

Raf and Dane exchange a look I can't decipher, and then I'm grabbing my phone from the nightstand and looking for myself.

It's a post made on her Instagram in collaboration with Dell.

Hey everyone,

Alright, let's talk about my relationship with Isaiah Johanssen. Yes, he is my coach, and understandably, our connection has raised some eyebrows. I know many of you are disappointed in me, but I'd like to share my side of the story.

Nine years ago, we were just two rugby players in college who became fast friends—friends who harbored feelings for the other and could never find the right time to express them. It didn't get easier after graduating. Life and circumstances got in the way. But when he accepted the position as head coach for the USA Valor, there was no denying that magnetic pull was still there.

Hiding our relationship to the team wasn't right, and I never intended to disrespect the institution of USA Valor. But sometimes, love has other plans and gives a big middle finger to the boundaries we set for ourselves.

I don't know what will happen with our positions on the team, but I sincerely apologize for the disappointment we have caused. I think I can speak for both of us when I say if we are allowed to come back, we promise to have the best interest of the team. Our roles as player and coach will be prioritized, just as they always were.

And if you believe the rumors that he was cheating on me, please see Dell's statement next.

Thank you for understanding and I hope you can forgive us, because I love sharing my life with you all. There's so much more I hope to someday share with you.

With love,
Robyn

When I flip to the next slide, it's a picture of us from a summer sevens tournament in college. Both of us are ragged and tired, but smiling at the camera with an arm around each other.

I remember that day. I remember feeling at peace when she first spotted me from across an empty field and ran into my arms like she always did. A wave of determination settles over me because I know...

It's my turn to run.

But there's more after that picture. The next slide is from Dell.

I'm going to be a lot more direct than Robyn.

Isaiah Johanssen used to be my client, then we became friends, then we became more. We're in love with each other and Robyn Cassidy. There was never cheating because we were all together. If polyamory is a new concept to you then do some research.

Yes, I used to make content for a certain spicy, subscription-based site, and I had never been ashamed of that until feelings emerged between me and Robyn. I was scared of what it would mean if people found out—scared of the shadow it might cast on her. But here we are with our dirty laundry airing because I refuse to keep us in the dark any longer.

I love Robyn Cassidy and Isaiah Johanssen with all my heart and we're not hiding it anymore. You can deal with it, or you can get out of the way.

With love,

Dell

"Holy shit," I whisper.

"Yeah," Dane says. "Seems like they haven't given up on you."

They also placed a huge bet that I would come back, because if I don't, then they just shot me in the foot. Now there's no way in hell I could walk into the Valor office today and lie to HR that all we shared was a kiss.

They have me right where they want me.

That means Robyn knows this could get her fired, and she's still going through with it. Holy hell. I can't let this be for naught.

"There's more," Jonah gesturing to my phone. "Just check your DMs. I sent you a bunch of stuff."

> @TheLondonHornets: *Isaiah Johanssen is a gentleman and a hell of a rugby player. Not as good as Robyn Cassidy, but maybe she could teach him a thing or two.* #WithYouWithLove

@ServingSerwaa: Let's remember former USA Valor fullback @JasonCrandle not only dated a porn star while playing for @USAValor but made videos with her and was lauded for it. #WithYouWithLove

@JasonCrandle: That's true. #WithYouWithLove

@Khaos(She/They): Listen, I know everything that happens on this team and even I didn't know they were in love. #WithYouWithLove

@ToniBaloney: U think she got preferential treatment? Ha! If u dont think we'd call him out on his BS as soon as that happened then ur delulu. #WithYouWithLove

@Casshole: No one works harder for this team than them. #WithYouWithLove

@WalesRugbyOfficial: If they don't play, we don't play. #WithYouWithLove

> @PhillyMensRugbyOffiicial: We will suspend all games until @USAValor reinstates both Coach Johanssen and Robyn Cassidy. #WithYouWithLove

Oh my god, there's an entire storm of rugby teams saying they won't play until we are given our positions back. Cities and countries all over. Pro and club level. Wales, Philly, San Diego, Argentina, Canada, Australia, New Zealand... even college teams. My entire team has made statements in support of us.

Even brands.

> @ADIDASNorthAmerica Hey Robyn Cassidy. We're #WithYouWithLove

> @CastleWhiskey Love is strength. #WithYouWithLove

> @PolarRandomHouseBooks Dibs on this memoir. #WithYouWithLove

"That's it," I smile and toss my phone aside before launching off the bed toward the bathroom. "I'm running this time."

Chapter 51
With You

Isaiah

When I pull into the parking lot of the Valor's training facility and offices, I don't see Robyn's Jeep, but that's probably because I'm twenty minutes early. Ever since I realized I'm the biggest idiot ever, I've been running.

I run into the lobby. I run up the stairs.

Robyn and I are supposed to be interviewed together, but when I spot two people from HR, Bob, and the President of USA Valor, Ken Cartwright already sitting in the glass conference room and looking at Robyn and Dell's statements on the monitor, I run again.

Every second counts.

"Excuse me," I huff, realizing now just how out of breath I am.

Dan from HR holds up his hand. "Isaiah, you have at least another fifteen—"

"If I step down as head coach," I interrupt as I step inside and the door closes behind me. "If I resign, will Robyn be able to keep her job?"

The four of them look between one another and the statements again. Ken, a white man well into his sixties with a crisp haircut and permanently stern face, looks at me. "Mr. Johanssen, do you understand the severity of this situation?"

"Yes, of course. The perceived power imbalance alone should be enough for me to lose my job."

Ken gestures to the monitor. "She says here that—"

"I know what they said and it's all true. I love her. I love him. More than this job—no offense, it was a great gig—but I will happily step down if it means she can keep her job. This is her livelihood, but it is just a job for me."

Ken turns to Dan, and they nod before everyone looks at me again. "She can keep her job if you resign."

"Done,[1]" I laugh.

A giddy energy bubbles from the soles of my feet and evaporates above me. I just quit a job most rugby players would dream of having, but I feel nothing but raw joy at my future. Is this what Dell always feels like? Making a decision no matter how big or small and flinging himself into it with abandon? I thought it would be a lot more terrifying. Maybe it would have been if I was doing it alone, but I'm not.

Robyn and Dell's public statements play in my mind.

They're with me.

They didn't give up on me.

And as I exit the conference room without another word, I turn and there, waiting in the lobby is my whole life.

Robyn and Dell. Watching me.

"Did you just do what I think you did?" she asks, her eyes round and gleaming with hope and unshed tears.

I stop short. "I did. You're gonna need a new head coach."

Her brow furrows. "But, I don't know if I still have a job."

I step closer. "You do. They agreed you could keep your position with the team if I resigned. They saw your state-ments—your wonderful, heartfelt statements—and I said they were true. Robyn," I say solemnly, swallowing a ner-vous lump before taking both of their hands in mine. "I made, quite possibly, the dumbest decision to leave us. There's no job more important than you two. I let fear take over, and it convinced me I was better off in the shadows. But I was a coward. So I... I took some inspiration from both of you."

Their hands squeeze mine, and the corner of Dell's

mouth turns up the slightest amount before I say to him, "I could hear your encouragement and feel your head-first energy."

Then I direct my gaze down to her. "I saw you running to me from across the field. I could feel the warmth of your smile. And you two made this decision so easy for me." Tears fall down our faces, but her smile has me floating. "Can you forgive me? I promise to never make you feel like this again. I promise to prioritize us before anything else. I promise to never let fear drive."

"Yes," she swallows. "I'm not going to let it drive me either. Every hit will be worth it."

My chest could explode from her forgiveness. My knees could buckle from the impact of her words. There isn't a doubt in my mind that I made the right call.

"And can you forgive me?" I ask Dell, his warm brown eyes filled as my heart punches harder than ever. "Can you forgive me for breaking her heart and breaking yours? I want it to be the three of us. Always and forever."

Staring at him in this moment is like looking down the barrel of a gun, and with every passing fraction of a second, I grow more antsy. If he doesn't forgive me, I would understand, but I wouldn't give up. I'd grovel until my dying breath. Hell, even if he does forgive me, I'll still grovel just so he can rest assured that I mean every word—that I believe in us.

All at once, Dell wipes the stream trickling down from his eye and smiles before wrapping both of us in his arms. "Of course, baby. We're with you."

---

1. *Could Have Been Me* by The Struts

Epilogue

Dell

Nine Months Later

"Shut up," Robyn hisses, slapping my tuxedo-covered arm and watching Zofia and Dominico toddle down the aisle dressed to the nines. Everyone in the church pews giggle as Zo stops in her tracks to dump all the petals in her basket halfway down the aisle. At the sound of the crowd's laughter, Zo's face scrunches and she cries, but Nico is there, wrapping his tiny arms around his twin sister to comfort her.

A collective *Aww* hushes over the crowd, including Robyn and myself, because how can you not? When the pair of them let go, they both ditch the flower basket and pillow holding the fake ring and walk hand-in-hand to their waiting mother and father at the end of the aisle. Raf's brother Joaquín stands as best man, and Isaiah stands next, followed by Dane and Jonah. Next to Angie is her friend Cora and her sister Ivy.

The twins give their parents a hug, and they're given to the grandparents in the front row before we all take a seat. Grabbing Robyn's hand, I place a chaste kiss on the back of it. She looks gorgeous in her pale-green slip dress. From the tip of her head to her toes, she's flawless, and she's every bit mine as we are hers.

When the priest begins the ceremony, he's only speaking in Spanish. Robyn and I exchange awkward glances because we don't know the language, but we *are* in Mexico, we should have seen that coming. Language barrier aside, the wedding is beautiful, and it doesn't take my understanding of the language to capture the essence. To see joy weep from their eyes and feel the couple's commitment to each other.

Robyn's painted nails dance along my palm, and I picture us up there standing with only Isaiah. *How wild a concept*—three people getting married to each other under the roof of a church. But the more I picture it, the more it isn't.

I know Robyn and Isaiah are the end game for me. The two of them are everything I ever wanted in a relationship—I just didn't know it was going to come in the form of two partners.

Isaiah catches my eye, and a little comment he once said passes through my mind yet again. About how he would dream about me fucking him.

"In my bed. In the back of a car. In a pool. On our honeymoon."

Our honeymoon.

I never forgot about that. I've only been thinking about ways to make it happen. I want to see my rings on their fingers—so I'm shooting my shot.

Today.

Robyn lays her head against my shoulder and exhales a contented sigh as Angie and Rafael recite their vows. There's a small curl to her painted lips, and the urge to kiss it buzzes through me. I love her happy.

It was no easy effort to get where we are now though, especially with her parents. Deidra and Chris Cassidy didn't exactly welcome me and Isaiah until there was overwhelming support from the media and her fan base. Conditional love is something I've never been used to, and neither has Isaiah. But she's been dealing with this dynamic for her whole life, and we get it—the love of a parent can be complex and nuanced. And sure, I was serious when I told Robyn I wanted to kill her mom for saying those awful things to her at her photoshoot, but there's too much tied up in their relationship to cut them out. Yet. Isaiah and I aren't keeping a mental tally or anything. No, nooo, we wouldn't do that. We wouldn't be waiting for the ideal time to strike—to suggest she cut her parents out of her life—if it means protecting our girl.

No, never.

For now though, we'll play nice as long as they place nice.

Robyn met my family between Christmas and the new year, and my parents were head over heels for her just like they are with Isaiah. My entire hometown is now trying to claim the place as Olympic Rugby Player Robyn Cassidy's hometown. The lie has been proudly displayed on billboards along the highway ever since she left.

Of course, my nephew Liam has been properly obsessed with Isaiah. During our last visit to Kentucky for his birthday, the three of us got the boy a year of piano lessons, but Isaiah didn't feel like it was enough. So, before we flew back to Philly, he took Liam to a musical instrument store where he picked out the cutest little guitar.

Zay is such a sucker for kids. He acts rough and tough, but those soft spots of his are the gooiest. I may have four percent body fat, but I love being one of his soft spots, too.

Since Isaiah stepped down from his position as head coach for the USA Valor, he's been sinking all his extra time and energy into With You Rugby, his consulting and training program with his buddy, Kermit. It's been growing like wildfire. It certainly helps that he's dating the most famous rugby player in the country. I love seeing him get so passionate about his work—his craft, really. He still has a heavy hand in the rugby community while coaching. Often, he'll talk through one of his team's problems with Robyn, who is all too happy to figure it out with him, and then the *team* is all too happy when Robyn stops by practice for a visit.

When the wedding ceremony ends, Robyn and I make our way to the picturesque hacienda where the reception will be, and Isaiah finds us soon after we arrive.

"You don't need to take pictures with the bridal party?" Robyn asks after he places a kiss on both of our cheeks. We're sitting on the edge of a reflecting pool, the sparkling, clear water behind us, and I'm already dying from the heat even after removing my tux coat.

"No, we got most of them out of the way before the wedding." Zay smiles. He takes a seat with Robyn in the middle, stealing a sip from her spicy margarita. "You two have me the rest of the night."

"I saw you shedding a tear up there during the wedding," I say with a cocked eyebrow and a smirk. "It was sweet."

Blush blooms over his cheeks and hides under his well-groomed beard before he shrugs. "My sister got married to one of my best friend's," he says. "I'm not made of stone."

"I wish we could get married," Robyn muses, her stare a million miles away. My heart skitters, and I'm pleased she's bringing this up right now. I didn't even have to lay my trap.

"We can," I tell her with confidence born from a lot of time thinking this through. Isaiah and Robyn both look at me. "It doesn't have to be legal to be real, does it?"

The two of them turn to look at each other, their bodies tensing in realization. "I guess not," she says. Zay blinks and draws his eyebrows together.

"What if we made that commitment to each other now?" I ask.

"Now?" Zay huffs.

I gesture toward the hacienda filled with Isaiah's friends

and family mingling with cocktails and deep laughter. Palm trees, hibiscus, and agave planted everywhere creating serene privacy.

"I'm not trying to piggyback on your sister's wedding, but... we could keep it a secret," I say, my voice low and smooth. We're public about our relationship now, but there's no denying how thrilling it was to sneak around and hide. Stolen kisses and secret sleepovers built tension, creating a naughty noise in our heads and lusty energy.

Robyn studies me, and a slow, faint smile creeps over her face. "You're serious."

With her hand in mine, I kiss it once again between, and it takes everything in me not to get down on one knee. But this is someone else's wedding, and my mama raised me better than that. "What do you say, darlin'? Will you marry me?"

"Of course I will!" she squeals. Before I can kiss her, she puts a hand to my chest and blocks it. "But not now."

"Wh—why not?"

She throws an arm out wide to the whole party. "Because I want this. I want the white dress and the bridesmaids and the whole shebang!" She turns back to me and holds my hands. "I know I'm your princess, but I want everyone else to see me like that on my wedding day, too."

God, I'm dumb sometimes. Of course she would want that, and I *want* to give her that. I want to give her anything she wants—anything that will make her happy.

I already know the answer, but I ask my beau anyway. "What do you think, Zay? Do you wanna marry our girl with me?"

"Of course I do," he laughs nervously.

"I have one condition." Both of them flick their shiny eyes to mine, but I look directly at him. "You have to marry me, too."

With that same smile he's had the whole day, now bigger

and brighter than ever, he stands up from the pool's edge and crosses to me. When he's between my legs, he caresses my face.

"Of course I'll marry you," he beams and lowers himself to kiss me. My entire body lights up like a Christmas tree—it's warm and twinkling and there's a choir of children singing.

Oh my god, I'm really going to not-marry marry these two.

A delicate, reassuring hand finds my thigh, and I sink deeper in love.

After a long, drugging kiss, Isaiah and I break apart. He stands straight up and looks around the venue before stepping in front of Robyn and kneeling. My heart jumps in my throat because he cannot be this dense to propose so publicly at his sister's wedding. But he's sly, this man. He bends over to adjust the strap of her heel as an excuse, and a radiant smile appears. "You're the last piece, Robyn. Will you marry me, if I marry him?"

His question to her rings through me, and I can see his long, hard-won desire manifesting before our very eyes with his sunshine friend from college. The two of them making that commitment to each other after years of longing is finally here.

One perfect, happy tear falls from her hazel eye and drops to her dress. "Yes, Isaiah. Let's finally get married." Still holding her ankle, he tilts his head up as she leans down to meet his promising lips and my heart explodes.

We're getting married!

The evening plays out like a dream, and I'm sure it would have been lovely if we hadn't just agreed to marry each other, but it's like I'm floating with them. I don't care that some of Rafael's Mexican family are watching the three of us with concerned looks as we dance and kiss all night long. I don't care that Jonah took his shirt off and jumped into the reflecting pool. I don't care that Dane's normal scowl is mysteriously replaced by a smile as he stands by the bar, watching Joaquín lower himself to the dance floor as everyone gets *a little bit softer now. A little bit softer now.*

I most certainly don't care that Robyn is dancing like a weirdo—like a beautiful, ridiculous weirdo.

She's our weirdo. She's our bad dancer.

And her kissing is just so bad, I think we'll have to spend the rest of our lives practicing with her.

When the private driver I hired shows up around midnight, the three of us, covered in sweat and bliss, pile into the back. And when our driver pulls up to a different hotel than the one Isaiah and Robyn thought we were going to, they catch their breaths.

"Where are we?" she asks as we make our way through the historic lobby.

"Well, I sort of had a different plan for us tonight, and this was the closest hotel that had the suite that I wanted."

"We had a suite in the first place," Isaiah adds.

"Yeah," I drawl. "But it wasn't exactly the one I wanted." The hotel front desk agent hands me the key and we head for the elevator. When we get to our floor and find the last room, their eyes round when they read the sign on the door.

Honeymoon Suite.

"Dell," Isaiah breathes, but I simply pull him inside as he pulls Robyn.

"I'm sorry. I may have had a different vision for how tonight's proposal was going to go. I may have jumped the gun." I flip on the light switches to reveal warm light casting over sandstone tile floors. Tan velvet drapes bracket large double doors that lead out to a private patio and illuminated pool. The arched ceiling glitters with teal and gold mosaic tile. There are ornate, deep red and brown rugs throughout, with a fireplace and small living room next to a large, inviting bed. On the table, champagne sits in a silver ice bucket next to three flutes.

"Dell," they both whisper in awe.

"It's pretty great, isn't it?"

"I love it," Robyn says.

Isaiah's warm hand cradles mine. "Someone was a little eager."

"I'll make sure we have an even better one on our actual honeymoon."

"And our stuff is already here?" Robyn asks excitedly when she peers around the corner.

I come up behind her, skimming her hips over the silk of her dress and pressing my growing erection into her backside. "You won't need any of that."

"What's this?" she asks, ignoring my efforts. Two small gift boxes sit on the dresser. She grabs one wrapped in cream and gold paper.

"Those would be your engagement rings. Though, I thought they'd be wedding rings tonight."

Beaming, Robyn snatches the black and gold box and hands it to Isaiah before hauling us to the bed and tearing her gift open like a five-year-old. As soon as the ring box is pulled from the box, she lets out a high-pitch squeal and flings it open to reveal a three-carat oval cut diamond ring.

"Holy shit! This is beautiful!"

"I'm glad you like it. It was my grandmother's. I had it redesigned to be a little more modern and... more like you."

Robyn nudges Isaiah, who's sitting there slack-jawed. "Open yours," she demands with crazy eyes.

He shakes out of it and tears into it. A single thick, gold band with a line of black diamonds running through the middle shines up at him from its cushion.

I really took a risk with his ring since I had no idea what kind of jewelry he likes. He always says he likes mine, but I didn't know how that translated to his style.

"If you don't like it, we can return it and get—"

As quick as my anxiety came on, it's squashed when he wraps me up in that delicious bear hug of his. "It's perfect," he murmurs into my neck, his full beard soft yet coarse against my skin. He pulls away just enough to find my eyes. "I can't believe you did all this. I never thought I'd ever be proposed to."

"Hey, what about me?" Robyn cuts in. "I asked you to make a marriage pact with me, didn't I?"

He chuckles, "You did, you're right. I just meant... you know."

I kiss him and touch his lower back. "I know."

He lets me pull out his dress shirt from the waist of his pants and take off his tie, his own erection growing with each deliberate pull. Robyn's already squirming next to us when I slough off his white shirt and gaze at his strong body—at his sweet belly, dusted with dark hair, that I love to snuggle into.

By the time we've completely divested ourselves of our clothes, we're revved up and ravenous. I'm so keyed up I have to promise them I'll take it slower for the next round, but I can't hold back any longer. The need to fully claim my fiancés claws at me like an addiction.

I lay my future husband on his back and position my future wife over him—their mouths fusing, their tongues rolling. Robyn's pretty little cunt searches for me behind her, while coating Isaiah's thick, bare shaft.

She's showing a lot more restraint than I am, but her needy, canting pussy isn't as needy as me. With a swift hand, I grab the rod between Isaiah's meaty legs and align it to her opening, guiding her down in a rough motion. They both groan the prettiest sound I could ever hear.

"Doesn't our future wife have the sweetest pussy?" I ask and before Isaiah replies, my tongue is lapping around his shaft and her lower lips.

"Yes," he rumbles, then spreads her ass for me.

Don't mind if I do...

Robyn gasps when I move my ministrations to her tight, puckered hole and feast. Isaiah slams into her—clap after clap, their skin thunders under me. She cries out our names and even through my desire-soaked brain, I wonder what those names will sound like in the future. Will we keep our last names? Will we share? Thinking through the possible combinations abruptly stops when I realize she's coming.

She rides his cock and my tongue until she's almost a pile of goo atop him, her legs shaking. That's when I sit up and push the head of my cock at her drenched and occupied cunt.

She hums, "Hurry. Please, Daddy. Just shove—*ahh! Yes!*"

She asked for it.

I thrust in as fast as she'll safely take me, my dick rocking in and out of her as Isaiah and I quickly find our rhythm. All that practice, you know?

I'm obsessed with this view of her stretching to fit us both—holding our lengths inside her so we can find our pleasure not only in her body, but with each other, too. I'm obsessed with her touching and writhing against our lover. Of her strong back and wide shoulders, flexing and rolling for my viewing pleasure. Of Isaiah's deep-blue eyes finding mine from beneath her—as if to reassure me, *Forever.*

Like I knew I would, I'm rapidly approaching my release, so I hastily find her clit and press in while teasing her saliva-coated back entrance with my other hand.

And there she goes, falling over the edge and crying out her climax. She rewards our cocks with her inner walls contracting, and neither of us last after that. We're both jerking and grunting through jet streams of cum, filling her up and claiming.

Claimed, my hindbrain sighs. *Mine.*

Robyn is giggling when I pull out. Sometimes she can get a little slap happy from a good dicking, and I like her like that. I like it even more when the two of them lay there and let me clean up, drinking every last drop from their bodies.

The pair of them close their eyes, but I'm far from done with them. Before Robyn can snuggle into Isaiah's body, I pick her up and take his hand to strut out of the room, through the double doors, and with no hesitation, jump into our private pool.

When we surface, Robyn's playfully slapping my shoulders and gasping at the temperature shock. It's not too cold, but it's definitely unexpected.

Laughter echoes through the night air as each of them koala me. With Isaiah on my chest and Robyn on my back, their legs wrap around me as we glide through the illuminated water, and float into our future.

Epilogue

Isaiah

One Year Later

A nervous energy pulses through my body unlike anything I've experienced before. I've played in massive stadiums but nothing of this magnitude. It's not even my game. But when Dell and I step through the tunnel and find our seats amongst our family and friends, all gathered to watch my wife play in her second Olympic Games, my blood electrifies as if I'm about to play, too.

"There she is," Dell's mom cheers as the USA Sevens team takes the field, Robyn leading the way. Everyone came for this—most of my family, Dell's parents, and of course Robyn's parents—and every one of us is wearing custom red, white, and blue apparel with Robyn's face plastered all over.

As the players begin their warmup, my husband squeezes my hand tight. "They're gonna take it all, I know it."

"It's only the first game," I remind him. "And the US has never won gold in rugby before, and she's been playing fifteens most of her career, and—"

"I know, but can't you feel it?" he asks with a manic grin.

"I can feel it!" Angie bellows behind us. This sets off a chain reaction through our section, and the whole stadium breaks out in the wave. The crowd ripples three tiers high, and it's impossible not to marvel at the magnitude of this day.

There was a time when I was too scared to tell her my feelings. There was a time I was too scared to let anyone know about us in fear she'd lose all the success she'd amassed. None of that matters anymore. My partners have shown me time and time again that good things come to me when I ask for them—when I open up and speak my truth. Good things come when I don't let my fears keep me from happiness. Sometimes I need reminding, and they're both always there, encouraging, holding, and loving me.

The jumbotron starts playing a segment where they feature individual players as they're warming up before the camera cuts to their family in the stadium. When it gets to Robyn, my gut clenches. Then there we are, Dell and I front and center. My whole body swells with pride before I hug my husband tight. There's a roar from the crowd as hands slap our backs as hard and as wild as our hearts beat.

When we break apart to look back at the giant display, the segment ends, only to be replaced by the newest ad campaign.

It's a double overlay image of Robyn. In one photo, she's wearing her rugby uniform, covered in sweat and dirt and determination. In the second image, transposed and slightly overlapping the first, she's wearing an amber evening gown and a sultry smile. One shoulder and a peak of her defined back are displayed. Low, near her hip, she holds a tumbler of brown liquor on ice.

Be anyone you want to be.
Castle Whiskey

Epilogue

Robyn

Fifteen Years Later

You know who doesn't give a shit that you're an Olympic medalist, TV show host, and model for major brands? Your own kids.

"Thanks, Mom," our nine year old son, Rain, says as I hand him his soccer cleats two minutes before his game starts.

"Hold up," I say, my hand circling his wrist. "There's a hug tax."

I know he's right on the cusp of thinking he's too old for such blatant displays of parental affection, but today is not that day, and he squeezes me in a quick hug.

That was worth the traffic.

I rushed home to get his cleats and made it back in just in time. Dell stayed back with our other son, River, who just turned seven yesterday. He's sitting in his own bag chair with Queen Charlotte, our pet hedgehog, and is reading one of the books we gave him for his birthday. We can't get this boy to like sports no matter how hard we try, so until he shows us interest one day, we're not going to push. My parents have already started making dumb remarks, but I'm right there with my husbands, defending our boy.

Regardless of what my parents think, our kids don't owe us shit.

While River is a quieter type who's into books and bugs and music, Rain is all sports and rough-housing. He's going to make a great rugby player one day—just as soon as he's old enough to play. For now, he's in soccer and trying to make it much more of a contact sport than it is.

Rain darts away to join his team, but the coach is heading straight for me and a little zap of lust sparks. When he stands before me, he's way closer than personal space should allow. "Thanks, baby," he murmurs and leans in for a kiss.

"Coach Isaiah," I giggle. "How inappropriate. There are children here."

"That's Coach Cassidy to you. I'll put another one in you if you keep looking that sexy."

All these years later and he can still make me blush.

And yes, they both took my last name.

"Enjoy the game," he says with a knowing waggle to his eyebrows and another quick kiss. He's a totally different man out there and he *knows* it gets me hot and bothered to watch him coach our son.

Here, with a dozen kids in red uniforms zipping by him, I'm reduced to nothing but hormones and desire. Heaven forbid one of the kids scrapes their knee—I'm toast—because he's there to wipe their tears and reassure them that they will, in fact, live to see another day.

"Thinking about reversing our vasectomies?" Dell chuckles as I take a seat next to him. He's been holding our primo spot amongst the other families in the sea of canvas bag chairs and metal bleachers.

I level him with pout under the bill of my ball cap.

After a pretty scary back injury when I was thirty-four, it was time to retire from professional rugby. Thankfully I had great doctors and an incredible personal trainer at my disposal, so I'm mostly put back together, but playing rugby is not in the cards for me anymore. Now I spend my days being a mother, hosting my third season of Poly Island (a Love Island spin-off featuring only polyamorous people), working various red carpet events as an anchor, modeling, and working alongside Isaiah with his training program.

Dell is still running his business, but it's grown just like his platforms. Personal Best Training has four locations and a staff of twenty, which means he has more free time to spend with our family.

And[1] what a family we have—our "maybe someday" family.

"If I said 'yes, get your vasectomy reversed,' what would you do?"

With that boyish grin that makes me weak and a complete disregard for my age, he leans over and plants the sweetest kiss on me. "I'd dive right in, darlin.'"

THE END

Enjoyed the playlist? Save it and listen to some bonus songs that I had on repeat while writing this book.

Didn't get enough of the Johanssen family?
Then get ready for Jonah's book! Preorder it now.
Read about Angie & Rafael in
Every Version of You.

Want to know all about Angie's friends Cora, Jay, and Marco? Read their story in The Structural Duet.
Structural Damage
Structural Support

---

1. Lil Boo Thang — Galantis Remix by Paul Russell & Galantis

Acknowledgements

Book number four—done.

I need to thank so many people for making this book happen, but first and foremost, I want to thank you, my dear reader. Thank you for taking a chance on me and on these characters who have been ruminating in my head for a long time.

There's a lot of myself and my husband in Isaiah and Robyn, and it makes me so happy to share part of our origin story with you. Remember that part about Isaiah never calling Robyn by her nickname? That really happened to me. I had a silly rugby nickname back in the day, and he was one of the only ruggers who never called me that. So, to my amazing husband, whom I met at a rugby tournament in college, who secretly had a thing for me—thank you. Thank you for shooting your shot. I love you so much.

To my alpha and beta readers, Brittni, Kenzie, Alex, Khaos, Priscilla, Marta, and Melly—thank you for your feedback. Being able to trust you with my unfinished manuscript is a huge deal, and I am forever grateful for you.

Thank you to Will for answering my demisexual questions. Sorry if I made you blush lol.

To all my former rugby teammates—there's a little bit of all of you in here. From my college team, Philly team, and Detroit team, you all mean so much to me. Thank you for all the memories and bruises.

To Siân (@booksofaginger) and Kristie (@read_between_the_wines)—thank you for all your help with plotting and character development. There were moments in this writing process that got me so stuck, and you were both so helpful and kind.

To all my family who's ashamed of what I'm writing about—I don't care. I'm going to keep doing it. To the rest of the family and friends who cheer me on—I love you.

Finally, thank you to my editors Dani, Sam, and Kate for polishing my story turd and making me feel good about it.

On to the next book!

About the author

Sloan Spencer lives in metro Detroit with her husband, two kiddos, and dogs. She loves nature, scandalous stories, and thick thighs. You can follow her on her social media accounts or visit her website (and sign up for her newsletter!):

Instagram & Threads: @sloan_spencer_author
TikTok: @sloanspencerauthor
Facebook: Sloan Spencer's Reader Group
Author website: sloanspencerbooks.com
Be sure to follow her on Goodreads and Amazon!